THE PETTICOAT PIRATE

IMMORTAL PIRATES BOOK 1

C.R. PUGH

Editor: Maddy Glenn, Softwood Self-Publishing - https://www.swspublishing.com/

Cover Artist: Christian Bentulan - https://coversbychristian.com/

Interior Formatter: Nicole Scarano - https://linktr.ee/NicoleScarano

CONTENTS

ONE

The two men gripping Josephine's arms sent her sprawling to the wood floor at her captor's feet. She cried out when her body hit the hard floor, pain surging up her spine and across her skin in waves. Black spots clouded her vision and her head swam, threatening to send her into a swoon. The skin on her back had been torn to shreds. Hair that was normally a soft brown had been darkened and matted down with sweat and blood. The gown she'd been wearing for the last two days was split open down the back where the pirate hunters had taken joy in flogging her with a cat-o'-nine-tails. The beating she'd taken had made her weak and her wounds were beginning to fester. The hunters had thought it quite a joke to use the cat on the daughter of a pirate; wasn't that the tool often used by pirates to punish their crew?

Gritting her teeth, Josephine managed to rise up onto her hands and knees, letting her head hang limp. A shiny, black pair of boots paced back and forth in front of her while five hunters stood silently against the walls. Upon capture, Josephine had been brought to an English fort on the shores of Manhattan. She now found herself in the office of some high-ranking officer in the military. They were all

1

dressed alike in their black suits and white cravats. They were so typically arrogant, all of them, not deigning to come down to their filthy dungeon, but bringing her up to this polished room to bleed all over the floor.

These pirate hunters were fools and nastier than any pirate Josephine had ever heard of. True immortal pirates never needed to resort to such brutality. In the eyes of these hunters, all pirates were the same - dishonest, thieving men who plundered other ships for gold. Ordinary pirates did not possess the magic of the sea. The bond between the captain and crew was forged by blood and magic, preventing any sort of betrayal. A mutinous heart would be discovered by the Captain before the crew was able to speak of their treachery. Her father's men were the most loyal of them all.

To these men, who worked for the British Crown, it did not matter. Hunters had made it their life's work to be rid of every last pirate and witch in the colonies and abroad. It was a hunter's paid profession. When Josephine had been captured two days ago, they had been lying in wait for her father, the Pirate of Blacktail Cove; the last surviving immortal pirate in this world.

"It seems, Miss Teversin," her captor began in his condescending tone, "that the tides have turned. Isn't that what pirates like to say?" He chuckled at his own joke. "Joseph Teversin - or should I call him the Pirate of Blacktail Cove - is coming here of his own accord. I knew he'd come for you eventually, though it surprises me that he has allowed you to suffer for so long. It was very foolish of you to visit the Bull's Head tavern. The place is always full of Loyalists and pirate hunters."

Tensing up at his words caused sharp, stabbing pains to run down every inch of her skin. A moan of anguish escaped her lips.

"Oh, do not despair, little half-pirate," he told her, feigning sympathy. "It will all be over soon."

Chills of dread ran up and down Josephine's spine, sending another wave of throbbing pain through her body. How had he known she was Blacktail's daughter or a pirate at all? Josephine had told them nothing, even throughout the worst of the torture they had delivered. Her father had protected her; kept her a secret from the world for fifteen years. Only the crew knew who and what she was.

Her father was coming, and it was only minutes before sundown. Tears pooled in Josephine's eyes. There was nothing she wouldn't do for her father, even take another beating, though it might just do her in.

"I know what you are thinking, Miss Teversin." He stopped just in front of her, his boots pointed at the windows. "It is nearly sunset. He had better hurry. Ah, I think I hear them now." Her captor pivoted to face the door.

The sound of boots pounding down the hallway had Josephine's ears perking up. She turned her face away from the window and looked back to the door, hoping she was mistaken - hoping *he* had been mistaken.

The door burst open, slamming back against the wall, and in walked her father, the Pirate of Blacktail Cove. Josephine's father was not even six feet tall, but he carried himself with such confidence, he could send even the tallest person running for the hills.

"Garreck Skulthorpe, I should have known it was you," Joseph snarled. When he turned his gaze upon his daughter, brown eyes identical to hers widened as they took in her ragged appearance and her raw and bleeding back. His jaw ticked, but the regret in his eyes revealed that he had known what was happening all along.

"I told your hunters that I would come!" Joseph growled. "This was not part of the agreement!"

The man called Skulthorpe raised his head in defiance. "I do apologize," he said with a haughty smirk. "Perhaps you should not have waited two days to make your deal."

A wave of peace washed over Josephine. Instinctively, she knew the magic in her father's blood was trying to soothe and speak to her.

Forgive me. His gruff voice sounded in her mind. Unshed tears filled his gaze.

Josephine peered at the windows out of the corner of her eyes. Sprays of orange filled the pink sky, signaling the final moments of the day. Emptiness descended upon her and tears began to fall. Josephine watched as dark storm clouds began to roll in out of nowhere.

"Let my daughter go. We made a deal."

"Yes, I did say that I would release her," said Skulthorpe. "But she *is* your blood, isn't she? A half-pirate. I am bound to the laws established by the Brotherhood."

"What are you saying?" He took a threatening step toward Skulthorpe but was jerked back by the hunters' grip on his upper arms.

"I will release her, but I cannot be responsible for what the hunters here" -he waved his hand around the room to the many men looking on- "will do to her once she is no longer in my custody."

Josephine's father lunged again. Condescending laughter filled the office, not only from the man called Skulthorpe, but some hunters as well. Skulthorpe had never been a man of his word when dealing with pirates and witches.

Anger began to bubble up inside Josephine. It seeped into her heart like poison, filling every empty crevice. The trees outside began to bend with the force of the wind.

"Josephine."

She turned her face up to her father. The sorrow she glimpsed in his eyes was almost unbearable. While tears continued to stream down her cheeks, he spoke to her mind again.

You must leave this place, Jo. Get out of here however you can. Do you understand?

Josephine nodded, but his words did nothing to smother her fury. Outside, the wind continued to circle around the building. Rain poured down from the sky in heavy waves. Pellets of water beat against the glass double doors leading to a balcony overlooking the beach.

Josephine? Oliver and the crew are waiting for you at the beach. Let them take you to Genevieve's in Charlestown. You will be safe there, my daughter. Oliver and Genny will protect you.

What about you, Father? Josephine cried out in her mind.

He smiled sadly. *Your mother and I will finally be together again.*

No, I need you. Tears trickled down Josephine's cheeks.

I will always be near you. Josephine's father glanced out the window at the raging storm, then back at her. *Promise me that this storm will not last for too long.*

Josephine broke down into sobs. The glass double doors burst open from the force of the winds outside. It took several hunters to close them again.

Promise me, Josephine. Be strong. Then he added, *I love you, Jo. You've always been my greatest treasure. Always.*

Josephine pinched her eyes shut and screamed out loud, "Father, no! You cannot do this!"

But it was too late. In her pirate's blood, she could feel the final rays of sun disappear. Her father was gone once she opened her eyes again. All that remained of him was a pile of sand on the floor.

Skulthorpe and even some of the hunters began chuckling. "At last," Skulthorpe muttered. "Another pirate bites the dust."

TWO

(3 years later)

OCTOBER 1773 ~ CHARLESTOWN, SOUTH CAROLINA

The Kraken's Lookout was a shabby alehouse located near the White Pearl Wharf, one of the busiest piers in Charlestown. Nathaniel Runik had never bothered visiting before because of the obscure location of this particular tavern and the guttersnipes that tended to frequent them.

So typical of these kinds of places, Nathaniel thought, swirling the rum around in his cup.

The dimly lit tavern was crowded and boisterous. Men of all ages were chugging back drinks and singing at the top of their lungs, celebrating the end of another day of their measly little lives. They were filthy, none of them having bothered to bathe or wash their ragged clothes for days it seemed. The combined scent of body odor, fish, and rum made Nathaniel want to gag.

But none of *them* concerned him at the moment. Nathaniel's eyes were locked on the slip of a girl he had been assigned to watch: Miss Josephine Teversin.

When Nathaniel's employer, Mr. Skulthorpe, had informed him of the Teversin girl and her connection to the Pirate of Blacktail Cove, he wasn't sure what he was expecting, but it was not her. He was prepared for someone more strapping. Ugly, even. Maybe a woman dressed in man's clothes or even a silly patch over one eye and gold teeth. This girl had plain brown hair piled up into an extremely messy knot at the crown of her head. Wavy tendrils had fallen from the knot to frame her face and when her eyes happened to glance in his direction, he could see they were a dull, muddy brown. She wore a dark blue dress that she barely filled out, with a white apron tied around her thin waist. Her clothes were plain and modest, without any frills or ruffles. She looked like a normal, although poor, girl, who could not be more than sixteen or seventeen years old.

There was also a French woman serving drinks to the men. *She* looked more the part of serving wench with her rich burgundy gown and extremely low neckline, as was the fashion in London and Paris. In comparison, the Teversin girl looked positively common. This could not possibly be the Josephine Teversin for which they were searching. Not to mention the fact that it was well past sunset and she was still alive. A true immortal pirate could not be caught on land after the sun had set or he would turn to sand on the spot. How could this be the daughter of the Pirate of Blacktail Cove?

The men finished their song and banged their mugs together, sloshing rum all over themselves, which made everyone, including the Teversin girl, erupt into gales of laughter.

Nathaniel scowled and slapped coins on the table to pay for his untouched drink. Rising from his seat, he shoved his tricorn down on his head and slipped out the door. If she was the daughter of a pirate, then he hated her already.

Nathaniel Runik was a hunter. And hunters killed pirates.

JOSEPHINE WAS ALERT the moment the dark stranger stood to leave the Kraken's Lookout. She'd been strangely aware of him the entire time he'd been sitting at his table. His stares made her blush, which annoyed her. For once, she was grateful that her Aunt Genevieve kept this tavern so poorly lit or someone might have noticed the color in her cheeks.

Aunt Genny sauntered over and stood beside Josephine at the bar. Genny's blonde hair was piled high on her head, shining like smooth butter in the candlelight. She wasn't really Josephine's aunt at all, just a friend of her father's. Genny had taken Josephine in three years ago when her father had died.

His death had been all Josephine's fault. Thinking of the pile of sand that had once been her beloved father had her heart twisting up into painful knots.

Ten years ago, at the young age of twenty, Aunt Genny had sailed to Charlestown from France with Josephine and her father. Joseph had helped her purchase the Kraken's Lookout to give her a new start in the colonies. Though she'd lived in Charlestown for many years, Genny continued to wear her most elegant Parisian dresses when she worked at the tavern. She always excused her frivolity as "good business etiquette" and said it attracted more customers. Josephine simply believed she was trying to attract a man.

Josephine couldn't help but envy the woman's beautiful garments: square-cut necklines trimmed with ruffles, brightly colored skirts and petticoats, matching shoes with elegant heels. Her hair was always curled and pinned up in the latest fashion. Josephine could have had all that when her father was alive. He had tried to spoil her terribly with hats, parasols, and all the latest frills, but she had been content to dress like the men. They never had to bother with pinching corsets, after all.

"He is a handsome fellow, that one," Genny said in her French accent, nodding to the door through which the stranger had just departed.

Josephine silently cursed as her cheeks flushed again. The man had been striking, but he was not the sort to visit a local tavern on the wharf. His skin wasn't darkened from working out on the docks like so many in Charlestown and his expensive black cloak suggested that he was a man of some wealth. The suit underneath was probably just as fine. His hair was black as a raven and tied neatly at the nape of his neck with a ribbon that matched his hair.

Josephine shrugged as she wiped down the bar. "I suppose." She was trying not to think about the dark shadow of stubble on his square jaw and how gracefully he had moved when he was striding out the door. Still, there was something about him, something familiar. Josephine couldn't quite put her finger on it.

"It is too bad he left," Genny said. "You could have spoken to him, *non?*"

"He didn't look like he wanted company, Aunt Genny."

"It would never do," she replied, dismissing her own advice with a wave of her hand. "Oliver - he would be too jealous."

Josephine scoffed. "Oliver wouldn't be jealous. He still sees me as a kid sister."

Genny snorted and rolled her eyes. "If you say so."

At a loss for words, Josephine walked away and began picking up empty mugs that the men were leaving behind. She would not argue with Genny about Oliver Blakely. Genny just wanted to match-make and Josephine couldn't be bothered with it. Oliver was nineteen years old, only a year older than Josephine, and he was certainly handsome. But he didn't think of her in *that* way.

"Oy, Angelfish!" shouted a deep voice from behind her. Fingers poked her ribs playfully.

Josephine yelped and whirled around, coming face to face with her oldest and dearest friend. Her heart beat a little faster at his nickname for her.

"Blimey, Oliver!" She swatted him with the dishrag in her hand. "Don't frighten me like that!"

Oliver gaped at her, feigning shock. "Such language, Angelfish," he said in a hushed voice, glancing around at the sailors still milling about inside the tavern. "People around here might think you were a pirate instead of a lady, eh?"

Josephine pinched her lips together. Old habits were certainly hard to break. Josephine's father had made sure her English was perfect, as good as any Englishman's, but she had grown up with a bunch of scallywags at sea. What did anyone expect?

"Don't say that so loud, Oliver," whispered Josephine, narrowing her eyes at him.

She turned on her heel and walked back to the bar. Before she could make it two steps, Oliver grabbed her by the elbow, pulled her close, and hissed, "And where's your bloody corset? Don't think I didn't notice, Jo."

Josephine gasped and smacked him with the dishrag again. "It's ungentlemanly to mention such things!"

"I ain't a gentleman, Angelfish, and well you know it," Oliver replied, grinning like an idiot.

"Oliver, you are positively beastly! You ought to be horse-whipped."

He threw back his head and laughed at her attempt to threaten him. Not that he should take her threats seriously. They had grown up together and had always been the best of friends. Her father had taken him aboard his ship and made him part of the crew at a young age, since he had no home or family. He was a hard worker and was there for Josephine at a time when she had truly needed a friend.

After her father had disintegrated into a pile of sand, Oliver had been the one to find her on the beach. No one could explain what had happened that night three years ago and Josephine did not discuss it with anyone. Not even Oliver.

While pretending to clean the bar, Josephine watched her friend through her lowered lashes. Oliver wasn't neatly put together like the dark, brooding stranger that had visited the tavern earlier. Oliver's shirt, though it was clean, was more beige than white from years of wear. Over his tunic, he wore a faded blue waistcoat, which he left unbuttoned, and his tan breeches were tucked into scuffed black boots. His skin was bronzed all over, eyes green like the sea. And unlike the polished stranger, Oliver's wheat-colored locks, though tied back with a ribbon, were windblown and tousled.

"Are you all right, Angelfish?"

Josephine's eyes snapped up to his. "Uh … of course."

Why was she feeling so nervous? It made her face heat up to think that Oliver might have known what she'd been pondering. Had he sensed her passing sadness or noticed her admiring gaze?

Josephine took a deep breath. *Oliver is just a friend. A very good friend, but nothing more.*

Her heart began to ache at the thought and the walls suddenly felt as if they were closing in on her. Josephine swallowed and, once more, pretended to wipe away imaginary spots and crumbs from the bar.

Oliver reached out and placed his calloused hand on top of hers. "Easy, Jo," he said softly. "You're rubbing a hole in the wood."

A corner of his mouth lifted in a half-smile, but Josephine could see the concern in his eyes. She was certain Oliver was aware of her turmoil and that it had nothing to do with him. It was a yearning she should have recognized, one that bubbled up from deep inside her pirate's blood. The familiar feeling came almost every evening after sunset. Like strings tugging on her heart, the sea beckoned her.

Josephine slid her hand out from under Oliver's, which left her feeling chilled. "Aunt Genny, I'm going out to get some air." Leaving her dishrag and apron behind, Josephine strode to the door of the tavern.

"You want any company?" Oliver called out.

At the same time, Aunt Genny asked, "Where are you going?"

Josephine forced a smile for the pair of them. They knew perfectly well where she was going. It was no secret what was happening to her. The pirate magic that had been dormant inside her as a small child was simmering to the surface now that she was older.

"No, thank you, Oliver." She turned to her Aunt Genny and added, "Out to the pier. I won't be long."

"If you're not back by midnight …" Oliver reminded her.

Josephine nodded, knowing he'd come looking for her if she didn't come back soon. Glancing back once more, she gave Oliver a small smile and escaped into the evening air, leaving the noisy tavern behind.

Josephine strolled along the cobblestone streets that overlooked the harbor. The autumn air was crisp with a hint of smoke from nearby chimneys. The dark water was smooth like glass out on the bay. There were a few sailors singing, gambling, and drinking on the docks, enjoying the evening before setting sail in the morning. They were a rough sort, but they wouldn't bother her. Being a pirate's daughter did have its advantages, like knowing how to fight with swords and daggers. Josephine was accurate with a pistol as well. Her father had taught her everything she'd need to know to survive in this world, and she always kept several blades hidden in the folds of her dress.

The White Pearl Wharf was the most popular place in Charlestown for ships to dock and it was Josephine's favorite escape. She strolled past brigantines and schooners that were roped to the dock. Their tall masts towered over her, as if they could scrape away the stars from the night sky. The creaking and swaying of the enormous ships brought back fond memories of sailing with her father. Josephine yearned for the days she ran barefoot upon the smooth wooden decks and climbed the masts so high she could nearly touch the clouds. She and Oliver would spend hours up in the crow's nest looking for dolphins, whales, and deserted islands. Her father's brig, the *Nepheria*, had been her home since she was a baby. Since he'd died, she had been stuck in this smothering town, surrounded by crowds of people and buildings. She'd always seen townspeople as trapped, and now it was she who was trapped among them.

Once she reached the edge of the pier, Josephine gazed out over the water and breathed in the salty air. The palms of her hands grew warm.

No, not again, Josephine thought.

The magic was trying to seep out of her skin. It frightened her. Josephine shook her hands and wiped them down her cloak, as if that would stop her magic from building up. Taking a deep breath, she concentrated on stuffing her powers deep down inside her where they could never break free.

The first time Josephine had lost control of her magic was three years ago.

While Skulthorpe and his hunters had been gloating over her

father's sand, Josephine had let out a blood-curdling scream that had silenced everyone in the room. Every window had shattered. The hurricane-force winds from outside began to circle within the room. A shard of glass sliced Skulthorpe across his cheek, sending him stumbling backward into the stone fireplace. His head hit the mantle and he was knocked unconscious.

Panic had ensued. Hunters barreled over one another in their attempts to flee, frightened of what Josephine might do to them. Her emotions had been out of control and so was the storm inside Skulthorpe's office. The wind had circled around Josephine, forming a protective ring of rainwater and glass. The hunters who had attempted to reach her had been cut to shreds.

In her grief, Josephine had collapsed to the wood floor, but the storm had carried on, as if some other force had taken up the reins on her behalf. The glass shards had scattered to the four walls and dropped to the floor. The salty water had licked up her father's sand and carried it out the windows to the sea. Josephine's limp form had been lifted up and cradled like a baby. Somehow, she'd ended up on the beach and in Oliver's waiting arms.

Oliver had told her afterward that he'd watched in awe as she'd been carried by the hurricane-force winds out of the second story window and down to the ocean, as if by magic. Oliver had never heard of a pirate being able to do that sort of thing.

Though her skin had eventually healed, leaving livid scars crisscrossing on her back, the wounds on her heart had not. Inside her pirate soul, it was as if Josephine had tethers, like lines that pulled the sails taut on a ship. Some of those ropes kept her firmly bound to the sea, just like any other pirate - the same ropes that called her to the pier every night. Josephine had no idea how long it might be before those tethers beckoned her home permanently. Those other lines had been cut free the day her father had died and continued to wave to and fro without any sort of anchor.

Her eyes pricked with the threat of tears, but she refused to let them fall again. Oliver would know immediately if she had been crying and would hover like a mother hen again. A heavy fog was already settling on the bay due to her misty eyes.

"Blast," she huffed, hastily wiping her eyes.

It had been Josephine's tears that had summoned the storm on the day of her father's passing. She had wept for weeks after watching her father disintegrate. It had resulted in a record number of hurricanes that season, which no one could explain. None of the crew had seen anything like it. Of course, there had never been a half-pirate before. Pirates were made by witches, not born. Although Joseph had searched for answers, there was no one who knew what magic a half-pirate might possess. Had she only inherited *some* of the magic or all of it and more? She was a conundrum.

Still not quite at peace, Josephine turned to make her way back to the tavern. The fog had not dissipated, but at least she had soothed her soul for the night. Busy pondering what to tell Oliver about the fog, Josephine was completely unprepared when a man stepped out of the mist, directly into her path. She fingered the dagger at her waist and her hands began to warm again at the possible threat. Maybe Oliver had followed her after all. Josephine was about to blister his ears about it when the man stepped forward. The expensive black cloak and dark, polished features brought her up short.

"Josephine Teversin?" His voice was as sophisticated as the rest of him.

Swallowing back her fear, Josephine answered, "I saw you in the tavern earlier, didn't I?"

Instead of explaining, he raised his arm out of his cloak and pointed what appeared to be a smallish pistol at her.

"Blast! You're a hunter!"

Instead of an explosive gunshot, she heard a quiet *thwap* when he pulled the trigger. Something sharp pricked her just below her collarbone.

Josephine gaped at the man. "Bilge-sucking landlubber! You really shot me!" She could have sworn she'd heard him chuckle at her outrage.

Josephine pulled the thing from her shoulder and attempted to examine it but her brain was turning to mush inside her head. She staggered as the world around her began to spin.

Sounding as drunk as a sailor, Josephine slurred, "I think ... I'm going ... to fall ... down." Then she ungracefully collapsed to the ground.

THREE

J osephine awoke in a darkened room, cold and alone with a
pounding headache. It took a moment for her head to clear and
remember exactly what had happened.

"That filthy bilge-rat," she muttered as it all came rushing back
to her.

The skin was a bit tender where the scoundrel had shot her in the
shoulder. Josephine massaged the spot with her fingers to relieve the
slight ache that remained. Reaching for her hidden weapons, Josephine
realized the hunter had taken the dagger at her waist. The blade that
was strapped to her thigh, under her petticoat, was still there. She
sighed in relief.

"At least he had the decency to keep his hands out from under my
skirts," Josephine grumbled to herself. The man was either careless or
underestimated her.

From what she could tell, the room was some sort of storage cellar.
The shelves along the brick walls were filled with dusty wine bottles.
The tiny ray of moonlight shining into the room was from a window
too small for Josephine to squeeze through.

"Blast!" Josephine rose to her feet to look for another means of
escape. Her head throbbed where she'd fallen on the pier. The black-

guard hadn't even had the courtesy of catching her. It was awfully rude of him.

Taking several deep breaths to calm her racing heart, Josephine took a turn about the room. There was a ladder on one wall, leading up to the main house through the low ceiling. On the opposite side of the room, three stairs led up to wooden double doors built at an angle. It was safe to assume that these doors led out into the back or side yard of the home. They were probably locked from the outside, but Josephine pushed against them with her shoulder to be sure. No luck.

Turning back to the ladder, Josephine frowned as she examined the trapdoor in the ceiling again. It seemed her only option was to climb up and escape through the house. Only a daft fool would wait around to see what the hunter had planned for her.

"So disappointing," Josephine sighed. The dark stranger had been so handsome.

Knowing immediately that her skirts would hinder her progress, Josephine tied them up around her legs like boys' knickers and proceeded to climb the rungs of the ladder. She wished she had her breeches on beneath her petticoat. They made matters much less tricky while moving about.

To Josephine's astonishment, the hatch wasn't locked after all. *What luck!*

But still, she took pause. If the man was a pirate hunter, surely there was someone guarding her? Or was she being overly dramatic? Would they underestimate her because she was a woman? Did the man assume that she would just sit tight and wait for him to come back? The man had known her name, so he probably knew all about her heritage as well.

Josephine inched the trapdoor up by the rusty hinges and risked a peek around. She found herself inside a small broom closet, just a bit larger than the trapdoor itself. Silent as a whisper, she climbed out onto the floor of the closet and closed the hatch beneath her. This room was much darker with no windows at all. Through the keyhole at the door, Josephine saw the kitchen. The room was large with expensive utensils and furniture. Josephine was most assuredly in a wealthier part of town or possibly a plantation home just outside Charlestown.

The wall to the left was almost entirely made of brick. A large fireplace and two bread ovens had been built into the wall and a black pot hung from the chimney crane. In the middle of the room, two British soldiers dressed in their pristine, red uniforms sat at the kitchen table facing each other, laughing and playing cards. Their tricorns had been placed on the table beside them.

The shorter of the two had a light complexion with red hair. He chuckled and slapped his cards to the table. "You cheated! Deal again."

The taller one with darker hair smirked as he gathered and shuffled the cards. "I don't have to cheat to win against *you*, Thomas."

Redheaded Thomas folded his arms across his chest. "We'll see about that, John."

John proceeded to deal the cards again. They were the only two men in the room as far as she could tell, but each soldier was armed with a sword and pistol. Both were regulars in the army and nearly as young as Oliver. Perhaps their youth was their weakness.

This is still going to be tricky.

Josephine surveyed the rest of the kitchen. To her right was a tall brown cupboard that held stacks of all kinds of dishes and serving pitchers. Beyond that was an open window. If she could somehow get past the two redcoats at the table, she could sneak through the window and escape.

Josephine rolled her eyes. "Brilliant," she whispered. "And how are you going to accomplish that?"

Her eyes shifted back to the two guards. Overpowering them was not an option and her stomach churned at the thought of using her blade to harm them. These men couldn't possibly know why they were holding her prisoner. They were not pirate hunters. They were merely taking orders.

It doesn't matter if I hurt them or not, Josephine silently conceded. If she escaped, their commanding officers would punish them or have them executed. Regardless, Josephine didn't want their blood on her hands.

Josephine recalled a lesson her father had once taught her. "Anything can be turned into a weapon, my daughter." Besides her dagger, there wasn't much to choose from. Josephine would need to use her wits to win this skirmish.

Gingerly, she tried to turn the knob, to no avail. She would have to pick the lock, one of the many skills she had gleaned from Oliver. Josephine yanked a pin out of her hair and got to work. In less than five minutes, the latch clicked free. Cringing at the noise, Josephine peeped through the keyhole. Her heart thudded hard as the men turned to stare straight toward her.

"Did you hear that?" Thomas asked his comrade.

"Yes," John replied, looking grim. He set the cards down on the table.

Thomas swiveled in his seat. "Think we should check on the girl?"

"I'll go. One girl won't be any trouble." John rose to his feet and strode toward the broom closet she was hiding in.

That's what you think.

The sound of the guard's boots drew close. Josephine rose to her feet and waited. When John twisted the knob, she shoved the door into his face. The man swore and fell backward to the floor.

"John!" Thomas shouted as he jumped to his feet.

Josephine grabbed a broom from the closet and swung the door open again. John was groaning on the floor, holding his hands over his nose.

"Don't let her get away, Thomas!"

The red-haired soldier charged toward her. Before he could seize her, Josephine jabbed the handle of the broom into his belly. Thomas grunted and doubled over. She whipped the broom around and bashed him in the head. The poor soldier fell unconscious to the wood floor.

John groaned and rolled to his knees, blood now dripping from his nose. Josephine didn't give him a chance to reach for a weapon. She swung the broomstick and knocked him out as well.

After setting down the broom, Josephine tiptoed around the table, her heart pounding in her ears. She was about to reach her freedom when another redcoat poked his head inside through the open window.

"John? Thomas?"

The soldier's blue eyes widened when he saw Josephine standing there gaping back at him.

His hand clamped down on her wrist. "You!"

Biting back a curse, Josephine grabbed one of the pitchers from the cupboard and smashed it into his temple. The man stumbled backward in a daze and dropped out of sight beneath the window sill.

Of course, escaping wouldn't be so simple. There were probably more redcoats outside. She'd have to find another way out. Tiptoeing to the main entrance of the kitchen, Josephine knelt down and peeked through the small crack under the door. Once she was certain no one was waiting for her on the other side, she slipped out.

The foyer of the house was dark and silent. A staircase to her right led up to the second floor and the front door was just ahead. Windows on each side of the door revealed two more redcoats pacing with their muskets on the front porch. They'd been too far away to hear the commotion, but they would soon find out about it.

Josephine turned to sprint up the stairs, but just as her boot hit the first stair, the floor began to rumble beneath her feet. Josephine gasped. Horses, and lots of them, were galloping closer and closer. She peered over her shoulder, out the foyer windows, to see two lines of soldiers riding down the front drive with torches. There were more than a dozen men and they would be at the house in a minute or two.

Why were redcoats riding toward this house? Was it some sort of British headquarters or meeting place? Josephine wasn't waiting around to find out. She ran up the stairs two at a time.

The second floor seemed to be empty. Josephine didn't bother checking each room. There was no time with those soldiers closing in, but these plantation homes were all the same. Parlors and libraries downstairs, with guest and sleeping quarters upstairs. The room she found at the back of the house had been transformed into a large gentleman's office of sorts. A shining, mahogany desk in the center of the room was cluttered with papers. A brick fireplace had been built into the back wall with two wingback chairs on either side of the hearth. The opposite wall was lined with bookshelves.

The impulse to nose about pulled Josephine into the room. She sifted through the papers quickly, looking for anything that stood out. It was all letters and bank notes and such. She pocketed the coins she found under the first stack of papers and then reached for another stack.

Below her, on the first floor, she heard the unmistakable sound of boots stomping through the house.

"Bring her up from below," one of the soldiers ordered. "Her presence has been requested by Mr. Skulthorpe."

Josephine's stomach dropped. Skulthorpe? Had she misheard him?

"It can't be," Josephine whispered to herself. Chills ran up her spine and every scar on her back seemed to burn with the memory of the evil man. The papers in her hands began to tremble.

Josephine knew she had no time to linger. Returning the stack of letters back to the desk, she scurried to the window. It was a long drop, but luckily there was a large oak tree not far from the side of the house. The tree's limbs stretched out from its thick trunk about thirty feet in all directions, some reaching into the sky, while others arched over and brushed the ground. It was the perfect climbing tree.

A careful look down assured her that no redcoats were standing guard below the window. They were all inside the house, searching for *her*.

"*She's escaped!*" another soldier shouted from downstairs. "Find her! Search every room!"

Boots pounded up the stairs to the second floor. Heart racing, Josephine ducked beneath the desk. Two or three soldiers strode through the upper rooms, searching.

A pair of boots slowly entered the office. Josephine's hands began to warm with her growing fear.

"Any sign of her, Wilkins?" a soldier asked from the hallway.

Wilkins, the man inside the office, spun on his heel and answered, "She's not here. The girl has probably escaped out of some window by now."

"Pity. I was hoping to see another pirate hang."

They both snickered. Josephine swallowed back the lump in her throat and curled her tingling fingers into fists to keep her magic at bay.

"You might get to see an execution sooner than you think, Corporal," Wilkins said. The two soldiers exited the room, their voices growing quieter as they traipsed down the stairs. "John and Thomas allowed the pirate to escape. Mr. Skulthorpe will have their heads for it."

Josephine let out the breath she'd been holding. Evading these soldiers did not ease the pinch of guilt she felt for the two young men she'd pummeled with that broom, but there was nothing to be done about it.

She crept to the window and jumped out onto the giant oak tree with ease. Arms and legs hooked around a thick branch, Josephine shimmied down the tree to the ground and took off into the shadows.

The scoundrel who had shot her on the pier was not the Skulthorpe she remembered. But if Skulthorpe had been involved in the abduction tonight, and that dark stranger was a pirate hunter, then she was no longer safe.

"IMPRESSIVE, ISN'T SHE, RUNIK?" Garreck Skulthorpe sneered.

Nathaniel Runik sniffed in disdain, but otherwise continued to sit silently atop his mount, flicking his leather whip against his thigh. Mr. Skulthorpe sat astride his own mount next to him, looking like a military general overseeing a field of battle, except his frock was black instead of red.

Mr. Skulthorpe's observation was spot on. The girl had passed the test. They'd been watching from a distance, waiting for her to emerge from somewhere, but he'd never expected a female to jump from a second-story window. He shouldn't be surprised by anything a pirate would do.

"Have I finally persuaded you?" asked Skulthorpe, peering at him out of the corner of his eye.

"You are quite confident in her abilities," replied Nathaniel. "Are you certain we should trust her?"

Skulthorpe placed the tips of his fingers together and held them to his lips in thought. He finally spoke, his words slow and pensive. "Of course we shouldn't trust the wench, but I believe she can be ... persuaded."

Nathaniel frowned. He was well aware of Skulthorpe's methods of persuasion.

"Follow her tomorrow," Skulthorpe suggested. "See where she goes, who her acquaintances are. Then bring her back. Tomorrow night, we'll have a chat with our little half-pirate." He began to chuckle as if he'd told a fantastic joke. "What a farce, Runik! A pirate in petticoats!"

FOUR

The next morning, Josephine rose early and donned her most horrid brown dress and white apron. A white ruffled cap covered her hair. Josephine stood in front of the mirror to judge her drab reflection.

"Brown hair, brown eyes, brown dress. I am extremely brown."

Aunt Genny would have a fit if she saw Josephine in this dress. Genny was always trying to convince her to wear more stylish clothes, but this dreadful gown would do well for today's outing. Josephine wasn't going out for a useless Sunday stroll or to try to attract attention. Blending in with the working crowd was of the utmost importance as she made her visit today. Josephine needed answers. What business had brought her worst enemy down to Charlestown and how had he known where to find her? Only one man might have that information and his shipping company was on a different wharf. A walk through the slums was the quickest route there and Josephine was sure the dark stranger would be trying to locate her. She would not be caught unaware this time. Daggers were strapped to her thighs under her skirt and there was even a sharp hat pin tucked into her hair that could be used as a weapon if need be.

Josephine checked her appearance one more time and then made her way out of the Kraken's Lookout to go see her old family friend, Captain Culligan.

NATHANIEL SPOTTED the Teversin girl as she departed the tavern. The waterfront street was busy with morning business and she was instantly swallowed up by the crowd. The girl was wearing a disguise of sorts, but he was not fooled at all. She had hidden her hair under a cap and was wearing a dress that was just as dreadful as the blue tattered garment she'd worn the previous evening. What stood out the most was that she carried no goods to sell or deliver, unlike every other vagrant on this wretched wharf.

Nathaniel followed from a distance and continued to track her into the worst part of Charlestown. An overwhelming sense of curiosity filled him. There were seedy-looking taverns, sawmills, butcher shops, and factories of all kinds. The roughest sort of men and women were loitering in the street, trying to sell their wares, and she continued to weave between them without knowing he was trailing her at all. Perhaps the girl was looking for a new place to stay after her ordeal last night. Perhaps she had some unfavorable contacts to which she could turn for help. He suspected the latter of the two.

Nathaniel's brows pinched together when the girl slowed her pace. *What is she up to?*

Veering off the road, Nathaniel pretended to inquire about some meat from a butcher. He instantly regretted it. The smell of bloody meat was overpowering, even in the midst of so much filth.

The Teversin girl was still in his peripheral vision, her white cap visible within the crowd. He crept along behind her, certain that she was still oblivious to his presence.

The screams of several females from down the crowded street caught Nathaniel's attention. *What's happening?* he thought, squinting through the glare of the midmorning sun. The crowd around Nathaniel began to run frantically and erupted into more screaming at the sound of ruffians on horseback charging down the street. Through the panicked mob, Nathaniel thought he could still see the white cap on the Teversin girl's head sprinting away from the melee. Once the four riders had passed by, he realized he'd lost sight of the girl completely.

"Out of my way! *Move!*" Nathaniel demanded as he elbowed his way through the pressing crowd. His effort to locate her was futile. Once the horses and their riders had cleared the scene, the morning bustle continued around him and Josephine Teversin was nowhere to be seen.

Cursing his bad luck, Nathaniel headed south, back to the White Pearl Wharf. He'd have to catch up with the Teversin girl at the Kraken's Lookout this evening.

___

From the narrow alley between two brothels, Josephine watched as her pursuer walked away, defeated. She'd known all morning that he'd been following her. Though he was wearing dull colors, the expensive suit he wore stood out like a sore thumb in this crowd of vagrants. If she ever came face to face with him again, she'd be sure to mention his shameful error. And underestimating her would be his biggest mistake of all.

"Better luck next time, hunter," Josephine said with her own arrogant smirk.

"Ready, Angelfish?"

Josephine jumped when Oliver spoke into her ear. He'd been standing right behind her. She spun on her heel and followed him farther into the shadows of the alley.

"Yes, of course, Oliver," she answered with a grin. "I do appreciate the distraction."

It was lucky Josephine had run into him on her way to Culligan's Wharf. She would have found a way to shake off the dark abductor somewhere here in the slums, but Oliver's help made things much easier. He'd discreetly made eye contact and recognized her father's old hand signal immediately.

"At your service," he said, taking a bow with a mischievous gleam

26

in his eyes. "And just who was that toff, Jo?" he asked, nodding his head toward the street.

Josephine peered over her shoulder one more time to make sure the scoundrel hadn't found her again. Gratefully, no one was there. "I'm not sure, but I'm on my way to visit the Captain to see if he knows anything about it."

Oliver frowned when she did not divulge more information, but didn't ask questions. Josephine bit her lip to tamp down the urge to reveal last night's adventure. It was after midnight by the time she arrived back at the Kraken's Lookout, but the tavern was crowded and Oliver had been too busy playing cards with the other sailors to notice what time she came strolling in. Oliver would only worry, so she said nothing.

Oliver's eyes cut down to Josephine's dress as they walked.

"Don't you dare make fun of me, Oliver. I needed a disguise."

"A maid in the governor's house?"

Josephine rolled her eyes. "It was this or a lady of loose morals."

"Oh, blimey, Angelfish," Oliver scolded half-heartedly. "I would've beat you senseless!"

She giggled and linked her elbow with his as they made their way through the slums, heading out to Culligan's Wharf.

FIVE

I t took another thirty minutes for Josephine and Oliver to reach the wharf. By then, it was nearly mid-morning and the quay was bustling with activity. On every docked ship there were men cleaning decks and repairing damages to the sails and rigging. Many were unloading fish and other cargo onto the docks. Josephine paused to admire the ships. Vessels of all sizes were tied to the wharf while others had been anchored in the calm water a short distance away.

Oliver nudged her with his shoulder when he noticed her appreciative gaze. "Are you missing them days, Angelfish?"

"Aye," Josephine answered.

"We all do."

She turned toward him, squinting from the morning sun. "Then why do you not find a new ship and crew?"

Oliver merely shrugged, but his expression hinted at some secret he wasn't telling her. A lump formed in her throat and guilt washed over her like a tidal wave. The wind picked up suddenly, whistling through the harbor, and overhead the clouds began to darken.

Oliver's hand came up to rest on her shoulder. "Angelfish," he whispered, interrupting her thoughts.

A sprinkling of rain began to fall as Josephine blinked back tears.

"I'm sorry," she said, wiping her eyes and breathing in deeply. The rain stopped at once. "I must get better control of this."

Oliver gave her a sad smile and led her down to the pier in silence.

Culligan's Shipping Company was posted on the building stationed directly in front of the docks. It was a warehouse where shipments were stored and inspected; those that had just been brought in by merchants or those about to be exported to other destinations. Josephine followed Oliver up the stairs of the warehouse and into what she assumed was the Captain's office. It astounded her that Culligan had given up sailing at all, as much as he loved it. Perhaps her father's death had changed things for him, too. Hopefully he was still keeping his ear to the ground for any British meddling in Charlestown affairs, specifically where it concerned pirates and hunters.

The sound of glass shattering greeted them as they entered the office.

"Cursing cockroaches, Jett! You spilled all the ink!"

The man called Jett was a thin, scraggly-looking fellow. Apparently, he'd dropped an entire inkwell. He was on his hands and knees, attempting to clean it up without much success. Captain Culligan was seated behind his desk, his head in his hands.

Josephine looked up at Oliver with a bemused grin and whispered, "Jett works as the Captain's assistant?"

"Aye," Oliver sighed.

"I don't recall him being such a klutz when he worked for Father."

"Jett's a fish out of water here on land. He was a master at rigging the sails."

Josephine frowned. "Oh, I see." Her heart ached that Jett hadn't found a ship to take him on, as skilled as he'd been.

"Apologies, Captain," Jett muttered, still trying to do something about the mess, although it seemed to just be getting worse. "I'll get you a new inkwell, sir. Right away, sir."

Captain Culligan looked up to say something else to Jett, but stopped suddenly, having seen Josephine and Oliver standing in the doorway. He was a large man and thicker around the middle than most in Charlestown. His hair was the deep auburn color she remembered and his dark blue suit was striking as well; something befitting a wealthy man. A ruffled linen cravat, waistcoat, silk stockings, and buckled shoes completed the expensive ensemble. Captain Culligan, former scallywag, had turned into a legitimate businessman.

"Josephine? Is that you, my girl?" Culligan whispered, like he was waking up from a dream. He stood and walked around the desk to stand in front of Josephine. He looked so different from the last time she'd seen him nearly three years ago. There weren't even holes in his stockings. "Blow me down and strap me to the mast, it *is* you!"

Josephine giggled as he pulled her into a hug and then offered her a seat. "Please, please, come in! Jett, just leave it for now and go find us something to eat and drink." Then he added, "Something besides rum!"

Jett wiped his hands on his breeches, leaving ink stains behind, and walked to the door. "Hello, Miss Teversin," he said, bowing to Josephine as he walked to the door.

"Hello, Jett," she smiled. "Nice to see you."

He stumbled at the door frame and then disappeared. Another loud crash sounded from the bottom of the stairwell.

Josephine looked at Culligan with wide eyes and pointed back toward the door. "Did he just ...?"

"Fall down the stairs?" Culligan answered with a roll of his eyes. "Aye, does it twice a day, at least. Come sit, Josephine, and tell me how you've been. Oliver, where'd you find this scamp?" He winked at her.

"Found her in the slums coming to see you, as it were," Oliver replied with a frown. His eyes cut over to Josephine. "Being followed by some rich Englishman, Cap."

Captain Culligan gave her a stern look. "What you been up to that's got you noticed, Josephine?"

"Not a thing!" Josephine sputtered. "I've only been working in the tavern with Aunt Genny. I swear it!" Josephine peered at Oliver out of the corner of her eye. He was watching her with such intensity it made her cheeks heat up. She lowered her eyes at his scrutiny.

"You're hiding something," Oliver said.

Josephine gasped. "I am not!"

"You lowered your eyes, Angelfish. You always do that when you try to hide something."

Josephine pursed her lips and looked away.

"You'd better tell us, Josephine, or we'll be thinking the worst," said Culligan.

"You must promise not to overreact," she said pointedly to Oliver.

Oliver folded his arms over his chest and waited. She confessed all that had happened when she had wandered out to the pier the night before. She even recalled the mention of Skulthorpe and the pirate hunter following her this morning.

"Bleeding scuttle-rats, Jo!" Oliver exclaimed, running a hand over his tawny hair.

Josephine flinched at his outburst. "Is this you *not* overreacting?"

He wagged his finger at her. "I knew I should've come with you to the pier last night."

"But I'm quite alright, as you can see."

Oliver glared at her, his lips tightening into a fine line. Perhaps her last statement was a bit naive.

"This is why I didn't tell you right away, Oliver. I knew you'd be cross with me."

"Cross? *Cross?*" he said, scowling fiercely. "That don't even begin to -"

"All right, you two," Culligan interrupted. "Let's save this spat for later."

"Oh, of course," Josephine agreed impertinently and turned to Oliver. "This evening, then, at the Kraken's Lookout?"

Scowling, Oliver pushed up out of his seat to pace behind her. Josephine was surprised at how angry he was. Didn't he realize she could take care of herself?

Culligan turned back to Josephine. "This hunter shot you in the shoulder, you say? But it wasn't a pistol."

"If he had shot me with a pistol, more damage would have been done."

"Like a bloody hole in the chest?" Oliver muttered behind her.

"Quite," Josephine answered, wincing at Oliver's retort. "It was some sort of poison. I slept an hour at least."

"And you're sure you heard the name …" Culligan leaned forward and dropped his voice to a whisper. "*Skulthorpe?*" His eyes darted back and forth like he was expecting Skulthorpe to pop his head into the room like a ghost upon hearing his own name.

"I'm positive," said Josephine. "And why are you whispering? Skulthorpe is not -"

Culligan shushed her and waved his hands for her silence. "Don't be saying the name too loud." He peeked at the window over his shoulder. "That man's got his spies, his *hunters*, everywhere. And you know good and well that *he's* the bloke that killed your father."

"I know." Josephine shivered again and Oliver placed his hand on her shoulder, warming her insides with his presence. She didn't dare look up at him, knowing she might cry again. "That's why I've come to see you, Captain. I thought you might have heard why he's in Charlestown. I thought his headquarters was in New York. At least it *was.*"

"That it is, Josephine, but the man's got a mighty long reach. He has his hunters scouring the colonies on the lookout for your kind."

"But I thought Father was the last. And … and me."

A thud and the sound of breaking glass sounded from the stairway.

"That'll be Jett with the tea and biscuits," Culligan announced just as Jett stumbled through the door carrying a tray. "I suppose you broke one of my cups?"

"Only one this time, Captain," he answered meekly.

Josephine beamed at him. "Thank you, Jett."

Jett gave her a bashful nod and nearly dropped the entire tray.

"Here, let me." Josephine rose from her seat and began to pour the tea. Neither Oliver nor Culligan wanted any. Josephine nearly gagged but somehow managed to swallow the bitter-tasting liquid. She coughed to cover her repulsion and added more sugar.

Jett had likely let it steep a bit too long, but Josephine suspected this tea was not imported from the East India Company. The fight with England over the tax on tea had been ongoing in the colonies since

May. Merchants were leaving the better quality British tea on the ships to rot while smuggling it illegally from the Dutch. The smuggled tea was cheap but it didn't taste as good.

She noticed Oliver sharing a smirk with Culligan. With a wicked gleam in her eye, Josephine said, "Really, Oliver. You must have a cup."

Oliver grinned and narrowed his eyes at her. "Already had too much today, Angelfish, but you drink as much as you want."

Stifling the urge to gag again, Josephine set down her cup without drinking another drop. "We really must be going, I suppose. But not before you tell me -"

Culligan stood abruptly, knocking over the chair he'd been sitting in, his eyes wide with fear. "You ought not be meddling, but if you're determined, then you'd best come with me."

After his startling interruption, Captain Culligan led them from the office, leaving Jett behind, fumbling with the foul-tasting tea. Josephine and Oliver trudged down the steps behind him, wondering what on earth was wrong.

"What was that all about?" Josephine asked the Captain.

"Didn't want to be saying too much in front of Jett. The less he knows about this business, the better ... for now."

The warehouse was filled with shipping containers of all sizes. Sailors were coming and going, busy with the morning's work of hauling the shipments in and out. As they passed the workers, they greeted Culligan with a jolly, "Morning Cully," then continued on as if the other two were not there at all.

In the back corner of the storage area, furthest from the entrance, sat large crates that were coated with dust. They looked as if they'd been sitting there for years and, a moment later, Josephine found out why. Hiding behind the stack of boxes was a secret hatch that led down to an even lower level.

"Oh lovely," Josephine murmured. "Another cellar."

Once he and Oliver had lifted the trapdoor, Culligan lit a candle and led the way down the rickety wooden steps. Oliver offered his hand to Josephine and they stepped down together. She did not let go of his hand right away, because this room was even more eerie than the cellar she had woken up in last night. Not only that, Oliver's warm hand felt quite nice around her own.

The ceiling was extremely low, just an inch above Josephine's head. Neither one of the men could stand up straight. It was dank and smelled like salt, as if the sea were just beyond the walls.

"What's down here, Cap?" Oliver whispered.

Culligan stalked to the back corner, the candle lighting his way with a soft orange glow in the dark. Two treasure chests were sitting side by side in the corner.

"Something I've been hiding for a little more than three years. Old Blacktail found them on a British merchant ship. Wasn't supposed to find it, methinks."

The lid creaked as Culligan opened it. Inside was a sizable amount of dirt, but sitting on top was the same smallish pistol the hunter had used on her. Josephine's breath caught when she saw the strange thing.

Culligan quirked an eyebrow at Josephine. "That be the pistol that shot you?"

"Aye, but how is it that you have one here? I've never seen the like before?"

The Captain scratched his bearded chin. "Best that we could figure, these here pistols shoot something about the size of a musket ball, but without the gunpowder."

She reached for the tiny thing. It fit neatly into the palm of her hand. "Whatever the man shot me with, it didn't look like a musket ball, but the size was comparable. Did you acquire any of the poison devices?"

Culligan shook his head. "Just the wee pistol. Seems rather a waste if you ask me."

"Whoever created these needed a weapon that was easy to conceal," said Josephine. Her shoulder tingled with the memory. "And they don't want their targets dead."

"Lucky for you," Oliver added.

Josephine nodded and returned the tiny pistol to its resting place. "What's in the other one?"

Culligan flipped up the lid of the second chest. Oliver and Josephine stared down at its contents, completely mystified.

"Is this a blooming joke?" asked Oliver, his brows furrowed in confusion.

The container was filled to the brim with all sorts of ladies' accessories: parasols, corsets, fans, shoes, handkerchiefs, and gloves.

"Blacktail told me the two chests was being guarded fiercely. Both of them. Said there was a letter inside the first one talking about how these ... er ... garments and the pistol were prototypes of some sort. They were to deliver the goods to Skulthorpe in New York for further testing." Culligan closed both chests once more.

Josephine snorted. "Oh, for goodness' sake, Captain. How could ladies' garments be any sort of prototype or *useful* in the hands of hunters? I doubt they know what to do with them."

Captain Culligan didn't argue and neither did Oliver, which was a first.

Oliver narrowed his eyes. "You said there was a letter inside one of the chests?"

"Aye," Culligan replied.

"What happened to it?" asked Josephine. "I wouldn't mind getting a look at it."

"Blacktail burned it," Culligan replied. "He delivered these here personally. Told me to never let anyone know they was here. Not two months later, he was bargaining for your life. I ain't touched them since. Wasn't till you got here mentioning Skulthorpe that I thought of them."

"Skulthorpe knew that Blacktail was hiding these things," Oliver stated.

Josephine turned to Culligan. "That's what you're saying, isn't it?" she added. "My father was murdered because he found these prototypes and *not* because he was the Pirate of Blacktail Cove?"

Culligan shrugged. "A bit of both, methinks."

"But the more pressing matter now is -"

"You've become the target," Oliver said, frowning at her again.

"Oliver, you cannot blame *me* for this. I knew nothing of these prototypes!"

Oliver opened his mouth to reply but was stopped by the sound of men shouting from the main floor above. They all glanced up in silence.

"Captain Culligan? We're here for inspections!" shouted someone in the warehouse.

Culligan blew out the candle quickly. "Bloody inspectors. Stay hidden till I get 'em out of here, eh?"

He hopped up the stairs to greet them, leaving Oliver and Josephine alone in the dark. It wasn't long before the darkness began to press in on Josephine. The smell of salt and moisture in the air took her back to a night when her father had hidden her below decks during a violent storm on the Atlantic. The *Nepheria* swayed and pitched with the rise and fall of the waves. The one candle her father had dared leave below decks with Josephine had toppled over and was snuffed out. Oliver had been on deck with the other men, so she'd been all alone.

Josephine pinched her eyes shut and felt herself stagger as if the room had begun to move like a ship at sea. A warm hand clamped down on her shoulder, steadying her.

"Oliver?" she whispered, clasping hold of his hand.

"Angelfish," Oliver murmured into her ear.

Josephine swallowed. She hadn't realized he'd been standing so close.

"Are you all right?" he asked. His close proximity was a welcome warmth.

"Topping, actually," Josephine replied sarcastically. "It's not every day a girl feels like her life is in danger."

Oliver gently squeezed her shoulder. "I'll look after you."

"I don't need looking after. I would much prefer some answers."

"What you need is a good kick in the breeches, Jo. You'd best not be putting your nose into British business."

Josephine gasped at his impudence.

Oliver continued, "And you need more weapons ..."

"My daggers will do, thank you."

"... a pistol, and a sword. And a disguise that'll hide more of your ... *assets*."

Josephine elbowed him in the ribs. "Keep your eyes off my *assets*, you ... you ... troglodyte!"

"Troglodyte?" Oliver said, snickering at her choice of insults. "Oy, that one hurt, Angelfish. Almost as much as your bony elbows. You need some better curses if you're going to call names. Like bilge-sucking toad or kraken's arse, or -"

"That will be quite enough of that, Oliver," said Josephine, trying to keep from giggling. "Growing up on a ship taught me plenty, thank you." Josephine added, "And my elbows are *not* bony!"

"Fine, Angelfish. They are very pleasant elbows."

Josephine thanked him for his facetious remark with another elbow in the ribs. Oliver grunted from the blow.

After another charged silence, Oliver asked her, "You think that toff will be waiting for you at the Kraken's Lookout?"

"I had thought that, yes." Josephine chewed on her lip and whispered, "Surely he wouldn't be so bold as to actually come into the tavern again. He'll be waiting in the alley or something. I worry for Aunt Genny. I don't want her involved in this."

"Don't worry," he said reassuringly. "I have me an idea or two. What do you say to a day on the docks with me? Maybe I can get my hands on a sloop and we can go out on the water for a bit, eh?"

"Oh, Oliver! You mean it?" Josephine beamed at the idea. "But what about the Captain? Your job? Won't you be missed?"

"You let me worry about that, Angelfish," said Oliver, squeezing her shoulder again.

Suddenly, Josephine's day seemed much, much brighter.

SIX

I t wasn't difficult for Oliver to beg off from his duties on the dock. He'd pulled Captain Culligan aside after the inspectors were gone and explained that he'd like to keep a weather eye on Josephine for a while. Culligan had agreed wholeheartedly and even offered to pay Oliver his regular wages just for watching out for her.

Culligan felt somewhat responsible for her since Joseph had died. Joseph was one of the few who had known Captain Culligan by his true name: Lewis Brown. Culligan had thought the name Captain Brown was a bit dull, so he'd changed it to something that inspired a little more fear and respect.

Oliver managed to round up a small sloop to take Josephine sailing into the Outer Harbor. He had always delighted in her smiles, and the thing that brought Josephine the most joy was sailing. The sloop was small enough for the two of them to handle. Josephine had even taken down her hair and kicked off her shoes and stockings for the short trip, just like the old days. She was a glorious sight to behold.

He'd had to mentally kick himself for staring so openly at her. Josephine was far too good for the likes of him. She'd been raised by a pirate, sure, but she was better than the lot of them.

It was impossible not to admire her. As they skimmed across the water, the wind whipped her hair out behind her. At the tavern, her locks seemed so dark, but the sun's rays brought out honey-colored strands that shimmered, and the gold flecks in her brown eyes sparkled as much as the choppy seawater. She was enchanting. A knot formed in his chest knowing she was completely out of his reach.

As the sun was setting, Oliver and Josephine found themselves walking back to the Kraken's Lookout again.

"Honestly, Oliver. Was this disguise necessary?"

Oliver gave her a lopsided grin. "You don't look half bad as a boy."

Josephine grimaced. "What you're really saying is that I don't possess enough of those *assets* you were mentioning earlier. That's what makes this disguise so believable."

"I didn't say that, Angelfish." Oliver didn't believe she had anything to be ashamed of in the least, but a sailor's ratty clothes tended to be baggy, so they worked perfectly. They'd tucked Josephine's hair under a scarf and dirtied her face a bit to cover her pale skin. "Do you still have that pistol I gave you?"

"Aye," she answered. "And, of course, you can see the sword sheathed on this blasted shoulder belt. It's a trifle heavy to wear."

"You'll get used to it."

"Get used to it?" Josephine gaped at him. "You cannot expect me to wear this thing all the time? I much prefer my daggers. They can *at least* be hidden."

"But you're much better with the sword, Angelfish."

"Oh, I suppose. If I must."

"Aye, you must," Oliver said with an impatient sigh. "If that blackguard happens to try and nab you from your bedroom, you slit his gullet or shoot him with the pistol, do you hear?"

Josephine shook her head at him. "Oliver, I don't know if I could *kill* the scoundrel. I've never done anyone in before. Perhaps you could take care of it for me?"

"That would require me to sleep in your room," he told her, peering down to see how she took that news.

"Yes, I suppose it would be improper for you to stay the night."

Oliver nearly groaned thinking about it.

"Do you see him?" he said, changing the subject.

"No, but that doesn't mean he isn't somewhere lurking. He is well-versed in the art of lurking."

Oliver barged into the tavern with Josephine on his heels, approaching Genny at once.

"Oliver!" Genny announced, clapping her hands in delight. "You are looking handsome this evening. But young Josephine is not here I'm afraid."

"I'm right here, Aunt Genny," Josephine grumbled, giving them both a peevish glare.

Genny's jaw dropped in astonishment. "Oh, darling, you look horrible in those clothes. Go! Go!" She shooed Josephine toward the stairs. "And do not come back down till you are decent!"

Oliver chuckled and pulled Josephine close before she could sneak up to her bedroom. "I'll be near tonight, Angelfish. If you need me, just scream."

JOSEPHINE TOOK off her sword belt and slung it across the room into the corner. Oh, she could just scream! Josephine couldn't have been more humiliated, and in front of Oliver, no less. When would Aunt Genny learn to keep her *horrible* comments to herself?

And Oliver! Josephine covered her heated face with her hands. Oliver had dressed her up as a boy and then complimented her on how boyish she looked. It was extremely disheartening.

Josephine ripped the scarf from her head, dunked it into the water basin by her bed, and scrubbed the dirt from her face.

At least he spoke highly of my swordsmanship, she thought. Her father had taught her well and Oliver could certainly attest to that. He and Josephine had practiced regularly when they were at sea.

Using the pistol was what worried Josephine most. Like the sword, she was more than capable of handling the weapon. She just didn't know if she had the stomach to pull the trigger when pointed at an actual person.

Once Josephine had gotten past her embarrassment, she checked her room for unwanted guests. When she was certain no one was hiding, she changed back into her simple blue dress from yesterday. She thought about returning to the tavern, but she couldn't bear to face Oliver after feeling so mortified. Slipping into bed, Josephine pulled the covers up to her chin and closed her eyes. Getting some shut-eye was best. The tavern would be crowded till after midnight. Surely the hunter wouldn't dare try anything until then. If he did come for her, she'd be armed and well-rested.

It wasn't at all difficult for Nathaniel to scale the wall of the inn and sneak through the open window of the Teversin girl's room. He'd been waiting patiently for her to return to the Kraken's Lookout, and she hadn't disappointed him. The disguise she wore was creative, but not enough to keep him from recognizing her. Once she was inside, she had lit a candle and shown him the way to her window. Nathaniel waited until after the French barmaid had locked up for the night before attempting to make the climb.

The girl's room was a tiny cubicle that one would commonly find at a disreputable inn. There was a wardrobe by the door, a standing mirror on the opposite corner, and a small bed next to the window where he stood. *If one could even call it a bed at all,* he thought snidely. It looked more like a cot one would find in a prison.

But in that bed was the girl he'd been given the task of retrieving. She was covered from head-to-toe with a rough woolen blanket. Nathaniel shouldn't have much trouble. Barnaby gave him plenty of the sleeping powder to use on her. Inhaling the tiniest bit would have her unconscious in seconds.

Pulling a small vial from his cloak, Nathaniel put a pinch of the powder into his palm. But as he was reaching for the covers, he felt the tiniest prick of a blade at his throat.

"Did you think that because I'm female, it would be easy to abduct me again?"

Nathaniel glanced down at the bed, then straightened and chuckled. She was back in her blue dress from the night before, but her hair was loose and fell in waves down her back. The girl looked incredibly pirate-like, in a charming sort of way.

"Very clever, Miss Teversin," he said in a congratulatory manner. "Very clever, indeed. Pillows under the covers. Well done! I don't believe I've seen such smooth trickery since my baby sister used this same maneuver to sneak down to the kitchen for some sweets."

"You mock me, sir, but my smooth tricks left you befuddled enough this morning."

Nathaniel froze and raised his brows in disbelief. "You *planned* that chaos? I do not believe you. How could you possibly?"

The girl gave him a smug smile. "I have my ways. And, I'll have you know, I'm quite adept with this sword and will not be taken easily."

Nathaniel looked her over, noticing her balanced stance and grip on the blade's handle. It seemed she was knowledgeable in swordplay, but he didn't have time for such nonsense. His movements were swift as he attempted to toss the sleeping powder into her face, but the girl was indeed quick with her sword. Josephine smacked the steel of the blade against his wrist, sending the powder in the wrong direction. With another flick, she'd relieved him of the vial as well. The flask dropped to the floor and shattered, ruining what remained of the powder. The tip of her sword pricked the underside of his chin before he could make another move.

"Miss Teversin, I believe I've underestimated you."

"And you always will, I imagine," she snapped. "Now get out of my room or I'll gut you like a fish."

Nathaniel smirked. "My dear, you should have taken your dear Oliver's advice tonight."

"Oh, yes?" she said, narrowing her eyes at him. "Do enlighten me, kind sir."

Nathaniel narrowed his eyes at the Teversin girl. If she had intended him harm, she would have stuck him with her blade while his back was turned. Last night, she had shown a considerable amount of restraint by only disabling the soldiers. Nathaniel had intentionally left the dagger in her possession to see what she would do.

Sensing the girl didn't have the stomach to truly injure anyone, Nathaniel lunged for her. He clasped her sword arm and overpowered her at once. As she struggled to loosen his hold, Nathaniel reached for his napshot and shot another dart into her arm.

He backed away quickly. "You should have slit my gullet while you had the chance."

The Teversin girl gasped and glared daggers at him. "Blast it all! You cheated and shot me again!"

The furious expression she wore was highly entertaining. He tucked the napshot safely inside his cloak, smoothed the wrinkles from his suit, and readjusted his gloves. All he had to do was wait for her to pass out. "Did you expect me to fight fairly with a pirate?"

"I suppose not, hunter."

Five seconds later, the girl's sword slipped from her grasp and fell to the floor. Her words slurred as she said, "Can you at least be a gentleman and catch me this time?"

He nodded his assent. "On my honor."

She swayed for another few seconds and then finally succumbed to the sleeping potion he'd injected. Scooping her up as promised, Nathaniel slung her over his shoulder to deliver her to Mr. Skulthorpe - *again*.

SEVEN

J osephine awoke alone again. This time, her head wasn't aching and the room wasn't completely dark. Several sconces on the walls had been lit, casting eerie shadows across the room.

"At least the scoundrel kept his word and didn't let me hit the blasted floor," she muttered, rubbing the tender spot on her arm where he'd shot her.

Lifting herself into a sitting position and looking around, Josephine was astonished by the grandeur of the room. This one room alone was as large as Aunt Genny's tavern and was fit for a king, or at least some other titled snob.

The four-poster bed she was lying on was covered in a rich burgundy spread, trimmed with gold. Matching velvet drapes hung like curtains around the bed, tied back with shiny gold ropes with tassels. A matching chaise had been placed on a red, blue, and gold floral rug at the end of the bed and a fire blazed in the ornate, mahogany fireplace on the opposite wall.

Josephine didn't feel like a captive at all, but a welcomed guest. Perhaps the hunter thought she would be so grateful waking up in a comfortable room that she would conveniently forget about escaping. Well, that was certainly not going to happen.

Josephine felt for her daggers. They were all accounted for, surprisingly. Was the hunter really so naive, underestimating her again? Why would he allow her to keep them? What was his game this time?

Taking a turn around this large guest room, Josephine, once again, did not see anything more useful than her daggers, so she drew one that had been strapped to her leg. She strode to the door. Before she could put a finger on the shiny brass knob, someone rapped loudly from the other side. Josephine jumped aside just in time for the door to swing open. A British soldier, in his bright red uniform, stormed into the room.

Without hesitation, Josephine bashed him in the back of the skull with the hilt of her dagger, knocking him out cold. The soldier hit the hardwood floor with a thud.

Josephine rolled her eyes at the unconscious man. "Could you be any louder?"

Relieving him of his sword, she crept out into the hall. The place must have been an absolute mansion because there were at least ten guest rooms in this one hallway. A crimson and navy patterned rug stretched from one end of the corridor to the other. Four-foot-tall portraits of wigged gentlemen - family members, no doubt - hung between each doorway and three shiny brass chandeliers hung from the ceiling.

Boots thundered up the stairs at the end of the hall. Josephine slipped into the nearest room to hide and wait. Two soldiers in their red uniforms jogged by, both wearing white wigs beneath their tricorns. One was a captain; the other, a private. Josephine debated whether she should continue to hide. Upon realizing she was missing, they would certainly raise an alarm. Sword in one hand and her dagger in the other, Josephine stepped out into the hallway to confront them.

The soldiers skidded to a halt when they spotted her.

The hallway was so narrow that only one of the men could engage her at a time. The captain stepped forward, drew his sword, and smiled. Josephine narrowed her eyes at his arrogance. The redcoat assumed he would win the duel without breaking a sweat.

"Just because I'm wearing this dress doesn't mean I'll lose."

The soldier looked her up and down. "You're going to trip over those skirts and injure yourself."

She snorted. "I don't think so."

Josephine bent her knees and lifted her sword arm, ready to prove him wrong. The redcoat chuckled at her smart remarks and advanced. Josephine bit her lip in concentration and focused on the man's blade. He attacked and then backed away a few times, testing her resolve and skill. Josephine shuffled backward and then forward again, matching his footwork step for step. She held her own against him until the soldier flicked the end of his sword at her, slicing right through her sleeve.

Josephine retreated a few steps and examined her shoulder. He could have drawn blood with that thrust ... but he didn't.

She gave him an accusing glare. "You're going easy on me."

"I was instructed *not* to kill you," he said with a cocky smirk. His sword hung down by his side.

Arrogant swine, Josephine thought.

But maybe he didn't have much to fear. She had never killed a man before.

"Do you surrender?" the soldier asked, startling Josephine out of her morbid thoughts.

Josephine scowled and advanced again. Surrender was not an option. Keeping a firm grip on her sword, Josephine battled back. She swiped her sword at him. The soldier jumped back against the wall, dodging the blade and smashing into a portrait hanging on the wall. He pushed off the wall with his elbow, sending the portrait crashing to the floor.

Painful vibrations shot up her arm each time their blades clanged together. Soon, Josephine began to tire. As she whirled to the left, she stumbled on the edge of the rug and hit the wall with her shoulder. The soldier spun and struck back. Josephine quickly adjusted her stance and parried his thrust. The gleam in his eyes revealed that he was aware of her weakened state.

Josephine shuffled backward again, putting distance between her and her opponent. Her heart was pounding and she was gasping for air.

The redcoat, breathing hard as well, lowered his sword and studied her.

"You've done yourself proud," he said. "But you cannot possibly defeat both of us."

A rush of anger coursed through Josephine at the thought of defeat. She had not asked for this. *They* had kidnapped *her*. In response to her fury, white-hot magic surged up through her torso, down her arms, and exploded from the palms of her hands. The soldiers were blown fifty feet down the hall and lay motionless on the floor. Even Josephine tumbled backward and landed on her rear. The sword and dagger that she'd been holding had shot out of her hands. The blades were sunk deep into the walls either side of her. The portraits on the walls had been charred and lay in pieces on the floor.

Josephine stared down at her hands, frightened and appalled at what she'd just done. "I killed them," she whispered.

Scrambling to her feet, Josephine turned and fled in the opposite direction, a sick feeling in her belly. She had to escape without losing control again.

At the end of the hallway, a wide staircase curved down to the first floor around a three-tiered, wrought iron chandelier. There was nowhere else to go. Josephine raced down the stairs, holding her skirts up around her knees to keep from tripping.

Nearly halfway down, she realized there were three more redcoats waiting for her at the bottom. Without thinking, Josephine grabbed the banister and leapt over the side. Grabbing hold of the bottom rung of the chandelier with both hands, she swung down to the floor, just as she used to do from the rigging of her father's ship. Josephine hit the floor rolling and was up and running seconds later, despite her skirts.

Josephine dashed to the back of the house into a ballroom but froze at the sight of red uniforms and the sound of muskets being cocked. There were at least twenty British soldiers, ten on each side of the room, all with their muskets aimed at her. There was no escaping this trap. Josephine stood still, fighting the urge to drop to the ground in exhaustion.

Amidst the sea of red uniforms, one black suit stood out. It was him. The hunter who'd kidnapped her, not once, but twice now. She could finally see him properly in the lit-up ballroom. He had the most startling silver-blue eyes, like the color of steel. They clashed brilliantly with his long, black lashes. There was an arrogant gleam in those eyes and a smirk on his face, as if he'd won some sort of game against her.

Josephine scowled, wondering if he'd still be grinning after she had thrown one of her daggers at him. She wouldn't kill the man, but perhaps a hole in the ear would teach him some manners.

A single, slow clap of applause sounded behind her and echoed across the room. "Well done," a man sneered. "Well done indeed, Miss Teversin."

Cold chills rippled up Josephine's spine at the sound of that taunting voice. It was one she remembered quite well. Gathering what little courage she had, Josephine lifted her chin and turned to face her father's executioner.

Garreck Skulthorpe.

He wore an extravagant suit of royal blue and gold trim, with a fancy ruffled neck cloth. The man was a bit younger than her father had been, maybe late thirties, but his pompous attitude and white wig made him seem older. He was a handsome man, even with the small scar on his cheek. One might believe him to be the perfect gentleman, if not for the cruelty in his dark eyes.

He placed his hands behind his back and looked down his nose at her like she was a bug that needed to be crushed beneath his heel. "You do not disappoint, my dear. Wasn't she brilliant, Runik?" Skulthorpe had directed the question to the man in black. When Josephine's head swiveled back to him, he was still glaring at her.

"Come, my dear, into the sitting room where we can be more comfortable," Skulthorpe announced, spinning on his heel and striding out of the ballroom. "Runik, bring her along."

The man called Runik gripped her elbow tightly and dragged her out of the ballroom, back toward the foyer where the chandelier was still swinging from her stunt. Oliver really was going to murder her when he found out about all this. She hoped she'd live long enough to give him the opportunity.

Runik read her thoughts exactly and murmured into her ear, "You should have killed me when you had the chance."

"Aye, I should have."

He merely chuckled and pulled her along. How could a man so devilishly handsome be such an evil little codfish?

Four soldiers were posted outside the double doors of the sitting room. Skulthorpe shut and latched them while Runik all but tossed her into the nearest chair.

Josephine was, once again, in awe of the grandeur of the chamber. The walls had been covered with sky-blue wallpaper and the fabric of the chairs and settee matched perfectly. The crown moldings along the edges of the ceiling had been trimmed in gold, and a brass chandelier hung from the middle of the room. The fireplace to Josephine's left was at least six feet tall with a mantel carved from white marble. Above the mantel hung a large clock showing the time to be one-thirty in the morning.

Is this Skulthorpe's home? Josephine wondered. *He must be awfully rich.*

Skulthorpe sat on the settee across from her. On the table between them sat tea and biscuits. Runik did not sit, but stood in the corner of the room with his arms folded across his chest. Josephine sat with a ramrod straight posture, suddenly feeling as if she were a lamb in the presence of two hungry lions. She lowered her eyes and ran her hands nervously through her mussed hair, waiting for them to get on with it.

"You really are a wonder, Miss Teversin, truly," said Skulthorpe, pouring two cups of tea. "Have some. There is very little of it in the colonies these days and you must be exhausted from your efforts." He held out the cup of tea on a saucer for her. "Come now, it's quite rude to refuse a perfectly good cup of tea from your host."

His words sounded cordial enough, but his eyes held a dangerous glint that dared her to cross him. Josephine took the cup of tea with barely steady hands.

After a minute or two of sipping in silence with the two men glaring at her, Josephine finally gathered the courage to ask, "Why have you not called for your hunters?"

"Hunters, Miss Teversin?"

"That is why I am here, is it not? I cannot imagine you have suddenly developed a soft spot for taking tea with someone who may or may not be a pirate."

Narrowing his eyes, Skulthorpe drawled, "Indeed. Regardless, I find that I am in need of your … particular skills."

Skulthorpe pushed up from the settee and began to wander about the room. "When I proposed my idea of hiring you, Runik was set against it. But who, in their right mind, would ever suspect a woman of …" he hesitated.

"Being a pirate?" Josephine finished for him.

"Yes, exactly!" He shook his finger in the air as if he'd come up with a brilliant idea.

Josephine snorted. "Mr. Skulthorpe, pirates do not wear petticoats."

"True enough. No immortal pirate has ever been a female, nor has any pirate ever fathered a child - at least that we know of. Be that as it may, you still have skills that I find useful," he said sharply. "You've shown that you are resourceful in a bind. You think quickly, move strategically, and you are not disinclined from getting dirty to accomplish the task at hand. Your skills with weapons are far superior to many grown men." Skulthorpe chuckled again. "The Corporal you clubbed is seeing stars and, just a moment ago, I saw Captain Norton staggering down the stairs. He is *still* catching his breath from your duel and he brags that he is an expert swordsman!"

Josephine pinched her lips together. Her swordsmanship was not the reason the captain was catching his breath. Regardless, she was relieved that she hadn't killed the two men after all.

"You exceeded my expectations, to be sure."

Josephine's brows dipped in confusion. "Expectations? For what purpose?"

Skulthorpe looked down at her again from where he'd been pacing. "We are men with the common purpose of secretly extracting and, when necessary, eliminating patriot radicals here in the colonies. We are called the Brotherhood. We enforce the ideologies that the British Crown has established here through clandestine undertakings."

"Secret agents for King George, then?" Josephine asked point blank.

Skulthorpe stopped and glanced at Runik, a baffled look on his face.

Brazenly rolling her eyes, she said, "I am not an imbecile, Mr. Skulthorpe. I know what words like *eliminate* and *clandestine* mean."

He nodded and took up his pacing again.

Josephine pressed for more information. "What about the hunters? Do they belong to this Brotherhood as well?"

Skulthorpe pressed his lips together in a sinister grin. "I believe there have been enough questions. You will begin tomorrow. Consider yourself on my payroll and under the direction of Nathaniel Runik here. He will give you your assignments and you will report only to him. Is that understood?"

"Payroll? To do what exactly?"

"Information gathering."

"You need *me* to gather information for *you?*" asked Josephine. "I thought you were secret operatives. Isn't that what *you* are supposed to be good at?"

His lip curled in contempt. "I do admit to some surprise that I would lower myself to obtaining the help of a pirate and common street urchin, but I will do what is necessary to achieve my goals."

She set her teacup down on the table. "And what if I don't want to be on your payroll?"

The dangerous glint was back in his eyes. "Miss Teversin, if you refuse my offer, you will be found guilty of piracy by association with the Pirate of Blacktail Cove. You will then be executed." His dark, wicked gaze swept over her again. "You may not be showing any signs of your pirate legacy, but that will not stop me from summoning the hunters. And it will not end there, Miss Teversin. If you do not complete *all* that I ask you to do, you can be sure that those you hold dear will be made to suffer."

The blood drained from Josephine's face.

"Quite, my dear," said Skulthorpe. "Think about your dear Aunt Genevieve and that boy ... Oliver, is it? You wouldn't want anything to happen to them, now would you?"

A lump had formed in Josephine's throat and her hands were shaking. As hard as she'd tried to keep Oliver and Genny out of this business, they were right in the middle of it. Of course, Skulthorpe *would* find out everything about her so that he could blackmail her into doing his bidding. The idea of him doing anything less would be laughable. However, he was somehow oblivious to her unpredictable powers. Did he believe the storm Josephine had conjured three years ago was a coincidence? If he wasn't aware of her strange magic, then she meant to keep it that way.

Josephine felt sick. It was obvious now that she had been deliberately herded into that ballroom. Everything she'd been through in the last two days had been nothing but a test; some evaluation of her cleverness and weaponry. They had toyed with her in some sort of twisted game and she had lost.

Josephine's heart sank in defeat as she met Skulthorpe's leering eyes. "It seems I have no choice in the matter."

"I am glad we understand each other. Runik, escort Miss Teversin back to her tavern. See that she is prepared for all that will be required."

Without a backward glance, Garreck Skulthorpe was striding through the double doors, leaving her alone with Mr. Runik. Josephine sat motionless, staring blankly at the doors and lost in her anxious thoughts over this fiasco.

"Come along, Miss Teversin," Mr. Runik said impatiently from the doorway.

Jolted back into the present, she blinked and shifted her eyes to find the dark rogue. His deep voice had an edge as sharp as his suit. He continued to glower. Feeling extremely put out over the last two days, she huffed and rose from her seat, following Mr. Runik to a carriage that was waiting for them in front of the estate.

Sitting across from one another, they rode in silence. The carriage moved along slowly, swaying with the gait of the horses and the bumps in the road. Josephine soon grew uncomfortable trying to keep steady against the motion of the coach, but also because of Mr. Runik's piercing glare.

Runik. The name sounded so familiar to her for some reason.

"What was that?" he snapped.

She hadn't realized she'd spoken aloud. Josephine cleared her throat and muttered, "It was nothing."

"Humph."

The dark scruff on the man's face was so striking that Josephine thought she might have to give herself a good knock on the head to keep from staring. *Especially since he's a villain, you fool!* she scolded herself silently. Instead of gaping at him like an idiot, Josephine toyed with the loose threads on her tattered dress. Unfortunately, this Runik fellow was not one to be ignored.

"Tell me, Miss Teversin, because I have been anxious to hear the truth: why would anyone *want* to become a pirate? It is not exactly a high rank to be achieved."

Stunned by the abrupt question, one that she had never been asked, Josephine did not answer right away. Her hesitation earned another patronizing query.

"Was that question too difficult for you to answer?"

Josephine pursed her lips at his condescending tone. "Honestly, I have no idea why men choose to be pirates."

"I find that hard to believe."

"I have only known one pirate and I wasn't born yet when he made his change. I cannot tell you what he was thinking at the time."

"Was it the gold, do you think?" he asked. "I've heard that immortal pirates are able to magically find whatever treasure they set their minds to."

Josephine bit her lip to keep from confirming that bit of truth. It was indeed a fact that true immortal pirates were able to track whatever treasure they deemed most important and, more often than not, material wealth was high on the list for many men. The rumor that pirates were merely gold-seekers and robbers was an easy one for people to accept, but it did not always make it true. Not every pirate believed that gold equals wealth.

She recalled what her father had said to her just minutes before he died, and her breath caught. *You've always been my greatest treasure. Always.* Josephine remembered the warmth in his brown eyes when he looked upon her every day and how he would hold her close and kiss her forehead before she lay down to sleep. He always showed such patience with her while teaching her new skills. The joy he wore on his face for all to see after she'd mastered the technique … all the riches in the world could never replace what they'd shared as father and daughter.

Swallowing the lump in her throat, she whispered with a quivering voice, "Not everyone's treasure is gold."

Ignoring her, Mr. Runik continued his barrage of questions. "What about those stories of pirates who plundered ships? Can you honestly look me in the eye and tell me that pirates have never ransacked a ship?"

Balling her hands into fists, Josephine could not resist defending her father. "There are a good many immortal pirates who are thieves. My father was not one of them. We were not swimming in gold, as you can plainly see." She gestured to her worn out gown. "Father was an honest merchant and an honorable man."

Mr. Runik chuckled. "An honest and honorable pirate?"

She gritted her teeth to keep from flaying him with her tongue. Unfortunately, there were a great many common pirates in the world who ransacked ships for gold and other items of value. That did not mean they had been changed to become a true immortal pirate. Immortal pirates were transformed by witches. If they had not made that transition, then they were just a common thug with no magic or long lifespan. Ordinary pirates knew nothing of the blood-bond between them and their crew, nor did they have to worry about being back at sea by sunset.

"And what about the ship?" he asked. "I have heard that a pirate's ship can magically sail the ocean without assistance. Whatever happened to your father's ship? I daresay it is sailing the Atlantic with no one on board!"

His mocking laugh was nearly her undoing. Biting her lip again, Josephine swallowed back her angry retorts. It was true that an immortal pirate's ship had magical qualities. If a pirate was separated from his ship for any reason, the ship could be called back to him. No crew was necessary. Common pirate ruffians did not possess this skill. Josephine had never seen it done before, but she believed what her father had taught her of the magic. Even so, there was no need to share those truths with this hunter, whose mission was to threaten her and those she loved. He'd already made the worst assumptions about her kind.

When the carriage rolled to a stop a short distance from the Kraken's Lookout, Josephine prepared to exit quickly, but Mr. Runik prevented her by holding out a small bag that jingled with coins.

"What's this?" She eyed him and then the coin purse.

"Your wages for the last two nights."

Before she could tell Mr. Runik where he could stick the coins, he'd flicked opened the door. "I will be in this spot precisely at noon tomorrow. Do not be late."

After Josephine was dismissed from the carriage with the coins in her hands, he shut the door in her face and signaled the driver to be off.

EIGHT

J osephine had been so angry over the events of the night and the
rather distasteful insinuations about her father that she very
nearly tossed the bag of coins into the harbor in a fit of rage.
Common sense prevailed, of course.

Back in her small room above the tavern, Josephine stared down at
the coin purse in her hand. *Perhaps I could save what I earn and
escape with Oliver and Genny,* Josephine thought. Money was money,
and secretly fleeing Charlestown and the colonies was more appealing
now than ever. The three of them could hide themselves somewhere
else - *anywhere* else - where Skulthorpe could never find them. But
then she would have to confess to Oliver exactly what was happening.
That was something she wasn't ready to do just yet.

The following morning, the sound of Josephine's bedroom door
banging open roused her instantly. She scrambled about for her dagger
and then stood upon the bed, almost expecting Runik back to kidnap
her again. Her dagger was raised to attack and she wouldn't hesitate
this time. That no-good scoundrel had shot her for the last time.

Through the mess of hair falling in front of her face, she saw that it
was only Oliver. His lips were pinched together. She couldn't decide
whether he was about to scold her or burst into laughter.

Lowering her blade and sweeping the hair from her eyes, she huffed, "Oliver, why are you barging in so early?"

"It ain't early, Angelfish. It's near mid-morning and you're usually up at the crack of dawn."

Josephine slapped her hands on her hips. "How do you know that?"

"Genny told me."

"Oh," Josephine squinted at the window, still trying to get her eyelids to open all the way. "What time is it?" Mr. Runik would report her to Skulthorpe if she was late on her very first day, and he would be sure to punish her, or Oliver, if she crossed him.

"It's about eight o'clock."

"Eight o'clock?" she cried. "That's not mid-morning, you ... kraken's arse!"

Oliver guffawed. "Rag-mop squid!"

Josephine gasped, picked up her pillow, and threw it at him. "I do not look like a rag-mop! Nor a squid!"

"Aye, you do!"

Oliver raked his sea-green eyes over her body. Realizing that she was only clad in her father's old shirt, heat crawled over her face and she quickly dropped down to cover herself with a blanket.

Chuckling, Oliver tossed the pillow back to the bed and then sat down in the chair by the window. Josephine shouldn't feel so uncomfortable in front of him. She'd grown up with him. He'd seen her scantily dressed before on the ship, but she had been a child then. This time seemed different to her. Josephine was suddenly feeling timid and had to swallow the lump in her throat before she could speak.

"I ... I didn't get much sleep last night. You know, from worrying."

"You lowered your eyes again, lass."

"I did not!" Josephine wailed. She had tried her best not to, anyway.

"Aye, you did," he sighed. "He got you again, didn't he? That's why you've got smudges under your eyes."

Josephine wiped at her eyes and ran her hands through her hair again.

Blast," he whispered, wiping a hand down over his face in frustration. The muscle in his jaw ticked. "Seems you got away just fine, eh?"

"Aye," she answered. It was killing her not to tell him everything, but she couldn't. She would not let him get involved in this trouble.

""It won't happen again, Oliver," she told him softly.

"You said that yesterday," he snapped. "And did I not tell you to shoot him? But you didn't, did you?"

"Trust me. After what happened last night, they were glad to be rid of me," she lied.

"Maybe you ought to stay someplace different for a bit."

"No, Oliver. I told you. They won't be back." Despite her fabrication, Josephine was able to look him in the eye. He held her stare, as if he was attempting to read her mind. He finally nodded as if satisfied that she was telling the truth. Now she had to come up with some lie to get rid of him. Josephine definitely could not tell him of her new employment with Skulthorpe. Oliver would lock her up and throw away the key. "I should get dressed then," she said. "Aunt Genny said something about shopping today. I think I might get a new gown. My blue one is getting worn out."

Oliver nodded at his cue to leave. Before closing the door, he looked back and asked, "You'll be with Genny all day?"

She nodded. Yet another lie.

"See you at the tavern tonight then, Angelfish." Oliver nodded and closed the door behind him.

Josephine dropped her head into her hands, riddled with guilt. She was already living with the guilt of her father's death. If the same thing happened to her best friend, she wouldn't survive.

Tucking all her regret away, Josephine got up and put on the old blue gown again. It wouldn't be difficult to talk Aunt Genny into going to the shops that morning to be measured for dresses. She'd been trying to get Josephine into nicer gowns for ages. Now that she had some extra money, she might as well do something useful with it. Her second motive was to make sure that she did not get caught in her lie.

NINE

S hopping was fun, Josephine had to admit. At first, she was nervous, especially when Aunt Genny had asked her where she had come by so much money.

"You are not doing anything … inappropriate, I hope?" Genny asked, eyeing her.

Josephine gaped at her. "Of course, not!"

"I was only asking, darling. Your father would jump out of the sea and murder me if you did something so scandalous."

Josephine's cheeks heated. "No. It was just a few generous tips in the tavern. I've been saving it." Josephine's heart pounded, waiting for Genny to accuse her of lying.

Genny merely smiled. "That dark, handsome stranger came back? He must be very rich!"

Dark, handsome hunter, you mean, Josephine thought.

Aunt Genny had talked her into purchasing two different gowns. One was going to be blue with white stripes, simply because blue was Josephine's favorite color. The other gown was rose-colored with a matching floral petticoat underneath. This one was Aunt Genny's favorite of course. She told Josephine that the gown would bring out the lovely shade of her hair. Josephine wasn't quite sure of that, but she had loved the material anyway.

The black carriage arrived just as Josephine was free from Genny's company. It had been only too easy to lie to her. She'd told Genny that she was going to be with Oliver all afternoon and Genny never even blinked. Well, maybe she had winked. And grinned. Josephine was fairly certain that Genny was matchmaking again. As if Josephine had any time for that today.

Mr. Runik opened the carriage door from the inside, but did not climb down to help her inside. "Miss Teversin," he said in greeting as she took the seat across from him.

"Mr. Runik," she replied in kind, though her voice was tainted with hostility. "Decided not to shoot me into submission today?"

"That has not yet been decided." He rapped his knuckles against the ceiling to signal the driver to move along.

Once in motion, Mr. Runik gave her a once over, but it was different from Oliver's flattering gaze. Runik's lip curled like he had just stepped in something offensive.

"Your gown. You will need to do something about that now that you are working for the Brotherhood."

Josephine pressed her hand to her heart, feigning insult. "Mr. Runik, my heart is simply breaking over your insults." Her words belied her true feelings, however. Josephine had never cared much how she dressed before, but she had to admit, it was a bit humiliating to be seen in such rags beside Runik. It was no wonder he did not get out of the carriage to hand her up.

He scowled. "Is this going to be your habit, Miss Teversin? Goading me with your sarcasm?"

"Only as long as you continue to look down your nose at me," she shot back. "I haven't had a lot of money to spend on gowns until recently. You'll be pleased to know that I was fitted for some this morning."

Runik gave her a puzzled frown. "Are you still angry?"

"Perhaps."

"Whatever for?"

Josephine gaped at him.

"Oh, come, Miss Teversin. You had more money in your pockets last night than you could have earned in three months at that tavern. You were not at all injured. I would have thought that a *pirate* would have found all this quite the adventure."

The sneer on his face made Josephine want to slap him. "Any other pirate, ordinary or immortal, might have shot you."

"Well, Miss Teversin, you must get past your displeasure with the situation since we are to be working together for a while."

After a minute of silence, Josephine asked him, "How long is a while?"

"Until you are no longer needed."

The blood drained from Josephine's face. Skulthorpe's idea of 'no longer needed' could mean a hole in the head. She swallowed and kept her silence on that terrifying thought.

They travelled north along the street next to the docks for a while and then turned west onto Broad Street, one of the more popular streets in Charlestown for business. The red-clay road was swarming with men and women. They kept to the edges of the road to avoid the horses and carriages. Some of them were out for a morning stroll while others strode purposefully toward their shops for a full day's work. The box-shaped buildings on each side of the road housed shops for cotton, textiles, housewares, and goods, such as tea, rice, and indigo. White signs hung over each entrance, printed with the owner's surname and his line of trade beneath it so that passersby could identify each store effortlessly. Soon, they turned north again onto King Street to head out of town.

"Where are we going?" Josephine dared to ask.

"Back to Mr. Skulthorpe's estate." When she blanched at his answer, he surprised her by adding, "If all goes smoothly then you will most likely not see him again. All of your direct orders will come from me."

Josephine breathed a sigh of relief at that news. If she never saw that man again, that would be all right with her. She looked out the window of the carriage, attempting to ignore Mr. Runik. It took all her willpower not to openly gawk at him. In the daylight, his features were even bolder, and though it was early in the day, he still had a shadow across his chin. She had a feeling that no matter how often he shaved, he would always have it.

To break the uncomfortable silence again, Josephine asked, "What sort of training am I doing today?"

"Haven't the foggiest," he answered with raised eyebrows. "We'll both find out when we arrive. Our team of tutors has been brought in to see that you are prepared in every way."

Josephine's brows knitted together, imagining something horrible. "I'm not going to be killing anyone, am I?"

"Of course not," Runik said, scoffing at the notion. "We do not need a female's help with *that* business. You will be gathering information only."

"Well, that's a relief," she replied, rolling her eyes. "I'm actually astonished you don't believe all pirates to be murderers as well."

Runik glared so coldly at Josephine that she flinched in response. She had no idea what had caused such a reaction, but she wisely kept her silence and turned her eyes to the window once more.

A few miles north of the city, the carriage made a sharp turn to the right. Josephine craned her neck out of the carriage window to get a glimpse of the elaborate estate that the darkness had hidden from her the night before. Tall oak trees lined each side of the road, creating an archway over the drive to the house. The carriage slowed to a halt. Once her feet were back on the ground, Josephine was staring up at Skulthorpe's three-story, plantation home. The mansion was white with black shutters. Six columns lined the front porch and a balcony overlooked the circle drive where the carriage was parked. The vast home seemed even larger in the light of day.

As they stepped inside the foyer, Josephine took in the lavish dwelling. The windows were open, letting in the sunlight and the cool autumn breeze. The shiny gold-plated ornaments in the halls glittered. The gold trim on the doorways and crown moldings shimmered as they strolled through the foyer. Josephine was led under the three-tiered chandelier and back to the ballroom, but no redcoats were waiting and distracting her from admiring the place.

The walls were a brilliant white against the shiny hardwood floors beneath their feet. Eight columns had been spaced around the edges of the rectangular room, separating the dance floor from the outer edge where onlookers would mingle. Arched windows lined the back wall and glass double doors led out to the veranda and the gardens beyond.

How could a mere Mister *afford all of this?* Josephine wondered. This place was as large as any duke or earl's country dwelling back in England, she was sure of it. Skulthorpe was a murdering fiend. It would not surprise Josephine if he was pilfering or blackmailing other aristocrats for his riches or someone extremely affluent in society was secretly funding his pirate-hunting efforts here in the American colonies.

The three tutors - two ladies and a gentleman - stood in the middle of the ballroom, likely waiting for her to stop gawking.

While she walked toward them, Runik glared down at her. "Be polite."

The older of the two ladies wore a white wig with a couple of spiral curls draped over her shoulder and seemed a very grandmotherly sort. The other woman wore her own raven hair in a loose but delicate knot at the crown of her head. She was as young as Josephine. Their gowns were very fine and the ladies were the definition of grace and beauty, making Josephine feel like a black sheep ... or at least a brown one. The man was finely dressed as well; a younger and less threatening version of Skulthorpe. He wore a white wig that flattered his handsome face and he was grinning from ear to ear. His hazel eyes sparkled from the sunshine beaming through the windows.

"Miss Teversin." Mr. Runik began introductions. He gestured to the lady with the white wig. "This is Madame Sophia Arment." Curtsies were exchanged. "And Miss Eleanor Bromley." More polite greetings. Madame Arment looked down her nose just as expertly as Runik. Miss Bromley gave a small smile and looked genuinely pleased to meet Josephine. "And Mister Beauregard Hopwood." The man bowed and smiled.

"You may call me Beau," he said, taking Josephine's hand and placing a kiss on her knuckles like a true gentleman. "None of this 'mister' nonsense. You'll make me feel like an old man, and I am *not* an old man." He winked at her.

"Pleasure to meet you all," Josephine said. She may have been smiling on the outside, but Josephine was on her guard. These people were employed by Skulthorpe. They were not her friends, however pleasant they seemed to be.

"Where are you from, Miss Teversin?" asked Madame Arment, surprising Josephine with an English accent, though her name sounded French.

"My father's family hailed from London, I believe," answered Josephine warily. She nearly added that her home had truly been aboard her father's ship, the *Nepheria*, but assumed Madame Arment would not think highly of that information.

"Her speech is impeccable, Mr. Runik," Sophia pointed out. "Skin needs whitening, and those freckles ..." She wrinkled her nose and shook her head like they were the most horrid things she'd ever seen. Circling around Josephine, inspecting her, Sophia added, "But her hair is clean and shiny. The neck is a wonderful length, very handsome. Posture will be improved upon when she is wearing the newer garments."

"Exactly what I was thinking, Madame," Miss Bromley interjected. "She has all the pieces." She approached Josephine and smiled again. "We just need to refine them all."

Sophia turned to Runik and waved him away with her fan. "We can take it from here, Mr. Runik."

"As you wish," he replied. Before leaving, he gripped Josephine's elbow. "A word, if you please. In private." Giving Josephine no chance to argue, he pulled her a distance away so they wouldn't be overheard. His icy glare could cleave a ship in two. "Miss Teversin, you are to be on your best behavior with them."

"Of course," said Josephine defensively. "I said that I would. I'm not a complete barbarian."

"And you are not to lash them with your sarcastic comments."

Josephine pinched her lips together to keep any from slipping out.

"Do *not* use your crude sailor profanities in front of them." He tightened his grip and pulled her closer so they were nearly nose to nose. "And do not, under any circumstances, attack them or try to escape." His fingers gripped her arm painfully. "Do you remember the agreement you made with Mr. Skulthorpe?"

The threat from last night was plain to hear in Runik's voice. It took a great deal of restraint to keep Josephine from striking the arrogance off his face, but she supposed that would fall under the 'bad behavior' category of this arrangement. Instead, she clenched her teeth together, giving him the most convincing smile she could muster. "I promise *not* to be my ... pirate self."

"Good."

Without so much as a *thank you* or *fare-thee-well*, he released her, adjusted his white gloves, and walked away, dismissing her completely.

TEN

Josephine turned back to her new companions, feeling a bit vexed by Mr. Runik's comments. Did he honestly believe that her manners were no better than some street urchin? Or was his animosity toward pirates in general? Definitely the latter of the two, she told herself. It could not be a personal vendetta against her. Mr. Runik didn't seem to be the type to be easily insulted, unless he had been offended by something she had said. The icy glare he'd given her in the coach gave her a bad feeling. Unfortunately, she could do nothing about it at present.

Thankfully, Mr. Hopwood - Beau - interrupted her thoughts before they could wander too far. "Don't worry your head about Mr. Runik," Beau told her quietly, taking her elbow. "He's a frowner, and no amount of sweets could change that." The man laughed, putting Josephine at ease.

Don't fall for their acts, Josephine. They work for the man who murdered Father.

"Stand up straight, child," Sophia ordered. "And don't frown. Ladies never frown. We keep our faces neutral unless we are pleased - then it is only a demure smile."

Josephine had no idea what a demure smile was supposed to look like, but she put her shoulders back as best she could and tried to relax her face. Madame Arment paced in front of her, Miss Bromley standing quietly to the side. Miss Bromley hadn't said much at all since they'd met, so Josephine assumed she was an assistant of sorts. Madame Arment was clearly in charge.

"We have been given instructions to turn you into something of a duchess," said Madame Arment, continuing to pace with her gloved hands folded in front of her. "You will learn to speak, stand, and walk properly, all in the most fashionable attire. You may believe this to be an easy task, but, let me assure you, it is not. You will learn to dress and act like a lady in civilized company. You will also learn the most modern dances with Beau as your partner."

"I simply love dancing," Miss Bromley told her. "It's one of my favorite things." .

"Except for a nice cup of hot chocolate," Beau added, waving his finger in the air.

"Oh, yes," Miss Bromley giggled. "Chocolate is divine."

Josephine had to bite the inside of her cheek to keep from grinning. If she wasn't careful, she was going to start to like them. Hot chocolate indeed!

Madame Arment gestured toward Miss Bromley. "Eleanor and I will be instructing you on fans and parasols and all their uses, social and otherwise."

Social and otherwise? *What did that mean?* Josephine wondered.

"And Beau, having been born and raised among the elite families in London, will advise you on the conversations and behavior of men during social engagements."

Beau bowed slightly to Josephine at the recognition. "At your service."

Sophia stopped pacing and eyed her. "Do you have any questions?"

"Not at present, Madame."

She nodded, seeming pleased. "There is no need to be so formal. In the company of others, it is appropriate to call me Madame Arment or Madame, but when we are here in a casual setting, Sophia will do. The same for Eleanor and Beau, although he despises being called Mr.

Hopwood. And we shall call you Josephine. If that will suit everyone?" She didn't wait for a response. "Now then, off we go."

Beau offered his elbow to Josephine as if she was truly a lady and she took it graciously. Eleanor smiled and took her other elbow. This familiarity was foreign to Josephine. She had never let anyone get this close except Oliver and Aunt Genny. Josephine pushed her unease to the back of her mind.

Linked arm in arm, the three of them followed Sophia to the far side of the ballroom and into a solarium. Nearly every wall of this new room was made of glass. The sun shone through, lighting up a vast collection of roses, tulips, daffodils, and hydrangeas - and those were only the flowers Josephine recognized.

"It's an indoor garden," Josephine remarked, pausing to admire the delicate yellow daffodils that were growing from a blue and yellow painted pot in front of her.

In a gentle voice, Eleanor said, "This is my favorite room. It always smells delicious!"

"Not as delicious as apple pie, Eleanor," Beau pointed out. He turned to Josephine and asked, "Have you had the pleasure of tasting apple pie?"

Josephine's brows pinched together. "I don't believe so."

"We must order some at once," Beau suggested. "The chef here makes a mouthwatering pie."

Eleanor leaned in and murmured in Josephine's ear, "Beau loves sweets. It's a wonder he isn't as large as a horse the way he eats."

"I heard that, Eleanor," Beau chided.

"Well, it's true!"

Josephine couldn't help but giggle at the two of them.

The fragrant scent of roses was replaced by wood polish and old books as they entered the library. Bookshelves lined almost every wall of the two-story room. Another large fireplace with a dark mahogany mantel had been built on the wall to Josephine's right. A wrought iron spiral staircase in the back corner led to the second level, and an iron railing wrapped around the square room along the second-floor balcony. Several chairs had been set about for reading and a chess set decorated a table in the corner. Near the hearth stood a gold statue of a horse and rider sitting on a pedestal. The rider appeared to be holding his sword extended, as if he was preparing to charge.

Sophia strode toward the gold statue and gestured for them to follow.

"What is she doing?" Josephine asked Eleanor.

"She's opening the door to Headquarters," she answered.

Josephine watched as Sophia tugged down on the sword arm. A latch released from somewhere inside the bookcase and, with a groan, the shelves split open, revealing a secret door.

"Come along," Sophia ordered, swinging the bookshelf open just wide enough for them to pass one at a time.

Eleanor led the way. Beau continued to escort Josephine and Sophia followed behind to close the door. The secret entrance took them to a tight spiral staircase that led downward and was lit up brightly by sconces. As they neared the bottom of the stairwell, Josephine heard the familiar ring of metal on metal.

"Is that ... sword fighting I hear?" Josephine asked Beau.

"Yes," he replied. "It's not even teatime and they already have their knickers in a twist."

"Beau, your manners!" Sophia gasped.

Josephine covered a giggle by clearing her throat. Questions filled her mind, but she didn't dare ask them. Her three tutors were working for the Brotherhood and Skulthorpe. Were they aware of the 'clandestine operations' that took place under the guise of British advancement here in the colonies? Josephine could only assume that they knew.

At the bottom of the steps, they entered a dimly lit room nearly three times as large as the Kraken's Lookout. Men were milling about everywhere. To her left, there were dozens of tables set up with all sorts of knick-knacks, papers, and potions.

Perhaps I need to do a little information-gathering of my own, thought Josephine as she studied the room around her.

The laboratory filled up almost the entire left side of Headquarters. Silver and gold pocket watches hung like ornaments from the wall. Josephine could hear them all ticking amidst the murmuring and shuffling of papers. Each of them twinkled under the glow of the sconces and oil lamps that were strategically placed to light up the room. Why have such mundane objects hanging all over the place? Surely, there was some special purpose for them? Josephine wanted to find out what.

The men working wore aprons, gloves, and goggles as they hunched over their individual projects. The scents wafting from the lab were a mixture of skunk and rotting fruit. Josephine could not fathom how something so foul could be useful. This place was likely where Mr. Runik's poison darts and mysterious powder had come from. Her fingers tingled with the need to explore - if she could only stomach the rancid smells.

Noticing her scrunched nose, Eleanor remarked, "It really is nauseating, isn't it? We try to steer clear of that area." She shrugged and pulled her away. "And the lab rats don't like us nosing about anyway."

In the back of the large room, about fifty feet away, was a dueling ring in which two men were fencing. Several others looked on and cheered every so often. Weapons hung on the walls that surrounded the ring, within reach for any who wished to practice. Josephine realized these men must be hunters and wondered if they knew who she was. Perhaps Skulthorpe had kept most of them in the dark about her recruitment. What would they do to her if they knew she was a pirate?

Josephine studied their faces from a distance, the tone and texture of their hair, their posture, and even their body language. None of these men were familiar to her, but after today, she would be able to identify these hunters if she ever met them on the street.

A table directly in the center of Headquarters captured Josephine's attention next. It looked like a model of a town. The tiny buildings had been constructed out of wood and painted in various shades to match the actual city.

"Is that Charlestown?" she asked, gaping at the model. She walked over to inspect and, sure enough, she found the White Pearl Wharf along one side of the table and several other buildings that she recognized from town.

"Remarkable, isn't it?" Eleanor said from beside her. "The detail is incredible."

"All it needs is little ships over here in the water!" Josephine pointed to her beloved pier.

"Don't touch that, missy!" A gentleman with work gloves and apron approached them at the table. He was surprisingly young, perhaps in his twenties. The man was only an inch or two taller than Josephine and was thin as an anchor line. Spectacles rested on the bridge of his nose, while a pair of work goggles covered his forehead. Black soot stained his nose and cheeks. His sandy brown hair was fashionably tied back at the nape of his neck with a ribbon.

Josephine felt sure that this man was indeed the evil genius behind the prototypes her father had stolen.

"Don't shout at her, Barnaby," Eleanor snapped, surprising Josephine. She seemed like such a timid thing. "She was only admiring the craftsmanship."

"And who might she be?" he asked Eleanor.

"This is Josephine Teversin. Josephine, this presumptuous man is Barnaby."

As soon as Eleanor announced her name, the room went silent and everyone turned to stare. The lab workers mostly seemed curious. The hunters glowered and began murmuring amongst themselves.

"Thank you for that, Eleanor," Josephine whispered, ducking her head.

Eleanor cringed. "Oops."

Barnaby just waved his hand as if it was nothing. "So, you're the Teversin girl we've been preparing for?"

Eleanor leaned closer to Josephine. "He's the mastermind behind all the inventions they come up with down here. You give him an idea and he can make it work."

"Oh, go on now, Miss Bromley," Barnaby said. "Don't be telling any tales. I do what I'm told and that's that. We'll be seeing you around, then. Good day."

Josephine watched the man walk away and then turned to Eleanor. "You've been preparing for me?"

"Yes, for weeks now."

Skulthorpe had been planning her abduction for weeks? How had he even known she was in Charlestown?

"You coming here has been the most excitement we've seen in ages," Beau said with a wink. "Now, come on, ladies. Sophia is waiting for us in the dressing room."

Beau grabbed hold of Josephine's hand and led her to this so-called dressing room, which happened to be straight across from the laboratory. The room was like an oversized closet just off the main area of Headquarters. This immense room was covered wall to wall in women's gowns, men's suits, and accessories for all occasions. There were muffs, scarves, hats, parasols, gloves, and shoes, in every color, everywhere. Josephine felt as if she'd just entered the queen's own dressing chamber. She stood frozen at the entrance, gawking at the sight of all the lovely clothes. *Am I going to get to wear some of these elegant things?*

Josephine's mind whirled with questions. Why did hunters have a dressing room filled with ladies' garments? Had this room been prepared specifically for her? Josephine had a brief vision of Culligan opening the old chest in his cellar, revealing the ladies' garments - prototypes.

Eleanor's voice cut through Josephine's thoughts. "This used to be merely for the men. They sometimes use costumes and disguises when they go on their missions."

"I see," Josephine replied. *That explains things*, she thought. *They added gowns just for me.*

Eleanor shut the door to the dressing room while Sophia began pulling a few items from the shelves. Beau had already walked over to a table that had been set up with tea and other refreshments and started filling a small plate.

"Come, ladies!" Beau called out. "These cakes look positively scrumptious."

Pressing her lips together, Josephine stared at the three tutors. Her father's murder hadn't been their fault, but she wouldn't be swayed by sweets and fancy dresses. Her father had informed her that immortal pirates had never shown favoritism toward any king or country and now Skulthorpe was forcing her to work against the Patriots in the colonies.

Josephine clenched her jaw. *I will not be a pawn in whatever game he is playing.* She vowed to find a way to foil Skulthorpe's plans and avenge her father's death.

ELEVEN

"You look perplexed," said Mr. Runik, breaking the silence in the carriage.

They hadn't said a word to each other since he'd barged into Headquarters and announced that her training was done for the evening. It was best that she not speak. If they attempted a conversation, Josephine was certain she would wind up in another argument with him. As they rode down the cobbled streets, she was content to watch the world pass by through the window so she wouldn't have to see Runik scowling at her.

"*You* look angry," Josephine pointed out then went right back to ignoring him. He was indeed glowering at her.

The truth was, she was overwhelmed and exhausted. To her astonishment, she'd enjoyed her time with her tutors, especially Beau and Eleanor. Beau was determined to put more meat on her bones with all the sweets he had continued to order from the kitchen and he was constantly saying something witty to make her laugh. Sophia ordered her about like a general, but Eleanor was there to gently redirect and model what she was to do. Her smiles were encouraging and contagious. On the other hand, Josephine was quite certain Madame Sophia never smiled.

All the facts and rules they insisted she memorize were spinning around inside her brain, giving her a terrible headache. Introductions, curtsies, sipping tea, and eating dinner properly. She had been instructed on how to sit correctly in a chair at the theatre, at the park, at a soiree, while playing cards, and any other place Josephine might sit when on assignment. According to Sophia, they were all completely different. It was almost too much to take in all at once. And when Josephine had snickered at how silly it all was, Sophia had given her a murderous glare. The next five minutes were spent berating Josephine about her ignorance and bad breeding. Eleanor had been kind afterward, not mentioning her blunder, and Beau - well, he was too busy stuffing himself with dessert and tea to notice her humiliation.

Josephine's father had come from a respectable family, but he had never expected her to know how to act at the theatre or a fancy ball. When would she have had the opportunity to go anywhere like that? Why would she even want to? How was she to know she would one day need those snobbish skills?

Not only was she made to feel like the worst sort of ruffian, as soon as she stepped out of the mansion that evening, Josephine sensed that she and Mr. Runik were being watched. Surely, there wasn't anyone else spying on her. There were plenty of eyes observing Josephine's behavior as it was; Runik, Sophia, Skulthorpe, and any of the other dozens of hunters on the grounds of the estate.

But perhaps it wasn't Josephine that those spying eyes were watching. It would not be surprising to find that Skulthorpe and his hunters had other enemies out there. Witches were still wary of the hunters and, of course, Skulthorpe had mentioned the Patriot rebels in the area. Either way, Josephine did not have enough brain power at the moment to ponder it all, nor did she have any mind to warn Runik. After shooting her with those poison darts and acting like a gargoyle since she'd met him, he was on his own.

"Did things not go well on your first day?" Runik inquired.

Josephine closed her eyes and pinched the bridge of her nose in irritation. "No daggers were thrown, if that's what you're asking."

Runik's eyes narrowed. "I was clear on the consequences if that were to happen, Miss Teversin."

"Madame Arment would probably retaliate in kind if I did anything of the sort."

The corner of Runik's mouth lifted. "I don't doubt it."

Neither spoke again until the carriage rolled to a stop near the White Pearl Wharf.

"Same time tomorrow, Miss Teversin."

That was her dismissal. Josephine's jaw clenched when Mr. Runik once again made no attempt to hand her down out of the carriage. He stayed rooted to his seat, staring out the opposite window. Determined not to let his cool demeanor bother her, she jumped from the carriage and made the short walk back to the Kraken's Lookout alone.

Despite their employment with Skulthorpe and the Brotherhood, Josephine was surprised to find she had enjoyed Beau and Eleanor's company. Josephine was more anxious about the dresses she was required to wear. She detested corsets, and the tasks Runik and Skulthorpe expected her to undertake would be more challenging in a stuffy ball gown and pinching heels.

Josephine was so wrapped up in her own thoughts that she nearly barreled into Oliver on her way up the backstairs of the tavern.

"Oh, hello, Oliver," she said, smiling weakly. She was not ready for this confrontation. She'd told him she would be with Aunt Genny all day and, clearly, she hadn't been. Oliver looked ready to throttle her, so Josephine slipped past him to quickly climb the stairs.

Oliver followed after her. "Where were you, Jo?"

Josephine faltered slightly but continued to smile. "Just out with friends." There, that wasn't such a lie. After all, Eleanor and Beau were friends - sort of.

"Friends?" Oliver asked, narrowing his eyes. "What friends?"

"I have other friends besides you," Josephine snapped. "We took tea and played cards," she said, which was mostly true. She had learned how to sit while playing cards. The actual game-playing was not to take place for a few days, according to Sophia. Josephine thought it best not to mention that she knew a few card games, but they were not the types of games aristocrats played.

Oliver kept giving her sideways glances as he walked the stairs beside her, but said nothing about her half-truth. Josephine had convinced herself that Oliver didn't need to know, and until she had something to worry about, she would say nothing of her new employment with Skulthorpe. There was nothing to do but bide her time. She'd do what was asked until they demanded she do something her conscience would not allow. Once that happened, she'd make a break for it. Somehow.

For the time being, she was going to enjoy the company and the food and hopefully get to try out some of the interesting devices in the laboratory. Josephine was also going to use her position to discover more about the mysterious weapons the British were creating. She was not a Patriot, but she felt sure, now that she had seen the laboratory, that those prototypes from Culligan's warehouse were for the Brotherhood. How her father had managed to snatch them or why he thought them important, she did not know. Perhaps more time at Headquarters would reveal some answers. Skulthorpe had hired her to gather information, and so she would.

Once they reached Josephine's room, she stopped to face Oliver in the doorway. Oliver's hand lifted toward her cheek, but at the last second, he shifted to rest it against the doorframe.

"Are you sure you're alright, Jo? There ain't nothing you want to tell me?"

Staring up at Oliver's sea-green eyes, she nearly confessed everything right then and there. He suspected something. It didn't help that the sea was calling to her like a Siren. The anxiety gripping her heart was enough to turn her into a blithering idiot and say whatever came to her mind. Josephine had to return to the water tonight or she'd go mad.

"Of … of course," she stammered. "Are you staying again?"

He nodded. "I'll be right next door if you need me."

With a trembling heart, Josephine nodded and bid him goodnight. Once she'd closed the door, she leaned her forehead against it and closed her eyes. She could feel Oliver's presence on the other side, as if he were waiting for her to open the door again and spill her secrets to him. Josephine nearly did just that, but after another minute, she finally heard the muffled sound of his boots retreating to his own quarters, leaving her alone with her lies.

TWELVE

"One more turn about the room," Madame Sophia ordered from the opposite end of the grand ballroom.

The urge to sigh was overwhelming, but Josephine could not have done it if she'd tried, since her corset was squeezing the breath out of her. The fancy shoes she was wearing made her feet ache, and she was growing weary of simply walking in circles around the ballroom. After two days of training, they had finally dressed her up in the finest gown she had ever worn. It was pale green, patterned with soft pink roses and a solid pink petticoat underneath. However, there was no lace flowing from the sleeves at the elbows, as she had seen Sophia wear.

"Lace is expensive," Sophia had pointed out. "If you slosh your tea, it might ruin it. Better to practice in something more modest."

Josephine tried not to take offense even though she wasn't a klutz like Jett. The dress was still lovely, with a simple pink ruffle on the sleeve instead of fine lace and pink ruffles lining the square cut neckline to match. Josephine might have, for once in her life, felt beautiful had she not been exposing so much of her - as Oliver would crudely say - assets. The neckline of the gown was cut so low, she was positive that what little she had was plunging out for all to see.

"Stop covering yourself with that fan, Josephine!" Sophia scolded her for the third time. "Your décolletage can be one of your greatest weapons. Beau, please escort her around this time."

After gaping like a fish and turning a deep crimson due to Sophia's provocative insinuation, Beau took her arm. "Don't you fret, Josephine," he said with a naughty grin. "I've seen much worse in France."

Josephine fanned herself rapidly to cool her heated face and tried to breathe in the awful corset. The plunging neckline of the dress was only a small part of her worries. Josephine had been jolted out of her sleep well before dawn because of a terrible nightmare. In the dream, Skulthorpe had commanded that she perform a perfect curtsy or she would be hanged. When attempting the curtsy, she had stumbled. Instead of catching herself, Josephine's hands had been bound behind her back, so she fell on her face. Runik appeared out of nowhere, hoisted her up off the floor, and carried her like a sack of potatoes to the town square.

With a noose dangling from her neck, Runik had glared at her and asked, "Why are you so angry? This was inevitable, you know."

Josephine had woken up in a cold sweat, her neck tingling from the feel of the rope.

"You look marvelous," Beau said, interrupting her ominous thoughts. "Green is a wonderful color on you. I think Eleanor and Sophia mean to dress you in gold next to match the gold sprinkles in your eyes. I happen to agree. You won't need a wig, either. Wigs are for older matrons. Your hair is too beautiful to cover up. It reminds me of dark honey or chocolate." He peered down at Josephine out of the corner of his eye. "You've had chocolate, haven't you? Delicious candy!"

Josephine tried to smile at his mention of food again and continued to frantically wave her fan.

"You're waving that fan too fast," Sophia called out.

Beau grabbed Josephine's hand to stop her mid-wave.

"I'm never going to get this, Beau," Josephine whispered, attempting to slow her movements when he finally released her fingers.

"You are doing well after so few days with us," he assured her, patting her hand. "Just keep your chin up. Pretend you are *dying* of utter boredom." Beau spun on his heel and gestured to Eleanor. Eleanor strode over at once. "Here, watch how Eleanor walks."

Eleanor proceeded to demonstrate how she should walk. Her hips swayed slightly and the expression she wore was one of complete disinterest and arrogance. She waved the fan as if she was weary from holding it in her hand. Once Eleanor had reached the other side of the room, she snapped it closed, turned, and strolled back the same way.

"That was excellent, Eleanor," Sophia announced. "Now, let's see you do it, Josephine."

Josephine smiled at Beau and Eleanor, trying to be gracious. Lifting her nose in the air, she took one more turn, working hard to look as bored as Eleanor had.

"That is much better." Sophia announced without an ounce of excitement over her achievement.

Despite Sophia's bitter praise, Josephine felt a surge of pleasure having finally accomplished something. Beau and Eleanor both gave her warm smiles.

Before Sophia could demand that she take another turn, the sound of the front door crashing open echoed into the ballroom. A moment later, Runik marched in donning his usual black suit and white cravat. His black tricorn was tucked under his arm.

"Madame Arment," he said by way of a greeting. Everyone bowed and curtsied politely. Runik glanced around the room. "Where is Miss Teversin?"

Josephine didn't know whether to laugh or cry. He had looked right at her. Had she looked so beggarly before that he did not even recognize her now?

Lifting her chin high, Josephine put on her best look of boredom with the perfect demure smile and approached him. She would not give him the satisfaction of knowing just how much he had humiliated her.

Stunning.

81

That was the only word that came to mind when Nathaniel finally recognized Miss Teversin. Madame Arment had turned her from a pirate into a princess, and for a moment, he was rendered speechless.

Her hair was pulled up into a stylish twist with curled tendrils framing her face. Her cheeks and lips were rosy. The sunlight beaming into the ballroom made her hair shine and her brown eyes sparkle. Nathaniel wondered how he had ever thought her plain. From head to toe, she was radiant.

He swallowed the lump that had lodged itself in his throat and straightened his shoulders, hiding his thoughts behind a cool exterior. "Miss Teversin, there has been a slight change of plans. Your first assignment will be tomorrow."

"Tomorrow?" Josephine croaked. All the color drained from her face in an instant. She opened her fan and began waving it frantically.

"Mind your composure, Miss Teversin," Madame Sophia ordered.

Josephine backed away from Nathaniel, shaking her head. "You know I won't be ready by then. It's only been three days!"

Nathaniel could only roll his eyes as Josephine lost her composure. She paced the floor a short distance away, still waving that silly fan and muttering all sorts of crude words not fit for anyone's ears. Nathaniel had never seen her so agitated.

"I need to sit down … but I probably won't be able to in this infernal corset!" he heard her say when she came within earshot.

"One should *never* mention one's undergarments in mixed company!" Madame Arment exclaimed in horror.

Smoothing his gloved thumb across his bottom lip, Nathaniel repressed a sudden urge to laugh. Josephine turned and began shaking her fan at him. "You had better be glad I'm not a fainter, because *if* I was …" Instead of finishing her thought, she opened her fan and began waving it to cool her face once again.

"Just breathe, Josephine," said Beau.

"Should I get the smelling salts?" Eleanor offered.

Nathaniel's lips twitched again. "No, I do not believe that will be necessary."

"She really was doing so well," Eleanor murmured.

"I'll go fetch some food," Beau announced. "Maybe some pie. That always helps." He turned and strode off to the kitchens.

"Leave us," Nathaniel ordered. "I will speak with her." He nodded to the two ladies and they retreated with Beau.

Nathaniel watched Josephine pace for a moment more before interrupting her muttered tirade.

"Miss Teversin, you are getting yourself worked up over nothing."

He thought about grabbing her and giving her a good shake, but she was not a typical lady. Heaven only knew how many daggers she had hidden in that dress. The little pirate would probably run him through without blinking an eye. Better to keep a distance.

"Easy for you to say," said Josephine, still fanning her heated face. Then she lowered her eyes and murmured, "It is not *your* neck on the line."

She said the words so softly, Nathaniel nearly missed them, but her meaning was clear. A heavy silence fell as Josephine turned her back to him. He had never seen her so troubled, not even on the nights she'd been captured and had attempted her escapes. At least, not until …

Realization washed over him. It wasn't until she had faced his employer, Garreck Skulthorpe, that she'd shown any fear. Josephine's demeanor had shifted swiftly that night as well.

Gritting his teeth together, Nathaniel silently scolded himself for instinctively wanting to protect her. He could not care about this woman's feelings.

Schooling his features into a mask of indifference, Nathaniel approached her cautiously. "It *is* nothing," he explained. "It's barely even an assignment. It's more of a trial, if you will." Josephine turned to face him again, her expression resembling that of a hunted deer.

Not a bad comparison, to be sure, he thought.

"I'm not ready," she replied, biting her bottom lip nervously.

Nathaniel hardened himself against her pleading eyes. She was a pirate. He could never forget that detail. There was a high probability that she was only manipulating him with her womanly charms. Especially now that she looked so ravishing.

Never forget what happens when you trust a pirate, he reminded himself.

"You have no choice but to be ready," he said, a hard edge to his words. "Come. Let us discuss the assignment."

Nathaniel surprised himself by offering his arm. The pale Josephine nodded and hesitantly took it, startling him even more. He escorted her out of the double-doors to the veranda, which led to various pebbled paths that encircled the lush gardens. Even in autumn, the grounds on Skulthorpe's estate were a sight to behold. He hoped they would have a calming effect on the girl.

No, she was not a girl. Josephine Teversin was definitely more mature than he'd previously thought - perhaps eighteen or nineteen. The usual modest and dingy attire she wore at the tavern did nothing for her shape. The gown she donned now revealed an elegant lady, at least in appearance.

Clearing his throat, Nathaniel put aside his idle thoughts. "Now then, Miss Teversin, the assignment. We have been invited to tea."

Josephine paused and scrunched her nose in confusion. "*I* have been invited? Who in Charlestown knows *me*?"

"They do not know you. I have mentioned you in passing to some acquaintances. They have requested for me to bring you along so they can meet you."

"Acquaintances? You mean targets."

"Not necessarily," Nathaniel said. "Do not jump to conclusions. They may not have any relevant information pertaining to the rebels."

"So, what does that mean? What is *my* assignment?"

"To come and have tea. Meet them." He turned to continue their stroll through the gardens. Keeping his eyes on the path was less distracting than watching the tendrils of hair sweeping across her neck and cheeks.

"That's all?" Josephine let out a deep sigh of relief and then murmured, "I can do that, at least."

"I wouldn't relax too much, Miss Teversin. There may be opportunities for snooping around and talking to servants, but you must be acquainted with them first. Many of our agents have been undercover with these Patriot groups and haven't learned anything new for a long time."

"What makes you think I'll be able to uncover anything?"

"As Mr. Skulthorpe mentioned before, we are hoping that, as a woman, you will succeed where the men have failed. You bring a new perspective, you see. A new variable to the equation."

Josephine frowned. "I see."

He turned to escort her back to the house. "Come. Mr. Hopwood probably has a full picnic of sweets awaiting you after your fit of hysterics."

Josephine closed her fan and smacked him on the shoulder. "I did not get hysterical."

"Then what would *you* call it?"

She lifted her chin. "A slight case of nerves."

"Just nerves, was it? You were set to swoon just moments ago."

"I would not have swooned. I told you, I'm not the fainting type. Although, I *am* going to demand that Eleanor loosen my stays a bit or I might very well faint from suffocating."

Nathaniel coughed to cover up his amusement. When Josephine wasn't deliberately baiting him, she really was quite comical. He might have actually liked her - under different circumstances, of course.

Just as Nathaniel had predicted, the trio of tutors had refreshments set out on the veranda and Beau was already indulging. Josephine released her hold on his arm and took a seat next to Eleanor.

"You looked lovely walking about on the grounds, my dear," said Sophia. "Don't you agree, Mr. Runik?"

"Quite improved," he answered, giving her form a once over again. Josephine was improved in many areas, none of which he planned on mentioning. "Madame Arment, I would suggest instructing Miss Teversin in taking tea properly."

Josephine's jaw dropped. "I don't need instruction on -"

Nathaniel cut her off mid-sentence. "The tea these colonials serve is pure swill, but one must be polite and observe the finer points of etiquette."

"I quite agree," Madame Arment replied.

"Good. Now, when you are finished here, we'll be on our way," Nathaniel gave them a half-bow. "I will be in the study."

DESPITE THE FEELING of dread in her stomach, Josephine finally ate a little something before Eleanor escorted her to change gowns again.

"It's really such a shame to put you back into this old thing," Eleanor muttered.

Josephine's cheeks heated at Eleanor's remark, but knew it to be true. She didn't want to go back to being plain old Josephine after having worn such an exquisite gown. It had been a long time since she had felt pretty. The compliments she had received from Beau and Eleanor warmed her insides.

"Did you see the way Mr. Runik was staring at you?" Eleanor said when they were finally in privacy of the dressing room.

"What? Oh, I'm quite accustomed to his glares," replied Josephine.

Eleanor placed a hand upon Josephine's arm. "Oh, Josephine, you do miss things sometimes. Mr. Runik was definitely *not* glaring at you. Not today." She giggled. "You do look fetching in this gown."

Josephine laughed hollowly. "You're imagining things."

"Think what you will, but I thought his eyes were going to pop out of his head when he saw you!"

In truth, she had noticed Runik gaping when he'd first recognized her, but his gray eyes had turned frosty a moment later. Josephine shook her head. Eleanor was as bad as Aunt Genny when it came to matchmaking. At least Oliver cared for her a bit and was not a pirate hunter. Someone of Runik's position would never allow himself to be attracted to someone like her, especially when he belonged to the Brotherhood. Josephine did not fear him, but he seemed to harbor a special grudge against her. She was a pirate. Josephine could never expect someone like him to overlook that point. Not to mention, he was the evil cockroach who had pulled her into this mess in the first place. There was no ignoring that, either.

The silence was uncomfortable on the carriage ride back to the wharf. Josephine stared out the window, like she always did, and tried to ignore Runik, and he responded in kind.

Chancing a peek in his direction, Josephine noticed a strand of his raven hair had come loose from his queue, curling over his forehead. It made him seem a bit younger and not quite so arrogant. If it was possible, Josephine thought he looked even more handsome - until she caught the look in his eyes. Ruthless, as always. Josephine wondered if he had ever been anything but a cold-hearted hunter.

THIRTEEN

The following day had Josephine's insides in knots. She had nearly bumped into Oliver when running from the Kraken's Lookout to the carriage. Avoiding her friend had made her late, so Runik was even more unpleasant than usual. To top it all off, she felt as if she was being watched again. The idea suddenly occurred to Josephine that this might be another piece of her pirate magic emerging, but she had not ever heard her father talk about having a sixth sense in that way. Of course, Father had never blasted anyone down a hallway, either. Josephine's powers were unique.

On the carriage ride to Skulthorpe's mansion, Josephine considered confiding in Mr. Runik about someone spying on them, but quickly decided against it. He would either think she was being paranoid or she had gone daft. *Actually*, she thought in dismay, *both may be true now that I'm working for the hunters.*

At the estate, Mr. Runik peppered Josephine relentlessly with information about her new alias. Afterward, her tutors whisked her away to make her presentable. Sophia decided on a sky-blue afternoon gown with pink trim. Everyone gushed over how brilliant she looked, and even Runik nodded his approval. He was wearing a suit that was designed to complement her dress, instead of his usual black attire. The waistcoat and breeches were a pristine white and his coat was a pale pink. The men from Josephine's world would rather drink nasty bilge water than wear such a refined suit with ruffles on the neckcloth and sleeves, but the pink was dashing next to Mr. Runik's dark features. His hair was tied back neatly with a ribbon and the black tricorn he intended to wear matched his buckled shoes.

While Eleanor was styling Josephine's hair into a small pouf on top of her head, Runik walked about and quizzed her about her new identity. Typically, the dressing room seemed quite large, but with all five of them inside, Runik's pacing was making Josephine dizzy.

"My name is Josephine Pinchley," she recited to Runik. "I'm a distant cousin of yours, orphaned when my parents died of sickness. I was sent here to the colonies to live with friends of the family. Ow!" yelped Josephine, as Eleanor yanked on her curls.

Runik halted his pacing to glower down at her. "What was that?" he snapped.

"Nothing," Josephine muttered. Attempting to ignore the painful hair-pulling, she continued ticking off the details one by one. "The people I'm staying with are the Smyths of Georgetown, just up the coast from Charlestown."

"Yes," Runik said with a nod. "Remember, the village is similar to Charlestown, so it will be easy to be vague about the details. Continue."

"I'm here to attend the Harvest Festival."

Runik paused again and heaved a frustrated sigh. "We hope. I have been working to obtain an invitation to the soiree. It is a prime opportunity for information to be passed between these Patriots."

Eleanor placed a ringlet of hair just over Josephine's shoulder and stepped back to inspect her work. "There! We are finished!"

Josephine breathed a sigh of relief. She was positive there were over a hundred pins holding the pouf in place and each one of them was stabbing her scalp.

"Don't forget your hat!" exclaimed Eleanor, striding over with a dainty straw hat that she'd retrieved from a shelf. A pink ribbon wrapped around the crown of the hat was tied in a bow under Josephine's chin to keep it from blowing away. The brim was small, but it angled down over her forehead to shield her face from the sun.

Beau beamed down at her. "You look marvelous! Better than any duchess."

Josephine grinned at their approval.

"All right," Josephine said, lifting her chin and turning to Runik. "I believe I'm ready. Or ... at least, I *look* ready."

Runik placed his own hat firmly on his head. "We must be on our way, then."

Astonishing Josephine once again, Runik held out his elbow to escort her back upstairs and to the front of the estate. This time, upon entering the carriage, he assisted her as if she were truly a lady. Perhaps he had forgotten who she was or had realized how cumbersome her dress would be ascending the step.

As the carriage jerked forward and began to move, Runik asked, "Why are you making that face?"

Josephine blinked and turned toward the window, wondering if she ought to say anything at all. His mood could shift faster than a hurricane.

Mr. Runik fidgeted in his seat. "If you are going to ridicule the color of the jacket I'm wearing, I'll just have you know -"

Josephine shook her head. "I think you look handsome." Heat flooded her cheeks and she nearly cursed out loud. She had not intended to be so forward. She quickly added, "But that's not what I was thinking." She could have sworn that his eyes had thawed for a second, but they quickly froze over again. Josephine did not want to uncover why he always looked at her so coldly. Pushing the errant thought away, she murmured, "You were being kind to me. That's all. It was ... unexpected."

"And you found it surprising that a gentleman could be kind?"

Josephine gave a hollow laugh. "Any kindness you bestow upon me is surprising." Looking out the window again, she wished she'd just kept quiet. There was no need to get into a spat now.

"This afternoon, you are playing the part of my distant cousin," he explained, as if instructing a child. "We must pretend we are family and show some affection toward one another. And, as a gentleman, it is appropriate to offer my arm and assistance."

Josephine pinched her lips together to keep from disagreeing. A true gentleman would never have blackmailed another, especially a lady, to do his dirty work. Even her father had taught her that much. He may have been a pirate, but he was more of a gentleman than Runik had shown himself to be.

The carriage rolled to a stop in front of a quaint town home, and Josephine's insides began to churn. The assignment had begun.

A wide-eyed, smiling woman with chestnut hair answered the door, her voice bubbling with excitement, while an older, gangly man hovered just behind her as they entered. "Oh, do come in! Do come in!"

The man behind her said, "Madam, I must insist -"

"Oh, Davis, it's all right!" she said brightly and waved him away. "This is our butler, Davis. Such a wonderful help, but I do so love answering the door for company!"

Josephine paused with uncertainty and glanced at Runik for guidance, but the woman had ushered them both inside before anyone could stop her. Apparently, this woman did not hold with formalities, which was extremely refreshing to Josephine.

While leading them into the parlor, she said, "I am Mrs. Graves, but you can call me Mattie, and you must be the wonderful young lady that Mr. Runik here has been telling us about!" She took Josephine's hand with a broad smile still plastered to her rosy face.

Runik stepped forward to do the introductions. "Yes, of course, Mrs. Graves. This is my distant cousin Josephine Pinchley, recently settled in Georgetown."

"Oh, pleased to meet you, my dear, and I know Mr. Runik will not change his ways but I insist that you call me Mattie." She leaned closer and whispered into Josephine's ear, "The men don't like it, so just call my husband Mr. Graves."

"How do you do?" said Josephine, trying to dip into a curtsy with

Mattie hanging onto her arm. For a moment, she thought she might actually stumble to the floor, her nightmare come to life. Luckily, she stayed on her feet.

The parlor in this home was a quarter of the size of Skulthorpe's sitting room. Two pastel yellow sofas faced each other in the middle of the room, adjacent to a small but adequate fireplace. There were no extravagant moldings or shiny ornaments other than a few sconces that decorated the walls in various places. It felt more like home to Josephine.

Mattie shook her finger at both Josephine and Runik. "There is no need to stand on ceremony in this house, dears. Now, let's all have a spot of tea. Mr. Graves will be along shortly."

Their hats were taken by the silent and waiting Mr. Davis and a thin maid with blond hair brought in a tray of tea, scones, raspberry tarts, and bread with butter.

"Janie, these look delicious! And don't you worry, dear, I'll pour the tea for our guests," Mattie said to the timid maid and shooed her back to the kitchen.

True to Mattie's word, Mr. Graves joined them a few minutes later, nearly bounding into the room. "My sweet Mattie, is it time for tea already? And Runik!" Mr. Graves turned to bow to Runik. "How good to see you, and you have brought your cousin. How marvelous!"

While busy pouring tea and serving pastries, Mattie began chattering amiably without stopping for breath. "Mr. Runik has told us so much about you, we feel as if we know you already. I am so dreadfully sorry to hear about your parents, my dear, but we mustn't focus on that sad news. Tell me, are you attending the Harvest Festival? The soiree to celebrate the festival is in two weeks. You simply *must* attend! Mr. Graves, darling, won't you see about two more invitations for this fine pair? They will have such a good time at the soiree!"

Mattie dominated the conversation completely, not giving anyone a chance to say much of anything, but Josephine liked her instantly. The vibrant woman was a bit shorter than Josephine and much healthier in weight, but the friendliest lady she'd ever encountered. Not at all the stuffy aristocrat she'd envisioned when Runik was tutoring her in manners. If it weren't for Mr. Runik eyeing her every move, she would almost feel relaxed about the whole ordeal.

Mr. Graves was quite the opposite. Tall, but not nearly as tall as Mr. Davis. His graying hair was tied into a messy queue, the locks in front curling up around his face and over his forehead, as if they just wouldn't be tamed. He was evidently enamored of his wife, which Josephine found charming. While Mattie served refreshments and talked, he seemed to take pleasure in simply watching, listening, and, when the occasion arose, laughing. Josephine could not help but smile at the pair.

Nothing remarkable happened during the visit. Mr. and Mrs. Graves were not at all interested in Miss Pinchley's past, for which she was grateful. Oliver had told her repeatedly that she was a terrible liar, and Josephine would have disliked telling a falsehood to such friendly people. They shared small talk mostly: discussing town affairs, gossip, and such. Nothing was mentioned of the Patriots or any hints of rebellions afoot.

Mr. Runik was a superb actor. He almost had Josephine believing they were friends. More than once, she found him smiling and sometimes even laughing, which made him seem like an agreeable person. Once during a conversation, he had reached out and grasped her hand tenderly and she had nearly spewed tea out of her mouth.

There was an opportunity for Josephine to freshen up - something ladies did frequently to Josephine's surprise - so Mrs. Graves escorted her to the bath closet. This was Josephine's opportunity to snoop about, as Runik had suggested.

After a few minutes, Josephine crept out of the bath closet, searched the hallway for Mr. Davis' prying eyes, and then snuck away. She padded down the hall, away from the parlor, her heart racing. Josephine had never been a spy before. Did spies typically feel like emptying the contents of their stomachs while on assignment?

Josephine swallowed and kept going. Only ten feet down the hall, she stumbled upon a library. Before anyone spotted her, she slipped inside the room. Bookshelves lined the wall adjacent to the door and two high-backed chairs faced the fireplace on the opposite wall. A small round table was situated between the two chairs and a pile of letters had been placed on it, probably by Mr. Davis. After peeking over her shoulder to make certain she was still alone, Josephine sifted through the letters. What was she even searching for? Mr. Runik had not given her specifics, but she felt sure she would know if something seemed out of place.

Every letter sent was from someone with the surname of Graves. Just family correspondence.

Blast, she thought, setting them down again. At least she hadn't found anything incriminating. Josephine liked Mattie Graves and didn't want to see her in trouble with Skulthorpe or the Brotherhood.

"Can I help you, my lady?"

Josephine gasped and spun around at the sound of Mr. Davis' dour voice. She clutched at her heart and tried to slow her breathing. "Oh, Mr. Davis, you gave me a fright." Her heart thudded in her chest as she quickly thought of an excuse to cover her blunder. "I'm so sorry. I took a wrong turn obviously and got lost. Mr. Runik is always telling me what a horrible sense of direction I have. But this library really is wonderful."

Mr. Davis cleared his throat and stepped to the side of the doorway and gestured for her to exit. "This way, Madam," he said without any inflection at all.

Josephine allowed him to lead her back to the parlor. Mr. and Mrs. Graves hadn't noticed anything out of the ordinary and continued on with their conversation. Of course, Runik had known all along what she'd been up to and looked as if he was ready to strangle her. Josephine sipped her tea and smiled innocently. *Yes, he is definitely going to throttle me later*, she thought.

"WHAT WERE YOU THINKING?" Nathaniel sputtered once they were inside the carriage and driving back to the estate. *"Or were you thinking at all?"*

Josephine flinched at his harsh words. "You were the one who told me to snoop."

"Not on your first visit and *not* when you haven't a clue what to look for!"

"Well, you didn't say that, did you? You should have made yourself clearer. Besides, nothing happened."

"You were *caught*," he said through gritted teeth.

"Oh, that," she said, waving her hand in dismissal. "I told the butler I was lost."

Nathaniel gaped at her. "The house is no bigger than that dressing room down in Headquarters. It is very likely he saw right through that *ridiculous* lie."

"Oh, do stop your worrying," she said with a sigh. "Most men think ladies are ninnies anyway." Josephine gave him a pointed look. "Wouldn't you agree?"

Nathaniel clenched his fists and scowled at her. "This is precisely why you should never have been asked to do this. There is too much at stake."

"I thought I got on quite well with the Graves," Josephine said, raising her chin in defiance. "They *did* invite me to the soiree. And their tea was *not* swill."

Nathaniel blinked in confusion. "What does that matter?"

"You said 'the tea these colonials serve is pure swill'. I was simply disagreeing with your opinion."

"Oh. Well, yes, it was better than I expected … *but that is entirely beside the point!*" Nathaniel shouted. "*Weeks* I have spent visiting them and buttering them up. They take one look at you and you've cinched an invitation for us to the soiree. It is quite maddening!"

"Are you cross because I was successful in acquiring an invitation?" Josephine asked, getting angry as well. "That's just silly. I still don't understand why they did not invite you in the first place. You're the son of a lord in England, aren't you? Perhaps they didn't want you there because you've been a curmudgeon."

"I am not a curmudgeon!"

"Yes, you're quite right. You are a charming man who never loses his temper," she said cheekily. "Do you know what I believe you should do, Mr. Runik?"

"I dare to wonder," he muttered.

"You should simply say 'thank you' and quit your huffing. Madame Arment would blister your ears for this behavior. And, honestly, I think you are looking under seashells."

"Looking under ...? What are you talking about now?"

"You are looking under seashells," she explained. "I love looking for seashells on the beach, but do you know what's under them? Nothing. You, Mr. Runik, are looking for *something* where there is *nothing*."

Nathaniel's jaw clenched. "That is quite enough out of you, Miss Teversin."

The girl kept silent the remainder of the ride and it took every minute of that time for Nathaniel to regain his cool composure. When they arrived at the mansion, Mr. Hopwood and Miss Bromley were there to greet them in the foyer.

"You have one hour to ready yourself," he said sharply. "Do you think you can manage to make it back to the tavern on your own without causing any more mayhem?"

Frowning, Josephine nodded silently. Seeing the hurt on Josephine's face, Nathaniel had to bite his tongue to keep from taking it all back. Having sympathies for a pirate - especially *this* pirate - was something he would not allow.

Miss Bromley hesitantly spoke up. "She will be ready, Mr. Runik."

"I will see her home," Beau chimed in, lifting his finger in the air to volunteer. "No need to worry, my dear." He gave Josephine an encouraging smile.

Nathaniel nodded to Beau, grateful for a respite from that duty for the night. He turned back to Josephine. "I will be picking you up at nine o'clock sharp in our usual spot by the White Pearl Wharf. Be dressed and ready. You will accompany me for a stroll in a park just north of town as part of your training. Mr. Hopwood, make sure there is a hearty luncheon waiting when she arrives back here at noon."

"Of course," said Beau, ignoring the obvious tension in the room.

"If you have no more questions, we are done for the day."

Turning on his heel, Nathaniel fled the room before he found himself shouting again. Or apologizing.

FOURTEEN

Early the next morning, Josephine was distraught over what she should do with her appearance. Normally, she would just wear her pitiful blue dress and do her hair up in a simple knot, but this morning she would be out with Mr. Runik. They would be in the park where anyone could see her. Even if it was only for training, he would be sure to wear his finest waistcoat and knee breeches. The dresses Josephine had ordered should be ready, only she had been too busy to pick them up. Josephine would look like a grubby street rat in her old blue dress. Pride demanded that she not be humiliated again by that insufferable sea urchin. Why she was suddenly so worried about what *he* thought was beyond her. Runik had made his position about Josephine - and pirates - perfectly clear.

"Oh, blast!" she exclaimed, finally slamming down her comb after unsuccessfully recreating the twist that Eleanor had done so easily. She needed help.

Josephine traipsed down the stairs to her Aunt Genevieve's quarters on the second floor and knocked on the door. When it cracked open, Genny stood in the doorway wearing a burgundy velvet dressing robe, her blond hair in a simple braid down her back.

"Josephine? Is there something wrong?"

"I need help, Aunt Genny," Josephine admitted with a sigh. "I'm going for a walk with someone and I have no idea what I'm to wear … or do with my awful hair." Josephine ran her hand over her unruly locks that tumbled down around her shoulders.

Aunt Genny beamed at Josephine. "You have come to the right place, darling!" She pulled Josephine through the door and closed it behind her. "Now tell me, what sort of someone is this? Is it a gentleman?" Aunt Genny's eyes sparkled in delight.

"Uh, yes." No need to tell her that the gentleman was not really a gentleman at all.

Genny clapped her hands in excitement and then looked in horror at Josephine's tattered gown. "Oh, then you must *not* wear that terrible thing!"

"I know, Aunt Genny. That's why I'm here, begging you for help."

"Lucky for you, I picked up your gowns in town yesterday. I think you will be much pleased!"

She pulled out two boxes from under her bed and lifted the lid of the first one. It was the blue and white striped gown - the one Josephine had picked herself. The material was so bright and clean, she almost hated to wear it at all.

"This one is nicer than I thought it would be, but for a walk in town with a beau, you must wear the pink."

Lifting the lid of the second box, Josephine was stunned. Aunt Genny had been right after all. *This* was the one she should wear. The shade of pink was soft and, though she had not been able to afford any lace, the pink ruffles that flowed down from the sleeves at the elbow were just as elegant.

"It's lovely, Aunt Genny," Josephine whispered and hugged her guardian.

"Just wait until you put it on," Genny added. "It will look even lovelier. You will look like an angel."

By the time Aunt Genny had finished with Josephine, she looked just as fetching as she had yesterday at the Graves' home. Even Madame Sophia would have been proud.

"Aunt Genny, you are a miracle-worker!"

Just when Josephine thought they had finished, Aunt Genny pulled out another smaller box.

"I took the liberty, darling," she said and proceeded to pull out a beautiful pink hat that matched the gown perfectly, trimmed with white feathers in the back.

"Aunt Genny, you shouldn't have," Josephine said breathily as Genny angled it on her head perfectly, securing it with a pin. "Is it French?"

"Of course, darling. All the best clothes come from France, *non*? Now you look perfect," Genny said with a grin. She handed Josephine her own white parasol and ushered her out the door. "Do not forget to give me all the details this evening!"

Josephine ducked her head and giggled almost all the way down the stairs. When she reached the bottom, she barreled right into Oliver, but this time she did not flee.

"Begging your pardon, Miss." Oliver nodded politely and side-stepped around her. Without a single glance, he turned his back on her and started up the stairs.

"Oliver! Are you just going to ignore me?"

Halting on the steps, he turned back to Josephine and gaped. "A-Angelfish," he stammered. "I ... didn't even recognize you." He looked her up and down and nearly stumbled on his way back down the stairs. "What's this you're wearing?"

"I told you - I bought new gowns with Aunt Genny," explained Josephine. "Do you like it?" Josephine twirled for him, smiling widely with pride.

Oliver approached slowly, with an almost predatory look in his eyes. It did not escape her notice that his eyes rested on the low neckline a little longer than was necessary. Josephine's face heated but she resisted the urge to cover herself.

"Well," he said, clearing his throat, "those hoops under your petticoat are so bloody wide, you're liable to get stuck trying to walk through the door."

Josephine's jaw dropped. "They are not *that* wide!"

He quirked an eyebrow and looked down at her chest again. "And your -" he waved his hand in front of the low neckline "- *assets* are showing a bit much, if you ask me."

Oliver grunted when she struck him in the leg with the parasol. "You should not be looking at my *assets*, as I've told you before!"

"Well, somebody's going to be!" he growled back.

Josephine flinched. "You're angry with me. Why?"

With fire burning in his green eyes, Oliver asked, "Where are you going, Jo?"

"That's none of your concern." Josephine tried to maintain eye-contact but her resolve shattered under his perceptive gaze.

Oliver replied more gently, "That's why I'm angry. You're hiding things from me. We've never had to keep secrets from one another. We've been an honest pair, eh?"

He backed Josephine into the wall and gently lifted her chin with his calloused fingers, forcing her to meet his eyes. His face was so close she could feel his breath on her lips, sending nervous flutters down her spine.

"You'd better watch yourself, Angelfish," he said. "I don't trust *him.*"

Josephine's stomach dropped. Before she could argue or explain, Oliver cupped her cheek with his hand, placing his thumb lightly over her lips.

"Don't," he whispered. "Just be careful. Promise me, Josephine."

With a trembling voice, she replied, "I promise."

Grazing her bottom lip once more with his thumb, Oliver turned and left the Kraken's Lookout, leaving Josephine in stunned silence.

JOSEPHINE, as always, stared out the window as she and Mr. Runik rode in the carriage again. They traveled west down Broad Street away from the White Pearl Wharf. Charlestown citizens were bustling down the edges of the dirt road toward their destinations as they did every morning.

Awkward or not, Josephine was thankful for the silence, because she couldn't bring herself to concentrate on the lesson that Runik had in store for her. Her mind was still whirling from the things Oliver had said. He'd known about Mr. Runik. Had it been Oliver spying on her that first day? Could he have known even then? Had he been watching over her from a distance, making sure no harm had come to her?

He's clever, Jo, she thought. *He was bound to figure it out sooner or later.*

Josephine wondered how long it would be before he attempted to intervene on her behalf. She was quite certain his last blood oath to her father had been to protect her. Oliver would die before he broke that oath, and that was exactly what she was afraid of.

"You are awfully quiet this morning," Mr. Runik remarked.

"That should please you," Josephine replied without any enthusiasm.

As much as she usually enjoyed irritating him, she was in no mood to talk or get into another quarrel with him. Oliver used to tell her that arguing with a pirate was much akin to beating one's head against a brick wall. Quarreling with a hunter was not much different. Pitting their stubborn natures against one another was going to end badly for her.

The carriage turned right onto King Street, headed to the northern part of Charlestown. Josephine placed her palms on the seat to brace herself for the sway of the carriage.

"Might I say how lovely you look this morning, Miss Teversin?"

This rare bit of flattery should have been cause for celebration.

"Compliments of Mr. Skulthorpe. Were you surprised that I could make myself pretty?"

"A pleasant surprise."

Turning back to the window, Josephine masked her emotions as best she could and changed the subject. "We're going to a park?"

"Yes," he replied. After a long pause he added, "Tell me, Miss Teversin, why you are constantly looking out the window. It is quite rude to ignore your company; one of the many points of social etiquette you must keep in mind."

Straightening away from the window, Josephine did her best to look him in the eye and keep her voice neutral. "I'm not trying to ignore you."

"Yes, you are. And you were yesterday and the day before that," he pointed out. "If we are not quarreling, then you are looking out that window, pretending I am not here. Perhaps it would be easier for us both if we agreed not to lie to one another?"

Josephine rolled her eyes. "Fine. I'm ignoring you."

Mr. Runik huffed like a spoiled child. "For what purpose, Miss Teversin? I am being pleasant enough this morning. I thought we could at least be civil."

"Civil?" Josephine laughed hollowly. "You want to be civil? After the things you said yesterday?"

"Humph," he retorted. "I'll admit to being a bit vexed, but I believe we would make a better team if we could at least hold a polite conversation. We are, after all, going to be working together for quite a few months. Maybe even years. Who's to say?"

Josephine's stomach clenched. *Years? I may not have years here on land.*

"For now, we must prepare for the soiree, which is in two weeks."

Josephine blinked and shook her head at the sudden change of topic. "The Harvest Festival soiree that we've been invited to attend?"

Mr. Runik nodded. "Have you attended before?"

"Of course not," she said snickering. "How would I have obtained an invitation?"

"That works in our favor then. No one will recognize you, with the exception of Mr. and Mrs. Graves and anyone else we might have tea with in the days to come."

"We might be invited to tea again?" Josephine's throat tightened up. She had been a bundle of nerves at the last one. It had only been Mattie and her cheerful disposition that had set her at ease.

"It's quite possible. I have many contacts that will be attending the soiree as well. Anyone who's anyone will be attending. The Festival will be outdoors for much of the day, as long as the weather holds. Then there will be tea and some entertainment during the late afternoon. Dinner will be served after dark. There will also be dancing."

Josephine blanched at that bit of news. "Dancing?"

"No need to panic," he reassured her. "Beau will teach you all the basic country dances that you will need to know. Most of the attendees will be English landowners, loyal to His Majesty, King George, but there will be many Colonial Patriots present as well. It is imperative that we fit in with them."

"*You* are going to be dancing at the soiree?" Josephine asked, eyes widening in surprise.

"Yes, Miss Teversin. Did you think I would just allow you to scamper off to the Festival without proper supervision?"

Josephine frowned at his insult and replied with an equal amount of sarcasm. "I don't know. It sounds like it might be too much fun for you. Perhaps Beau should escort me instead."

Runik barked out a laugh, which was completely out of character for him. Josephine's eyes widened again at seeing Nathaniel Runik's face look so cheerful, even if it was at her expense. For one moment, his eyes shone brightly and a dimple appeared on his cheek that she would never have known was there.

With a lopsided grin still on his face, Runik said, "I would like to see what the two of you could accomplish together."

"At least Beau and I would have some fun. He makes me laugh," she pointed out, smirking back at him. "And you underestimate Beau. I think he's sharper than he makes himself appear. You intelligencers all think you have to be stuffy and serious."

At that remark, Nathaniel snorted in amusement.

"Mr. Runik, did you just snort?" Josephine accused, gaping at him. "Madame Arment has lectured me repeatedly about how snorting is impolite. And here you are, *snorting*. I did not think aristocratic cock-roaches could lower themselves to make such an error in social etiquette."

"Aristocratic cockroaches? Miss Teversin, you simply can*not* talk this way when you are with company. Ladies do not speak like … like …"

"Like what?"

He folded his arms across his chest. "Like pirates."

"Pirates do not wear petticoats," said Josephine in the most sickly-sweet voice she could muster, just to aggravate him.

"So you keep saying."

Before Josephine could continue goading him, the carriage rolled to a stop.

"Ah, we are here." Mr. Runik stepped down from the carriage and placed his black tricorn on his head. Then he held out his hand for her like a proper gentleman. Refusing his help was awfully tempting, but Josephine thought it might be a bit childish. Placing her hand in his, she stepped down into the sun.

Of course, now that she was out of the carriage, she could not get the parasol to unfold. "Oh, open up you bloody, blasted thing!" she muttered.

"Miss Teversin, *we are in public!*" The muscle in Runik's jaw ticked. "Ladies do not say 'bloody' or 'blast'. Are you incapable of controlling that mouth for one morning?"

"Here, then," she said as she shoved the infernal thing into his arms. "You do it, if you're so smart."

"Oh, for heaven's sake," he barked. "You can sail a ship but not open a simple thing like this?" He muttered to himself as he bent to the task, possibly just to prove what an imbecile she was.

"I think it might be stuck," Josephine pointed out as Runik fumbled with the parasol. "This is precisely why Beau would be useful on an assignment. You are as much of an idiot with these things as I am. And no one was even looking until you started shouting at me."

Less than a minute later, Josephine was delighted to hear him cursing the parasol.

"Oh, Mr. Runik!" Pretending to feel faint, she fanned her face with her hands and continued to goad him. "What language! My delicate ears can take no more!" She planted her hands on her waist. "Your mouth is just as foul as mine, thank you very much."

Straightening up again, Runik scowled down at her, flung her parasol back inside the carriage, and slammed the door behind them.

"Wait!" she exclaimed as he dragged her away by the elbow. "Are we just leaving it there?"

"You can do without just this once. You've been gallivanting around Charlestown without a parasol for some time now, as I recall."

"But that's different. Really, Mr. Runik, it just isn't done."

Mr. Runik stopped to glare at her, yet again. "What does it matter if you cannot open the silly contraption?"

"Because Sophia will murder me if I get anymore freckles."

"What, may I ask, is wrong with your freckles?"

The sincerity in his voice surprised her so much that she gave him the truth. "I've never given them much thought," she said with a shrug. "But you and Sophia are supposed to be turning me into a lady. And ladies aren't supposed to have freckles."

"Well," he began, taking her hand and looping it under his elbow. "If Madame Arment murders you, then you will be excused from your next assignment."

It was a relief for Josephine to finally be back at the Skulthorpe estate. The irony of it was not lost on her. Runik's ever changing mood had nearly driven Josephine over the edge. One minute he was charming and the next he was glaring cold daggers at her. He had to have some sort of grudge against her, or maybe all pirates. Josephine couldn't sort it out. At first, Josephine had not noticed the shift in him because she was completely mesmerized by the park. It had been as beautiful as a painting. Then Mr. Runik had opened his mouth to lecture her, and that was where her good humor had come to an abrupt end.

Thankfully, Beau came through on the incredible luncheon. Sandwiches, scones, warm bread, honey, jam, and tea had been set out for them in the ballroom where they would soon be attempting to dance.

Beau made himself busy with all the food while Eleanor questioned her about the training and Mr. Runik. "Did you have a lovely time with him?"

Josephine squashed the urge to roll her eyes. Eleanor had been nothing but gracious and didn't deserve Josephine's sarcasm, unlike some chowder-headed mules. "It was ... interesting. The park was lovely. The gardens were my favorite." Josephine glanced around the room. "Where is Sophia? I thought she would be here to oversee the dancing."

"No, no, my dear girl!" Beau announced. "Dancing is for Eleanor and me to teach. Grab a dish, my dear. You look a bit green … but absolutely dashing in that pink. Excellent color on you." Beau continued to blather on while filling his tiny saucer with apple tarts, sugar wafer cookies, and orange biscuits.

Eleanor grinned. "Sophia said something about having errands and sending a message to someone. Now, don't change the subject. How was your walk in the park with Mr. Runik? Give us all the details!"

"Eleanor, I told you before," Josephine said. "Mr. Runik does not fancy me. I'm too lowborn for him."

Eleanor sipped her tea and studied Josephine for a moment. "I don't know how you can be sure of that. And you are not lowborn. The Teversins are well thought of in London, from what I remember."

"You mean my father's family," Josephine muttered, inwardly cringing.

Even if he had wanted to, Joseph wouldn't have been able to rejoin polite society as an immortal pirate, and Josephine, pirate or not, was positive she *never* could. She had no idea who her mother was. The woman could have been a tavern doxy for all she knew. She would never be welcomed into the upper class fold with the other elite families, regardless of her family name.

Not only that, it was possible her father had outlived his siblings, since his magic had given him a longer lifespan. Heaven only knew if any of his immediate family were still alive. If they *were* alive, they resided in London, and Josephine had no intention of travelling there.

"Ladies, these orange biscuits are positively divine when covered in honey," Beau interrupted.

Josephine chuckled and spooned some honey onto her biscuit as he suggested. She was not disappointed. The biscuit melted on her tongue and the honey gave it such a sweet flavor, Josephine was sure it would make her sick if she ate too much. "That *is* delicious."

"Beau is right, you do look handsome today," Eleanor agreed. "That gown is becoming on you."

Josephine lowered her eyes. She really hated when they fawned over her looks. Maybe she was pretty enough, but the beauty they saw was merely because of all they had done to change her. An image of Oliver sprang to mind and the way he had berated her this morning. He had never actually said she was ugly, but it was clear he didn't appreciate what she had done to herself at all. Josephine set down her half-eaten bread and honey, a wave of nausea washing over her at the thought.

Eleanor continued without pause. "Beau and I *had* agreed that you should wear gold to the ball next week, but now I might reconsider seeing this color on you."

"But I told her she'd look stunning in gold, Eleanor," Beau exclaimed. He turned back to Josephine. "Didn't I tell you? The pink is lovely, but gold will bring out the golden flecks in your eyes. You will have every man in the room falling at your feet!"

Eleanor giggled. Josephine was sure she was turning ten shades of red. She didn't want every man falling at her feet. In truth, she didn't know if there was any man that would dare to court her. There had been men, boys mostly, that had called on her at the tavern, but they never came more than once. Maybe she was too much of an odd duckling for anyone.

Mentally scolding herself, Josephine forced her mind back to the present. "When will we begin dancing?"

Beau spoke up immediately. "As soon as we have filled ourselves with yummy things, we are free to dance the afternoon away."

It was Josephine's turn to giggle. Standing up and dusting the crumbs from her lap, Josephine announced. "Well, I am ready when you are!"

Three hours and two sore feet later, Josephine had not been successful in what Beau considered to be the easiest of all the country reels. Still, she had two more weeks of torture to endure. With Beau and Eleanor's encouraging remarks, and a whole lot of luck, she would master this thing called dancing.

FIFTEEN

After running into Josephine at the Kraken's Lookout, Oliver decided to make his way back to Culligan's Wharf to speak with the Captain. Joseph Teversin and Cully had been close friends. Joseph would have trusted him implicitly. After getting a peek at the two chests in Cully's cellar, Oliver was certain there was more to the story between Josephine and Skulthorpe.

Josephine.

A thrill of delight ran through him again, thinking about how beautiful she'd looked today. Oliver could stare at her for hours, no matter what she wore. But his temper had gotten the better of him this morning. Knowing she was dolled up for some other man, some English toff - he'd completely lost his head. Just the thought of anyone else setting their eyes on her made him want to beat someone to a bloody pulp.

Without knocking, Oliver raced up the stairs to Culligan's office.

"Cap?" he called out.

Culligan stood up behind his desk. "Oliver, my lad. Good to see you!" When he noticed Oliver's grave expression, he sobered immediately. "I take it you're not here for a social call. Is Josephine all right?"

"Ain't sure, Cap."

Taking a seat, he filled Culligan in on everything that had happened since the last time they'd spoken. Culligan paced back and forth behind his desk, listening intently, showing no outward signs of shock over Josephine's second abduction, the trip to the mansion in the country, or Josephine getting dressed up for the same bloke that had been stalking her.

"Are you sure you're not in a tiff because she's with some other gentleman?" Culligan asked, eyeing him.

Oliver rolled his eyes. "I don't believe she'd be stupid enough to fancy someone who shot her. Josephine's never been secretive with me before, even with suitors. If that's all it is, she would've told me."

Culligan chuckled, stroking his beard. "Does she know that you pounded all them suitors to the dust so they wouldn't come calling again?"

Oliver's fingers tightened into fists at the memory. "None of them were good enough for her."

"Tell me, lad, who *is* good enough for her?"

Oliver met Culligan's knowing gaze, not bothering to answer him. The Captain knew ruddy well that he didn't want anyone touching his beautiful Jo.

"Tell me everything you know about Garreck Skulthorpe," Oliver demanded. "Anything you've found out about why he's here. I ain't seen him with Jo yet, but she's been meeting with a hunter. She *knows* he's a hunter and still she goes. My gut's telling me that Skulthorpe is here and he's been threatening her."

Culligan halted his pacing and muttered a curse. "How deep into this mess do you really want to go, Oliver? This is dangerous business."

There was no hesitation when Oliver replied, "It's Josephine. I'll go as deep as I have to, Cap. I ain't letting Jo get hurt by that villain. Not again."

Culligan lowered his voice and said, "Then we ain't talking here. Come with me."

NATHANIEL WAS at the Skulthorpe estate promptly at four o'clock to take Josephine home, but unfortunately, Josephine's ill-humor had not improved since that morning. She sulked in silence across from him in the carriage and stared out the window.

Nathaniel was certain Josephine was the most vexing woman he had ever met. Typically, ladies he encountered were superficial, thinking only of parties, gowns, and embroidery. They were simple-minded and predictable, but not this little pirate. The girl was completely uncouth at times, thanks to her upbringing, but she had gumption, he supposed. Or was she being disagreeable on purpose? Her outrageous and sometimes vulgar comments made him want to shout at her. And he would, if he didn't have such an undeniable urge to laugh. Aristocratic cockroach indeed.

It did not help in the slightest that he found her so beautiful. He would be a fool not to think so and an even bigger fool for acting on it. When she had entered the carriage at the White Pearl Wharf earlier that morning, it had taken all his self-control not to react. He had been furious at the effect she'd had on him, and when she mentioned her freckles, Nathaniel had to bite his tongue to keep from mentioning how fetching they were on her pert little nose. It was imperative that he keep his distance.

Remember what she is, Nathaniel thought. *Remember what her father has done.*

That reminder had been enough to get his wayward thoughts under control again.

The walk in the park had been a test on Josephine's observation skills. At the soiree, it would be of utmost importance not to become preoccupied with the gossip and dancing while she was supposed to be spying on the Patriots. Nathaniel talked to her, distracting her as much as possible, as they strolled down the paths. He had instructed her on holding appropriate conversations with the social elite - which topics were safe and which were to be avoided. After a time, he'd stopped and interrogated her to see how closely she had observed her surroundings.

Josephine had visibly swallowed. "Well, there aren't as many people about as I thought there would be. The docks are swarming with sailors and merchants doing business."

"The wealthy have no need to be up and about so early. They tend to sleep the morning away," he said. "More people will be here this afternoon."

Josephine's nose scrunched, but she went on. "There are a lot of places to hide for an ambush, especially in the shrubs along those narrow paths through the garden. Anyone could jump out and rob us."

That detail hadn't been exactly what he was looking for, but perhaps as a pirate, she'd been taught to be wary of traps. Nathaniel cleared his throat. "What about the woman we passed earlier by the fountain? What color was her gown?"

Josephine's brows pinched together and her eyes shifted to the left as she tried to recall the simple detail. "Her gown? I have no idea. But her dog has fleas."

"Fleas? How do you know?"

"Didn't you see how the poor thing kept stopping to scratch?" Josephine turned and narrowed her eyes at Nathaniel. "I did notice that she had her parasol."

Nathaniel coughed to cover his amusement. "Right. What about the man under the maple tree, sitting on the park bench?"

"Oh, yes! I remember him. I think he might have been spying on us."

Nathaniel's eyebrows shot up. Josephine was right of course. Martin was one of the three hunters he'd assigned to keep watch while they were walking. "Why do you think he's a spy?"

"The black suit," she said.

"A lot of men wear black suits."

Josephine shrugged. "It's not just the suit. If he hadn't been wearing black, I wouldn't have noticed his odd behavior. For one thing, he looked like he was reading, but he never turned any pages. And whenever we passed by, he shifted so his body was angled toward us."

Nathaniel gritted his teeth. He was going to blister Martin's ears when they returned to the Skulthorpe estate. The man was new to the Brotherhood, but it was no excuse for not being more discreet.

He didn't blame Josephine for noticing him. The woman walking her dog was no threat, so Josephine had ignored her for the most part.

"And the riders over there," Josephine said, pointing to the large field in the distance. "They seemed to be riding in circles. I've seen the same two or three riders go past every few minutes. I don't understand that."

"Men of society often go riding to be seen," Nathaniel confessed.

It was the same in London. Men and women of the *ton* would walk or take carriage rides in Hyde Park for no other purpose than to be seen by other wealthy members of society and mothers would parade their debutante daughters around for eligible men.

Nathaniel shook his head and turned his attention back to the task at hand. "What about the people up on the hill?"

"The ones having a picnic?" asked Josephine. "It's a lovely day for one. Not a lot of wind and the sky is clear."

"What about the couple?" Nathaniel hissed, beginning to lose his patience at Josephine's babbling. "What did you notice?"

"They had entirely too much food for just two people," Josephine pointed out. "Wasteful, if you ask me."

"I didn't ask."

For Josephine's first attempt, it hadn't been a total disaster. The things she'd noticed had been a bit unusual. Most women would notice the color of a dress instead of fleas, but Josephine was no ordinary woman. *They were details a pirate would take note of*, Nathaniel thought.

Perhaps he had jumped to conclusions yesterday evening when he'd bluntly told her that bringing her into the Brotherhood fold had been a mistake. Josephine was perfectly aware of her surroundings.

As the carriage moseyed down the cobblestone streets, Josephine was once again staring out the tiny window. A frown darkened her lovely face. He knew he ought not to engage her, but the urge to know her thoughts overcame him.

"Why, may I ask, do you look so troubled?"

Josephine shrugged, but did not face him. "I'm not very good at dancing, that's all. And my feet are hurting."

"Mmm. Well, perhaps tomorrow morning you should rest," he said. "Skipping one morning won't hurt. I'll pick you up at noon like before and we'll resume my part in the training the morning after."

Nathaniel gloated to himself, certain that his decision would make her happy, but she was not smiling when she squared her shoulders to face him.

"Please, Mr. Runik," she said. "I am extremely exhausted and in no mood for you to patronize me."

"I was trying to be a gentleman. If you would rather -"

"I would rather you just make up your mind."

"Make up my mind about what?" he asked.

Cocking her head to one side, Josephine looked at him thoughtfully. "You are like a jellyfish."

"I beg your pardon?" choked Nathaniel.

"Have you ever seen a jellyfish up close?"

Nathaniel couldn't keep up with the woman's train of thought. Why on earth would she be prattling on about jellyfish?

His lip curled in disdain. "I don't believe so, Miss Teversin. I am not a sailor, nor do I care much for sea water or creatures of the ocean."

"Jellyfish are very tricky creatures. From a distance, they are beautiful. Graceful."

Nathaniel smirked. "You think me beautiful?"

Eyes flashing, Josephine continued without answering him. "They wait patiently for their prey to be lulled into a false sense of security. The prey moves closer, because how could such a beautiful creature be dangerous? And that's when it happens. The tentacles underneath the jellyfish's soft outer shell begin to wrap themselves around the prey, trapping them. The bite of their sting is agony, causing the prey to struggle, entangling them more and more until they are paralyzed in the jellyfish's deadly grip. They are beautiful, but they cannot be trusted."

Josephine glared at him. "It is foolish of me to believe that I could ever trust you. When I'm quiet, it doesn't suit you, but when I open my mouth and speak - that doesn't suit you either. You say you want to work well as a team and be civil, but when you look at me, your eyes are cold and full of disgust. I have done my utmost to do as you ask during training and assignments, and, granted, I barely know what I'm doing, but you have nothing to give back but condescending remarks and insults. These last few days I have seen these rare moments of kindness in you, so I have been trying to be friendly in return, attempting to joke with you, but then the moment passes and you're back to hating me again. It was naïve of me to forget who you are and that you work for someone like Garreck Skulthorpe."

"Mr. Skulthorpe is a brilliant and cunning man. Any man loyal to the Crown would be honored to work for him."

"Don't bother defending Skulthorpe to me. I know exactly who that man is, probably better than you."

Josephine relaxed against the back of the seat, done with the quarrel. Gritting his teeth, Nathaniel knew that he ought to let the opportunity pass, but his stubborn nature could not resist getting in the last word.

"That's highly doubtful."

Piercing him with another furious glare, Josephine sat forward and began to scold him yet again.

"I know that the only reason you joined that silly Brotherhood of British imbeciles is because you are the youngest brother in a wealthy titled family. Since you are not the eldest, you will not receive the title or the inheritance, so you were forced to find other means to make your fortune. It was the same with my father. He was a third son. But he chose to be his own man. He worked hard and saved everything he had so that one day he could have his own ship. He never wanted to live by another man's leave. We may have been scallywags, the dirtiest scum beneath your shiny, aristocratic boots, but *we* never took orders from anyone."

Nathaniel crossed his arms over his chest to keep from strangling the woman. "Even if it meant being changed into a pirate? Is that the price of being a happy man? To become a criminal?"

"My father was a good man. Not a common criminal," she argued. "And you're one to talk, hunter! Skulthorpe openly admits that this Brotherhood of yours is in the business of lying, stealing, and *killing* on occasion," accused Josephine, ticking the crimes off on her fingers. "And yet, you do not call yourself a criminal. Hypocrisy at its finest. You can try to convince yourself of Mr. Skulthorpe's greatness. His *brilliance*. But he is nothing but a cruel man. If you continue to work for that blackguard, you are going to end up just like him."

"And it would be an honor!"

Josephine snorted, irritating him further. "Has he really pulled the wool over your eyes so well? Skulthorpe plays his role of the honorable gentleman, but he has his own agenda. You can be sure of that."

The carriage lurched to a stop, but before Josephine could bolt, he gripped her arm and hissed in her ear, "Be very careful, Miss Teversin. You do not know who you are dealing with."

"I know exactly who I'm dealing with, unfortunately," she replied. "He is a murderer."

"Just like your father?"

Josephine jerked her arm out of his grasp and gave him a scathing look. "My father never murdered anyone."

Nathaniel watched with a clenched jaw as the insolent girl disappeared into the shadows of the Kraken's Lookout. Overhead, storm clouds threatened, and drops of rain began to splatter on the carriage. He closed the door and urged the driver to make haste before the downpour.

He'd never let himself become so unhinged before. What made him even angrier was that she had, in fact, pegged him accurately. He was the fourth son to an Earl and would not inherit a thing. No land, no title, no wealth. If he wanted anything, he was going to have to earn it all.

Joining the army was one of the few options available to those without a title and he had done so as soon as he had turned sixteen, just five years ago. It was a trifle too young to join but Nathaniel's dark facial hair made him appear older. He was an officer for three years before Mr. Skulthorpe had begun to recruit him. His father had been dead-set against it, but Nathaniel had sworn that he would make some-thing of himself. The risk was greater, but so was the pay and prestige.

When word was sent that his father was suddenly killed by a pirate, it had sealed his fate with the hunters. If Josephine Teversin thought he was suddenly going to forget about that transgression, she was sorely mistaken.

SIXTEEN

C ulligan took Oliver back to his run-down townhome in the heart of the slums. There at his work table, they sat together, shuffling through old papers that Joseph had left in the Captain's possession.

"Cap," Oliver speculated, looking around the filthy place. "I'd have thought you'd have enough gold to buy yourself a nicer place than this, and a maid to tidy things up."

Culligan never looked up from reading his papers. "I don't spend my gold on land and houses, lad. I spend it on large ships and loyal crew."

"Aye, that's true enough," he agreed. Oliver didn't spend his own earnings on a nice place, either. In fact, his one-room flat was located in a miserable part of town not far from here, but at least he kept his place free of dust and cobwebs. It wouldn't surprise him to see a ghost walking through Culligan's place.

Sifting through the various letters and shipping statements, Oliver asked, "So what's in these papers you think we're supposed to find?"

"Just a hunch." He handed a stack of letters to Oliver. "Here, take these."

"What am I looking for?"

"Letters from three years ago," said Culligan.

Oliver froze with the papers in hand, realization setting in. "It was Skulthorpe who captured Josephine that night, wasn't it, Cap?"

Culligan paused in his reading and frowned at him. "Aye. She didn't tell you?"

Shaking his head, Oliver replied, "I knew it was pirate hunters, but I didn't know it was *him*. Jo never said a word after that night, either. Like she's trying to block it out."

The Captain stroked his beard thoughtfully and then got back to reading his papers. They sat in silence for a while, skimming through the letters, but Oliver could find nothing to help them.

Slamming the papers back down on the table, Oliver heaved a frustrated sigh. "I don't think these papers are -"

Culligan jumped from his seat. "Here's what I been looking for, lad! These letters here are from a man named James to Joseph Teversin." Cully pointed at the discarded stack of papers. "Most of these here are worthless - nothing worth hiding - but these ..." His eyes glittered in excitement.

"James?" Oliver repeated. The memory surrounding the name was vague, but he did recall Joseph telling him something about a James that he'd been in touch with. Unfortunately, Oliver was never told anything more. "James is an awfully common name, Cully. Everyone is named James, here *and* in England. Are you sure that's what you're looking for?"

Culligan pointed to the letter in his hand. "Aye. James says here that he needed old Blacktail's help. Something to do with his son in England being in a bit of trouble. Says here that James had been in hiding from the Brotherhood."

"Brotherhood?"

"Secret group, the Brotherhood. British spies, working for the Crown," explained Culligan. "Specifically targeting Patriot groups that stand against England. Trying to quell the rebellion that rumor says is growing in size."

"The rebellion is mostly up north, ain't it?" Oliver inquired.

"It's spreading quickly, especially with the new taxes the Crown has placed on the colonies over the last few years," Culligan explained. "People say it ain't right."

Oliver's brows pinched. "What does all this have to do with Skulthorpe and the hunters?"

"The hunters kill pirates exclusively. The immortal pirates have always wreaked havoc on British trade routes."

"Which helps the colonials," Oliver muttered.

"Aye! Common pirates are bad enough for the British merchant vessels, but immortal pirate ships move faster because of their magic, so merchants here can get their goods quicker, from a different source, and *cheaper*. Like tea. That tea tax the British have been pushing on us here has got a lot of merchants seeing red. They're getting their tea somewhere else."

Oliver snorted. "Your tea ain't any good though, Cap. Almost ain't worth drinking."

"True enough, lad, but it's cheaper to buy."

Oliver stood up to pace across the room. "So, the hunters eliminate the threat of the pirates and go on controlling the prices of imported goods. Where is this Brotherhood tied in?"

Culligan shook the papers at him. "The bleeding Brotherhood owns the hunters, of course! They're all in it together, and I believe Skulthorpe runs the lot of 'em."

Oliver rubbed his forehead. "What does he want? We're still missing something."

Cully scratched at his beard again. "I don't hear as much as I used to, since I stopped sailing myself, but Skulthorpe had his hands in a lot of pockets at one time. Here and in London. Was well-known for having a lot of unsavory contacts. He was commissioned here by King George personally, or so I heard. There was talk, just before the Pirate Purge years back, that the King was afraid the pirates and witches would join sides with the colonials. Then there'd be nothing and no one to stop the colonials from breaking loose from his grand empire."

"The pirates and witches ain't never taken sides with a king or country. Seems a bit mad to think they would now."

As if he thought someone might overhear, Cully whispered, "Some also say that the King's wits may be a bit addled. Just rumor, mind you."

"It still don't explain what this bloke wants with Jo," Oliver stated. "Why not kill her? Why not rid the world of one more immortal pirate? That's always been the hunters' way. What does he want with her?"

Before Oliver had time to ponder all this new information, the Captain shoved the letters into his hands. "Here. Take these and read 'em carefully. There's something about this man, James - I'm certain. As soon as Joseph found out that Josephine had been caught, he brought these here to me with no explanation. Just said to hide 'em. They been in this drawer collecting dust since that day. I ain't sure where Josephine fits into all this, but there has to be some explanation behind it all. Jo may be the one that can tell you."

Running his hand over his hair, Oliver said, "I'm going to talk to her, then."

"Good luck to you," Culligan said sympathetically.

Outside, thunder sounded in the distance. Jumping to the window, Oliver watched dark clouds roll into the harbor at a speed that was too rapid to be natural.

"Blast," Oliver muttered. There was only one reason why a storm would be forming so quickly over Charlestown. "Thanks for the help, Cap, but I best be going," he said, stuffing the letters into his waistcoat pocket.

Culligan nodded. "I'll keep my ear to the ground. Dig up what I can."

With grim determination, Oliver raced back to the Kraken's Lookout through the pouring rain. His Josephine was hurting, and nothing was going to stop him from being by her side.

JUST AS JOSEPHINE was finally getting her emotions under control again, a soaking wet Oliver burst through her bedroom door. Water dripped from his hair and clothes, creating a puddle on the floor.

"Blimey, Oliver!" she yelled, quickly wiping away the last of her tears. "Don't you know how to knock?"

Josephine had changed from her lovely gown into a boy's shirt and knee breeches. Her bare feet were tucked under her as she sat curled up on her bed, hugging a pillow to her chest. Josephine squirmed nervously at being dressed so indecently, even though she had never cared before. Things had been different between the two of them this week, so she wasn't positive how he would react to seeing her like this.

Slamming the door behind him, Oliver crossed the room to tower over her, showering her with water at the same time.

Raising her hands to shield her face, she cried, "Oliver Blakely, you are getting me all wet!"

"What did he do to you?" he demanded to know, ignoring her complaint.

She got up and padded barefoot across the room to find him a towel out of the wardrobe. "What are you talking about?"

Oliver followed her with his eyes. "You know bloody well what I'm talking about, Jo. It has been pouring outside for nearly an hour. I know you've been crying. You better tell me what that bilge scum did to you. Did he touch you? I'll rip his black heart from his chest and feed it to the fish!"

Josephine paused midway through the tirade to stare at her old friend. He was a sight to behold in his fury. The muscles in his cheeks were clenched and his eyes had darkened to the color of a stormy sea. In that moment, his personality and temperament reminded her so much of her father. She didn't doubt Oliver's desire to pounce on anyone who threatened to harm her. The thought of it sent butterflies fluttering through her belly.

Josephine handed him a towel and he began drying himself. When he removed his waistcoat and boots, she flushed and walked back to the bed, hoping that Oliver hadn't noticed her odd behavior.

"No, he didn't touch me. He didn't do anything."

"Why don't I believe you?" Oliver asked.

With a sigh, she plopped back down on her bed. "He yelled at me. I yelled back. That's all."

"Josephine Teversin, you lowered your eyes again."

"It was just an argument." Josephine lifted her eyes to his. "He said some things about Father. And me."

"And?"

"And I didn't care for what he said. He called Father a murderer, so I blistered his ears and ran before I could cry in front of him. He only hurt my feelings. Nothing more."

Tossing his tricorn into the chair, Oliver paced the floor while Josephine rubbed her aching feet. She still was not accustomed to those shoes pinching her toes, and the dancing all afternoon had not done them any good.

The bed sank as Oliver sat down beside her, causing Josephine to nervously straighten up and hide her naked feet. His nearness made her heart beat a little faster, and it took everything she had to keep her breathing under control. As a distraction, she started freeing the pins that were jammed into her scalp.

"Josephine?" Oliver began.

Josephine continued to yank at her hair as she waited for him to continue, but he merely stared as she made a mess of her hair.

"Blast these pins!" she muttered.

"You're going to end up with a bloody bird's nest if you don't let me do that." He swatted her hands away. His fingers moved through her thick waves, gently pulling pins and loosening the knot that Aunt Genny had so expertly fashioned that morning.

"Thank you," whispered Josephine. Trying to keep from squirming at his touch, she cleared her throat and attempted to change the subject again. "Were you going to say something?"

His fingers paused only for a split second before they continued working and combing through her locks. "Aye," he said grimly. "I need you to tell me what's going on. Who is that bloke that comes to pick you up every morning and what does he want? The truth, Jo."

She stiffened. Could she risk telling him? Skulthorpe hadn't ordered her not to say anything. Josephine had just chosen not to so that Oliver wouldn't worry or do anything rash.

"Do you not trust me, Josephine?" said Oliver gently, resting his warm hand on the nape of her neck. He rubbed slow circles with his thumb, sending shivers down her spine.

Reluctantly, she turned to face him again, meeting his steady gaze. "Of course, I trust you. That's not the reason I haven't told you."

"Will that bloke hurt you?"

Josephine shook her head. "I don't think *he* would."

Oliver's body visibly stiffened at her response. "Garreck Skulthorpe. *He'll* hurt you."

Josephine's voice shook as she said, "And you and Aunt Genny."

Rising from the bed, Oliver took up his pacing again. "Bloody hell, Jo. You should've told me from the start."

"I couldn't risk it! I didn't know what he would do if he found out that I'd told you - and you know I can take care of myself!"

"As can I, Jo!" Oliver shouted. "How do you think it feels to watch you saunter off with that hunter, knowing you might never come back?"

Josephine gasped. "You *were* following me! I thought I felt someone watching."

The muscle in Oliver's jaw clenched in fury.

"Fine," she huffed, folding her arms over her chest. "I'll admit it was foolish of me to think that you couldn't handle the truth, but what about Aunt Genny? I don't want her hurt."

"Genny is more than capable of looking after herself."

Josephine frowned. "What do you mean?"

"Genny's a witch."

Josephine's jaw dropped. "A witch? She never told *me* that! And how is it that *you* know?"

Oliver shrugged. "She don't go around boasting about it, Jo. She probably thought you knew all along. I did."

She rubbed her forehead. "Did Father know?"

"Of course," he replied. "Why do you think he sent you here to live with her?"

Josephine straightened up with a sudden thought. "Oh! She's not my mum, is she?"

"Jo, do you think your father would keep you from your own mum if she were alive?"

She slouched down in disappointment. "It was only a thought. I'm under some sort of spell of protection, then?"

"Several. And a spell to hide your whereabouts from hunters."

"Well, that didn't seem to work, did it?"

"Only another powerful witch could have managed to find you," Oliver said, still sounding angry with her. "Which means Skulthorpe must have one working for him."

"But I thought the hunters killed witches as well as pirates?"

"The last time I checked," Oliver replied. "But *you* are a pirate and *you* are still breathing. I don't think he's playing by his own rules anymore. Makes me wonder what he's up to, having a pirate and a witch on the payroll." After a few more circles around the room, Oliver asked, "So why has he not killed you?"

"He's hired me to be one of his spies," she muttered reluctantly, peeking up at him to see his reaction.

"You're blooming joking! A spy?"

Josephine flinched at the bite in his words. "It's not been that bad, actually. They're teaching me to be a lady of society. Though Mr. Runik is a ..." She searched for the proper insult.

"A kraken's arse?"

"Yes, quite."

"Why do they want you?" he asked. "They can't find some other lady of society to be their spy?"

"How many upper-class ladies do you know that can do the things I can do?"

"So Skulthorpe chose you specifically," Oliver murmured, taking up his pacing once more. "Interesting."

"It's not so bad really. My tutors have been kind enough. And the food is excellent!" Josephine grinned at him, trying to lighten the mood. She hated seeing her friend so irate with her.

Oliver stopped and glowered at her. "The food? You're being pretty cavalier for someone strolling around town with the enemy."

"Oliver ..."

"That hunter could put a musket ball through your heart at any time and you're talking about food!" Oliver growled.

"It was just a joke."

"*This ain't a joke, Jo!*" he shouted. "Your father gave his life to get you out of Skulthorpe's hands, and here you are … working for him and *joking* about it!" The look he gave her was filled with disgust.

"I'm being careful, Oliver."

"You can't trust them, Jo," he shot back, ignoring her. "No matter how nice they appear to be. Hunters can't be trusted!"

"I know that!" she barked.

Oliver marched to the chair in the corner of the room, snatched up his wet tricorn and waistcoat, and strode to the door.

"W-what are you doing?" Josephine stammered, watching him pull on his damp boots.

"I'm going down to the tavern. I don't think I can stomach talking about this with you right now."

"Oliver," Josephine said, rising from the bed. "I'm sorry."

Giving her one last look of disappointment, Oliver stomped out, slamming the door behind him.

SEVENTEEN

I n the dark alley behind the theater district, Garreck Skulthorpe
stood alert as he waited for the witch. He'd taken a chance, hiring
her a year ago, but he'd had to take drastic measures to find the little
half-pirate that had escaped him and his hunters three years ago.

His obsession with finding her had only grown over time, and it
gave him great pleasure knowing that he now controlled her. Like a
puppet-master pulling strings, she was his little marionette, obeying his
every whim. Only when he had achieved his goal would he put an end
to her; the last of the pirate breed.

Yes, she *was* the last. Good riddance. His hunters had combed the
seas and could find no more. Skulthorpe smiled with delight at what he
had accomplished. Then he would be onto bigger things than witches
and pirates.

His thoughts were interrupted by the sound of footsteps entering
the alley. Fingering his pistol, he turned to meet the cloaked woman.

"Witch?"

"Who else?" she said impatiently.

"Well?" he demanded.

"All is going as planned."

"The girl?"

The witch sniffed. "She'll suit our needs."

"And our surprise for the Harvest soiree?"

"It will be a night to remember."

"Good," Skulthorpe gloated. "And did she finally confess all to that boy?"

She tilted her head at an angle. "Yes. Why do you care if she did or not?"

"It is essential to my plans. Now go." He waved the witch away. "And do not be discovered."

The witch merely chuckled. "She has no idea. Trust me."

***

DOWN IN THE Kraken's Lookout, Oliver sat alone at the far end of the bar and stared down into his mead. The candles hanging on the walls flickered as workers and sailors filed in and out of the entrance to the tavern. The room smelled of fish, rum, and pipe-smoke. Normally, Oliver would join the others in their merriment, but he wasn't in the mood.

Genny paced back and forth behind the bar, filling mugs with rum or mead for the men to drink after a hard day's work. She walked past him, quirked her eyebrow at his untouched drink, and then strode off to serve another round to the sailors who just sauntered up to the bar. The furtive looks she kept giving Oliver were making him squirm.

Why was he so upset with Josephine? He had known the whole time that she'd been hiding things. He'd followed her to that mansion every day and stood watch within the oak trees, making certain his Josephine walked out each evening. Her blasé reaction to the situation had set him off. She wasn't the slightest bit worried about her own safety. It was maddening. Every explanation she gave had made him more and more furious. Before Oliver could say anything to Jo that he might regret, he'd stormed out of her room to cool off.

The door to the Kraken's Lookout opened and shut with a bang.

The scent of rain wafted in. Oliver swiveled around on his barstool to find two rough-looking blokes entering the tavern.

"Blimey, this is the second squall we've had today," one of the lads said.

"Aye, very strange," the other replied.

They made their way up to the bar to get a drink, but Oliver continued to stare out the front window. The street lamps cast an eerie orange glow over the bay road. Leaves swirled outside while men and women ran by looking for cover from the approaching storm.

"What are you still doing here?" Genny barked.

Oliver whirled around to face her. She glared at him with her hands planted on her hips.

"Do not stare at me like a simpleton, Oliver. You know what this storm means." She gestured to the window.

"Aye," he replied in a gruff whisper, brows furrowing. Josephine was hurting again. This time *he* had caused it. If he continued to sit there like a slug, things wouldn't get sorted between them.

"Get out of here, then," Genny huffed, ripping the mug out of his hands before he could take his first gulp. "*I* can't very well leave the tavern as busy as it is. Shoo, shoo."

Oliver held his hands up in surrender. "All right, I'm going."

Slipping off his barstool, Oliver trudged to the stairs that led up to the second and third floors and headed up. Once he reached the door to Josephine's room, he lifted his hand to knock and then hesitated with his fist just an inch away from the wood. He shuffled his feet and ran his hand over his face, knowing he was being a fool. Josephine was probably lying on the bed, weeping into her pillow, and he was standing out here, nervous as an untried lad.

Finally working up his courage, Oliver rapped on the door three times and murmured, "Angelfish?" He waited, fidgeting with his hat for a moment. There was no response and no movement from inside her room. Inching the door open, Oliver said a bit louder, "Josephine? Are you there?" No one answered.

Oliver entered her room and glanced around. For one terrifying moment, Oliver thought she might have been abducted by that hunter again, but it seemed unlikely since Jo had been going with the bloke willingly each day.

The wind whistled through her cracked window, the storm winds picking up speed. Oliver cursed, spun on his heel, and sprinted back down the stairs.

Josephine had gone to the pier.

JOSEPHINE SPRINTED across the cobblestone street and down to the end of the wooden dock of the White Pearl Wharf, clutching the collar of her hooded cloak. She'd been feeling claustrophobic even while Oliver had been speaking with her. After he'd stormed out, her need to be by the ocean had tripled.

The night air was getting cooler in the autumn months and there was a lingering mist over the docks from the rainstorm she'd created earlier. Her heart pounded and her hands grew warm with her barely-caged magic. Lightning flashed inside the distant storm clouds that were rolling in off the Atlantic. The smell of rain and salty sea on the wind whipped around her.

She ignored the sailors who were finishing up work on their ships or carrying goods to the warehouses along the docks. Some onlookers whistled at her, while others smiled, hoping she might stop to show her favor. She pushed past a couple of men who were striding toward the taverns to find shelter from the storm.

Josephine skidded to a halt at the edge of the pier. A gust of wind pushed her backward, keeping her from tumbling headfirst into the water.

She struggled to breathe. Was this her pirate magic, churning inside her, fighting to break free? Her father had never spoken of feeling this way. But he'd been changed into a pirate by a witch - her Aunt Genny, most likely. Josephine had been born of a pirate and … who? Was her mother a human? Another witch? Who knew what kind of powers Josephine had or even how to control them? Oliver had not even known.

Josephine's heart twisted. She had really let Oliver down. Had she severed the tie between them for good? Could he ever trust her again? Her bottom lip trembled and her eyes stung with the threat of tears. Lightning flashed again, this time a little closer. The clouds were moving toward Charlestown at an unnatural speed; the effect of her emotional turmoil.

"Breathe, Josephine," she whispered to herself, inhaling deeply and closing her eyes. "Get control." The wind continued to swirl around her and a few raindrops splattered on her cheeks.

"Angelfish?"

She spun around. Oliver's tall, lean form was striding toward her. His shoulder-length hair had come loose from its ribbon and his mouth was turned down in a worried frown.

"You followed me," she choked.

"Aye." He approached her at the edge of the pier.

The way Oliver stared at her made her heart race again. Josephine's stomach flipped over and she found her own eyes lingering on his mouth and his broad chest.

"I ... I'm so sorry, Oliver," said Josephine, tears pooling in her eyes against her will.

Oliver stepped closer and cupped her face in his hand. "You know I can't stay mad at you, Josephine. I ... was more furious at myself, anyway."

"Why?"

Oliver gazed off at the looming storm clouds and pinched his lips together. "Because I failed you once, Jo, and it nearly killed me. I don't want anything to happen to you again."

His voice had an edge to it. Josephine knew he was talking about the night she'd been captured by Skulthorpe three years ago.

Josephine took a step back and Oliver's hand fell from her cheek. "That wasn't your doing."

Oliver's eyes found hers again. "If I'd have been there ..."

Swallowing back the bile that was threatening to rise up in her throat, Josephine asked, "Why are you bringing this up?"

He placed his hands on his hips. "Because Cully found letters from a man named James that were sent to your father from three years ago."

Josphine's eyes widened and the blood drained from her face. "That could be anyone, Oliver. Father had many friends and business associates."

"But *this* man was asking for Joseph's help. He was in trouble with the Brotherhood." Oliver took a step toward her. "I want to know the truth, Jo. If I'm to protect you, to *help* you with these hunters and their game, I need you to tell me what happened with Skulthorpe. What happened that night, Angelfish?"

Josephine turned to look out at the water, unable to face him. Her stomach roiled at the memory.

"We were docked in New York to deliver molasses, sugar, and tobacco. You and Father, and a few others, took the goods to the warehouses. That was when we got a message from him - from James," she said, her voice trembling. "He'd written to Father several times asking for help. Father would never tell me why, but I knew it was important by the way he reacted each time he received a letter. They'd been corresponding for over a year." Josephine kept her eyes fixed on the choppy waters, knowing that she might break down if she looked at her friend. "Somehow, he knew we were docked in New York and sent a messenger with a note wanting to meet at a tavern not too far from the docks. I thought I could handle it. It was simple enough to retrieve him, only when I got to the place ..."

"The hunters were there waiting?" Oliver asked.

She nodded, blinking back tears. "I'm sure they were waiting for Father."

Oliver cursed under his breath and ran a hand down his face. Tiny raindrops began to sprinkle all around the two of them as a single tear trailed down Josephine's cheek.

Josephine let her eyelids drop. "It was all my fault."

Oliver grabbed her up in his arms and Josephine wept into his chest. She clung to him as the rain came down harder, soaking them both to the bone.

"Don't, Jo," he said his breath warm in her ear. "It ain't your fault."

"I got him killed!" she sobbed into the crook of his neck.

"No!" Oliver vehemently said, squeezing her tighter. "That ain't true and you know it. If you hadn't gone to the tavern, your father would have been there and would've been killed anyway."

"You should have stopped him!" she cried. "Father should never have turned himself in! He could have found another way."

Oliver gently released her and held her at arm's length, his hands cupping her cheeks. "Josephine, you know how determined your father was. Once he got an idea in his head, there was no stopping him." His eyes looked out to the river, then cut back to Josephine. "The crew and me, we tried to persuade him to let us help, but he made us swear a blood oath. He made us swear not to interfere. You know we can't go against an oath once we've taken it. He didn't want to put any of us in danger."

Josephine's face crumpled, hearing those words. He was right. Her father would never have done anything so selfish.

Oliver pulled her into his arms again and gently stroked her hair.

"I don't know why he didn't try to free you some other way," he said softly into her ear. "Maybe by dying, his magic transferred to you, Josephine. Maybe that's why you were able to escape out that window the way you did." He shook his head. "I could be wrong, but whatever the reason for his going alone to rescue you, I trusted him. He knew what he was doing. I would've done the same, Jo. I would've done anything to save you."

They stood for long minutes, letting the rain soak them through, until Oliver finally suggested they go back inside.

"Cripes, Angelfish, you're going to catch your death." Oliver looked down at her and rubbed her arms to warm her. He tucked Josephine under his arm and started walking back to the Kraken's Lookout.

Josephine leaned into his warmth. "It's my own fault for making it rain again."

She chuckled, but Oliver didn't seem to be in the mood for jokes. To be perfectly honest, she didn't know what was going on in her friend's mind. It was as if he'd withdrawn from her, like he had the morning he'd railed at her because of her gown.

They walked back to the Kraken's Lookout together in silence. It was a relief to finally have confided in him. Josephine only hoped she would not come to regret it.

EIGHTEEN

The days leading up to the dreaded soiree seemed to be getting shorter and shorter, while Josephine grew more and more anxious. No amount of Beau's sweets or Eleanor's soft-spoken encouragement could calm her nerves. Even Sophia was acting less like a general and more like a mothering hen as the dinner party drew near.

Two invitations to tea had come during the week, which Runik would not allow her to avoid. Josephine had been under strict instructions not to leave her seat or do anything untoward during the hour of the visit. Throughout each social call, she sat as stiff as a ship's mast and let Mr. Runik do all the talking. He, on the other hand, was doing his best to keep her at a cold distance since they had argued. They only spoke to each other when absolutely necessary or when they were in lessons.

It didn't help one bit that Josephine had not seen Oliver since that night at the pier. She trained all day to be a genteel lady and came back to the Kraken's Lookout to sit alone in her room or work in the tavern with Aunt Genny, who had wisely chosen not to speak of Josephine's sullen mood. Genny's sad smiles and sympathetic gazes told Josephine that she was aware something was terribly wrong.

Josephine could hardly speak two words to Aunt Genny, either.

Knowing that her friend and guardian had been a witch all along was discomfiting to say the least. It bothered her for some reason, but she didn't know why. It wasn't as if Josephine didn't possess magic of her own. Perhaps it was simply the secrecy that irritated her.

To make matters even more frustrating, Josephine hadn't had a single opportunity to snoop around the mansion. Because she'd been so frazzled, Beau and Eleanor wouldn't leave her alone for a moment of privacy. She wasn't sure whether they were trying to comfort her or make sure she didn't run from the mansion screaming, never to return.

The only bright spot in this whole mess was that Skulthorpe had not shown his face since the night she'd been coerced into his service. He was surely checking up on her through Runik or the rogue witch, whoever she was. Josephine hoped above all that the witch was not one of the trio of tutors. Spending time with them, Beau and Eleanor especially, had become one of her favorite parts of this whole kerfuffle. A betrayal of one of them might just send Josephine over the edge.

"Well done," Sophia remarked after another dance lesson. "I think you are fit enough for the soiree, my dear."

Josephine sighed and shook her head. "It is gracious of you to lie, Madame Sophia, but I know that was my worst turn yet." Taking another deep breath, Josephine sat down to rest her feet. The soiree was tomorrow. She had to be ready to play the part.

The unmistakable clicking of Runik's bootheels caused everyone to turn toward the entrance of the ballroom.

"Mr. Runik, you are early," Sophia pointed out.

"Yes," he replied, giving Josephine one of his icy glares. "I thought it best to give Miss Teversin the remainder of the evening to rest. Tomorrow, we will go over the particulars of the assignment and make her presentable for the evening. How is she faring with the reels?"

"Her dancing is much improved," Beau announced. "If she has a strong partner, she will be tremendous!" He smiled widely at Josephine, trying to lift her spirits.

Mr. Runik turned to walk out and called over his shoulder, "Very well. Come along, Miss Teversin."

Taking Josephine's hand, Beau lifted her to her feet and gave her a quick peck on the cheek. "Rest well, my dear. You will be marvelous!"

Lifting the corners of her mouth in a forced smile, Josephine curtsied to the trio and left without a word.

Josephine tossed and turned the entire night, waking from nightmares that alternated between Oliver, Genny, and herself; all having been murdered by Skulthorpe with Runik looking on, wearing his usual haughty smirk.

Dressing with care, Josephine readied herself for the trying day ahead of her. She could do this. She had done trickier things before, but her friends' lives had not been in jeopardy. Those adventures had been purely voluntary, usually with Oliver in on the scheme. She was all alone now, with no one to see her through. It was highly doubtful that Mr. Runik would come to her rescue if she happened to get into trouble.

Leaving her hair in a loose braid for Eleanor to fashion, Josephine swallowed nervously and made her way down to meet Mr. Runik's carriage.

NATHANIEL WAS ABOUT to storm into the Kraken's Lookout to fetch Josephine when she finally emerged from the tavern. Halting his pacing at once, he opened the carriage door and offered his hand. Neither of them bothered with greetings.

Once inside the coach, he noticed how ill she looked. Her face was white as a ghost and there were dark circles beneath her eyes. He shouldn't comment or comfort her. She was only a means to an end, wasn't she? However, his polite nature won out.

"It will be alright, Miss Teversin. I would not allow you to do this assignment if I didn't believe you were truly ready. And I will be there the entire time."

She nodded, but didn't reply or even look at him. This had been the way of things for days and it bothered him. He found that he missed her spirited banter, her quick wit. Heaven knew he would get none of that tonight at the soiree. Ladies and gentlemen all prattled on about the weather as if there were nothing else on earth to talk about. It was utter nonsense, as Josephine had so succinctly pointed out during one of their walks in the park.

Upon arriving at the Skulthorpe manor, Nathaniel led the quiet Josephine down to Headquarters where Beau and Eleanor whisked her away to dress her. One hour later, she came out looking ravishing. It took all of Nathaniel's willpower not to openly gawk at her, and it was becoming more and more difficult to hide his attraction under his cool exterior.

"Doesn't the gold gown look wonderful with her hair," Eleanor beamed. "Oh, I do love this color on you, Josephine!"

"Yes, I quite agree," Sophia stated matter-of-factly. "And that is not all, Josephine. We must arm you."

Josephine's brows pinched together. "Arm me? With daggers?"

"You'll be able to hide one or two blades, though you should not need them," said Nathaniel. "There are a few other weapons that Barnaby has ready for you."

"Like that pistol you shot me with?" She seemed to perk up at the thought.

Nathaniel pulled the tiny weapon from his waistcoat pocket. "Unfortunately, you will not be able to properly conceal the napshot in that bodice of yours. You will have other weapons."

"Napshot?" Josephine raised an eyebrow.

"Down for a nap with one shot," he explained with a smirk.

Thankfully, some color came back into her cheeks at his silly pun.

"Let's not keep Barnaby waiting," Beau suggested. "He gets crabby when he's running behind, you know."

JOSEPHINE WAS NEARLY BURSTING with excitement. She could hardly wait to see what gadgets Barnaby had created for her to use, although it made her anxious to think that she might need a weapon at a soiree. Even so, it was the only thing that she had been anticipating throughout this assignment.

Barnaby was waiting for them at his lab table with his usual sooty apron tied around his neck. His goggles and gloves rested on the table beside him and in his hands was a lady's fan. Without so much as a greeting, he handed it to Josephine.

Josephine turned the accessory over in her hands. It was just like any other fan she had ever seen - about twelve inches long. Josephine spread the fan open to reveal a cream and gold printed leaf that coordinated with her gown.

"*That* is not just any fan, missy," Barnaby explained, his eyes lighting up. "It shoots poisoned darts. It's loaded with three. All you do is press this pearl button at the base. It triggers just like Mr. Runik's shooter."

Now that she was paying close attention, Josephine could see that the spine of the fan was indeed hollow. The fan itself flicked open and closed with ease in her fingers. No one would be able to see anything out of the ordinary. The female version of the napshot, she silently observed.

"Now this here ..." Barnaby grabbed another gold trinket from the table, "... looks like a pocket watch, but it has several uses for you."

Josephine's eyes shifted to the back wall where all the pocket watches hung, glimmering in the candlelight. *So, those were prototypes as well,* she thought.

Opening the front cover of the small gold watch, he began pointing out the different crystals that decorated the face. "Here at three o'clock, pressing this crystal will release a pin that will pick any lock."

Josephine cleared her throat. "I can already pick locks."

"I heard." Barnaby grinned. "This will be easier than a hair pin. Trust me."

Josephine nodded and watched in amazement as Barnaby demonstrated its release. Then he folded the tiny piece of metal back into place.

"Now, I won't be demonstrating six o'clock, but I'll just tell you," said Barnaby. "When you press that crystal, it opens a tiny compartment that contains a sleeping powder. Just blow it into your target's face and they'll be out before they know it."

Josephine narrowed her eyes and looked at Mr. Runik. His expression revealed nothing, but she knew it was the same powder he had tried to use on her. Of course, she had proven that the powder could be turned against her or easily avoided, so she silently vowed to use it only as a last resort.

He went on to nine o'clock. "Once you press this crystal, the minute hand will point North. In case you get lost."

"What about twelve o'clock?" Josephine was almost afraid to ask, but excited to know as well.

"The twelve o'clock crystal will enable the explosive device within."

Josephine's head popped up and her eyes widened. "Explosive device?"

"It's only active when you push the crystal, but yes," he said. "You should have about ten seconds of wait time before the thing goes off. Just make sure you're not holding it in your hand, missy. Don't want to lose one of those," he said jokingly. "It won't destroy anything as large as a building, but it should create enough havoc for a proper distraction."

No one seemed to be as startled as Josephine was. An explosive device? This was getting rather serious. What if she set it off on accident? She would handle this pocket watch with extreme caution. Barnaby closed the watch, concealing the crystals around its face, and Josephine tucked it carefully into the small pocket of her skirt.

The trunk full of women's accessories from the Captain's cellar suddenly came to mind. Josephine knew without a doubt that those prototypes had been meant for her or some other female spy that Skulthorpe had been attempting to recruit. Josephine only hoped she would survive this assignment so she could inspect them all. She also wondered if she was the only female agent working for Mr. Skulthorpe. Had he hired other women to work under cover? What had happened to them?

"Now, Miss Teversin," said Mr. Runik, folding his arms across his chest. "Let's discuss your assignment."

NINETEEN

J osephine checked all her concealed weapons for what seemed like the hundredth time that afternoon on the carriage ride to Sturch Manor, where the soiree was to be held. The estate was located in the countryside outside Charlestown.

"Stop your fidgeting, Miss Teversin," said Runik. "Everything will be fine. Remember, you are my cousin, Miss Josephine Pinchley. You should see a few faces you recognize from our appointments this past week. As you said before, you got on well with Mrs. Graves, so she should introduce you to people." Giving her a once over, he added, "Try to relax. You are as stiff as a board."

"You can blame that on my corset," she muttered, rubbing her waist.

"Are your laces too tight?" he asked. "I'll not have you fainting."

Josephine snorted. "I won't faint. And what could you do about it if they *were* too tight?"

"Touché. Now remember, your job is to find out all you can about any Patriot plans. Listen in to conversations. Even the wives of some of these Sons of Liberty may talk amongst themselves, so keep your ears open. There will be a great number of the Patriots here tonight, which might give them an opportunity to pass information. They could be meeting tonight after the soiree, or even during. Do not forget, you will be extremely useful in perusing the estate at leisure when, as a lady, you excuse yourself to go and powder your nose - or whatever it is that ladies do when they leave the ballroom."

"Did you just roll your eyes?" Josephine mocked.

Runik smirked at her. "Possibly."

"Well, it's quite rude, or so I've been told on countless occasions."

His gray eyes danced with laughter. *How handsome he would be if he wasn't always so cold to me.* But it would not last. Sooner or later, he would revert back to his usual cool demeanor.

Before long, they were pulling into the circle drive of Sturch Manor. It was just as grand as Skulthorpe's vast estate. Carriages were lined up to drop off the guests at the front steps, and, when it was their turn, Runik actually waited for the door to be opened for them. Once he'd stepped down, he helped her out of the coach.

"Remember," he murmured in her ear. "It's all about appearances. Try to blend in."

Smiling demurely, as Sophia had instructed her, Josephine took a deep breath and nodded. She could do this. Mr. Runik led her through the foyer and into the ballroom. No one had seemed to take notice of them yet, for which she was grateful.

"I never thought to ask, why are you not using an alternate name?" she whispered.

"Because my father used to sit in the House of Lords," he told her. "He was a very influential man in London. That is why the Patriots have been attempting to ... well ... they either want to recruit me or tar and feather me."

"Tar and feather you? Would they really do that?"

"Difficult to say. It's worse in the northern colonies than it is here. Especially Boston. The Sons of Liberty have been inciting anarchy since a few colonials were killed three years ago."

Josephine swallowed. Having been in hiding for the last three years, she was quite unaware of how volatile things had become in the colonies. "You said your father used to sit in the House of Lords? He doesn't now?"

"He's dead," he explained quietly.

Josephine frowned. "I'm sorry."

"Enough of this," he hissed. "It's time to work. Come. I believe I see the Graves."

With that, they were off to mingle with the crowd. Most of the women looked uninterested in her arrival, or maybe they were just looking down their nose at her. Josephine was certain she looked just as lovely as they did, all in thanks to her trio of friends. It was the men who made her nervous. Most of them seemed to be gawking at any young attractive lady - Josephine included. One man in particular made Josephine uneasy. He had large red cheeks and an even larger middle. His breath reeked of liquor already and he openly stared at Josephine's chest, all while licking his lips. The man's clammy hands on hers made her skin crawl. The sudden urge to jerk her hand out of his and slam her small fist into his nose crossed her mind, but Josephine didn't think that would go over well with Runik. Josephine pulled her hand out of his grip and gave him a polite smile. She intended to keep her distance from the puffy man or she might be forced to use the sleeping darts on him.

"Miss Pinchley?"

Runik gave Josephine a nudge to remind her that she was, in fact, Miss Pinchley.

"Oh, I beg your pardon," Josephine stammered. "I was just thinking about how fine the weather is this evening."

A groan escaped Runik. Fortunately, it was Mattie and her husband, Mr. Graves, there to greet them. Neither of them seemed fussed by her blunder.

"It *is* a fine evening, to be sure," Mattie replied with her wide smile and rosy cheeks. She donned a lovely emerald green gown and a gold comb had been tucked into her chestnut hair. "Would you like to find some refreshments with me, Miss Pinchley? We'll leave the men to their politics," she giggled into her fan.

She linked arms with Josephine and led her away from Mr. Runik. Josephine did not have any inkling if this was customary or not, but since it wasn't *her* suggestion, she shrugged and went along with

Mattie. A peek over her shoulder convinced her that Runik was not at all concerned. He was already engrossed in his own conversation with Mr. Graves and another gentleman, paying her no heed.

"Don't worry about your man, dearie," Mattie told her sweetly, sweeping past a group of women who were all glaring daggers at Josephine. "We'll have you back by Mr. Runik's side after everyone has gotten a chance to stare at and interrogate you!" Mattie giggled again.

"Oh, he's ..." Josephine started to correct her about Runik being *her* man, but decided not to bother. Let Mattie think what she wanted. Plus, it might keep Mr. Puffy away from Josephine if people thought she was attached to Mr. Runik.

Mattie went on without a pause. "And don't worry about those debutantes staring at you," she murmured into Josephine's ear. "They are only jealous of new competition, my dear."

"But I'm not -"

"And poor Mr. Runik. He's had a rough go of it. I would like to see him settled down already. We were *so* pleased when he mentioned you. Mr. Graves and I wanted to meet you immediately! It's so difficult finding a truly good match these days."

Josephine nearly snorted at being described as an acceptable match for Runik. If Mattie knew how Josephine and Runik quarreled or that Josephine was an immortal pirate, she would be devastated. But Josephine was grateful that Mattie was not talking about the weather. Perhaps men had no notion of what women talked about, since they did not include ladies in their own conversations.

"A rough go of it?" Josephine pressed. Whether her intrigue was polite or not, she didn't care.

"Well, the death of his father, you know. They say he was murdered," Mattie whispered, as if she was speaking of a great scandal. "Shot by bandits or something of the kind here in the colonies. Did you not know that, my dear? I am so terribly sorry." Mattie patted Josephine's hand. "We were appalled to hear of it. Poor Mr. Runik was still in England, in the army at the time, I believe. I'm glad he came to the colonies for a change of scenery. It will do him some good, especially now that he has such a wonderful young lady in his life!"

Josephine blushed at the suggestion. She began fanning herself, hoping to cool her heated cheeks. Once she realized what she was doing, she froze mid-wave and nearly cursed out loud. *What if I send a dart flying across the room by accident?* There had been no time to test the thing, so she had no idea how easily the darts might be triggered. Slowly and carefully closing the fan, Josephine turned her attention back to what Mattie had been telling her.

"Yes, of course. That must have been ... difficult for his family," she stammered, gripping the fan in her fist, hoping she wouldn't set it off. Josephine was failing miserably already and the night had just begun. It was a good thing Mattie did not need her to respond very often. The woman was quite content to keep the conversation going.

"This party is just the thing we needed. Don't you agree?" Mattie exclaimed. "Dancing! Now, are you going to be joining in with the dancing, my dear? Mr. Runik looks as if he knows his way around the dance floor!" she said in a sing-song voice. She gave Josephine a wink.

Josephine's face burned again at Mattie's insinuation. "Oh ... um ... I don't know."

She bit back another curse. There was a very real possibility that she was making an absolute fool of herself. Mr. Runik was probably watching her from afar, just waiting to pounce on all her blunders. That was, if the pocket watch she carried in her skirt didn't explode by accident. Josephine was not a clumsy person, but it was unnerving to know that her gown could go up in flames with a careless flick of her fingers.

They reached the table together and accepted glasses of punch from the server as another group of ladies joined them. The women were gossiping and people-watching. Josephine did the same. Sipping her punch and listening to the ladies prattle on, she let her eyes wander over the crowd, searching for anything of importance. The dancing had not yet begun, so everyone stood at the edges of the ballroom.

Refilling her punch, Josephine feigned interest in the ladies' chattering, but they were talking about their dance cards and dresses. At last, she spotted something that might be of some importance. Two of the Patriots that Runik had pointed out had just hidden themselves behind one of the larger pillars at the edge of the ballroom.

If that's not secretive, I don't know what is, Josephine thought, carefully opening her fan again to hide her face, as the other ladies were doing.

Edging away from the table to get a better view, she noticed them murmuring to each other for a moment, and then a note passed from one gentleman to the other. If Josephine had not been paying attention, she might have missed the exchange altogether. The man accepting the note was taller than Oliver. He wore a fashionable wig, like many of the men in the room, so there was no way to distinguish him from the rest, except for his remarkable size. Josephine never took her eyes off of her mark as he slipped the note into his pocket and made his way back into the noise of the party.

She had to find some way to get the note, for she was sure this was something Runik would expect her to retrieve. Exhibiting her finest expression of boredom, Josephine began strolling in his direction.

She considered all her options. She had an idea, but it was mad. Runik would likely think her completely daft for going through with it. As a lady, she couldn't force an introduction and it was simply not correct to approach him without a male presence leading the conversation.

While keeping watch on the tall gent out of the corner of her eye, she found Runik still engaged in conversation with the same men as before. As if he knew she was watching him, Runik made eye contact and winked at her. Josephine nearly choked on her punch. To make matters worse, he grinned, which was completely out of character for him. Josephine scowled at him in return, but his smile merely widened.

She narrowed her eyes at him. *Perhaps a dart* accidentally *shooting across the room and into his backside isn't a horrible idea.*

Josephine sighed, resigning herself to what must be done. It actually worked in her favor that she was such a bundle of nerves. Her hands were trembling already and her face heated as she moseyed over to her mark. Still attempting to be nonchalant, she sipped her punch and waved her fan the way Beau had taught her. Just ten more feet.

Without warning, the man she'd been targeting turned to face her. Josephine hadn't expected that. She froze and stared at him. *Oh, blast!* She thought, holding her breath. *Do something!*

Looking down his nose at her, he said, "My lady?"

He stared expectantly down at Josephine, so she did what she'd planned to do all along - pretend to faint.

Josephine closed her eyes and staggered forward. The wigged Patriot reached out to catch her as she fell into him. The punch glass she'd been carrying made a spectacular crash on the hardwood floor and every lady and gentleman in the vicinity joined the man in trying to revive her from her 'swoon'.

"Smelling salts!" the Patriot called out. "Does someone have smelling salts?"

Apparently, someone did have a bottle of the awful liquid, for Josephine inhaled and immediately began to gag.

"There, I think she's coming to," Mr. Runik announced.

Josephine opened her eyes to see Runik and the Patriot, along with Mattie and a few other concerned faces staring down at her. Josephine blushed again at lying on the floor in such a humiliating state. It had all been worth it, however. She'd plucked the note clean from the Patriot's pocket in the melee.

"Well, you've finally decided to wake up, have you?" said Mr. Runik.

"Oh, Miss Pinchley, are you all right?" Mattie wailed, hovering over their shoulders. "I had no idea that she felt unwell or I would never have allowed her to leave my side. This is simply awful! She must sit down or get some fresh air at once. Mr. Runik? Mr. Howard? Would you be so kind?"

"I think some fresh air is just the ticket," the Patriot called Mr. Howard suggested.

Josephine suffered a momentary pang of guilt from having picked his pocket. There was kindness in his eyes and the note may not have anything to do with the rebel cause.

"I quite agree, Mr. Howard," Runik replied. "Up you go then, Miss

Pinchley. Let's take a stroll outside to sit a spell. The cool night air will do you good."

Together, the men lifted her to her feet. Josephine inwardly cringed, knowing how ungraceful she must have looked, going down like that. Sophia would have been appalled to see her sprawled out on the floor, especially in this nice gown. What if she'd torn her lovely dress or mussed her hair? Opening her fan, she continued the ruse until she and Runik were safely ensconced on the veranda.

"That's quite enough fanning, Miss *Pinchley*," Runik said with a chuckle. "Did you get it?"

Josephine blinked up at him. "What?"

"The note. Did you get it?"

She was speechless. Runik must have been watching more closely than she'd imagined.

Silently, he extended his hand, checking their surroundings once more to make sure they were alone.

"You codfish," she growled, pulling the paper out from under the neckline of her dress and handing it over. "I've never done anything so humiliating."

He gave her a roguish grin. "You were brilliant and vastly entertaining, I might add. I nearly forgot to play my part of the concerned cousin!"

Josephine's lips twitched. She didn't know whether to strike the smirk off Runik's face or laugh over the whole ordeal.

Runik tapped his finger against his temple. "I told you. A new variable in the equation. A man could not have done what you just did. But you need to work on your faint. I am sure your tutors can teach you a few tricks."

Josephine huffed and folded her arms over her middle. "Well? Was it something useful or did I disgrace myself for nothing?"

"Yes," he answered. "Yes, it is useful, I believe. It's a cipher, but I believe we will be able to sort it out."

"Cipher?"

"A sort of code that I have seen used before," he replied, offering his elbow. "Come along. Now that you are recovered, we should have a dance. And Mrs. Graves is correct. I am an excellent dancer."

Josephine narrowed her eyes at Runik, even as she took his arm. "How did you hear that?"

"I am a spy," he murmured in her ear. "I can read lips very well. Would you like to know all the things people are saying about you?"

"No, I don't believe I do."

Runik laughed and escorted her back inside the ballroom.

TWENTY

R unik led Josephine out onto the dance floor where other couples were lining up for a reel. The music began and, after the first few turns around the room, weaving through the lines of dancers, Josephine relaxed and actually began to enjoy herself. Josephine's gold gown shimmered under the candlelight of the crystal chandeliers hanging overhead while she twirled and swayed to the music. The Graves danced near them in the line, and Mattie's laughter was contagious. Josephine smiled brightly at Mr. Runik as they circled each other, not caring a whit that he looked so serious and a bit bewildered.

Once the song finished and the couples bowed and curtsied to each other, another man approached and tapped Runik on the shoulder.

"May I have the next dance?"

Runik looked the stranger up and down with his calculating gray eyes, as if trying to find a flaw of any kind. "I do not believe we've met."

"Brown," the man bowed elegantly to them both. "Mr. Lewis Brown."

Josephine curtsied, but she couldn't stop staring at the man. He *was* handsome in his own way, but that wasn't it at all. His green eyes matched Oliver's exactly. The name Lewis Brown was not familiar to her and she knew that Oliver had no living relations, so the man couldn't be a brother. It was silly of her to even consider. A lot of people had green eyes.

Runik continued introductions. "Mr. Brown, may I present Miss Josephine Pinchley."

He bowed to her and held out a hand. "May I have the pleasure, Miss Pinchley?"

His green eyes held her captive for a second before she was able to answer. Mentally shaking herself out of her stupor, Josephine stammered, "Oh … yes! Yes, of course."

Neither of them spoke as they danced the reel, but Josephine was breathless by the time they finished. Those familiar eyes never left hers. A vision of Oliver flashed before her, his blonde hair tousled in the wind, the muscles in his arms and back straining as he pulled the lines of the sails. She missed Oliver's easy smile and the way he carried himself with a relaxed confidence instead of a brooding arrogance, as Runik did. All at once, she was wishing it were Oliver here with her instead of either of these gentlemen. But that would have been impossible. Oliver didn't own fancy garments such as these and he surely didn't know how to dance like this, either.

As the dance came to an end, all the ladies and gentlemen took their bows, but Mr. Brown took Josephine's hand in both of his and whispered, "I do hope that we'll be able to do that again one day." He bowed over her hand and placed his lips softly to her fingers. Heat crept into her cheeks and a lump formed in her throat. Mr. Brown didn't wait for her to respond. He turned on his heel and disappeared into the crowd, leaving her speechless.

Josephine danced again and again with different strangers, but none acted as curiously, or as familiar, as Mr. Brown. The country dances didn't invite much conversation, so Josephine was excused from talking about the weather. After her fourth or fifth dance, Josephine began to grow weary. Her shoes were pinching her toes and she was beginning to sweat from the press of so many people in one room. Josephine hadn't done any other snooping since the fainting disaster, so she excused herself from the ballroom. A group of giggling females were headed into a hallway off the ballroom, so Josephine followed after them.

After taking a few minutes to freshen up, she returned to the hallway to find it deserted. The sconces were lit, providing enough light to see, but the quiet hallway was still filled with shadows. Josephine felt for her daggers again and took a deep breath. There was nothing here to frighten her, she tried to tell herself.

"Well, hello again," a man drawled behind her.

Josephine tensed, recognizing the slurred speech immediately. Mr. Puffy had followed her into the corridor and was closer than she would have liked him to be. How had he snuck up on her, being as drunk as he was? Perhaps he'd been hiding out in the shadows waiting for any unsuspecting female.

Clearing her throat, Josephine asked, "May I help you with something?"

Where is my blasted fan? she wondered. Had she left it in the powder room? Finally, she felt it in the pocket of her skirt, but it was caught on the material and wouldn't be budged.

Like a predator stalking his prey, the pudgy man moved closer. He licked his lips as he had done so blatantly out in the ballroom and his bloodshot eyes roamed over her body.

"Oh, yes, my pretty thing," he slurred. "You *can* help me with something."

Bile rose up in the back of her throat. She was positive she could take care of herself, but she preferred not to hurt anyone here at the soiree if she could help it.

"I think I need to be heading back now," she said more forcefully.

The man grasped her forearm in a painful hold before she could sidestep him. Josephine's instincts took over immediately. She curled her fingers into a fist and struck him square in the face, as Oliver had taught her to do with men who were too forward. He recoiled and held his hands over his mouth and nose.

"You broke my nose!" he shouted. Blood trickled down between his fingers.

Josephine turned to make a run for it, but somehow, he managed to grab her again.

"Let go, you bug-brained baboon! You're completely pissed!" she bellowed, not caring who heard her coarse language.

This time, Josephine kicked him in the shin. He retaliated by back-handing her across the face, snapping her head back, and jogging her senses a bit. Josephine yelped and her face stung from the force of the blow.

A loud bellow, much like a raging bull, filled the hall. Josephine's assailant was suddenly yanked off her. Lewis Brown had come to her rescue out of nowhere. Grabbing the puffy man by the collar, Mr. Brown gave him a solid punch to the jaw, knocking him out cold, and sending him sprawling to the floor.

Shaking his hand, Mr. Brown turned to Josephine, who was still breathing hard and rubbing her tender cheek. There would be a mighty large bruise tomorrow.

"You should not have come here alone." Mr. Brown reached for her chin and tilted it toward the light. "Are you all right?"

Josephine stared at the man as he inspected her bruised face. Though she was still a bit shaken, she wasn't compelled to recoil from his touch. There was something about Mr. Brown. Josephine couldn't put her finger on it, but she knew she could trust him.

With a frown, Mr. Brown said, "He's been staring at you all evening. You'd best get back to the ballroom."

"Thank you … for coming to my assistance, Mr. Brown."

The man nodded in acknowledgement, but instead of escorting her back to the ballroom, he turned and headed in the opposite direction, disappearing into the shadows. Josephine took a few steps toward the sounds of the soiree, knowing she ought to do as Mr. Brown had said. Enough trouble had found her this evening. Josephine halted and stared down the hall after Mr. Brown.

What business does he have in this empty hallway? Mr. Brown was definitely up to something. Against her better judgment, Josephine followed him. After passing several empty guest rooms, she padded up a narrow stairway leading to the second floor of the mansion.

Josephine held her breath. The wood groaned beneath her feet with every step. Even the slightest sound seemed to echo loudly in the silence.

On the second floor, the hallway looked much like the others, except for the light streaming out from underneath a closed door fifty feet to her left. Josephine crept toward the room. Was Mr. Brown in conference with the rebel group? Was that why he'd come this way? Or was this the secret meeting that Runik had been telling her about?

Ear to the door, Josephine held her breath as she listened. The voices were muffled but could still be heard talking.

"I do not agree with these methods," she heard one gentleman argue. It was not Mr. Brown, nor anyone else she recognized. The second man she recognized immediately. It was the snide voice of Garreck Skulthorpe.

"Trust me," he said persuasively. "You must look at the bigger picture. Losing a few lives will be worth it if it helps us with our cause."

"But these men and women -"

"Anyone killed will be martyrs for the rebellion!" Skulthorpe barked. "We will do what needs to be done. And what are you whining about, anyway? It's not as if you have to lift a finger. The plan is already in place. Now go. I cannot linger. I'm not supposed to be here at all, you fool."

Backing away quickly, Josephine knew she must hide so she was not caught snooping on Skulthorpe himself. The latch of the door clicked open. He would not thank her for this; in fact, her neck began to tingle at the thought of a noose wrapped around it.

Turning to make a run for it, Josephine didn't get two steps before she was jerked into the dark room just next door. She didn't see who grabbed her. He had pulled her into his muscular body and dragged her backward, his large hand clamped down over her mouth. The man pulled her deeper into the shadows, his hold unbreakable. Was there no end to men grabbing her tonight?

"Quiet," he hissed into her ear. His voice was so familiar to her. "I'm not going to hurt you, Josephine."

She stilled immediately when he spoke her name and, together, they watched silently as Skulthorpe and the other gentleman moved past without noticing them in the shadows.

Once the hallway was quiet, he released her. Quickly pushing away from the man, Josephine turned to face him, but it wasn't who she was expecting.

"Mr. Brown? What are you doing here?" she demanded. "And how do you know my name?"

"No time for explanations," he said. "I think we'd best be going."

He grabbed her by the hand and dragged her from the room.

TWENTY-ONE

N athaniel had seen Josephine leave the ballroom, and it *was* he who had suggested she do a bit of snooping around under the guise of going to the lady's room. But an hour had nearly passed and she was nowhere to be seen in the ballroom. Surely, she knew that it wouldn't do to be gone for such a length of time.

Perhaps she's made her escape.

Nathaniel shook his head. It was a ridiculous thought. Josephine knew the consequences of disobeying his instructions. That boy, Oliver, and her Aunt Genevieve would pay for that mistake, and she would never do anything to put them in jeopardy.

Excusing himself from the gentlemen in his group, Nathaniel marched out of the ballroom and into the corridor where he'd seen the ladies escape to all evening. He checked each room and shouted Josephine's name, but she didn't answer. It wasn't until Nathaniel began to smell smoke that he started to worry.

Nathaniel paused and looked in both directions. The hallway was getting hazy. *This much smoke couldn't possibly be from the kitchens,* he thought. His stomach sank with the realization that the house was on fire.

Nathaniel covered his mouth with his handkerchief and sprinted back to the ballroom, which was thick with black smoke as well. The guests were coughing and screaming, while running frantically toward the exit. Red and orange flames were climbing up the back of the ballroom by the veranda.

How did the house catch fire? This was no accident. A guest would have sounded an alarm much sooner if someone had dropped a pipe or cigar. *Have Patriots rebels done this?*

Nathaniel spotted the Graves in the thick of the mob and pushed toward them.

"Have you seen Josephine?" he asked them, his stomach clenching in dread.

Mattie yelped as a man with wide, terrified eyes rammed into her from behind. Mr. Graves pushed him away.

"I haven't seen her since she was dancing, Mr. Runik!" Mattie shouted over the noise. "Oh, I do hope you find her!" Mr. Graves clung to his wife, desperate to keep her at his side. The crowd swallowed them up, pushing them through the corridors and away from the deadly smoke.

In the ballroom, fire had engulfed the back wall. Someone had torched the building from the outside. *Or a witch is responsible,* Nathaniel thought. Only a fire made from magic could consume the manor this rapidly.

He could not leave without Josephine. Had it not been for the smoke, he would have stayed to search the ballroom, but it seemed that everyone had already escaped.

Keeping his mouth and nose covered by his handkerchief, Nathaniel raced through the house, shouting Josephine's name, searching every room he could find. The hallways were empty, save for a few stragglers - mostly maids who hadn't figured out what was going on.

As Nathaniel passed them in the corridor, he barked, "The house is on fire! Run!" He continued to search rooms as the servants cried out and hurried toward the exits.

He burst through another door, revealing an empty and smoke-free guest room. "Josephine!" he shouted. No one answered.

Hot ribbons of gray and black ash slowly seeped into the room, like poison spreading through the bloodstream. After stripping off his frock and waistcoat, Nathaniel took a deep breath of the remaining clean air, covered his mouth again, and ducked back into the smoky haze. Black dust stung his eyes and invaded his lungs. Nathaniel's eyes watered as he coughed and choked on the ash in the air.

I need to find an exit, Nathaniel thought, resisting the urge to panic. *Which way is the ballroom?*

He looked left and right down the hallway, but the thick cloud of deadly smoke had left him disoriented. Finding his way back to the front entrance was a lost cause. The fire had likely destroyed the ballroom and spread into the foyer by now. The east and west wings of the estate would be in danger next if they weren't already burning.

Nathaniel headed right, where the air looked clearer. He hadn't made it twenty feet when he tripped over something large lying across the carpet. Nathaniel fell to his hands and knees. With the smoke obscuring his vision, he reached out to determine what had made him stumble. From what little he could see and feel, it was a body, but one much too large around the middle to be Josephine. The unconscious man's face was bruised and blood dripped from his nose as if he'd been in a fight. He thought the man's name might be Mr. Murphy. What was he doing out here in the hallway?

Nathaniel's chest tightened. *Josephine could be wounded or knocked out somewhere, just like this man.*

To Nathaniel's right, the house groaned. The eerie sound was followed by a crash as beams from the high ceilings collapsed. The temperature in the corridor was rising steadily, and, through the dark haze, he could see bursts of gold and red rising up along the walls in the heavy darkness. The fire from the ballroom was catching up to him.

Nathaniel reluctantly threw Murphy over his shoulder and pushed himself to his feet. Smoke continued to billow into the hall. Portraits and tapestries hanging on the walls were seared by the scorching flames and falling to the floor as they succumbed to the destructive blaze.

"*Josephine!*" Nathaniel bellowed one last time. He coughed as his lungs did their best to expel the ash he was inhaling.

The fire crackled in the distance and the house groaned, threatening collapse. Those were the only sounds Nathaniel could hear. Continuing to search for Josephine was useless. Nathaniel would lose his own life trying to find her. Josephine had either fled or she was dead, consumed by the smoke and flames.

Nathaniel strode down the corridor, away from the growing fire. His lungs burned with the need for fresh air. When he turned the corner, he skidded to a halt. Flames were licking up the walls on this end of the corridor as well. Nathaniel was surrounded.

Suddenly, the house groaned again. Nathaniel leapt back just as the ceiling collapsed where he'd been standing a second before. In his haste to get out of the way, he dropped Mr. Murphy. The unconscious man's breeches immediately caught fire from the falling debris.

Murphy must have felt his leg burning because he chose that moment to wake up from his slumber and began to scream. "Fire! I'm on fire! Get it off!" He frantically kicked his legs, but the flames only spread more quickly across his clothing.

Grabbing the gentleman by his collar, Nathaniel dragged him into a guest room and slammed the door behind them.

"My leg! It's burning!" Murphy shrieked.

Nathaniel sprinted to the window and jerked down the drapes. "Be still, man," he shouted at Murphy. He crossed the room again and used the curtains to smother the flames dancing across Murphy's leg. "There. The fire is out. Now ..." Nathaniel rose to his feet and looked around the room. "... we need to get out of here."

Smoke began to trickle beneath the crack under the door, but they were safe from the blaze for the moment. Nathaniel strode to the window and flung it open. They were on the east side of the house. Flames were ravaging the wings on either side of them.

Nathaniel looked back at Mr. Murphy. The gentleman was still sitting on the floor. He'd finally stopped yelling, but he was now sobbing and staring at his charred breeches. Tears were starting to trickle down his face.

"Get hold of yourself, man!" Nathaniel barked, marching over to the pudgy man. "You'll have a nasty burn, but you won't lose your legs. Get up! I'm not carrying you another step." Nathaniel grabbed him under the arms and hauled him to his feet.

"I can't. I can't," Murphy blubbered.

Nathaniel pulled him to the window's ledge.

Murphy cried out again. "I'm afraid of heights! I can't do it!"

Nathaniel rolled his eyes and shoved him out the window. "We're on the first floor, you buffoon! And I'm not staying here and being burned alive because of a coward like you."

Murphy's knees buckled when he hit the bushes and he rolled onto his back. He lay there, still sniveling, as Nathaniel climbed out the window.

"Get up and run, you idiot!" Nathaniel ordered. He heaved Murphy to his feet again and, carrying the bulk of the man's weight, helped him rejoin the remaining guests at the front of the house.

Once Murphy was safely among the guests and being treated by the local doctor, who had luckily attended the soiree, Nathaniel continued to search the crowds for Josephine. There was no sign of her.

He waited until most of the guests were gone, hoping he might spot her, but there was no use in staying any longer. He sent up a prayer that she had made it to safety and then made his way back home in his own carriage.

Questions plagued his mind. There were always people waiting for opportunities to cause chaos. The colonials had been protesting and rioting in many of the larger towns for years over the slight increase in taxes. But surely the colonials wouldn't burn down the home of one of their own Patriot comrades?

What if the fire *had* been started by a witch? Witches had been hunted by the Brotherhood and colonials alike. Since the Puritans in Salem had tried their best to exterminate witches in the Massachusetts Bay Colony, some may still hold a grudge against the colonials.

Nathaniel rubbed his forehead as the carriage rocked back and forth on the road. He was nearly home and there were still too many questions that needed answering. The soiree had ended in disaster, and he was determined to find out why.

THE NIGHT WAS quiet except for the cicadas singing in the trees all around Josephine. Lightning bugs glimmered every so often in the distance, as if they were stars sent down from the sky, and the full moon above was a brilliant white, lighting up the road ahead of her. But Josephine could not enjoy any of it due to being dragged relentlessly down the road by Mr. Brown.

Smoke had been filling the hallways when they made their escape. Sturch Manor was burning and, as they fled into the dark, Josephine could still see the orange glow of the flames in the distance. Why Mr. Brown had taken it upon himself to see her safe from the carnage, she didn't know. He showed no signs of stopping, even though they were safe from the attack.

"Slow down, please," she pleaded. "You're hurting my arm, sir. And my feet! These shoes are not exactly made for running."

Chuckling, he slowed to a walk, but did not release her.

"You can let go now, Mr. Brown. I believe we're safe. Not that my safety is any of your concern." Josephine gasped when she recalled Mr. Runik. "My escort! We left him!"

Josephine didn't feel quite as much panic as her voice revealed, but this stranger need not know that. Had they left Runik to die in the fire? He might be an arrogant snob, but no one deserved to perish in such a terrible way. *Surely, he made it out on his own*, she reassured herself.

She attempted to turn back to look for Runik and nearly had her arm wrenched from its socket.

"We need to keep moving."

It was then that Josephine realized that Mr. Brown's voice had drastically changed since their dance and the dreadful encounter in the hallway. He sounded more like …

"Wait. Stop!" Josephine twisted her arm out of his hand.

Mr. Brown turned to face her, his expression hidden in the shadows of the night.

"Who are you really? Why do you sound so familiar?"

He took a step toward her, but Josephine backed away.

"It's me, Angelfish. It's Oliver."

"Oliver Blakely?" Josephine frowned in confusion. "Why do you look different? How? You sound like Oliver, but your appearance ..."

"Oh, blimey, I forgot." He loosened his cravat and unbuttoned his shirt. Underneath was some sort of amulet that he'd been wearing around his neck. When he removed it, the glamour melted away, revealing the man she had always known, though a bit more polished. "I almost forgot I didn't look like myself!" He chuckled softly.

Josephine was dumbstruck. It was no wonder his eyes looked familiar to her. For a second, she was relieved to find that it had been Oliver all along. Recalling how he'd held her during the dance, kissed her hand, and whispered those soft words to her - it had been Oliver who had done all those things. Her heart beat a little faster at the memory. She remembered the puffy man and the way Mr. Brown - or Oliver, rather - had come to her rescue. Even though Josephine knew logically that she should be grateful for his intervention, she was angry instead.

When the corners of her mouth turned down in a frown, Oliver's smile faltered. "Jo?"

Oliver reached for her but she smacked his hand away. "What were you doing at the soiree?"

"Angelfish, I -"

"I haven't seen you in days and now you come here to spy on me?"

"I wasn't spying. I was there to help."

Josephine shook her head. "I didn't need your help or your protection. I can take care of myself."

Knowing it was childish, Josephine spun around and stomped away. Before she could make it two steps, Oliver grabbed her wrist again and dragged her off the road into the trees.

"What are you doing, you two-faced eel? Are you going to give me a good thrashing then?" She grabbed her full skirts with her free hand to keep from tripping as she jogged along behind him through the brush.

"I ought to tan your hide, you little hellion," he snapped over his shoulder.

She gasped. "You wouldn't dare! Let go, Oliver!"

Once they had reached the shelter of the woods, he released her. He loomed over her, his jaw clenched and eyes hardened. "You can take care of yourself, eh? What about that toff that had his hands on you? Were you taking care of yourself then, Josephine?"

She stubbornly folded her arms across her chest. "That drunken toadstool? I got in a good punch! I didn't want to *kill* the man!"

"I'm glad you were being so thoughtful. Unfortunately, he wasn't doing you the same courtesy. That's going to be a sound black eye tomorrow morning." He gestured to her face.

Josephine pressed her fingers to her cheek and winced. A bruise was already forming.

Oliver nodded. "Aye. And he wasn't going to stop there."

"I was handling it!"

Oliver ignored her. "And when you were eavesdropping on those blokes on the second floor? You were as good as caught, and you know it! How about getting out of the bloody mansion when it went up in flames? I know a magical fire when I see one and so do you. It was set by a witch."

"Even if the fire was set by a witch, you don't know they were after me," argued Josephine. "I know I would have been fine, Oliver."

"But *I* didn't know it!" he roared, gripping her shoulders. "Why are you not taking this seriously? Do you not know by now, Josephine Teversin, that it would kill me if anything happened to you?"

Josephine shoved him and he stumbled backward. "Yes, let's not forget about your last blood oath."

Oliver's brows drew together. "What are you talking about, Jo?"

She scowled at him. Blood oaths sworn to an immortal pirate had to be fulfilled. It was part of the magic they possessed. If the oath was broken, the punishment was instant death - not by the pirate, but by the magic. When she was younger, Josephine's father had told her that unscrupulous pirates abused their magic, trapping men with the pledges they made, taking advantage of their mortality in the worst way. She knew her father had hardly ever asked his crew to swear blood oaths because the cost was steep. He'd valued his sailors and never wanted to betray their trust.

If Oliver had sworn an oath to protect her and he failed ...

"Don't act like you don't know." She jabbed her finger at him. "You should never have taken that oath to my father if I was going to be this much trouble for you!"

Oliver flinched, as if she'd struck him. "You think I took a *blood oath* to protect you?" His voice was gravelly with emotion. "Why would you think that?"

Realization washed over Josephine like a tidal wave and heat tinged her cheeks. It was true that Oliver had never once mentioned what his final promise to her father had been. She had only assumed that her father had asked that one thing from him.

"You've been following me, sleeping in the room next to me at the tavern, and practically hovering over me every day. And then coming here tonight ..." She shook her head. "When Father came for me, he told me that you would protect me. But you didn't pledge anything at all. Did you?" Josephine covered her face with her hands in humiliation and hurt. "I'm such a fool."

He pried her hands from her face with gentle hands. "Do you honestly believe it would take a blood oath for me to look out for you?"

"But you stayed here with me. I know you miss sailing as much as I do. Why would you stay here if you could have found another ship to call home?"

Oliver grazed his knuckles down the side of her face. "Because I care for you, Jo. You mean more to me than anything in this world. Even sailing. I ain't leaving this continent unless you're with me."

Josephine shook her head, not daring to believe him. "Don't say things like that if you don't mean it, Oliver."

He slowly drew her into his arms. "I've cared for you almost since we first met, Angelfish," He chuckled into her hair. "You were a trifle pain in the arse, and still are sometimes." After a moment, he stepped back and held her at arm's length. "I would've given him my oath had he asked, Jo. But he didn't need to. Joseph knew I'd *never* abandon you. He knew I'd follow you to the ends of the earth to keep you safe." Tightening his grip on her shoulders, he added, "And whether you like it or not, I'm going to protect you to my dying breath."

Slowly and tentatively, he cradled her face with his hands. Her breath quickened as he lightly outlined her mouth with his thumb. Equal amounts of fear and excitement filled her, somehow knowing that this moment would change things forever between them.

Oliver placed butterfly kisses on her eyelids, her nose, and then the corner of her mouth. Their breath mingled while he waited, giving her one final chance to pull away. Then, finally, he brushed his lips over hers. Forceful winds whipped all around her as he kissed her. The loose tethers in her soul latched onto him so tightly it was almost painful. It was a force that she could not control and had no intention of stopping. This connection was even greater than her longing for the open water. It was terrifying and magnificent all at once. Josephine was sure no one had ever experienced anything quite like this.

Far too soon, Oliver was pulling away, leaving Josephine breathless and hanging on to his waistcoat for dear life.

"Was that normal?" Her voice was still husky from the flood of emotions still whirling inside her. She raised an eyebrow. "Never mind. I don't think I want to hear about any other kissing exploits you've had."

Oliver burst into laughter and hugged her tightly. "Aye, you'd best not be asking then!" He chuckled playfully as she punched him on the shoulder. When he pressed another soft kiss to Josephine's lips, a gust of air circled them again.

Oliver glanced around curiously. "Are you doing that?"

Josephine ducked her head. "Not on purpose. I suppose the weather changes whenever any of my emotions surface. At least it's not raining."

"Are you still concerned about your escort?" He rolled his eyes.

"My escort? Oh." Josephine looked over her shoulder at the orange glow in the distance. "I don't suppose I should care. I was sure I heard Skulthorpe's voice in that meeting and Mr. Runik works for him."

"Aye, so if Skulthorpe meant to start that bloody fire …"

"Maybe they'll think I'm dead." Her eyes widened. "If they think I'm dead, we could leave."

Oliver narrowed his eyes, considering her suggestion. "Aye, maybe."

"We could get on a ship and sail away. We could go anywhere!" The thought of the two of them finally setting sail together made her so happy she thought her heart might just burst.

"And what about Genny?"

"You're right. We can't leave Aunt Genny behind." Josephine's shoulders sagged. "Would she leave the Kraken's Lookout?"

"We can talk to her about it tomorrow." He placed a kiss on her forehead and linked their fingers. "Come on. Let's get out of here."

TWENTY-TWO

H and in hand, Josephine and Oliver made their way to the slums of Charlestown. In fact, it was the same street where Oliver had caused a ruckus when Runik had been following her. Could that have been just a couple of weeks ago? It seemed like much longer than that.

"I must know, Oliver," Josephine questioned as they walked. "How is it that you knew how to dance so well? And talk like a noble? I honestly didn't think you had it in you."

Grinning, Oliver told her, "Where do you think I've been all this week? Been preparing." He shrugged. "Wasn't too hard once I let Genny get hold of me! She found it all exciting, conjuring the glamour and all."

They both chuckled.

"Yes, she does have a tendency to go overboard."

Oliver gently squeezed her fingers. "I was sure you recognized me."

"It was your eyes. They *were* familiar. Aunt Genny did a marvelous job with the disguise."

The taverns and bawdy houses were still booming and would continue to be busy throughout the night in this seedy area. The air reeked of cheap perfume, tobacco, and rum. The mills and shops along the street had closed earlier in the evening.

"Is this where you live?" Josephine asked him finally.

Oliver nodded. "I live in a flat just above that place there," he pointed just ahead at a large tavern with several women skulking about on the front porch and greeting the passersby with giggles and waves.

When Josephine realized which building he was referring to, she froze in her tracks. "You live in a house of ill-repute?"

"Josephine -"

"You live with a bunch of tavern doxies?" Josephine scowled up at him. "Have you been ... *cavorting* with those ... *women*?"

"No, little jealous shrew," he chuckled, bringing her in for a comforting embrace. "And they ain't what you think. They're witches, Jo, and this is their home. They disguise themselves behind this charade. The townsfolk won't take notice of a brothel like they would a coven of witches."

That did not comfort Josephine at all. It was still a horde of women that could be flirting their way into Oliver's arms. This brush with jealousy astonished her. She had never seen Oliver with another lady. Was this how Oliver felt when she had been courted by other men?

"Jo, I've never had eyes for any of them," he told her gently. "Never wanted anyone but you. I pay to live here because I know their charm to disguise the place protects me as well."

Swallowing back her jealousy, she finally nodded. "I still don't like it," she muttered, frowning up at him.

"I can see that." He placed a kiss upon her forehead and smiled. "Come along, Angelfish." He laughed again and led her into the run-down, three-story witch-house.

The inside of the place was not what Josephine was expecting. Gold sconces were lit along each wall, illuminating the floral rugs on the floors. Two burgundy sofas faced each other in the sitting room. A white vase filled with sprigs of feathery fountain grass, along with orange mums, had been placed on the coffee table between the sofas. In the back corner of the sitting room was a settee and a small side table, where a candle was burning, filling the room with the scent of cinnamon.

Three witches sat on the sofas, warming themselves by the fire and speaking in low voices. Others came and went, roaming the halls and the kitchen. They were not provocatively dressed as she'd imagined. Instead, they appeared to be conservative women in modest dresses. One or two wore dark cloaks over their garments, but all in all, they looked rather like an ordinary group of well-mannered ladies.

Oliver greeted a few of them, but didn't stop for pleasantries. Never letting go of Josephine's hand, he led her up the two flights of steps to his one-room flat on the top floor. It was a cozy room and much nicer than Josephine's at the Kraken's Lookout.

There was a large open window that overlooked the street, and, in the distance, she could see the docks where Culligan's Wharf was located. A chocolate brown rug covered most of the wood floor and a wardrobe stood tall against the wall opposite the bed. Everything was neat and put in its place; the mark of a true sailor.

What had Josephine in knots was the bed. It was twice the size of hers. Heat flooded her face at the thought that Oliver might want to sleep beside her. She'd slept beside him before on her father's ship, but they'd been in separate hammocks. It was much less intimate than this.

Unaware of her reticence, Oliver walked to the wardrobe standing across from the bed, pulling off his neckcloth and waistcoat along the way. "You take the bed. I'll make a pallet on the floor."

Josephine breathed a quiet sigh of relief. "I don't mind sleeping on the floor. This is your room."

Oliver snorted. "I ain't making you sleep on the floor, Angelfish. I thought it'd be safer, you staying here under the witches' charms. I'll send one of them to Genny to let her know you're safe."

"Yes, that's probably best."

"And, as lovely as they are, you ain't going to be sleeping in those petticoats." Pillaging through his wardrobe, Oliver pulled out a shirt and some breeches for her. "I know they're a mite big, but they'll do. Aye?"

"Of course. Thank you," she stammered, still trying to overcome her nervous flutters. "Can you help me with my laces?"Clutching his clothes to her chest, she cringed at how much her voice shook.

Time seemed to stand still as the question hung in the air. They both knew that she was asking him to help undress her and that he'd never done such a thing for her before. Josephine swallowed back her apprehension and turned around to get it over with. Someone had to do it. Josephine certainly couldn't reach them herself. She supposed she could ask Oliver to fetch one of the witches to assist her, but she didn't want one of those strange women up in his room.

Oliver approached and carefully loosened the ribbons that held her dress and corset in place. Josephine held her breath as his warm fingers grazed her shift, the only material covering her flesh beneath the gown.

"I'll never understand ladies and all these laces," she said, sounding a bit out of breath. "It's so much work."

Oliver's fingers stilled against the small of her back. "Not that much."

His breath was warm on the back of her neck, sending shivers up her spine. As she turned to face him, Oliver cleared his throat and took a step back. "I'll leave you to the rest while I get that message sent."

OLIVER SENT TEMPEST, the coven leader, out to the Kraken's Lookout to give Genny the message and his warning. He didn't trust any of the other girls with the message, and if anyone was lying in wait, Tempest could certainly handle herself. He only hoped that Genny was ready for any kind of threat.

After sending his message, he'd paced the floor for at least ten minutes to give Josephine plenty of time to undress. When he returned to his room, she was sitting at the window sill, staring out at the docks. Wearing the boys' clothes while her hair was still pinned was so fetching, Oliver couldn't help but silently stare.

"Are you just going to stand there?" she asked, still facing the window.

"How did you know I was here?"

Giggling, she turned to peer at him over her shoulder. "I don't know, I just … sensed you standing there."

"You heard the door open."

Josephine shook her head. "I felt you outside the door."

Oliver scratched the back of his neck thoughtfully. "Your father could do that too."

She looked out the window again. "I don't think it's the same. You had a blood bond with my father. You haven't taken one from me. This feels different." Josephine paused to find the right words. "It feels as if the connection is just between you and me." She shook her head, waving the thought away. "It doesn't matter."

Stepping over to the window, Oliver nodded toward the harbor. "Do you need to go out there?" Oliver knew she was restless for the sea these days. It was only a matter of time before she was called home for eternity.

"I'm fine tonight," she said. "Taking off that corset helped. You know how I loathe them. Are you worried I'll turn into a pile of dust?"

"Nah. It's after dark already." Oliver cleared his throat and asked, "If you don't mind, I'm going to get into some different clothes now."

"Oh, of course."

Josephine promptly turned her back so that he could shed his own fancy garments and put on a fresh set of breeches. Leaving his upper body bare, he ran his hands through his hair and tied it back neatly again.

"You can turn around again." When she did, Oliver chuckled in amusement at the color that crept into her cheeks. "Why are you blushing, Angelfish? You saw me without a shirt plenty when we was at sea."

"That was different."

He sat down beside her on the window sill. "I'm still me. Same as I always was. And you was never shy with me before."

"You weren't kissing me before."

"Would you like me to stop?"

"No!"

The quick response had Oliver's heart beating faster.

"I do ... I mean, I don't ..." Josephine sputtered. "I was never sure of how you felt. Aunt Genny tried to tell me again and again that ..." Her words trailed away, still flustered. "The way you would look at me sometimes ... and then you'd be angry and withdraw. I just didn't think ..." She sighed and slapped her forehead. "Blast! I can't even finish a sentence!"

Grinning at her awkwardness, Oliver took one of her hands in his. "I wanted to tell you how I felt for a long time, but I thought it best to keep a distance. You're too highborn for the likes of me. And that ain't being nice, it's the bloody truth."

"Too highborn?" Josephine said with a snort. "If anyone is a misfit, it's me! A pirate with a first-class name, talks like a scallywag half the time, and also a woman. I don't fit in anywhere!" She jabbed an accusing finger into his chest. "And you failed to mention why you've been so furious with me."

"I wasn't furious. Maybe a bit annoyed."

Josephine rolled her eyes. "Annoyed, then. Why didn't you like my dress that morning I bumped into you? It hurt my feelings."

He closed his eyes and smiled, remembering that day perfectly. "You was the most beautiful thing I'd ever seen, Angelfish. I was *annoyed* that it was for someone else."

"You didn't think that he and I -"

"It crossed my mind a time or two, when I wasn't thinking the hunter was hurting you. That's why I was a bit cross." He caressed her bruised cheek with the back of his fingers. "When I saw that bloke hit you tonight ..." The muscles in his jaw ticked. "I thought I was going to kill him."

Josephine swallowed. "He might be dead now ... from the fire."

"A lot of people could've been hurt tonight," Oliver pointed out. "My only concern is to keep *you* safe, Jo."

"I'm so sorry," she whispered, lowering her eyes in shame. "I never meant to worry you."

Oliver squeezed her hand in response. "I felt the same the night your father died, when I saw the scars that were left on your back." His voice cracked. "I swore it would never happen to you again."

"So, it wasn't about the dress?" she said, grinning.

"Josephine, you are an impertinent wee brat." He tweaked her nose and then cupped her cheeks with his hands. "Gown or sailor's rags, you have always been the most beautiful thing I've ever seen."

Then he claimed her mouth again. His heart pounded as she tentatively placed her hands on his bare shoulders. Her fingers fluttered down to his arms and then his chest. It was the most wonderful touch he'd ever experienced. And it definitely had been worth the wait.

PROMISING TO STAY CLOSE, Oliver insisted she lie down on his bed to get some sleep. When she awoke a few hours later, it was not quite morning, but Oliver was gone. He'd left a fire burning in the fireplace and had covered her with a soft blanket. Josephine snuggled into the bed and smiled widely, thinking about their kiss.

Her smile melted away when she noticed the stack of papers on the bedside table that hadn't been there earlier. Josephine swung her legs over the side of the bed and touched her feet to the plush rug. Grabbing the candle by the bed, she padded across the floor to the fireplace, carefully lit the wick, and returned to the table. Josephine set the candle down and reached for the papers.

They were letters addressed to her father. Oliver had mentioned letters between the man named James and her father, but he'd not given her a chance to look at them. Josephine hated thinking about the day she had gone to fetch James and wound up in the hands of the hunters. What she'd witnessed ... what had happened to poor James would stay with her forever.

Sinking back down on the bed, Josephine began to read and didn't stop until she'd read all six letters. By the end of the last letter, Josephine's stomach was churning.

The door to the room creaked open. Josephine peered over her shoulder to find Oliver carrying a tray laden with bread, butter, jam, cheese, and a pot of fresh tea.

"Oh, good," he said. "You're awake! I brought ..." Oliver stopped mid-sentence once he noticed the stricken look upon her face and the letters in her hand. "I'm sorry, Jo. I should've put them away so you didn't have to read them. I didn't mean to upset you by leaving them there."

Josephine rose from the bed and faced him. "It's not that."

He set the tray down on his small dining table and folded his arms across his chest. "Then what is it?"

She swallowed the lump that had formed in her throat. "This man … James. He had a son."

"Aye?"

"James was writing to Father because he was trying to protect his son from the Brotherhood."

Oliver's brow pinched together. "Aye, I read that too."

Josephine went on. "James signed each letter. He signed them all *James Runik.*" She held out the letter for Oliver to see.

"I don't understand what you're telling me, Jo."

"His name is James *Runik*," she stated emphatically. "The man I've been working with - the hunter who works for Garreck Skulthorpe? His name is Nathaniel *Runik*. That cannot be a coincidence."

Oliver muttered a curse as he snatched the letters from her.

"Quite," Josephine answered, wanting to curse as well. "The Brotherhood wasn't hunting for his son. They were recruiting him."

TWENTY-THREE

With only a small semblance of a plan, Josephine and Oliver decided to make their way back to the Kraken's Lookout early that morning, mostly so that Josephine could get back into her old blue dress. She much preferred the boy's clothes, but her ideas of comfort were not appreciated in a city like Charlestown. Upper-class women dressed extravagantly in heavy velvets and multiple layers of undergarments and hoops, despite the terrible heat of summer. Even the working women dressed modestly in skirts at least, though they were much simpler in material, colors, and cut.

Even though it was just after dawn, people were already swarming Broad Street, opening their shops, or distributing goods from the docks. It was the busiest road in Charlestown and ran perpendicular to the docks. As Josephine and Oliver drew closer to the wharf, the street grew more crowded. Men, and even young boys, raced east toward the street that ran along the wharf.

"What's going on?" Josephine whispered to her companion. "Where is everyone going?"

"Might be a ship coming in or someone's been arrested. You know how people like to gawk at things like that."

As they turned off Broad Street and south onto the bay road, a cold wave of nausea churned in Josephine's gut.

She stopped in her tracks. "Oliver, something's not right. I feel very strange."

"What do you mean?"

"I mean, I have an odd feeling in here." She pointed to her belly. "Something I've never felt before."

His brows knitted together. "Could your pirate blood be telling you something?"

Josephine closed her eyes and concentrated on the sensation that was suddenly rushing through her. "Maybe."

"Do you feel like you're conjuring the magic?"

She shook her head. "I'm not a witch. I don't conjure."

Oliver rolled his eyes. "You know what I mean."

"It feels like ... a warning."

People were still running down the bay road, all headed south in the direction of the Kraken's Lookout. Rounding the bend, about a hundred yards from Genny's tavern, a mob had formed. At least a hundred people had gathered, shouting and jeering about something. The few women who had joined them were throwing rotten fruit and other objects. Men were shoving each other and fights were breaking out. Smoke rose into the air somewhere beyond the crowd.

Oliver held her hand as they cautiously approached the mob.

"It's another protest," Oliver muttered.

There had been plenty of unrest in the colonies since the Crown had raised taxes on imports. It really hurt colonial trade and pushed many merchants to smuggle in their goods from elsewhere.

Josephine stared at the smoke. "There's a fire. Oliver ..."

"I see it."

Josephine let go of Oliver's hand and sprinted toward the horde of angry colonials.

"Wait! Jo!" Oliver sprinted after her.

But she kept running toward the danger. She had a feeling that something dreadful had happened. The chill inside her was growing colder, warning her to stay far away.

Then Josephine knew.

Aunt Genny.

"No!" she cried as she pushed into the crowd. Bodies pressed in on all sides. The smell of sweat, blood, and smoke overwhelmed her senses.

"Josephine, stop!" she heard Oliver yell from somewhere behind her. She'd lost him in the throng of people.

A man to her right raised his fist and screamed, "String them up!"

"First they raise our taxes and then they raze our businesses to the ground!" another man bellowed from just behind her.

Josephine skidded to a halt. She finally caught a glimpse of why everyone was raging. The Kraken's Lookout was engulfed in flames. Black smoke billowed out of the windows and doors, into the morning sky. The wood cracked loudly, collapsing from within.

Covering her mouth with her hands, Josephine let out a blood-curdling scream. No one noticed over the shouts of the protesters.

A couple of men crashed into Josephine, nearly sending her sprawling to the ground. Hands grabbed her waist and yanked her back against a solid, warm body. Josephine struggled to tear herself away, kicking and flailing. Was it a hunter coming to abduct her again? Had the Brotherhood caused this carnage?

"Jo, it's me! It's Oliver!" he shouted into her ear.

He dragged her back into the shadows between two shops, away from the mob.

"But Aunt Genny!" Josephine wailed, struggling to break free. "She's inside!"

"Josephine, if she *is* in there, there ain't nothing we can do now. It's too late."

In her heart, Josephine knew Oliver was right. The entire tavern was destroyed. There was nothing to be done to save it or Genny, if she had been asleep in her bed. And even if she'd wanted, there was no way for Josephine to reach the tavern to see for herself. The horde was growing more violent by the minute. Sailors were joining the foray, armed with clubs. A pistol fired and many people began to flee in terror, trampling other less-fortunate citizens beneath their boots.

"She could still be alive," said Oliver, trying to reassure her. "Genny has her ways, being a witch. If she's alive, she'll find us, Jo."

Josephine covered her mouth with her hands. "He did this," she whimpered. "Skulthorpe did this."

"You're probably right, Jo. If he is responsible, then it means he has reason to believe you escaped the soiree last night. We must make him believe you were in there, that you're dead, too. Let's go to Cully's. Now."

The feeling of imminent danger remained as they hurried back to Culligan's wharf. Josephine let the cold feeling in her belly linger, for she knew that if she turned to anger and grief, she would surely bring a hurricane down on Charlestown.

There was only one thing to do. Josephine knew she would not rest until the deaths of her father and Aunt Genny were made right. None of them deserved what had been done to them.

Later that day, the two of them sat with Captain Culligan in his dilapidated townhome. Josephine had not allowed herself to cry at all, which she knew was bothering Oliver. He seemed to be watching her every move, waiting for her to break down. She kept her composure and let her mind be consumed with ideas for what to do next.

Unfortunately, Oliver was not at all accommodating. At every attempt to come up with a reasonable plan, he immediately dismissed it.

"Putting yourself in danger is not acceptable, Jo."

"Sneaking into Skulthorpe's mansion is not that dangerous for me," Josephine argued.

"He'll know you're alive if you go traipsing through the place."

"Skulthorpe hasn't even been at the mansion since the night he forced me into his service. No one else has any clue about what took place last night and this morning!"

"Except for that bloody witch," said Oliver. "The witch was probably the one responsible for both those blasted fires, and well you know it, Josephine. You can't even tell me who the witch is!" He surged out of his chair and began pacing. "The witch could've disguised herself as a man if she's as powerful as we think. She could be *Runik* for all you know!"

"That is completely absurd!" she shouted back at him.

"How do you know?"

Josephine paused and pinched her lips together. There was no way to explain to Oliver why she believed Runik could never be the witch. She just ... had a feeling. "I just know," she simply stated.

Oliver shrugged. "Well, the answer's still no. There'll be no more arguing from you."

"Then how are we ever going to find out anything? And don't forget that the witch will know I'm alive eventually, if she's able to track me down with a spell."

Scratching his beard, Culligan chimed in. "If they think you died in that fire, the one last night or this morning, then they may not feel the need to track you."

"Aye," Oliver agreed. "Let's hope they're none the wiser about their mistake for a while. That'll give us the time we need to disappear. And what about that toff? Runik?"

"What about him?" Josephine asked.

"Do you think he knew about any of this?"

Josephine snorted. "You mean if he's not the witch?"

"Aye," Oliver drawled, rolling his eyes at her sarcasm.

Josephine wanted to answer no immediately, but hesitated. "I can't say for sure. He was at Sturch Manor when it caught fire. It doesn't seem likely that he would plan something like that and put himself in danger. However, he could have slipped away before it all happened. He's so loyal to Skulthorpe." Josephine rubbed her temples. "There's no way to know for certain."

Having no other ideas or arguments, they continued to think in silence. Josephine wracked her brain for another plan that might be possible without taking too much risk or allowing Oliver to accompany her. His presence at Skulthorpe's estate would definitely attract atten-tion. They'd be killed or imprisoned by the hunters before they could get to the entrance to Headquarters.

Josephine longed to snoop around down there. Not that Skulthorpe would ever leave evidence of his whereabouts or business where anyone could see. She simply wanted to inspect Barnaby's fabulous inventions. Josephine fingered the pocket watch and fan that she'd kept with her from the soiree assignment. She'd fled the party with Oliver before getting a chance to use them.

A thought suddenly came to Josephine. She straightened up in her seat and her eyes widened.

"What is it?" Oliver asked, watching her closely.

"I know where we could find more information that's not at the Skulthorpe estate."

NATHANIEL WORKED long hours that day. Decoding the ciphered message was his first priority and was easily managed. He consulted with the other hunters about the Sturch Manor incident, but none of them had any information that was useful. Most concluded that the fire was magic-made, but he'd already known that bit. It was an exceedingly frustrating day. Not to mention that Beau and Eleanor were beside themselves at the loss of Josephine. They could not be consoled, no matter how stoic he and Madame Sophia remained.

If he'd had any doubts about her being lost to the fire at the soiree, she most certainly had been killed this morning. He'd gone to the Kraken's Lookout at noon, the time he usually picked her up, but was horrified to find that it had been burned to the ground. He'd stood there staring, too stunned to move or even breathe. Not even the framework of the tavern remained. It had been completely destroyed, along with whoever was inside. A crowd was standing on the street, speculating over the fallen structure. A few women were tending to injuries. Some people were bleeding from head wounds, while others held their ribs or arms.

Nathaniel reached out to stop a woman who was walking by. "What happened here?"

The woman gave him a wary look. "That tavern there burnt to the ground, Sir. Then a riot broke out." The woman strode away quickly and he did not stop her.

A wave of regret washed over him at the loss. Josephine may have been a pirate, but did she deserve this fate? To be burned alive in her bed? He supposed it did not matter. Skulthorpe was set against all pirates and witches and would see them all dead eventually.

Nathaniel shoved his feelings away and returned to Skulthorpe's estate to report in, deliver the deciphered note, and find out his next assignment. There was still work to do, even without Josephine. They would just have to find a way to thwart these Patriots without her. He felt certain the Patriots were growing in number and moving to strike against the Crown's governing body here in the colonies. The list that Josephine had procured told him as much. There were many new names on the list that he did not recognize. The Patriots were expanding, protesting every shipment of tea that arrived. The rebels in Charlestown had stolen another shipment just last month, and none of the hunters could figure out where they were hiding it. The fire at the soiree would only incite the colonials further. The entire ordeal was giving Nathaniel a terrible headache.

Once his work was done for the day, he spent his remaining hours at the estate, fencing with the other hunters, mostly to avoid Beau and Eleanor. Beau couldn't stop eating cakes, certain that the sweets would make him feel better, and Eleanor's tears were driving Nathaniel to distraction.

The swordplay helped relieve Nathaniel's tension for a while, but when the day grew dark, and the sparring ended, he was still troubled. As nightfall approached, he emerged from Headquarters and rode in a carriage back to his small plantation home. Without fail, his staff were still moving about, making ready for his arrival.

"Cup o' tea for you, dear?" his housekeeper asked him when he arrived.

Nathaniel nodded. "I will be in the downstairs study."

He shucked his frock, gloves, and tricorn and set them aside. Someone would surely put them away. Or not. It mattered little.

A fire was burning in the study, ready for him as always. Usually, he would pick out a book from his extensive library or light a cigar to pass the time, but tonight, Nathaniel could do neither with any enjoyment. Slouching on the sofa, he stared at the fire with his head in his hands. Josephine and the fire at the tavern consumed his thoughts.

The floorboards creaked behind him, announcing someone's entrance into the room.

"Just set the tea on the table, thank you," he said, without bothering to look.

"As you wish," replied a familiar voice that did not belong to his housekeeper.

Before Nathaniel could turn to look, he heard the *thwap* of his napshot firing and felt a prick on the side of his neck. He knew it was only a matter of seconds until he passed out, but in those few seconds, Nathaniel simply sat there and laughed. Once again, he had underestimated the little pirate. And he was grateful for it.

GARRECK SKULTHORPE WAS ONCE AGAIN WAITING in the shadows for news that his plan had succeeded. The witch did not disappoint. The hood of her cloak darkened her face with a shadow.

"Is it done?" he asked without greeting her.

"Of course."

Skulthorpe narrowed his eyes at her. "You saw the remains? There can be no mistakes this time."

She sighed impatiently. "The witch is dead. Your little pirate is completely alone. Except for that boy, of course."

"Don't worry. I have plans for him," he smiled arrogantly. "Get back to work. Everything is coming together perfectly."

The witch sniffed. "Do you honestly think you can single-handedly start a war? That seems like such a waste of time and money."

"That is not your concern, is it?" he snapped.

"I just don't understand why you are keeping the girl alive at all," she commented. "What does she have to do with any of this?"

He chuckled. "Absolutely nothing."

"Then why use her?" the witch asked him.

"It amuses me to watch her suffer," he snarled at her. He had grown tired of her questions. "Get back to work. There is still much to do."

The witch nodded and walked away without a sound.

It was true that there was no underlying purpose for using the Teversin girl in his plans. He simply enjoyed having the upper hand. He wanted her to suffer for simply being what she was, and he wanted his revenge on her for escaping him. No pirate had ever escaped him once they had become a target. The Pirate of Blacktail Cove was the only pirate to evade him for so long. That thorn still pricked his pride from time to time, and Josephine Teversin would suffer for it before she met her end.

TWENTY-FOUR

J osephine and Oliver searched every square inch of Runik's country home, coming up with only bits and pieces of information that proved to be quite useless. Runik was downstairs, still asleep and tied to a chair in his study. They would deal with him soon enough.

It had all come together in Josephine's mind - Nathaniel Runik's home was where they had trapped her in the cellar the first night of her abduction. Skulthorpe and Runik had needed a quiet, secluded place that was out of town and easily guarded during her test.

Oliver had been acting strange all evening, ever since Josephine had come up with the plan.

"I still don't understand why we don't just kill the bloke," he grumbled.

"Because I believe that if Father were still alive, he would still be trying to save him. If we kill him, that will make us like Skulthorpe, and I *refuse* to lower myself to the status of bottom-dweller."

"And what if it was a matter of life or death? What if it was a choice between you and Skulthorpe himself?" Oliver countered. "You're telling me that you wouldn't kill him to save your own skin?"

Josephine paused in her search. "I don't know. I suppose I'll find out sooner or later, right?"

"Well, we ain't found nothing much that's useful here." Oliver stacked up the papers again and marched to the door of the office. "I say we go interrogate the prisoner now."

Josephine sighed. "Let's go, then."

When they entered the downstairs study, Runik was groaning. He struggled against his bonds for a moment and then stilled, focusing his attention on Josephine and Oliver.

The two of them sat down on the sofa opposite Runik. Oliver pulled out his pistol and rested it on his lap.

"Do you think that's necessary?" Josephine whispered to Oliver.

Oliver's hardened eyes never left Runik. "He's a *hunter*." He spat the word out like a curse. "It's more than necessary."

Josephine shook her head and turned to their captive once more. She tried not to squirm in her seat as she and Mr. Runik locked eyes. She was still in the boy's clothes Oliver had given her, since her dresses had all gone up in flames with her aunt's tavern. He didn't give her his disdaining look that was typically reserved for her. His eyes held a different emotion tonight. She couldn't pinpoint exactly what it was, but the usual coldness wasn't there.

"You're not cursing us to our graves," Oliver stated.

Runik's eyes never left Josephine. "I believe I probably deserve this. I *am* wondering, Miss Teversin, how it is you got your hands on my napshot."

Josephine flicked open the fan that Barnaby had entrusted to her and waved it lazily in front of her face.

"Ah, I see," Runik said with a smirk. "And my household staff? Surely they heard you."

Josephine pulled out Barnaby's pocket watch. "They are all asleep. Pirates do enjoy an adventure."

Runik's face sobered and his dark brows pinched together. "I thought you were dead. I looked for you at the soiree. Then I went to the tavern yesterday morning, hoping ... but the tavern was destroyed."

After tucking the devices away again, Josephine had to mentally shake herself at Runik's sudden show of concern. Could he really have been worried for her?

"I did manage to escape both," she said, keeping her responses vague. "Did you know that fire was going to happen?"

"No."

Josephine had trouble believing him. "Even the fire at the Kraken's Lookout?"

"I knew nothing. I swear it."

"And why should we believe you?" Oliver drawled, his index finger tapping the pistol.

"I was simply following orders," Runik snapped.

"Aye, you're good at that, aren't you?"

Runik sighed. "There was nothing in the plans that included destroying you, Miss Teversin. Mr. Skulthorpe was adamant that he wanted your help in retrieving sensitive Patriot information. That was all."

Josephine narrowed her eyes. "Perhaps you're right, Oliver. He doesn't have any useful information. Maybe we should just shoot him."

Oliver cocked his eyebrow at her, but then rose from his seat and pulled back the hammer on his pistol.

Mr. Runik's eyes widened. "I beg your pardon! Would you really shoot an unarmed man, Miss Teversin?"

"I happen to think it's a fine idea," Oliver mumbled.

"I told you I had nothing to do with the fires!"

"Yes, there is that," Josephine muttered, folding her arms across her chest. "I hate to say it, but maybe we should give him a chance to tell us what else he knows."

"Aye. Then we can shoot him." Oliver sat back down and slouched back lazily, releasing the hammer.

Josephine grinned. Oliver was playing along beautifully with her plan.

"Mr. Runik, did you know that Skulthorpe hired a witch into his service?"

Runik burst into laughter. Once he realized that neither Josephine nor Oliver had joined in, his amusement faded away. "You're serious. How did you come by that information?"

"That's our business," Oliver told him.

"Now, now, Oliver," Josephine said. "His surprise seemed genuine. Perhaps he's entitled to *some* information in return." Turning to Oliver, she asked, "Wouldn't you agree?"

"Perhaps." Oliver fingered his pistol again. "Both fires were started by a witch."

"And you think she was hired by Mr. Skulthorpe?"

Josephine frowned. "Wait. You knew a witch started that fire at the soiree?"

Runik rolled his eyes. "I am not a complete idiot."

"That's still to be decided," said Oliver.

Clearing her throat to keep from laughing, Josephine gestured for Mr. Runik to continue.

"The fire spread too quickly for it not to have been enhanced by some sort of spell," Runik explained. "But that does not explain why you think the witch could be employed by Mr. Skulthorpe. He hunts down and kills witches."

"Aye, and he supposedly kills pirates too," Oliver replied.

"Quite so," Runik agreed.

Oliver jumped to his feet and cocked the pistol again. "I say we shoot him now, Jo. Do you think sharks enjoy English meat?"

"Let's not be hasty, Oliver."

"Well, he's shot you plenty, aye?"

Oliver's fingers were curled into a fist at his side and the muscle in his jaw was clenched. A fire was burning behind his green eyes. Josephine had thought he was pretending, but perhaps he *did* want to injure Mr. Runik.

"Now, see here," Runik huffed. "I merely put her to sleep. I didn't mortally wound the girl."

Oliver pressed the barrel of his pistol into Nathaniel's shoulder and glowered down at him.

"Oliver, please. There's no need to shed more blood."

"We'll just injure him. There's plenty of places to shoot a musket ball that won't kill him." Oliver took aim at Runik's kneecap. "Like here. Shooting him in the knee will loosen his tongue, don't you think?"

"Now, be reasonable!" Runik was leaning as far back in his chair as he could manage, as if that would put some distance between them.

"Oliver, do sit down," Josephine said. "Let's wait and see if his information proves useful." She turned back to Runik. "Now, then. What do you know of the witch?"

"I don't know anything about her," Runik barked. "I've already admitted that I knew the fire at the soiree was caused by some witch, but I thought it was just a coincidence. Someone out to injure a few Patriots or just cause mayhem. *Your* kind are good at that," he sneered. "Maybe it was another *pirate*."

Oliver poked the barrel of his pistol into Runik's cheek. "You'd best watch your tongue."

Josephine ignored Runik's barb. "And the tavern too? Do you think *that* was a coincidence, as well? If you say yes, then I think you might deserve to be shot."

"Of course, I don't. At least … not now." Runik's lips parted slightly as realization dawned on him. "Your Aunt Genevieve was in the tavern."

Josephine looked away and covered her mouth with her hand to hide her trembling lower lip. She would not shed tears in front of him.

After a long minute of uncomfortable silence, she blurted out, "Skulthorpe was at the soiree."

Runik shook his head. "That's not possible. He would have told -"

"*You* told me to snoop around, so I did. And did I not tell you once before that Skulthorpe has his own agenda?"

Lips tightening into a fine line, Runik held his silence.

"From what I heard," she continued, "he was in a meeting with a man. A Patriot."

"Impossible."

"In fact, it sounded very much like he was the one who ordered the destruction of Sturch Manor. Did you know about that?"

Oliver shoved the pistol into Runik's cheek again. "Don't even think about lying."

"I swear to you, I knew nothing," Runik said through gritted teeth.

Josephine considered Runik's steel-blue eyes for a moment. They had hardened from Oliver's threats, but they didn't seem dishonest or cold. In all their time together, Josephine had never known Runik to lie to her, even when the truth made her want to strike him.

"All right," she said. "I believe you."

Oliver released the hammer once more and took his seat beside Josephine.

"Will that be all then, Miss Teversin? As much as I enjoy being tied to this chair and threatened, I would much prefer to have a brandy and retire for the evening. If you'd be so kind."

"There is one more thing I would like to know," Josephine said.

"Yes?"

Josephine took a moment to brace herself before asking, "Why did you become a hunter?"

The simple question brought the coldness back to Runik's eyes in a flash. "I was an officer in the British Army for three years when I was approached by Mr. Skulthorpe. He told me of the position, but I wasn't interested at the time. I had no desire to come to the colonies. My family was in England, so I politely refused his offer." Runik's icy gaze never left hers. "Then my father disappeared."

Josephine swallowed the lump in her throat. "His name was James?"

"Yes. Perhaps you know the rest of the story, Miss Teversin. He came to the colonies on government business. He was having an early dinner in New York, at an inn near the coast. A pirate murdered him while he was staying there."

All the blood drained from Josephine's face. She felt Oliver's eyes on her, but he wisely kept his silence.

"And not just any pirate, Miss Teversin," Runik snarled. "It was your father. The Pirate of Blacktail Cove."

TWENTY-FIVE

B ack at Oliver's flat, Josephine was wearing a path on the rug from her pacing. They'd left Runik seething at his small country home, one hand free and a knife to cut the rest of his bonds. This kindness had been above and beyond, according to Oliver, who was certain that shooting the hunter was the better option. The other alternative was leaving him tied up completely until one of the staff members woke to find him. Josephine had not wanted to be that cruel to him after hearing his tale. Her stomach was still reeling with sickness.

"Why didn't you tell me, Jo?"

Oliver sat in the chair in the corner, elbows on his knees, watching her circle the room. She glanced at him out of the corner of her eye, but the pity lurking behind his sea-green eyes was too much to bear.

Josephine kept her eyes on the floor. "I don't know."

"James Runik was the same man that your father was supposed to meet in New York?"

"Aye."

"What really happened to him? Cause I know your father had nothing to do with his death. He was with me. Was it hunters?"

A lump formed in Josephine's throat at the memory of that night. She nodded.

Oliver ran his hand over his blond hair. "So why does that Runik fellow believe your father did it?"

"Because that's likely what Skulthorpe told him. It's easy for him to twist the story to suit his needs."

And it also explained why Runik held such a deep hatred for pirates - Josephine in particular. The cold looks he always gave her was because of this.

"I don't understand why you left Runik alive, Jo," said Oliver, interrupting her sullen thoughts. "I hope it don't come back to bite us in the arse."

"As do I," she murmured, biting her bottom lip. "But I have to believe that it's what Father would do. He would never stop trying to save him, Oliver. He would never see a person as a lost cause - not anyone. You know that."

"Aye," Oliver replied, running his hand through his loose hair. "Always picking up strays wherever he went, eh?"

Just as Josephine was making another turn around the room, Oliver jumped up from the chair and wrapped his arms around her, pressing his warm chest against her back. "Now I understand why you hate it when I walk in circles." He chuckled into the crook of her neck, sending tingles down her spine.

Closing her eyes, Josephine linked her fingers with his and let his strength seep into her.

"I cannot help but feel that *all* of this is my fault," she finally admitted. Oliver's arms tightened around her. "It's true, Oliver. If I hadn't taken matters into my own hands that night, both Father and James might still be alive. Nathaniel would never have joined the hunters, either. He might even be our friend."

"That's debatable," Oliver mumbled.

Josephine ignored him. "And Aunt Genny ..." A sob hitched in her throat.

"You'll worry yourself to death over what might've been, Jo."

"I know. We cannot let Skulthorpe get away with it," she said with firm resolve.

"We'll find a way, Jo. I promise." he agreed. "Let's get some rest tonight, and tomorrow we'll come up with a new plan. One that ain't gonna get you killed."

JOSEPHINE AWOKE WITH A START. It was not even close to sunup, and everything was silent. Something heavy was draped across her body, and she realized that she was snuggled up against Oliver. At some point during the night, he'd left the pallet on the floor and joined her on the bed. He was at least on top of the covers while she was beneath them. Her head rested on his chest and one of his arms curled around her protectively. But Josephine did not believe that was what had stirred her from her slumber.

She felt it again. The icy sensation she'd felt the other day was beginning to build up again.

"Oliver!" she whispered urgently, giving him a shake. Josephine raised up on one elbow to look around.

"Mmm," he groaned, still half asleep.

"Wake up, Oliver," she whispered. "Something's happening." Josephine nudged him again, placing a finger over his lips so he wouldn't speak.

Finally registering her distress, Oliver sat up with a start and glanced around his room. "What is it?"

"I feel cold again," she whispered, crawling out of bed to find her boots. "We should leave. Quickly! Something's coming."

They scurried around to dress and collect what they could to make their escape. The chill coursing through Josephine was getting colder. "Hurry!"

Once they'd collected all their weapons and her devices, Oliver led Josephine to the wardrobe and opened it wide.

"We can't both fit in there," Josephine hissed.

"It's a secret passage, Jo. Get in and I'll shut the doors behind us."

Climbing inside the wardrobe, she realized that behind his row of clothes, there was indeed a bolt-hole out of the room. Oliver shut the outer wardrobe doors, pulled her even further inside, and then slid a rusty iron bar through the back of the trapdoor, locking them inside the dark passage.

Grasping her hand, Oliver led the way down the narrow corridor. "Do you still feel it?" Oliver whispered over his shoulder.

"Aye. It hasn't gotten worse ... yet." Josephine felt him nod in the dark and took another step. "I don't hear anything."

Oliver paused and listened for a moment, then cursed under his breath.

"The coven?" Josephine whispered.

"Aye. They're gone."

"Something more powerful than they are?"

He frowned over his shoulder at her. "Or we've been betrayed."

Oliver had claimed that the witches had placed charms and protective enchantments around the place. But Skulthorpe's witch might have driven out the coven that lived here or found her way around the charms. Could she be such a powerful witch?

"We're on our own. Come on, and mind the steps," he whispered, descending down the old boards of the staircase.

The trapdoor behind them rattled and Josephine gasped in terror. The iron latch held, but at the same time, Josephine felt like a bolt of ice pierced through her middle. Oliver swore as she doubled over in agony.

"Jo?"

"Keep going!" she said, still panting through the sting of cold.

Oliver edged open the next door cautiously, peeked out, and then swung it wide, letting in the cool night air. Still two stories up, Josephine followed Oliver down an old wooden ladder. It had been fixed to the side of the building, leading to the alley behind all the shops. She was nearly at the bottom when another rush of frigid cold struck her like a dagger. Losing her grip on the rungs, Josephine tumbled to the ground, landing hard on her side.

"Josephine!" Oliver cried, frantically gathering her up.

Still scrambling to their feet to flee, the silence of the dark alley was filled with a wicked cackle.

"My, my, my," the woman sneered. "You fell into my trap perfectly."

TWENTY-SIX

"The devil take that girl!" Nathaniel muttered to himself for at least the third time that night.

The better part of the last two hours had been spent pacing around his study, staring at the settee, and cursing the devious pirate who had occupied a seat on its cushions earlier. Josephine certainly knew how to get him riled. Asking him about his father had been the final straw. And she'd had the audacity to act as if she hadn't known anything about it!

Nathaniel sighed and rubbed his aching forehead. The talk about Mr. Skulthorpe hiring a witch was nagging him. Josephine had been a lot of things in the few weeks he'd known her, and they had antagonized each other relentlessly, but she did not have a false bone in her body. She could have been mistaken in what she had heard at the soiree, but evidence of two magical fires in one night was too much of a coincidence for there not to be some truth to her story. There was a witch out there. Whether she was working for the Brotherhood or not made no difference. Nathaniel would find her.

With a new quest looming before him, Nathaniel knew he must arm himself accordingly. He took the stairs two at a time, entered his upstairs office, and began rummaging through his desk drawers.

"There you are," he said, pulling forth a black onyx crystal that hung from a thin hemp cord like a medallion. Many of his fellow hunters possessed one of the smooth stones. The crystal detected magic, humming against the skin when one grew close to the magic-wielder. It was an invaluable tool for hunting witches, and this one had been given to him by Skulthorpe himself just a year ago.

Arming himself with a couple of pistols and daggers, his napshot, a few explosive pocket watches, and the medallion, Nathaniel saddled his horse and rode back to town.

The crystal buzzed with excitement as he drew closer. The medallion led him down the clay streets to one of the most run-down districts in Charlestown. The streets were still teeming with lower class citizens and sailors, probably out gambling or spending their wages on the most deplorable things, but he sensed that these folks were not what the onyx was detecting.

Tying his mount in front of a busy tavern, Nathaniel took off on foot, listening closely to the hum of the crystal. It led him to a three-story brothel that appeared to be empty, which seemed odd when every other tavern and shop was alive with activity. After picking the lock with one of his handy pocket watch pins, he drew his pistol and cautiously entered the building. It was clear for anyone to see that whoever had lived here had fled in a hurry. Chairs were overturned and food remained half-eaten on the table. A vase of flowers had been knocked over, spilling water on the coffee table and carpet. Drawers hung open as if they'd grabbed whatever valuables they could get their hands on and left the rest behind.

Nathaniel heard a muffled sound coming from the back of the old place and a flare of energy surged through the onyx.

The witch was near.

JOSEPHINE SCRAMBLED up off the ground and stood beside Oliver to face the witch. It was evident the woman had driven out all the occupants of the house and tricked them into fleeing. They were completely exposed and vulnerable. Oliver pulled a pistol from his belt, but Josephine knew with certainty that this witch was probably powerful enough to evade a musket ball.

"What do you want, witch?" Josephine demanded.

The witch's laughter echoed up and down the alley as she emerged from the shadows, covered with a dark cloak - completely unrecognizable.

The sound of her chuckling enraged Josephine. There had only ever been one other time she'd felt this kind of fury spark in her soul. Garreck Skulthorpe had laughed in that same maniacal way after her father had turned to sand. Josephine would not let him win again. She would not watch another person she loved be torn from her life. She'd already lost Aunt Genny. If she lost Oliver tonight, she would never forgive herself. Josephine let those thoughts take over and the fury burn brighter.

"Steady, Josephine," Oliver murmured, but it was too late.

The storm inside Josephine was already raging out of control, just as it had three years ago. The wind whipped wildly around them, swirling through Josephine's loose hair and whistling down the alley.

"So the little bird is going to try some magic?" the witch sneered, cackling again. The woman lifted her arms and began to conjure. Black smoke, like soot, began to form a cocoon around her as she muttered her spell. The smoke was completely unaffected by the storm that continued to swell around them.

Oliver took aim and fired his pistol at the witch. She disappeared with a twist, avoiding the shot easily, just as Josephine had expected. She reappeared three feet to the left, smiling as if this were just a game.

"She's conjuring again," Josephine warned Oliver as the black smoke began to form.

"Aye," he answered. "What's the plan, Jo?"

"You think I have a plan?"

"Well, you got this storm brewing, so that's something, eh?"

"I don't really know what I'm doing!" she hissed so the witch wouldn't hear. "It's just happening!"

Oliver reloaded his pistol, careful not to let his gunpowder blow away. "We can't let that smoke get to us or we're done for."

"The smoke disappears when she does," Josephine pointed out.

Both pistols loaded, Oliver aimed and fired one at the witch again. The woman twisted and disappeared as she had done before, reappearing again a split second later.

But it would not be long before they were out of time. The black smoke was forming again. Josephine could not lose Oliver. Another wave of fury surged through her body at that horrifying thought. The scars on her back prickled, her hands heated with magic, and her mind began to relive the moment her father had dissolved into sand. A wail of despair pierced the air and every window in the alley shattered.

OLIVER DROPPED TO HIS KNEES, yanking Josephine down beside him as every window in the vicinity blasted out of its pane. He covered her with his body, but the shards of glass never came close. Instead of showering down on them and shredding them to pieces, they formed a giant swirling ring, like a hurricane; the three of them protected inside the eye. Oliver had only seen Josephine brew this magical storm once before, but he'd not been in the midst of it.

A burst of lightning split the sky overhead and struck the alley, nearly cleaving the witch in two. The blast of white light blinded Oliver for a few seconds while the witch screeched with rage. Blinking a few times to recover his vision, he turned to see that she had managed to avoid the blast with her magical disappearing act and that her hood had fallen away from her face. Two more bolts of lightning came streaking down out of the sky, blinding him again. But not before he saw the witch's face.

No, it can't be her, he thought as he shielded his face with his arm.

The thunder that sounded after each bolt was a deafening roar that shook the ground.

Once the thunder had subsided, another blast sounded in the alley near the witch. It wasn't lightning - it sounded more like a cannon.

Oliver threw his body over Josephine's once more as smoke and stone exploded in every direction. The witch bellowed in outrage. Two more of the cannon-booms reverberated through the alley. Oliver protected his face and Josephine's vulnerable form as debris shot into the air and showered down on them both.

The circle of glass converged on the witch, growing smaller and smaller, leaving Oliver and Josephine on the outer rim of the funnel. The witch was furious, cursing loudly and attempting to conjure, only to be thwarted again and again by the mayhem around her.

"*This is not over!*" she shrieked. With a whirl, the witch was gone from the alley.

Oliver drew his pistol again and surveyed their surroundings. The lightning stopped when the witch departed, but the glass still swirled menacingly. He ached to go after the witch, but protecting Josephine was more important.

"Jo," he spoke to her softly, giving her shoulder a shake. She was still on her knees, arms crossed protectively over her chest, and eyes closed tightly. Oliver cupped her face in his hands and attempted to break whatever spell she was under. "Angelfish, it's over. She's gone."

Josephine didn't hear him.

The sound of light footsteps running toward them had Oliver on high alert once more. Cocking the hammer back on his pistol, Oliver stood protectively in front of Josephine to meet whoever was coming, witch or not.

"Oliver!"

The familiar French accent nearly sent him to his knees.

"Genny?"

Striding toward them, Genevieve had never looked so put together. Not a silvery white hair out of place or a speck of dirt on her clothes or skin. She wore one of her French gowns and a deep purple, velvet cloak.

"How did you ...? How in the bloody blazes ...?" he stammered, latching onto her arm as though she might not be real. "We thought you were dead, Genny!"

"I am so truly sorry, Oliver. It was necessary to hide myself. I've been tracking that horrible woman …" She tsked and then knelt down beside Josephine.

"Genny, it's me who should be sorry about everything." Oliver crouched down next to her, wiping a hand down his tired face.

Genny's brows knitted together. "Whatever for?"

"That woman's name is Tempest. She's the High Witch over this coven here," he pointed to his building. "I thought I recognized her voice, but I got a look at her face. She's been protecting my flat with protective charms for years." Oliver ran a hand through his hair and swore under his breath. "And I sent her to you with a message, not knowing …"

Genny placed a hand on his shoulder, though it did nothing to comfort him.

"She is a powerful witch, but so am I, *mon ami*." Genny scrunched up her nose in disgust. "I could smell her coming a mile away. Stupid woman," she spat. She ran her hands over Josephine's windblown tresses. "Josephine, where have you gone?"

Josephine remained frozen in place.

Oliver eyed Genny curiously. "What do you mean 'gone'?"

"I think her power was too much for her tonight," she explained. "She has retreated inside her own mind. Perhaps I will put her to sleep? Allow her mind to rest?"

Oliver nodded, knowing that Genny was asking for his permission before touching his Jo. She placed a gentle hand on Josephine's back and muttered a few indistinguishable words. Josephine relaxed into Oliver's embrace. The wind ceased immediately and the splinters of glass splashed to the ground.

"We shall take her someplace safe." A bit louder, Genny called out, "And the dear boy who is hiding may also come out, *oui*?"

Oliver tensed as Nathaniel Runik stepped out of the dark, his boots crunching on the glass. If Oliver hadn't been busy cradling Josephine in his arms, he would have stood to challenge him.

What is that hunter doing here? Oliver thought.

"Did she faint?" asked Runik.

Perhaps Oliver *should* give him a good beating. "Of course not, you pompous swine. She ain't the type to swoon."

"So she told me," Runik huffed.

"Gentlemen," Genny interrupted. "It is clear that, for the moment, we are all on the same side, *oui*? Those explosions, those were your doing?" she asked Runik.

Runik nodded.

"What were you doing here in the first place?" Oliver asked. "Coming back to kill Jo now that she ain't in your service?"

A guilty look flashed across Runik's face, but it was gone a second later, replaced by an icy glare.

"Actually, Mr. Blakely, I was witch-hunting." Runik brushed the dust from his black jacket and tugged on his gloves out of habit. "After you two renegades left my estate, I thought I would see for myself if Miss Teversin's information was accurate. And it was lucky for you both that I arrived when I did." He turned to Genny. "You are also a witch?"

"*Oui*, but I am a good witch."

Genny winked at Runik, but the hunter's lip curled in response. Oliver could only chuckle at the exchange.

Genny shook her finger at Runik. "That woman is a very powerful witch. And evil. And *stupid*."

"Aye," Oliver cut in. "And you'll not be killing Genny neither, is that clear? And just how did you manage to find us anyway?"

Runik cleared his throat nervously and pulled a hemp cord out of his cravat that he'd been wearing around his neck. A dark medallion hung from the cord.

"Oh, you wicked, *wicked* man!" Genny rushed to him and held the smooth black stone in her palm.

"What is that, Genny?" Oliver asked, still holding a sleeping Josephine across his lap.

"It's an onyx crystal," she answered. "Hunters have been *stealing* these from us for years."

"I beg your pardon," Nathaniel choked. "Mr. Skulthorpe gave this medallion to me."

"*Oui*, but where did *he* get it from, *monsieur*?" she inquired, raising an eyebrow at him. "These are made by witches to give to pirates we create. The onyx gives us a bond. The pirate would be able to find their creator no matter where she goes. If there was a need, of course. Not all witches do this … but this one," she fingered the crystal. "This one belonged to me before that evil hag tampered with the spell I placed upon it."

Genny looked down at Josephine sadly, then back to Runik. "I can sense that you are angry about wearing a pirate's onyx, but I must insist you continue to do so. It will warn you if that witch is near."

"And what if that medallion starts to hum and it ain't that witch?" Oliver asked, concerned. "What if it's you instead of Tempest?"

"*Non*, he would know it was me." She turned to Runik. "It feels different when I am near, is this not so?"

"It is only warm to the touch now that it is only you near," Runik admitted, though it seemed to gall him to do so.

"There you have it," she said with a flippant wave of her hand. "The onyx recognizes me. You are welcome, my dear boy!"

Oliver smirked at Runik's discomfort.

"Why don't you do us all a bloody favor and hunt Tempest down before she finishes Josephine for good?" Oliver said to Runik. "Then we can all get on with our lives."

Furrowing his eyebrows, Runik asked, "Tempest?"

"That's the witch's name," Oliver explained. "She's the High Witch of this coven here." He nodded in the direction of the building Nathaniel had come from.

"And you were living under the same roof as a full coven? That was foolish."

"The three of us were safe enough until you and that Skulthorpe showed up in town!" Oliver barked back.

"Gentlemen, please!" Genny interrupted. "This is not the time. We must leave before that woman returns. We should get some rest and then we will be able to discuss this intelligently, *oui*?"

"The safest place for Miss Teversin would be the Skulthorpe estate," Runik suggested.

Oliver lifted Josephine in his arms effortlessly. "I don't think so. I didn't trust you before, and I still don't trust you. I ain't putting her straight into the jaws of them redcoats and hunters."

Without waiting for an argument, Oliver turned on his heel and walked away from the alley and Nathaniel Runik.

TWENTY-SEVEN

Over an hour had passed since they'd parted ways in the alley. Nathaniel Runik returned to his home to pretend as if nothing out of the ordinary had happened. Oliver and Genevieve took Josephine to Captain Culligan's townhome near the docks so that she would be near the healing water if and when she needed it.

Genny pursed her lips when she saw the state of Culligan's townhouse. Before allowing Oliver to carry Josephine up to a guest room, Genny swept through every room of the house, casting charms and spells to cleanse the place of dust and cobwebs.

"Blimey," Culligan muttered. He glanced around at his now-spotless townhouse with wide, disbelieving eyes.

"The benefits of being a witch, *oui*?" Genny said with a clever grin.

Oliver made Josephine comfortable in a bedroom on the second floor, furthest from the front door. The room was no bigger than Josephine's had been at the Kraken's Lookout. A wardrobe, one small oak chair, and a bed barely wide enough for two people were the only furnishings.

Oliver tucked Josephine under the covers and dragged the wooden chair closer to sit beside her. He wasn't leaving her alone for a second.

Genny strolled into the tiny room an hour later. "Oliver, you should get some rest. Once Josephine comes out of her sleep, we can decide what's to be done."

"I've a good mind to take her away from Charlestown while she's sleeping and can't argue with me."

"*Oui*, she has a mind of her own, that one," she said with a wink. "Just one of the reasons why you love her."

Oliver held Josephine's hand in his and stroked her soft skin with his calloused fingers. *What am I going to do with you, Angelfish?*

Josephine's nineteenth birthday was coming soon, in just a few months. Every morning, Oliver woke with the fear that Josephine had dissolved into sand while she slept because she was living on land. Perhaps that particular immortal pirate law did not apply to her because she was only half a pirate. And what was Josephine's other half? The weather-changing magic she possessed was a sure sign that she was quite a bit *more* than just a pirate. She had powers that Joseph hadn't wielded. The identity of Josephine's mother remained a mystery to everyone except Joseph, who had taken it to his grave. The dreaded unknown was a curse.

Then there was that Runik fellow. Oliver ran his hands over his tousled hair and muttered a curse.

Oliver peered at Genny out of the corner of his eye. She was standing at the foot of the bed, gazing down at Josephine with motherly love in her eyes.

"I still think you should've kept quiet about where we was going," Oliver said. "I don't trust that Runik bloke. He's as slippery as an eel. He might've run back to Skulthorpe and given him our whereabouts."

Genny tsked him. "You must have some faith, dear boy. He would not have helped us if he was not wavering a bit in his loyalty to that horrible man." She padded around to the opposite side of the bed from Oliver and sat down on the edge of the mattress. "Besides, *mon ami*, I put a charm around the building to warn me if anyone comes near. Friend or foe."

"I still can't believe you're alive," Oliver said with a sigh. "Josephine has been beside herself for days over you."

Genny smiled reassuringly. "I am not so easy to kill. But that stupid woman will know that I am alive now, so we must be cautious."

Oliver scowled, thinking about Tempest and her betrayal. Was Tempest somehow connected to the witch who was employed by Skulthorpe? His next thought made his stomach sink. "You don't think …"

"Think what? What is it, Oliver?"

Oliver wiped a hand down his face. "Could Tempest be the same witch that's working for Skulthorpe? Do you think she's disguised herself and slipped in among those hunters?"

"It is possible," Genny replied. "The woman would not need a disguise. Josephine has never met Tempest, *oui*?"

"No, she hasn't. And I find it hard to believe there's more than one witch causing so much destruction in town."

The thought of his Josephine being in danger turned his stomach, but it also reminded him of something he'd been curious about. "Tell me, Genny, why you looked so sad when you saw that black stone. You looked at Jo like you were grieving."

"That onyx belonged to Josephine's father. I gave it to him when I changed him. I know that for certain." She stood and began to pace the floor. "That is how they found Josephine."

"Blimey, you're right," Oliver mumbled. "They had the means to track you and found Jo as well. They knew you'd be together. Blast!"

Oliver continued to caress Josephine's hand with his fingers, studying her in the candlelight. The onyx troubled him. What rightfully belonged to Josephine had been used against her. All of Joseph's valuables should have been given to his daughter, his heir, *before* he'd turned himself over to the hunters. Joseph would have given it to Oliver or another member of the crew to deliver to her. Her father never would have allowed the hunters a chance to steal something so valuable or dangerous to her.

Oliver murmured to himself, "How did Runik wind up with the onyx?"

NATHANIEL WOKE with the dawn not knowing what awaited him at Skulthorpe's estate. He donned his black attire and white cravat. *You must appear as if nothing out of the ordinary has happened,* the French woman had said to him. Nathaniel sniffed haughtily at the memory. As if a hunter, a professional spy for the British Crown, did not know how to play his part. He did not need advice from a witch.

Descending from the carriage at the Skulthorpe estate, Nathaniel fingered the onyx he had hidden under his shirt and silently cursed. He ought to take the thing off and send it to the bottom of the river. For three years, Nathaniel had clung to his hatred of the Pirate of Blacktail Cove. How could he doubt his employer - a fellow hunter - and trust the daughter of a murderer?

The sound of his boot heels clicking on the marble floors echoed through the empty hall. At this time of morning, only Barnaby would be at the mansion. Nathaniel was always the first hunter to arrive to make sure things were in order. Following his routine to the letter, he marched toward the entrance of Headquarters, gave the golden statue a tug, and descended the staircase.

Barnaby was at work in his lab, of course. Having never seen him leave, Nathaniel was quite certain the man must sleep here in this dungeon. It was dreadful to even think it, but perhaps he enjoyed the solitude of Headquarters.

Barnaby went on with his work without lifting his head to acknowledge Nathaniel's arrival. He knew Nathaniel had no use for customary greetings or small talk. Finishing his work was his first priority. Striding over to the table, Nathaniel watched the man tamper with some new device, twisting and tweaking what looked to be spectacles for reading.

"I designed these to allow you to see in the dark," Barnaby explained without even making eye contact. He lifted the specs and turned them this way and that for Nathaniel to get a good look. "See how the lenses are tinted? See for yourself, Mr. Runik."

Handling them gingerly, lest they break, Nathaniel held them up to the light to inspect them. It was a ridiculous idea, but Barnaby was always coming up with unusual ideas that turned out to be brilliant.

The tiny pistol he'd named 'napshot' was one in particular that had come in handy when he wanted to stun instead of kill.

Barnaby snuffed out the candles one by one until the room went black, and Nathaniel placed the spectacles on his face.

"Well?" Barnaby inquired.

"Marvelous," Nathaniel murmured, not quite able to believe he could actually see. "Everything is clear. I know that it is quite dark, but I can still see everything perfectly."

"Excellent." The gifted scientist shuffled around to light the candles once more. "There are two pairs of them. One for you and one for Miss Teversin."

It took a moment for Nathaniel to grasp what the man had just said. "I beg your pardon?"

"These are for the next assignment. Mr. Skulthorpe himself conscripted these; not that it was so difficult to work up. But now that we know that Miss Teversin has come to no harm, her duties will continue accordingly."

Barnaby sidled over to the lab table and began to tinker with some other contraption, leaving Nathaniel with a sinking feeling in his gut. Carefully returning the spectacles to the table, he exited Headquarters and made his way to the study, where he would meet with Mr. Skulthorpe for updates and assignments.

The study was quiet when he arrived, but there was already a tray of scones, biscuits, and tea set out for them. Nathaniel circled the room and stood by the window, hands clasped behind his back, as if nothing were amiss at all. Skulthorpe would expect him to know that Josephine was perhaps grieving for her aunt the day she was supposedly missing, but alive all the same. It had been Nathaniel's responsibility to see to her behavior and safety at the soiree, so Skulthorpe would have expected Nathaniel to see her home. That also meant Josephine would have been in the tavern as the fire started.

Perhaps the witch was working alone and Skulthorpe knew nothing about the Kraken's Lookout being destroyed. How did that explain the fire at Sturch Manor? If what Josephine had revealed to him was true, Skulthorpe had planned the fire at Sturch Manor. What was his employer's purpose in that? To cause chaos? To incite more colonials to rise up in rebellion? Nathaniel leaned toward the latter. But what of Josephine's accusation that he was consorting with Patriots who had been declared enemies of the Crown?

Nathaniel heaved a sigh of frustration. There were more questions than answers, and before he could even begin to sort through them all, Garreck Skulthorpe appeared at the entrance to the study.

"Runik!" he announced upon his entry.

He plopped down on the settee as one of the young maids walked in to pour their tea. She then curtsied and scurried out.

"What a couple of days it has been," Skulthorpe said after the maid was gone. He picked up the teacup and took a sip.

Mr. Skulthorpe looked like a British officer in his bright red jacket and white waistcoat underneath. It made Nathaniel long for the days of regular army life back in England, when things were less complicated. If he had stayed, he would have been promoted to Captain by now.

"Did Mr. Barnaby show you his newest invention?"

Nathaniel sat down across from him and added two sugar cubes to his own cup of tea. "Of course. They are excellent."

"I thought so," Skulthorpe chuckled while smearing some jam on a biscuit from the tray. After swallowing a mouthful, he got right to the point. "Your new assignment will be in one week's time. There is to be a masquerade ball to be held at the Willow Stone Place. And as you know, Alden Howard and his father, Jasper, are said to be in the inner circle of these Patriots here in Charlestown."

Nathaniel's stomach clenched a bit. This masquerade ball would be a grand affair; one that he was not sure Josephine would be ready for in mere days. Anyone who was someone in Charlestown, and other prominent cities as well, would be in attendance. This was likely a cover for the Patriots to all get together under one roof and discuss their agenda. He imagined a few of the names from the list Josephine had procured would be present as well.

Skulthorpe went on without a pause. "Both Jasper and Alden come from good blood in England. One would think they would be staunch Loyalists, but apparently, they've been living in these horrid colonies for too many years. Little do they know, everything they own will be forfeit to the Crown if they continue to support these Patriots."

Still sipping his tea, Nathaniel remained silent while Skulthorpe took his last bite and wiped his fingers on a napkin.

"So, Runik, the plan for you and Miss Teversin is to get close to the Howards - Alden in particular. Secure an invitation to one of these secret meetings and find out about their plans."

Runik sniffed. "I'm sure I could do that without Miss Teversin's presence. Her behavior at the soiree was ... unpredictable."

Skulthorpe eyed him with skepticism. "Did she succeed in her assignment?"

"Yes," he answered quickly. "It is her methods that are troubling." He rolled his eyes at the memory of her attempt at fainting.

"Well, Miss Teversin will not be allowed into the secret society meeting of course, but I have a different assignment for her while you are occupied."

Nathaniel stifled a groan. If the two of them were forced to go to this masquerade, it was certain to be a disaster, especially with a vengeful witch on the loose.

"I have been hearing from different Loyalist groups - some hunters, others strictly civilian - that the Patriots have been planning something. Something public and large-scale that will send a clear message to His Majesty King George. They have not been happy with the taxes that he has imposed on imported tea." He raised his teacup in a mock salute and took a sip. "We have gathered no intelligence as to the nature of this little act of rebellion, but I believe there should be talk of it at the ball. Miss Teversin's assignment will be to discover their plans, using any and all means necessary."

Skulthorpe was watching him sharply, so he set down his empty cup and leaned back as if he hadn't a care in the world. The old Nathaniel, the one who had hated Josephine with a passion, would not have cared if she succeeded or failed her assignment. Putting on his best arrogant expression, Nathaniel replied, "Consider it done."

"Excellent. I will be setting sail to New York as soon as you bring word to my ship. I will expect a full briefing as soon as the ball is finished." He gave Nathaniel a look that brooked no argument.

"As you wish."

"Off you go, then," said Skulthorpe with a more pleasant smile. "You have things to do; pirates to train." He chuckled.

Before Nathaniel could rise from his chair, Skulthorpe held out his hand. "I believe you have the note that the pirate intercepted?"

Reaching into his inside pocket, Nathaniel pulled out a small square of paper. "It was written in cipher, but here is what I decoded."

Never taking his eyes off Skulthorpe as he handed it over, Nathaniel wondered if he hadn't just made a serious error.

TWENTY-EIGHT

J osephine bolted upright in the bed, sputtering and gasping for air. She'd been caught in a terrifying dream of drowning in freezing water. Relief coursed through her when she realized she wasn't trapped beneath the dark water of the ocean after all. She shivered and looked around. Water was dripping from her brown hair and the duvet was cold and wet.

Why am I soaking wet? Josephine wondered, wiping away the water streaming down her face. Josephine glanced around to find Oliver standing beside her bed, holding an empty bucket, his expression a mixture of guilt and relief.

"Stinking, spineless *barnacle!*" She threw one of her damp pillows at him in protest. "Why did you dump water on me?"

Dodging the pillow easily, he knelt down beside the bed and planted a kiss firmly on her lips. "Angelfish! You have no idea what I was going through watching you sleep for so long. I thought it was high time we did something."

"So, you decided *this* was the best way to wake me up?" She gestured to the empty bucket.

Oliver scratched the back of his neck. "Well, I …"

He didn't get a chance to explain because the door swung open and Aunt Genny sauntered inside. Josephine's jaw dropped open.

"Is she awake?" Genny inquired. Once she had gotten a good look at Josephine, she turned her exasperated face to Oliver. "I told you not to do it that way. She is not a fish!"

"Your way didn't sound like it was gonna work, so I improvised a bit. And it worked, didn't it? She's awake now, ain't she?"

"I told you to put the water on a cloth and dab her face," Genny replied. "Not dump it over her head. She looks like a drowned kitten!"

"Aunt Genny?" Josephine gasped. Jumping up from the bed, she raced across the room, and flung her arms around Genny's neck in a fierce embrace. Tears welled up in Josephine's eyes. "I thought you were dead. The tavern ... the *fire!*"

Despite Josephine's wet clothes, Genny held her close. "My darling girl. That witch will not get the best of me." Once Josephine had released her, Genny quirked her eyebrow at Oliver. "You did not tell her I was alive?" She shook her head and muttered something in French.

Oliver shrugged. "You barged in before I had the chance."

Josephine couldn't take her eyes off Genny. The woman's silvery-blonde hair was pinned on top of her head and she was wearing a dark blue dress with black trim. The dress was a darker color than Josephine had ever seen Genny wear before, but nothing else about her was out of place. A lump formed in Josephine's throat. She'd never been so happy and relieved to see her guardian.

"Everything is all right now, darling." Genny squeezed Josephine's hand and patted her wet cheek.

Josephine glanced around the unfamiliar room. "Where are we, by the way?"

"Captain Cully's place," Oliver answered.

She glanced between Oliver and Genny and rubbed her forehead. "What happened? The last thing I remember was the lightning ... and feeling Oliver next to me. Then everything went dark. I could hear Skulthorpe laughing." Josephine closed her eyes and swallowed the lump in her throat. "After that, it was quiet and I was alone in the dark."

"You have lots of questions, I am certain. But let us find you something to eat and some dry clothes first, *oui?* And perhaps we take a walk down to the river. You need to regain your strength."

"My strength?" Josephine asked. "I'm in a bit of shock over you being alive, but I feel right as rain."

Oliver stepped up behind Josephine. "You used a lot of your magic last night."

Josephine's brows pinched together and she placed a hand over her aching belly. Now that he'd mentioned it, her body was a bit shaky and weak, but she'd thought it was from hunger. Panic began to take hold and her heart beat faster, knowing that her powers had been completely out of control again last night.

Genny drew Josephine into her arms again. "Do not be afraid."

"I could have killed you or Oliver," Josephine choked.

"I doubt your magic would let you do that," said Oliver. "It was protecting you from Tempest. Protecting *both* of us. With help from Genny and that Runik bloke, we made it out all right."

Josephine pulled away from Genny and gaped at Oliver. "Tempest? And *Mr. Runik?*"

"There is much to tell you," Genny said with a doting smile. "But first, we take care of *you*."

———

JOSEPHINE AND GENNY strolled north down the cobblestone street by the wharf. They'd left Oliver and Culligan behind, much to Oliver's dismay. He hadn't wanted to let Josephine out of his sight, but Genny insisted she would protect them both.

Schooners and brigs had been tied to the docks. Sailors strode purposefully on the decks of each ship, cleaning or making repairs, while other men delivered their imports to warehouses along the bay street. The sailors and merchants shouted out orders and crude remarks to each other amidst the cries of seagulls that circled the masts of each ship. The eastern wind brought with it the smell of seawater and fish; a scent that Josephine had always embraced. Further out in the Cooper River, ships had either dropped their sails and anchors to await their turn to dock or their white sails had been unfurled to head downriver to the Atlantic.

No one took notice as the two women in cloaks passed by the docks. They continued north along the coast until they'd left the hustle and bustle of the wharfs behind. Genny led the way to a cove that was a few miles north of Captain Culligan's docking area.

A small wooden dock had been built, extending out into the cove, probably for fishermen. Two small rowboats had been tied to the end of the wooden walkway. Reeds and cattails lined the shores of the inlet. Ducks swam aimlessly across the smooth water, quacking to each other and, every once in a while, dipping their smooth heads beneath the water to capture fish for their dinner.

These smaller inlets of water were popular with men and children who knew how to swim. There was less risk of being swept out to sea by the river's powerful current, and the larger ships did not sail into these shallower regions. Today, however, no one was swimming. During the month of October, the water was much too cold for most. But not Josephine.

"Do you expect me to swim naked?" Josephine whispered to Genny, blushing to her roots.

"Darling girl, just swim in your shirt. There is no one here to see."

Josephine took one last nervous glance around the isolated cove and then took off her black cloak. She stripped down to the tunic Oliver had loaned her and sat down on the edge of the dock, dangling her legs over the side. Her toes skimmed the surface of the water, sending a chill up her body.

Genny sat down beside her, tucking her legs and skirts beneath her. "Is it too cold?"

"It's a bit chilly, but the water will feel quite warm once I jump in," Josephine assured her. The ability to manage her own body temperature while swimming in the ocean was just another oddity that she had discovered by accident.

While sailing across the Atlantic several years back, Josephine had been careless climbing the ratlines up to the masts. She'd never had any difficulty climbing the rigging, but that chilly February day had been particularly windy. The brig was cruising through the choppy waters and suddenly pitched. It was not out of the ordinary for a ship to tilt so far or so swiftly, but it had taken Josephine by surprise. With the help of an ill-timed gust of wind, Josephine lost her grip on the ropes and fell twenty feet down into the water.

Terror had coursed through Josephine as she hit the freezing water. People drowned out at sea because they were pulled under by the crushing waves or died of frostbite. She kicked frantically for the surface, hoping that someone had noticed her fall. The *Nepheria* was at full canvas, moving a little faster than full-speed - aided by her father's pirate magic. The ship would be long gone in a matter of seconds.

Her head broke the surface just as another wave crashed over her, dragging her under again before she could draw a breath. Submerged beneath the waves once more, Josephine suddenly realized that the water was not as cold as it should have been. At first, she believed it was her own fear and adrenaline that was numbing her senses, but another few seconds passed and Josephine still felt no chill. Either the seawater, or her own body, had warmed to a comfortable temperature, protecting her flesh. So enthralled with this new phenomenon, Josephine almost hadn't registered that her lungs had stopped burning with the need for more air. In fact, she was having no trouble breathing. It was as if she had gills like a fish.

The peculiar moment had ended too soon. An unnatural current of water began pulling her toward the surface and her father's ship, which had dropped canvas two hundred feet away from her. Like a cannonball exploding out of a cannon, the strange force shot Josephine up out of the water and through the air. She landed on the unforgiving deck with a thud, water splashing down around her.

Once Josephine was safely onboard, she'd had the inexplicable urge to giggle, but she choked it back when she caught sight of her father. He and Oliver hadn't been amused by any of it. Their faces were stark white with fear as they sprinted toward her. Her father had, of course, felt her distress in his soul and ordered the crew to halt the ship at once. He'd hugged her, blistered her ears for her carelessness, and then locked her down in his own quarters for two days. When Josephine had asked her father later if his magic had forced her out of the water, he had merely pinched his lips together and shook his head.

A fish splashing at the surface of the river startled Josephine back to the present. Tamping down the sorrow that had crept up on her, she peered at Genny out of the corner of her eye.

"Aunt Genny, does it seem odd to you that I have magic above and beyond that of a pirate?"

"You are one of a kind, darling. Extraordinary. Look at all the things you can do."

"I can't control my powers. I nearly killed a couple of redcoats at Skulthorpe's mansion. I'm going to end up hurting someone."

"Impossible. You will learn," Genny said confidently. "It is in your blood."

"I wish I understood why my magic is so different to Father's."

Genny looked at her thoughtfully. "I imagine that bit of magic is inherited from your mother."

Josephine lowered her eyes and tucked her hair behind her ears. "I suppose Father didn't tell you about her?"

Genny shook her head. "He was secretive about the whole affair."

"Secretive?" Josephine gasped. "Was he with a married woman?"

"Of course not, darling. He was much too honorable for that." She wagged her finger at Josephine. "I do know that much."

I wish I knew more about her, Josephine thought.

Her heart twisted into a painful knot. It was difficult to decide if the ache in her chest was due to grief or a craving for the water. The tethers connecting her to the sea grew taut and she could wait no longer. Pushing off the dock, she slipped into the water.

As soon as Josephine plunged beneath the surface, the water warmed around her flesh, just as she'd expected. Relief from the knot in her chest was immediate and the hollow ache in her stomach disappeared. Immortal pirates had always depended on the ocean for their healing - physically, and in Josephine's case, emotionally. Josephine's other magical tricks were something else entirely. Her father had never been able to breathe underwater or cause a hurricane with his tears. Whatever magic Josephine possessed had not come from her father alone.

The small inlet of river water was not as clear as some of the coves she had seen in the Caribbean, but it would do. Josephine swam deeper. The riverbed was only thirty feet beneath the surface and was covered by smooth, round stones. Sunlight shone through the blue-green water and schools of silvery-gray fish swam in circles, unperturbed by Josephine's presence.

After swimming around the cove a few times, Josephine kicked for the surface again. She expected to feel that magical force shooting her out of the water like last time, but nothing happened. Had it only appeared because she had been out in open water or because of the imminent threat to her safety? Josephine suspected the latter.

Her head broke the surface to find Genny smiling down at her.

"Feeling better?"

"Much," Josephine agreed. She swam to the dock and climbed out, feeling whole again. Water spilled from her hair and shirt, creating a puddle beneath her. "Do you remember the first time you took me swimming? You thought I was drowning!" she said, snickering.

Genny slapped her hands on her tiny waist. "You gave me a fright, you reckless scamp! You stayed under that water for several minutes without coming up for breath. What was I to think?"

Josephine stifled another round of giggles, watching her Aunt Genny huffing and gesturing wildly. Her French accent grew thicker the more exasperated she became.

"I promised Joseph that I would see you safe," she muttered. "What would he say if I let you drown in the first few months?"

Josephine grinned. Once she'd wrung the excess water out of her hair, she struggled back into her trousers and boots, though her skin was still damp.

Genny wrapped the dark cloak around Josephine's shoulders and said, "Let's go and dry your wet hair, darling. You will catch your death."

BACK AT CAPTAIN Culligan's townhouse, Josephine and Genny found Oliver pacing in the foyer, waiting impatiently for them. The moment he set eyes on Josephine, he strode toward her with a gleam in his eyes and swooped in to capture her lips.

Aunt Genny cleared her throat. "I will just be washing up. Don't mind me."

Oliver ended the kiss and rested his forehead against hers. "I've been worried for you, Jo."

"We weren't gone that long, Oliver."

"I felt funny while you were away," he admitted. "Not having you near ... I felt like my insides were reaching for you."

Josephine gulped.

"You feel it too, don't you?" Oliver whispered. "You said something about it back at my flat the other day. Is it ... a blood-bond? Like what I had with Joseph?"

She shook her head, heat flooding her cheeks. "I-I told you, I think this is different."

Oliver linked his fingers with hers and led her into the parlor. The fire was blazing in the hearth. Josephine stepped closer to it to dry her hair and body. While she dragged her fingers through her wet tangles, she noticed the apprehension in Oliver's green eyes.

"Oliver, what's wrong?"

He shuffled his feet and ducked his head. "That bloke, Runik, came to call."

Josephine froze. "What did he want?"

"I hate to be telling you this, since you thought you were free of that spy business."

"Oliver?"

"Skulthorpe knows you're alive and expects you at the estate at noon."

The blood drained from Josephine's face and she dropped onto the settee by the fireplace. "That's in just a few hours."

"Aye. Runik said he wasn't surprised to know it. Said Skulthorpe has spies everywhere, probably watching the both of you."

"Or that stupid woman - that witch - is spying on you," Genny remarked as she entered the parlor carrying another tray of bread, cheese, and tea. "We must think about this, *oui?* How can you show yourself at that place with that witch on the loose?"

Josephine picked up a slice of bread and took a small bite. "But we know who the witch is, don't we?"

"That don't keep her from having a disguise," Oliver pointed out. "Even *I* managed it. She could be anyone at that estate. But that ain't the point, Jo."

"Then what is the point?" she snapped.

Oliver folded his arms over his chest and glared at Josephine. "I ain't gonna let you be dragged back into that mess, Josephine."

Josephine crossed the room and wrapped her arms around Oliver's waist, resting her head on his chest. "I told you I wasn't going to run from him again," she said softly.

Sighing in aggravation, Oliver finally allowed his arms to enfold her and kissed the top of her head. "I don't want you hurt, love. I'm afraid if you go, you'll be falling into a trap, and there'll be no way for me or Genny to be there to help you."

"You wish you could be there?" Josephine said, not quite a question.

"Aye."

She pulled back and looked up at Oliver, beaming. "I have a brilliant idea, then."

TWENTY-NINE

Mr. Runik collected Josephine a block away from Culligan's townhouse at eleven o'clock sharp. Josephine had been forced to wear one of Genny's new ready-made dresses, since both of their wardrobes had been destroyed. Genny had a few more curves than Josephine, so she spent the entire ride fidgeting and yanking on her dress to keep it in place.

"Can you not sit still?" Runik complained.

Josephine glared at him, "Don't start. I was poor before you coerced me into Skulthorpe's service. Now that the tavern's gone, I am completely destitute. It was this gown or filthy boys' clothes."

The neckline was even lower than the gowns she'd worn at Skulthorpe's estate, so Josephine had wrapped a thin shawl around her shoulders and across the neckline to cover herself. The material was a bright pink velvet. She'd seen many wealthy women wearing bright colors like this in Charlestown, but it was not a color that Josephine fancied for herself.

She squirmed again, readjusting her corset. "And I think one of my daggers is jabbing me. I'll likely be dead in an hour from slowly bleeding to death. Will you be so kind as to apologize to my Aunt

Genny for ruining her dress? And I won't be able to attend the masquerade, either. You'll have to soldier on without me."

Runik rolled his eyes at her overly dramatic remarks. "How many daggers do you have hidden under that dress?"

"Enough," she said. "You're lucky Oliver didn't force me to carry a sword. That would have been a lovely addition to this velvet, don't you agree?"

Runik's jaw was clenched tight, but she didn't care. She wanted to annoy him so much that he would flee the estate as soon as he dropped her at the front steps.

When she saw her three tutors in Skulthorpe's ballroom, she broke into a wide smile.

"Oh, Josephine!" Beau strode over and drew her into a tight hug. "Oh, we thought you were …" He pinched his lips together and couldn't finish his sentence. "So silly of me, I know," he held her at arm's length and grinned. "You are made of sterner stuff than those ruffians think!"

"Beau, really!" Sophia scolded. "Do not say 'ruffians'." She turned her stern gaze on Josephine and Mr. Runik. "We are certainly relieved that it was only a misunderstanding."

Josephine nodded. "Of course."

Eleanor approached and began leading her away from Runik. "We're ever so glad you're safe, Josephine. We were worried sick."

Beau sidled up to her other side. "It has been dead boring here without you, my girl. And what on earth are you wearing?" His narrowed eyes traveled down to her petticoats and back up to the shawl crossed over her chest. "That's something … isn't it?"

"We really must do something about this gown," Eleanor added.

Josephine grinned. "Yes, please. It's not my gown. Just a loan."

Beau nodded. "Of course. I knew you had better taste than this."

They continued to escort her down to Headquarters, talking all the while. Runik was gone, and Josephine was all alone again. Sophia's demeanor made Josephine nervous, but she always had a stern way about her. That did not mean that she was an evil witch.

Beau and Eleanor exchanged Genny's ill-fitting gown for one much more to Josephine's liking. It was a soft yellow with white trim around the neckline and sleeves.

Back in the ballroom, Josephine was practicing her dances relentlessly with Beau as her partner when Nathaniel Runik walked in once more and sat down to watch. No one seemed to care that he was present. But Josephine relaxed at the sight of him.

"Do you think I could rest my feet a bit before we start the next reel?" Josephine suggested to Madame Sophia.

Sophia sniffed. "I don't suppose there's any harm. Beau, do we have any refreshments?"

"What kind of question is that?" His jovial voice echoed through the room.

Taking advantage of the distraction, Josephine hurried over and sat down next to Runik.

"Well?" she inquired.

"It's me, Angelfish."

"Blimey," she whispered. "That's incredible, Oliver."

Aunt Genny had done it. She'd created a glamour that allowed Oliver to disguise himself as Mr. Runik. Now, he could walk freely throughout the estate without questions being raised. The only difference Josephine could see was the warmth in *this* Mr. Runik's steel-gray eyes.

"You must look at me more coldly," she reminded him. "Runik believes my father murdered his father. Remember?"

"Aye," he agreed. "How's this?" He glared daggers at her, which sent a chill up her spine.

"Um, yes, that's ... quite good," she stammered. "The real Runik should be back again by four o'clock, so just make sure you are well away before then or someone may notice."

"Don't you worry about me, love." He was looking at her warmly again. "Just don't go kissing him when it's not me, eh?"

Josephine let out a nervous giggle. "Of course not." The way Nathaniel Runik's face was eyeing her sent butterflies fluttering through her stomach.

"Aye, well, you better get back," he said. "Eleanor and Sophia are watching us closely. I'd wager anything it's one of them two."

"It doesn't have to be any one of them," Josephine scolded. "Don't be so judgmental."

"Go on, Jo. I'll be waiting at Cully's."

When Josephine rejoined the trio, Eleanor nodded her head toward Mr. Runik.

"It's odd that he's watching your training today," she remarked, sipping some tea.

Luckily, Josephine had prepared her lies ahead of time. "He's worried I'm going to make a fool of myself at the ball." This was not altogether untrue.

Beau and Eleanor chuckled, but Sophia's somber expression never changed.

"And why would he think such a thing?" Beau asked her.

Josephine proceeded to tell them the events of the soiree, leaving Oliver out completely. No one needed to know how she had actually escaped the flames.

She had Beau in stitches by the time she was done.

"Stop!" he exclaimed, holding his middle to keep from doubling over with laughter. "No, you didn't, Josephine! You actually pretended to faint?" He guffawed loudly, sending Josephine and Eleanor into smothered giggles as well.

"Sophia, we simply must teach this girl how to faint properly if she is going to use it on assignments," he chuckled, gently nudging her with his elbow.

Sophia pursed her lips. "It would be best if you stayed on two feet."

After Beau had calmed down, they proceeded to learn a new but popular reel that Josephine would be expected to know at the Howard's ball next weekend. Then they instructed her on social etiquette at a more formal dinner.

An hour later, Runik - the real Runik - stepped back into the ballroom and decreed it time to be on their way. Oliver had slipped out before they had finished their dancing, when the trio would be less likely to notice his absence.

Their deception was going to be tricky, keeping the real Nathaniel Runik in the dark and keeping anyone else from finding out about Oliver. But it was worth it to have someone she trusted close by this week. Josephine was nervous enough as it was with the masquerade happening so soon.

While riding back to the tavern, Nathaniel revealed her specific assignment.

"Discover what the Sons of Liberty are up to next ... by any and all means necessary?" Josephine sputtered. "What does that mean? How in heaven's name am I going to get that kind of information? This is not going to be as easy as fainting and picking someone's pocket."

Runik did not seem bothered at all by her impossible mission. He was completely relaxed, thoughtfully rubbing the dark scruff on his chin and gazing out the window.

"Do you realize the man you fainted on was Alden Howard himself? We will have to make sure he does not recognize you. I would not think he would accuse a woman of meddling in secret operations, but if he does realize it was you who stole his note, it will be a problem." After a pause, Runik finally looked up to meet her eyes. "Stop worrying. We'll come up with a plan. Remember your training. You will have a few of Barnaby's devices at your disposal as well. You will not be without resources."

"Resources," Josephine murmured to herself. An idea began to form inside her mind. Perhaps it was time to dig up those old prototypes that Captain Culligan was hiding in his warehouse. "Speaking of resources, Mr. Runik," she said in a more polite tone. "Did your medallion indicate anything today?"

"It buzzed frequently at the estate, but unfortunately, I could not pinpoint who the witch might be without being obvious about it."

"Pity," she said.

Runik's eyes dropped to Josephine's dress. "What do you plan to wear tomorrow?"

"I don't have anything else. Perhaps I could get an advance on my wages? Unless you would like me to wear this ... um ..." She gestured to her ill-fitting gown.

"Offensive gown? I believe those are the words you were looking for."

"No need to be rude about it," she replied. "This dress suits Aunt Genny's tastes just fine."

Mr. Runik sniffed, but reached into his pocket to produce some coins.

"Thank you ... Mr. Runik," she said graciously.

She had almost called him by his first name, which would have been improper. Josephine had been thinking of him as Nathaniel since she'd discovered the truth about him and his father. But they were not friends. There was no trust between them, at least not yet. And if Runik ever found out the truth about his father's untimely death, then there certainly never would be.

THIRTY

The week passed by without a hitch. Oliver had used his new disguise to freely enter the estate every day. The trio kept on in their usual manner, and the day before the masquerade, Josephine was wound tighter than a main sail. It was time to put her plan into action for the night of the ball. And it started with Beau.

After training was done for the day, Josephine cornered Beau in the dressing room out of earshot of Eleanor and Sophia. Oliver was still not convinced of the tutors' innocence, but Josephine had already decided that Beau was trustworthy and the perfect man for the job. Despite Runik's opinion, Josephine thought Beau would make an excellent operative.

Beau looked up and gave her an encouraging smile when she approached. "Everything will be alright, my dear. Do you believe that?"

"Yes," she said, returning his smile. "I believe it will. And I promise I won't try to faint again."

Beau chortled. "You will be marvelous." Grasping both her hands in his, he added, "I hope you know that I have enjoyed every moment of training you. And you undoubtedly will be the most gorgeous lady at the ball."

Her smile widened. "From that first day Beau, I have truly felt like we have been fast friends," she admitted. "Do you believe everything happens for a reason?"

"Absolutely." He kissed her knuckles.

"Then, as a friend, I need to ask you for an enormous favor," she pleaded. "I need your help."

Beau squeezed her hands. "I'm at your service."

Josephine lowered her voice and asked, "Do you think you can get into the masquerade on Saturday?"

Beau looked around like a sneak thief to see if anyone was eavesdropping. Pulling her close, he whispered, "Without a doubt. Tell me the plan!"

OLIVER HELD on to Josephine's hand a bit tighter that night as they walked the streets to Cully's warehouse. Josephine wanted to take a closer look at the prototypes that Joseph had risked his life for, and Cully suggested they meet him after his office had closed for the evening.

She was dressed in some of Oliver's clothes, but was covered from shoulders to boots with a cloak Genny had loaned her. Her hair was pulled back in a long braid and hidden under the collar of her tunic. All Oliver wanted to do was hold Josephine close. He'd been waiting a long time to have the chance, but he felt as if time was slipping away from him somehow. The masquerade the next day was giving him a bad feeling in his gut. Josephine had assured him that everything was quiet at the estate and their plan to disrupt Skulthorpe's assignment was coming together almost perfectly.

That was what bothered him most. The water was always calm just before a storm. But he did not speak his fears aloud to Josephine. He would be there to make sure she made it out safely. She was his only priority. Messages had already been sent to Joseph's old crew to be ready. Captain Culligan had a ship standing by in the harbor for their escape. They could sail anywhere and be out of Skulthorpe's grasp forever.

Cully was waiting for them with a candle just inside the entrance to his shipping company's warehouse. He was still garbed in his fancy waistcoat, breeches, and buckled shoes, but his hair was falling loose from its queue due to the hustle and bustle of the day's goings-on.

"Evening, you two scamps," he grinned in the flickering light.

"Hello, Captain." Josephine smiled and hugged him.

He led them into the darkest corner of the warehouse. The shadows from the dim light danced along the walls, making the place look sinister, as if something or someone might jump out from behind one of the many containers stacked in rows. Oliver kept a hand on the pistol tucked in his belt and an eye on Josephine, who walked ahead of him. The old trap door creaked and sent a cloud of dust into the air as they opened it. The three of them descended the wooden stairs into the dark hole once again.

Josephine ignored the chest with the pistol and went straight to the chest with the lady's garments. "You don't want to carry that wee pistol to the ball?"

"I don't have any darts for it," she replied. "I'd have to rob Barnaby's lab, and even if I did, I wouldn't know where to look. Besides, I have my fan with two darts left."

"What are you looking for then?" Oliver asked her.

Pulling out each of the items one by one, she looked up briefly and replied, "Anything useful. I have a feeling these things are not just ladies' undergarments and accessories. Captain Culligan, you said my father called them prototypes?"

"Aye, he did," Cully nodded.

"I think these may be special devices, like Runik's pistol or my fan. They were meant to do something besides the obvious." She picked up the lady's corset. "Take this, for instance."

They watched Josephine inspect the corset, turning it this way and that, and running her fingers along the material. The strangest thing about it was its color. While corsets tended to be white, this one was black.

"It's much heavier than a normal corset," she muttered.

Oliver chuckled. "We'll take your word for it, love."

"No, really, feel this material," she held out the corset to him, inviting him to touch it.

Josephine was right. It wasn't made with the usual silk or even the cheap cotton often used in the colonies. Could it be …

"Jo, it feels slick. Like … metal." Oliver studied the garment again. "Here, Cully, bring the candle closer. Blimey, it *is* metal. Some bloke shaped this metal into tiny threads and wove them together like cotton. Do you think …?" He didn't want to hope, but Josephine's eyes had already lit up.

"Could it be protection against musket balls?" Josephine was nearly bouncing with excitement. "This is genius! The corset does cover most of the important internal organs."

"I'd like to point out that it don't cover your head or your heart, Jo," Oliver argued.

"A corset covers most of the heart, and even so, that is still seventy-five or eighty percent of my torso protected," she calculated. "If it actually does what we think. Let's test it!"

"Josephine," Cully jumped in. "We can't shoot a pistol down here!"

"Aye," Oliver agreed. "And I ain't shooting nobody, especially you."

"I didn't mean to shoot me," she huffed. "Maybe just throw a dagger at it. If it repels even a dagger being thrown … that's something, too. Right?"

After five minutes of arguing, Josephine finally agreed not to wear the corset for this test throw. The men would simply hold it up like a target on the wall. Josephine was good with daggers, but that did not keep Cully from closing his eyes when Josephine's blade flew toward them. The woosh of the dagger was followed by a ping, as the blade ricocheted off the corset and clattered to the floor. The weave of metal strands held perfectly. There was not even a dent in the corset to mark that it had been hit.

"This is *brilliant!*" Josephine admired. "What else is hiding in here?" She clapped and knelt down next to the chest.

Oliver stood back and grinned as Josephine pulled more garments out. It wasn't wise to come between a pirate and new-found treasure.

———————

JOSEPHINE WAS in better humor after rummaging through the chest. It had been full of interesting devices, and she was convinced a few of them might actually prove to be useful the night of the ball. Even though she had hated corsets in the past, wearing the protective metal corset they'd unearthed would make her feel more secure.

A pair of beautiful gloves from the chest had a spool of retractable cord installed within the material. The strong, flexible cord had been extremely thin and long enough to enable Josephine to climb down from a second story window if need be. They had all been amazed at how the wire was hidden in the very design of the gloves, making it impossible to detect. It would have to be a one-time use, unless there was someone to release the cord, but Josephine could simply take the gloves off and be done with them. It would be a shame to lose them, but at least she wouldn't have to shimmy down a tree in her ball gown.

Along with the pocket watch, her fan, and whatever else Barnaby had designed for her, she would be armed and ready for almost anything. The only item in the chest that could not be identified was a strand of white pearls, though Josephine decided to take them along anyway.

"You ain't wearing them pearls without knowing what they do," Oliver had argued. "What if something sets them off and they strangle you to death?"

He made an excellent argument, so Josephine decided to somehow ask Barnaby about them without being too conspicuous.

"If I don't find out their use, then I simply won't wear them," she had assured Oliver. "But they are lovely, aren't they?"

"You're lovely with or without pearls, Angelfish," he'd said with warmth in his green eyes. It had made her heart race, and for once in her life, she hoped that she would be able to settle down soon. Well, as settled as a ship could be on the open water, of course. She was beginning to envision her future, sailing through the Atlantic again with Oliver by her side. Could she be hoping for too much?

One thing at a time, Josephine. First, she had to get through the masquerade unscathed. After that, she would be free of Skulthorpe and his hunters for good. That was her hope.

"Jo, you need to get some rest." Oliver was lying on his side on top of the bed covers and patting the spot beside him.

They had brought their supplies back to the Captain's townhome. Genny had left the pair a while ago to go to bed. Everything was ready.

Josephine nestled down under the covers while Oliver remained on top of them, as was their habit this week. They refused to stay separated, so this was the bargain they had made with Aunt Genny. She thought it was highly improper for the two of them to sleep together and then mentioned something about weddings. Thinking about being married to Oliver sent chills up and down Josephine's back.

"It will be alright, my Jo," he whispered in her ear from behind her.

"That wasn't why I ..." she started to say.

"That wasn't why what?" Oliver asked.

Josephine's heart pounded. She suddenly didn't want to explain why she'd been shivering. "Never mind."

"We've prepared for the worst," he reassured her. "Genny will be manning the outskirts of the manor, spreading charms and making sure the witch doesn't barge in on the party. You said Beau was on board with your plan, aye?"

"Yes. He said he was," she answered. "And even if he doesn't show, I should be able to accomplish things without him."

"And I'll be there too."

"As Lewis Brown first. Then you'll change into Runik?" She bit down on her lip, trying to shake her nervous jitters. "Are you sure you want to impersonate Runik at the ball?"

"Aye, and stop worrying," he murmured, then placed a soft kiss behind her ear. "I'll be careful, and I won't let nothing happen to you, love."

"I know," she whispered, shivering now in response to his hands in her hair.

"Do you mind me doing this?" he asked, combing his fingers down the length of her hair again and again.

"Not at all." She cleared her throat. "There is something I must say, Oliver."

His hands paused in her hair. "Don't you dare, Jo."

She half turned to look back at him. "I beg your pardon?"

"You're about to say your goodbyes to me and I ain't gonna be hearing them."

"I was not saying goodbye," she huffed. "I was merely going to say that I'm sorry."

"What for?"

"I'm sorry it took me so long to … show you how much I care for you."

Oliver sighed, ruffling her hair a bit with a puff of his breath. "That sounded a lot like goodbye, love. But you're not to feel sorry about nothing. I was the one who kept my distance. I thought you deserved better than the likes of me."

"I've already made it clear what I think of that opinion."

"Aye, you did," he agreed. "But one day, Jo, I promise I'll be good enough for you."

Josephine opened her mouth to argue but Oliver captured her words with a kiss.

"Enough talk," he whispered, tweaking her nose. "Time to sleep. You can argue with me tomorrow."

Josephine nodded and let her eyes fall shut, grateful that Oliver was there with her despite the unpredictable day ahead.

GARRECK SKULTHORPE MET the witch behind the theater, as he always did for his weekly updates on their progress. He had almost grown tired of his game with the little half-pirate and would be well rid of her after the masquerade, along with a few other targets.

"Is everything set for tomorrow night?" Skulthorpe inquired of his witch.

"Of course," she sneered. "None of them suspect anything. Least of all that pirate."

Skulthorpe chuckled. "Cheers." And he turned on his heel and stalked away into the shadows, grinning like a shark who was about to close in on his prey.

THIRTY-ONE

"Just wait until you see it!" Beau said with a mischievous grin. "You are going to absolutely *adore* the costume we've designed for you!" He and Eleanor linked elbows with her, dragging her away from the silent Mr. Runik to conduct the final fitting.

"I thought this was a masquerade?" Josephine asked. "Would I not simply be wearing a mask?"

"Oh, no, dear," Eleanor replied. "Masquerades are costume parties. The idea is to see if you can identify everyone despite their costumes and masks. It's so much fun!"

"And a perfect chance for you to remain anonymous while on your assignment!" mentioned Beau.

When they reached the entrance to the dressing chamber, Beau leapt behind her and covered her eyes with his hands. Eleanor led them the rest of the way into the room.

"Are you ready, Josephine?" Eleanor asked, brimming with excitement.

When Beau lifted his hands from Josephine's eyes, she was stunned speechless. After a moment of staring and pointing at her costume, she stammered, "Am I going as …? Is that …?" Josephine had no words to describe what she was seeing.

"Oh, we hoped you wouldn't mind," Eleanor said, wringing her hands.

Beau stepped up beside Josephine and waved his hand dramatically through the air as if he was presenting her with a showcased piece of art. "We were going for 'Enchanting Villain'. Do you like it?"

"It's perfect!" Josephine smiled, completely overwhelmed. They had designed a masterpiece just for her. She would be going to the masquerade as a pirate.

Beau clapped enthusiastically. "Let's get you dressed! I cannot wait to see you in our *piece de resistance*! You will be splendid."

With that, Eleanor and Beau were scurrying around and stripping her down to her underclothes. Having been so distracted with the costume, Josephine had completely forgotten about her new protective corset. They would have to be blind to miss it, since the undergarment was black as sin.

"Did Barnaby have a corset made for you?" Eleanor asked at once. "I remember him talking about one he'd made before but it was lost many years ago." She fingered the slick metal material with her finger. "Would we not have known about a new one, Beau?"

Josephine stared at her own reflection in the mirror, fighting to keep her composure. This was an amateur mistake on her part, having not thought up an excuse for it.

Beau never faltered. "Mr. Runik retrieved it from Barnaby himself a few nights ago, I believe." He winked at Josephine once Eleanor's back was turned. Josephine smiled her appreciation but her insides froze over. Why was Beau lying to Eleanor for her? Regardless, she was grateful for his intervention. The trust she had placed in him was growing stronger by the minute.

Once they had finished, Josephine was wearing a flawless white tunic with fashionable ruffles around the collar. The ruffles even extended down to her chest in place of the commonly worn cravat. The sleeves were loose, perfect for moving her arms about and brandishing a sword without being hindered by inflexible material. Even the ruffles along the cuffs had Josephine grinning. Her father had always had a weakness for them.

A black linen waistcoat was layered over the tunic, but not just any waistcoat that fit the straight lines of a man. This buttoned-up vest hugged every one of Josephine's curves, and in place of petticoats were black linen knee breeches and shiny black boots, cuffed just below the knee.

"Are you certain that I'll be decent?" Josephine inquired doubtfully. "These garments are stunning and they are ever so comfortable, but … did Mr. Runik approve this?"

Beau took a step back and inspected her from head to toe. "Oh, don't you worry your pretty little head about Mr. Runik. We designed a coat to cover *all* your *deliciousness.*"

Blushing to her roots, Josephine quickly turned her back and took a seat for what she knew was the next item of business: her hair. It took no time at all for Eleanor to smooth Josephine's locks back into a small pouf on top of her head. Two spiral curls had been draped over her shoulder as well. The black buccaneer's hat was the most handsome she'd ever seen. It fit down over her hair perfectly. The wide brim curved up on one side and an enormous white ostrich feather sprouted from the crown. Every day of his pirate life, her father had worn a hat similar to this. Josephine's eyes began to prick with the threat of tears for this rare privilege to emulate him.

Beau brought out the coat. Josephine was, once again, stunned into silence at the sight of it. The velvet of the garment was a deep burgundy and had intricate designs embroidered around the edges with shiny gold threads. It resembled a soldier's frock, except this one was long enough to reach her ankles, like a proper skirt. And, like the waistcoat, it had been tailored for Josephine's feminine curves. It was the most exquisite garment she had ever seen.

"There, you see," Eleanor chimed in after helping Josephine slip on the coat. "It looks like a gown from the waist down, so no one will notice what is underneath. There are not any hoops, which is not typically the thing, but see there are pleats on the hips and in the rear to hide some of your form."

"Unless you do something indecent," Beau teased. "And just look at all the embroidery. Our seamstresses worked every night this week to complete it."

He ran his hand along the lapels and edges of the gorgeous garment, showing off the designs sewn into the material. It certainly was striking. The gold trim would be rich enough to suggest Josephine was of some status in society, but still subtle enough that she would blend in with the shadows if need be.

Josephine looked again at her reflection in the mirror. The coat covered her legs and boots while she was standing still, but it did not close completely in the front.

Seeing her dubious expression, Eleanor spoke up to ease her mind. "Josephine, do not think anything of it. You should see some of the old biddies' costumes that go to these parties. Some of them are far more indecent than this. You'll see."

Beau heartily agreed, "Oh, yes! I remember in London, this one little vixen showed up in nothing but -"

"That is quite enough." The three of them turned to find Madame Sophia standing like a general in the doorway.

"Eleanor, will you please check with Barnaby about any last-minute accessories and see if there is any tea? Thank you."

Eleanor exited quickly, Sophia's severe tone brooking no argument. As soon as she was gone, Sophia marched forward to Josephine.

"Quickly, Beau, there is not much time," she ordered without taking her eyes off Josephine's. "Eleanor will be back in a moment."

Josephine's throat tightened. What was going on? Why was Sophia worried about Eleanor coming back too soon? Surely they didn't believe she was an enemy?

Beau walked purposefully to one of the wardrobes and pulled out a thin black belt with a holster attached.

Josephine gasped, "Is that a pistol?"

"Yes, my dear," Sophia said sharply.

Beau began to fasten the belt around her waist so that the pistol was hidden at the small of her back under her coat.

"A *real* pistol?" Josephine hissed.

"Yes!" Sophia and Beau answered together.

"You think I'll need -"

Sophia did not let her complete her inquiry. "Beau, the cutlass."

This time, Josephine's jaw dropped open with excitement. Beau draped a black leather sword belt over her shoulder.

While adjusting the belt to fit her, Beau explained, "The sword they made for your costume was useless. It was just for looks. We replaced it with a real blade."

"It's so light," Josephine remarked. "Are you certain it's real?"

"Yes, my dear," Sophia answered. "It feels light because it was made for a lady. You."

"But ... but, why? And why did you send Eleanor away?"

"Listen to me, Josephine." Sophia gripped both of her shoulders and looked her dead in the eye. "You must accomplish your mission."

Completely befuddled, Josephine answered, "Of course. I -"

"*Not* the Brotherhood's mission," she nearly growled. "*Your* mission ... to defeat Skulthorpe. You must succeed. Do you understand? It is your destiny."

Sophia and Beau both stared at her like she held the answers to some dark secret. Josephine was grateful that she could trust the two tutors, but how did Sophia know what she'd been planning? Had Beau been feeding her information? Were they both Patriots, working undercover as spies against the Brotherhood? And what did she mean by *destiny?*

Josephine's mind was spinning. "Why are you hiding these things from Eleanor?" she asked.

"She's not one of us," Madame Sophia replied.

Josephine swallowed. This could be a trap. Was she making a colossal mistake trusting Sophia and Beau? Regardless of who they really worked for, it was clear they didn't trust Eleanor. There was no time to waste thinking about it. She retrieved the string of pearls and gloves from her cast-aside garments, hoping that her instincts were right about Beau and Sophia.

"What about these things?" she said quickly, knowing time was short before Eleanor would return.

Sophia inspected the gloves and turned her approving eyes to

Josephine. "I don't want anything to inhibit your nimble fingers tonight. Hide the gloves in your coat pocket. You can use them later if you need them." Josephine tucked them away as Sophia held the pearls up to the light of the candle. After a bit of scrutiny, Sophia clasped them around Josephine's neck, hiding them under the ruffles of her shirt. "These pearls are like the pocket watch. Once you break the strand and the pearls slide away, a timer will be activated from the inside. One pearl could be used at a time or all of them at once. You will have somewhere between three and five seconds before they explode. Use them carefully."

Beau brought her two finely-made daggers. While she was tucking them into her boots, he reminded her, "Just make sure none of those pearls fall down your tunic!"

Josephine tried to laugh but all that came out was a nervous giggle. Their conversation ceased when Eleanor returned with the tray of tea. Josephine's stomach clenched, afraid that Eleanor would be able to see all the weapons she was hiding.

"Did Barnaby have anything of use?" Sophia inquired of Eleanor.

"He wants to discuss it with Josephine himself," she replied.

"Of course." Sophia turned to Josephine. "Let's not keep him waiting. After you, Miss Teversin."

The tea was left forgotten on the table.

THIRTY-TWO

Nathaniel appraised Josephine's costume for the masquerade as they rode along in the carriage. "You look like a villain. Very fitting." The glare Josephine sent his way through her mask made him smirk.

"As do you."

Nathaniel frowned at that statement. "*I* am not dressed as a rogue pirate, Miss Teversin."

"No," she agreed. "*You* look like a hunter."

He smiled with satisfaction. "Thank you."

Josephine snorted. "It wasn't a compliment."

Nathaniel tugged on his gloves and smoothed his coat. It was true, hunters typically wore a black suit with white cravats while working, but this was not his attire. The trio had prepared a black suit with gold trim along the edges that matched the trim on Josephine's costume.

"In truth, I feel like a highwayman in this mask."

Josephine barked out a laugh. "A pirate and a highwayman. We *are* a pair, aren't we?"

The twinkle in her eye made him want to smile. Never had his cool demeanor been so shaken as when he'd seen Josephine's pirate ensemble. She walked taller with an air of confidence he had not seen in her before. Perhaps her pirate spirit could truly never be broken, as Skulthorpe wanted. But was that what *he* wanted? The idea of crushing Josephine as they'd first planned did not sit well with him now that he'd come to know her.

After a few moments of enduring a charged silence and the sway of the coach, Nathaniel attempted to draw her back into conversation - very unlike him. He cleared his throat to shake the odd feeling. "Did Barnaby familiarize you with the night vision lenses?"

"Of course. They're simple enough." Josephine lifted her hand to her temple by the edge of her mask and shifted the tiny lever that was hidden there. "Lever up - night vision. Lever back down - no lens at all. I cannot believe he designed these. Do you think we will actually need them?"

Nathaniel shrugged. "Possibly. There are extensive gardens behind Willow Stone Place that would be excellent spots for an ambush or a secret rendezvous."

"Secret rendezvous?" Josephine smirked and waggled her eyebrows. "For Patriots or lovers?"

"Possibly both, but we are focusing our attention on the Patriots," he huffed. "Miss Teversin, are you trying to annoy me with your jokes?"

Josephine sighed dramatically. "You are entirely too serious. It is not my fault that my sense of humor annoys you. Besides, you are the one who is tense. What's wrong with you?"

"Tonight *must* go well. Are you prepared for what must be done?"

"Of course not. But ... I have a plan," she said with a firm nod.

Nathaniel's brows shot up. "Oh, really? And what is this plan?"

"To just go where the wind carries me." She swept her hand out away from her body as if it were floating along a breeze.

"That is not a plan!"

"Exactly!" she exclaimed, wagging her finger at him. "My plan is to ... not plan. It's a *non*-plan."

He closed his eyes and pinched the bridge of his nose. "Please tell me this is just your odd sense of humor."

"I'm being completely serious. At the soiree, I was ready to hyperventilate because I feared things might go terribly awry. Well … if there is no set plan, then I cannot be nervous. Thinking on my feet and reacting to what's in front of me is one of my many talents. That's why you brought me into the Brotherhood fold, isn't that so?"

"Quite right, but -"

"Then stop being so nervous," said Josephine. "Our goal is clear. The path of acquiring it is just a bit fuzzy. 'Any and all means necessary.' Isn't that what Skulthorpe told you? I'm simply leaving all doors of opportunity open."

Nathaniel pinched his lips together. It wasn't a horrible idea, but his need for a well-thought-out strategy was protesting it all the same. What Josephine suggested sounded very much like a pirate thing to do. It was dangerous.

With a disgruntled expression, Josephine added, "*And* I have promised everyone at least ten times that I will not attempt to faint again."

The memory of Josephine's comical faint at the soiree flashed through his mind and he started chuckling. He had been holding his laughter in for weeks. That outrageous remark finally did him in.

He looked up to find Josephine gaping at him like a fish and it made him laugh even harder. Soon enough, Josephine was giggling bashfully behind her fan. Once he had finished his snickering, Nathaniel's heart felt lighter than it had in a long time. When he happened to glance at Josephine again, she was watching him with a contemplative look upon her face.

"What is it?" he asked.

"I need to tell you something, Nathaniel," she said, daring for the first time, to call him by his first name.

He cleared his throat and shifted in his seat. "Miss Teversin, you needn't -"

"I understand why you've hated me. But I want you to know that I have never hated you." She paused, biting her lip thoughtfully. "You are … a giant pain in the arse. That's what Oliver would say," she said, grinning. "But he says the same about me, so perhaps you and I are too much alike for our own good."

"Miss Teversin -"

"You're a good man," she whispered, interrupting him again. "Garreck Skulthorpe has tried to bury that in you. Don't let him succeed."

Nathaniel could not look away from her pleading, innocent brown eyes, and in that moment, it was as if a dark veil had suddenly been lifted from his sight. The animosity he had felt toward this woman had been so strong it had consumed him. Tonight, that grudge against her was gone. It had melted away so subtly that he hadn't noticed until that moment. The Pirate of Blacktail Cove was dead and gone. Revenge on his daughter would not bring Nathaniel's father back. It would simply be another wrong that could not be made right again.

But she was a pirate. The hunter's code demanded that she be put down the same as all other pirates before her. Her pirate legacy would continue to be a threat to the Crown and the English interests in the American colonies. Was that enough reason to punish one innocent woman who had not chosen this path, but had simply been born into it?

A battle waged inside Nathaniel's mind as the carriage arrived at the old Willow Stone Place.

"Nathaniel?"

"Here we are," he said, ignoring her. Nathaniel could not stand to listen to any more of her pleas when his loyalties were faltering. Keeping his head clear tonight was of utmost importance. He would sort out the rest later.

Nathaniel descended the coach first and offered Josephine his hand. Instead of remaining stiff and reserved as was his usual habit, he tucked her hand under his elbow and smiled down at her.

"Remember, your name is Josephine Pinchley."

"Of course," she whispered, smiling demurely as Sophia had taught her. "And if you keep holding me so close, the rumors from the soiree are bound to get worse."

"What rumors?"

"That we are not cousins at all ... and *betrothed*."

Nathaniel snorted, causing Josephine to giggle.

"That will give everyone something to gossip about, won't it?" He grinned and escorted her inside.

Looking down at Josephine, her eyes wide behind her mask and a smile on her face, his decision became all too clear. She was not a killer and certainly not responsible for her father's actions. There was no cruelty within this woman, regardless of what Mr. Skulthorpe had told him about pirates. Whatever plans Skulthorpe had for her, he vowed to put a stop to them. After this assignment, he would help her leave the continent, no matter the cost - to the cause or to himself. He owed her that much.

Jasper Howard and his son, Alden, were standing at the entrance to the ballroom, greeting guests. They were both dressed in simpler attire, as Nathaniel was, though their masks were more extravagant. Jasper's looked like the face of a gargoyle, while Alden's was some sort of bird with a giant beak for a nose.

"Those things are hideous," Josephine murmured in Nathaniel's ear as they approached the two men.

"For once, we are in full agreement."

The exchange of introductions went smoothly, much to Nathaniel's relief. He had been holding his breath as Josephine dipped into a perfect curtsey and graciously accepted a kiss on the hand from Alden, but there seemed to be no sign of recognition on his part.

"Runik, I hoped we'd see more of you in town this week," Jasper, the elder of the two, informed him.

His son, Alden, agreed, "Yes, we'll be having brandy and playing cards later this evening if you've a mind to join us."

"I look forward to it," said Nathaniel. He bowed stiffly, sure that this was his invitation into the Patriot group. Progress was finally being made.

Leaving the two Patriots to greet their other guests, Nathaniel and Josephine strolled into the ballroom.

"Oh heavens, Nathaniel. The costumes ..." Josephine gaped. "Eleanor and Beau were right."

"Some of them are atrocious, aren't they?" he said, looking around the ballroom. "You are lucky Madame made you respectable-looking."

A woman ambled by in a pink satin get-up that wasn't quite a dress. Her tacky costume was ill-fitting. The bodice was too tight for her full waist, while the sleeves and skirt ballooned out like giant cream puffs. The woman's mask was pink as well, with a round snout over her nose.

"Oh!" Josephine gasped. "Is that woman dressed as …?"

"A pig? Yes, unfortunately for the rest of us."

"I'm glad Sophia did not dress me up in something like that," she whispered.

Nathaniel was in full agreement. Pirate or not, he was proud to have Josephine on his arm and not one of these other women. Another woman passed by them, dressed in a bright blue and purple dress. Peacock feathers trimmed the neckline of the gown and her shiny gold mask. A few men had dressed like court jesters with black and red suits. Most of the crowd simply carried their masks on a stem, only covering their faces for a minute or two before removing them to laugh and chat with their friends.

Nathaniel escorted Josephine through the crowd with their mission at the forefront of his mind. He spotted Mr. and Mrs. Graves speaking to Phineas Berry, Abraham Talbot, and their wives toward the back of the ballroom.

His pirate companion had not noticed the Graves just yet. She was still riveted by all the ostentatious costumes.

"You can gawk later," Nathaniel hissed, squeezing her hand.

"Sorry," she whispered. "They're just so distracting."

Once he had Josephine's attention, he steered her toward Mr. and Mrs. Graves and the others, speaking softly into her ear. "These men with the Graves are believed to be in the inner circle of the Patriot rebels here in Charlestown. Keep your ears open while conversing with their wives."

Josephine nodded and put on her best smile as they approached.

JOSEPHINE'S HEART thudded hard against her ribs. Phase one of her non-plan had already been set in motion. Preparing for tonight, she'd remembered quite well what Nathaniel had said about Alden Howard;

that he was the gent whose pocket she'd picked at the soiree. She also recalled the kindness in his eyes. If she was going up against Skulthorpe, she would need some inside help and Alden seemed like an honorable man. If she gave him some valuable information, perhaps he might be forthcoming as well. It was dangerous and she knew Nathaniel would be furious if he knew what Josephine had planned. Her one hope was to find enough damning information on Skulthorpe to convince Nathaniel that he should leave the Brotherhood behind. She'd made a mess of things with James, but she would finish what her father had started - she would save Nathaniel.

Josephine had come prepared to meet with Alden Howard. Slipping him the note had been tricky - making sure Nathaniel did not see and hoping that Alden would not give her away. Alden had taken the note from her flawlessly while kissing her hand during introductions. Josephine had seen the glint of recognition in his eyes immediately, so she trusted he would find her when the time was right.

Or he'll have his Patriot friends publicly arrest me and string me up in the square, Josphine thought. Beneath the five layers Josephine was wearing, she was beginning to sweat and it wasn't from the heat. Had she made a terrible mistake?

"There's nothing to be done about it now," she muttered under her breath.

"What was that?" Nathaniel asked as they approached his acquaintances.

Josephine shook her head. "Nothing."

Taking a deep breath, she gripped Nathaniel's arm a bit tighter as they continued on. She opened her special-made fan and waved it to cool her face. She would never understand how ladies could tolerate all the layers they wore to these extravagant events. If Josephine survived the night, she swore she would never wear such things again. Pirate life did have its perks. Not conforming to society's fashion trends was one of them.

Mattie Graves spotted Josephine and Nathaniel when they were still twenty feet away. She broke away from her husband, strode toward them, and grasped Josephine's hands. Her lovely gown was sky blue, and purple and blue feathers lined the top edge of her silver mask.

"Oh, my dear Miss Pinchley!" Mattie threw her arms around Josephine's neck to hug her.

"How did you recognize me?" Josephine asked once Mattie had released her. She adjusted her buccaneer's hat to make sure it sat straight on her head after Mattie's embrace.

"I didn't," she admitted with a grin. "I recognized Mr. Runik." Mattie's smile melted away, distress taking its place. "Mr. Graves and I were so worried after the soiree, but I see your Mr. Runik found you after all. We're so relieved you weren't harmed. What a catastrophe that was!"

Mattie's warm smile and delightful enthusiasm soothed Josephine's jitters at once. Josephine grinned and allowed Mattie to fuss over her.

"Come, Miss Pinchley," said Mattie, pulling her toward Mr. Graves and the others in their group. "Meet our friends!"

After introductions were made, Josephine curtsied and then began to study each of her new acquaintances.

Mr. Talbot was a slender man with blond hair. A black cape covered his red suit and a shiny gold mask covered half his face. His wife, Sarah, was a dainty woman with dark brown hair and eyes the color of bluebells. Her dress was almost white, with layers of feathers cascading down her skirt, making her look like a swan. Mr. Berry was an older gentleman with a white powdered wig, and his dark blue suit was more sensible than the other costumes. A pewter-colored mask was his only embellishment. Margaret Berry's tresses had been powdered to a bluish gray and was styled into a tall pouf on her head. The style was made complete with a bright pink feather that matched her gown.

"Come ladies," Mattie said, flicking a purple feather out of her face. "Let's let the men talk about their politics. You know they can't help themselves." Mattie linked arms with Josephine and steered her a few paces away from the men.

Margaret chuckled, her voice deep and husky. "It's true. Especially after the news."

Josephine asked, "News? What news?"

Sarah narrowed her blue eyes at Josephine. "You don't know? Mr. Runik didn't tell you?"

"Miss Pinchley has been staying in Georgetown," Mattie said to the other ladies, as if that explained everything.

Margaret added, "And they are not married. Just because we eavesdrop on our husband's business meetings, doesn't mean everyone does!"

Mattie, Sarah, and Margaret all giggled, but Josephine's heart began to beat harder. Nathaniel had told her that the wives of these Patriots might have valuable information. Was she about to find out something important? Were these ladies really speaking freely in front of Josephine, who was practically a stranger to them?

"There's a shipment coming," Mattie said to Josephine. "That's what my husband heard from Governor Bull."

"More than one shipment, I'd wager," Margaret pointed out.

A tingle of anticipation and dread rippled up Josephine's spine. Was this another shipment of those secret prototypes, like the ones her father had stolen? She perked her ears so she wouldn't miss a word.

"Too true, Margaret," Mattie said, nodding. "Everyone in the colonies enjoys their tea. It's going to be difficult to rally people to the cause when the tax on tea isn't even that high."

Tea? Josephine's brows knitted together. Why were the ladies concerned about shipments of tea? 'The cause' they spoke of could only mean the rebellion, but what was so important about shipments of tea?

"Mr. Adams will be particularly put out by the whole thing," Mattie continued. "Heaven knows what they'll do up in Boston."

Who was Mr. Adams of Boston? Josephine tucked that information away.

"It's best we not say anything more," Margaret suggested. "If we're overheard by any listening ears, it would be bad for our husbands and the cause."

Josephine's throat constricted. She was well-aware of what had happened to those who had gone against England, especially when caught by the Brotherhood. Her father had lost his life for stealing a couple of chests that belonged to Skulthorpe. What would happen to Mattie or the other Patriots if they were found to be traitors to the British Crown? They'd lose everything.

The crowd around them was growing louder with every passing minute, so Josephine didn't think anyone had been paying attention to their conversation. They didn't know that Nathaniel could read lips, nor did they realize that Josephine herself was gathering information. It was possible that the ladies weren't discussing anything important at all. Perhaps that was why they were speaking so freely, but Margaret's warning meant they suspected Loyalists were in their midst.

After a few more minutes of small talk, the orchestra began to play. Mattie clapped enthusiastically. "Oh, the music! Let's dance, shall we?"

Mattie strode over and yanked Mr. Graves away from the other men. Giggling like a schoolgirl, she pulled him to the dance floor. Mr. Talbot escorted Sarah to line up for the reel as well, though with a little more grace and dignity. Josephine smiled as she watched the dancers step, dip, and twirl to the rhythm of the music.

A moment later, Josephine felt Margaret sidle up next to her.

"Are you not going to dance, Miss Pinchley?" Margaret asked.

Josephine looked around for Nathaniel. He was still engrossed in conversation with a few other men. "I'll sit this one out."

Margaret lowered her stemmed mask and pursed her lips, continuing to watch the guests as they began to move to the music. "Are you enjoying your stay in Georgetown, Miss Pinchley?"

Josephine cleared her throat and lowered her eyes. "Yes, of course," she lied.

"I have a nephew who lives in Georgetown."

"That's nice."

"I visit … often," Margaret said, putting emphasis on the final word.

Josephine felt her throat tighten up. She resisted the urge to nervously fiddle with her fan.

"I pride myself on knowing a lot of people," Margaret continued. "I know many families who live in Georgetown. And yet, no one has mentioned an orphan moving from England. That's the sort of thing people in town enjoy gossiping about."

Frozen in place, Josephine felt the blood drain from her face. *The woman can't know about my ruse. Can she?* Her fingers warmed, the magic instinctively wanting to protect her from danger. She clenched her fists to keep her unpredictable power at bay.

Searching the room for some way to escape Margaret's keen intuition, Josephine's gaze landed on a tall man with a bird-like mask. It was Alden Howard - and he was headed her way. His dark eyes were locked with Josephine's as he weaved through the crowd. She felt her blood run cold.

Both Alden and Margaret know about me, Josephine thought. *He's coming to expose me and take me away.*

The older woman turned to Josephine. She was eerily calm, as if she didn't have a clue what trouble awaited Josephine. The tallest man in the room continued to stride toward them, exuding indisputable authority with every step he took. Josephine wrapped her arms around her middle to keep her hands from trembling.

"I might be making too much of this," Margaret said. "But I fear that's not the case. Is it?"

Josephine gulped. She couldn't tear her gaze away from Mr. Howard, who was bearing down on them. The hooked beak of his mask was like a sinister omen - the face of a vulture sent to pick her bones once she was dead.

"Mrs. Graves says we can trust you, Miss Pinchley," said Margaret. "I hope she's right."

"I'd never do anything to hurt Mr. and Mrs. Graves," Josephine replied with a shaky voice. And she meant every word. No matter what happened, she would never betray her friends who had been nothing but kind to her.

Margaret narrowed her eyes. "We shall see." She turned on her heel and walked away from Josephine.

Now standing alone, Josephine watched with wide eyes as Mr. Howard stopped directly in front of her. Half the man's face was covered, but she could see that his mouth was turned down in a frown.

Josephine risked a peek over her shoulder at Nathaniel. He was still engaged in conversation with the other gentlemen in his group, but his steel-gray eyes were fixed on her. With a subtle shake of her head, she warned Nathaniel to stay out of it and let her handle the situation.

"Miss Pinchley."

"Mr. Howard," Josephine croaked. She curtsied to the host with her heart hammering in her chest.

To her surprise, he held out his gloved hand and asked, "Would you care to dance?"

THIRTY-THREE

Josephine reluctantly took Mr. Howard's hand. She glanced around, searching for Nathaniel again. Her escort's eyes were filled with concern and something else she couldn't put her finger on.

This wasn't part of her non-plan, but she cast her fear aside. This was what she'd bargained for when she'd decided to go where the wind carried her. However, this blustering wind was hurling her straight onto the dance floor to make a fool of herself. The guests were lining up for a Virginia Reel, which, thankfully, was one of the simpler country dances in the colonies.

The ladies curtsied while the men bowed to begin the dance. Still uneasy from Margaret's warning, Josephine stumbled over her feet twice.

"Steady," Mr. Howard said, reaching for her hands for the next turn. When they drew close, he murmured, "Even pirates can dance."

Josephine's eyes flew up to his face. *Surely, he's just saying that because of the costume*, she thought, but Alden's eyes sparkled with mischief.

She and Alden stood motionless, waiting for their turn to dance their way up and down the line. After a few moments, they were moving again, clasping hands and shuffling down the line of dancers.

While they were shoulder to shoulder, Josephine whispered, "You're not going to expose me?"

"Why would I do that?" he replied without missing a beat. "You haven't done anything wrong. Yet."

They spun away from each other for the next turn in the reel. Through most of the dance, they stood opposite each other, unable to speak for being overheard. It was maddening to wait so long to continue their covert discussion. Behind his gaudy mask, Alden watched her with calculating eyes. After what seemed like an eternity, they stepped forward, took each other's hands, and sashayed down the line for a second time.

Gripping her hand firmly, Alden murmured, "You're taking a risk."

"I have to."

He squeezed her hand. "And your employer?"

"I'm not loyal to him," she whispered.

The dance forced them apart again. They continued the reel in silence, coming together and stepping back. He didn't speak to her again until the final turn.

"Wait two more dances, then meet me in the garden," Alden said quietly.

Her heart still racing, Josephine nodded.

The reel finally ended with bows and curtsies. Josephine took a deep breath as another gentleman stepped forward to ask her to dance the next reel. Phase one of her non-plan was complete. There was no turning back now.

INWARDLY SEETHING, Nathaniel watched from the edge of the dance floor as Josephine danced with Alden Howard and then another gentleman by the name of Mr. Hamilton. He didn't understand why he was so cross. Josephine was free to dance with whomever she liked.

Nathaniel clenched his jaw. *Is Mr. Hamilton trying to look down her tunic?* He grabbed a glass of wine from the next servant who passed by and took two large gulps. *Get a hold of yourself, man.*

Barely waiting until the dance was over, Nathaniel strode toward Mr. Hamilton and tapped him on the shoulder. "Mind if I cut in?"

Nathaniel didn't give him the chance to answer. He curled his arm around Josephine's waist and steered her away from the dance floor, leaving Mr. Hamilton sputtering in confusion behind them.

"We are not here to dance, Miss *Pinchley*," he hissed once they were alone.

"Don't be such an ogre," Josephine replied. "You said 'any and all means necessary'."

He peered down at her curiously. "So you gleaned some useful information, did you?"

"That remains to be seen. Are you thirsty?"

Nathaniel thought about the wine he'd just quaffed and shook his head. One glass of wine was enough. He needed a clear head this evening.

"Well, I'm parched. Let's find some punch." Josephine took his elbow.

While strolling through the abundance of masks and costumes toward the refreshment table, Nathaniel heard a familiar voice and halted at once. He couldn't quite put his finger on it, but the sound of that silly, booming voice was one he knew well.

"Josephine, did you hear that?"

"What is it?" she asked half-heartedly.

Peering through the crowd, he said, "That man sounds just like Mr. Hopwood."

"Who?"

"Beau," he replied. "Your tutor. I hear his voice." He grasped Josephine's wrist and pulled her through the crowd toward the sound of the man's familiar bellowing.

"You think it's Beau? Are you sure? There are a lot of people here."

Nathaniel spotted him. Beau Hopwood was standing at the edge of the dance floor wearing a sky-blue frock and powdered white wig. His sparkling black mask had been attached to a handle, which he held down by his waist as he talked with a group of ladies. The man wasn't even trying to hide. Nathaniel pushed through the guests, even elbowing a few to get them to move out of his way. Hearing the commotion, Beau turned and made eye contact with Nathaniel. He gasped, as if he were a thief that had just been caught, spun on his heel, and fled in the opposite direction.

"What is this nonsense?" Nathaniel muttered. "Where does he think he's going?"

As Beau weaved in and out of the pressing crowd, so did Nathaniel, dragging Josephine along behind him. It galled Nathaniel that he had to chase after the fool in order to get explanations.

"Mr. Hopwood," Nathaniel called out. "Stop at once."

Of course, the tutor didn't stop. Once Beau reached the ballroom doors, he darted left down a corridor. Nathaniel dropped Josephine's hand and chased after him. He knew he was making a scene, but that was the least of his worries. Mr. Hopwood's presence at the masque was not expected. Any deviation to their mission raised Nathaniel's suspicions.

By the time Nathaniel reached the hallway, Beau had disappeared. Nathaniel had no desire to search every room and closet. Accepting defeat for the moment, Nathaniel tugged on his gloves, straightened his coat, and returned to the ballroom. He would simply interrogate Beau once everyone had convened back at the Skulthorpe manor.

The guests of the party were back to gossiping and flirting, with glasses of wine and punch in their hands. The spectacle that Nathaniel had caused a moment ago was long forgotten in the merriment.

But when he searched the room for his companion, he realized Josephine was nowhere to be found.

PHASE two of Josephine's non-plan had been successful. Beau had played his part expertly, giving her a chance to slip away. As soon as Nathaniel had released her, Josephine had made sure he was quite distracted before sneaking out to the veranda overlooking the back lawn. Already, she was feeling guilty over her deception after what had passed between them in the carriage. Josephine was certain that she'd finally reached him behind his cool exterior. Her heart grew heavy, knowing that he could quickly rescind the frail measure of trust he'd extended. The ultimate goal tonight was freeing them both from Skulthorpe's grasp. Swallowing the last shred of doubt, Josephine went forward with phase three of her non-plan.

Lowering the night vision lenses, Josephine stepped out onto the lawn and began walking toward the tall shrubs that grew along the outer edge of the gardens; the best place for one of those secret rendezvous she had teased Nathaniel about. Willow Stone Place was nearly as elegant as Skulthorpe's estate, with its symmetrically patterned gardens, but there were indeed many shrubs on the outskirts of the paths that created more shadows for hiding.

Once she had reached the dark shadows of the hedges, Josephine glanced around nervously. These bushes were the perfect place for an ambush. Her palms began to warm at the thought of danger lurking about.

"No, not now," Josephine muttered, shaking her hands out and curling her fingers into fists. Josephine was about to pull one of her daggers free from her boot when a twig snapped beneath a heavy boot.

"Miss Pirate."

With a gasp, Josephine spun around. "Oh, it's you, Mr. Howard."

"Indeed." He gave her a half-bow and lifted the birdlike mask from his face. "I'm impressed with your skills. Even Mr. Runik did not notice you slipping me the note, but it was not necessary, my dear. Madame Arment informed me that you might be willing to speak with me."

Slapping her hands on her hips, Josephine huffed, "Well, Sophia did not inform me about you. I only just found out today that she's a double agent."

"She has risked much, infiltrating the enemy's camp. She advised me that you were trustworthy." Crossing his arms over his chest, Alden gave her a doubtful look. "Though I am not a man to trust so easily. What do you think to gain by meeting with me?"

With firm resolve, she looked him in the eye. "I'm here for information. In exchange, I have information for you."

"Really? And what information do you think you have that the Patriots don't already know about?"

Josephine raised her eyebrows. "Did you know that Skulthorpe is double-crossing you? He's not the man you think he is."

"Skulthorpe is a snake," Alden growled. "There are a few Patriots who have been fooled by him. But not me."

"Was that *you* meeting with him at the soiree?" asked Josephine.

"No," he said with a frown. "That was another acquaintance of mine, though I wouldn't mind knowing how you found out about that private conference. I, on the other hand, was busy being duped … by a pickpocket." His eyes twinkled in amusement. "Madame Arment warned me about that as well. The look on your face just before you went down in a faint was priceless." Alden chuckled with delight.

A groan escaped her. "So everyone keeps saying. Your note was worthless then?"

"The Sons of Liberty are not so foolish as to write down our plans. Ciphers are easily broken by intelligent men, and there are little thieving fingers everywhere," he joked. "It was merely a list of random names."

"I should have known that all along," mumbled Josephine. "Would Skulthorpe have known it was a fake?" Worry slithered into her mind again. If Skulthorpe knew that the information was false, then why did he not let Nathaniel know? Maybe he did know and was deliberately keeping it from her.

A mocking smile formed on his face. "It is likely he figured it out, which is why he sent both of you again this evening."

"You know everything then?" Josephine snorted and threw her hands up in defeat. "Then what in the bloody blazes am I doing here?" she muttered to herself. She glared at Alden when he chuckled again.

"You really are delightfully amusing," he said with a grin.

"Madame Arment was not wrong about that. What is your mission tonight? Why did Garreck Skulthorpe send you?"

"He knows the Patriots have something planned - something extravagant, it sounded like. My orders were to find out what it is."

Alden raised his chin and looked down at her with a murderous glint in his eyes. "And you think I'm just going to tell you?"

"Of course not. In fact, it would be best if you didn't. I've been told that I'm not a good liar, and I want to honestly say that I don't know anything if I'm questioned."

Alden chuckled. "Smart girl."

Josephine rolled her eyes. "Honestly, it wouldn't surprise me if Skulthorpe already knows your plans and is merely toying with Mr. Runik and me. All I know is that whatever the Patriots are planning, he's onto you. You need to be careful. He intends to do away with any Patriot rebels he gets his hands on."

"Have you decided to join the Patriot rebels against England?"

She snorted. "I'm on my own side."

He gave her a lopsided grin. "Spoken like a true pirate."

Josephine blanched at his mention of pirates. She shook her head and replied, "I'll help anyone who stands against Garreck Skulthorpe."

"Are you standing against that hunter who brought you here tonight?"

Josephine pursed her lips. "Listen, I know you might believe otherwise, but Mr. Runik is -"

Alden stepped toward her, and his voice held a furious edge. "Are you going to try and convince me that Mr. Runik is innocent of his crimes against the people of Charlestown?"

"Mr. Howard, Runik was coerced into the Brotherhood. He just doesn't know it. Did you know his father? James Runik?"

Alden blinked at the sudden change in topic. "I knew of him. He was a member of the House of Lords if I recall correctly. What does that have to do with -"

"Mr. Skulthorpe was after him … and had him murdered three years ago, but I don't know why. I was hoping you might know something about it."

Alden Howard stared down at her for a moment, considering her words. "The House of Lords advises the King of England on certain matters. If Garreck Skulthorpe was threatening one of the Lords, I can imagine he was attempting to sway them for some purpose."

"At the soiree, I heard him speak of the rebellion as if he supported it."

"Wars are expensive, Miss Teversin," he said, raising his brows. "That's one of the reasons taxes were raised here in the colonies – to pay for the last one. Parliament decided to impose those taxes. Skulthorpe might have been hoping the Lords would persuade King George to fund this new war as well."

Josephine sighed. "And when James Runik didn't comply, he killed him."

"It's quite possible," Alden agreed. "You care about that hunter, don't you? What is he to you?"

Josephine hesitated, her face growing hot under Alden's scrutiny. "I ... well ... let's just say I won't rest easy until both of us are free of Skulthorpe's shackles. My father died trying to save Nathaniel Runik. I'm going to see that through."

"You should be careful just the same," he warned. "The Brotherhood and their hunters - they play for keeps."

"Yes, I'm aware of that dreadful fact," she muttered, mostly to herself.

Alden studied her carefully. "Is there anything else you'd like to share? I fear our time is growing short. Mr. Runik will be looking for you, I'm sure."

"We found out that the fire at the soiree was set by magic. Did you know?" Josephine asked. "A witch works for him."

His eyebrows shot up. "No, I didn't know that, but it doesn't surprise me. Do you know who it is?"

"A friend of mine told me her name is Tempest," Josephine replied. "She's dangerous. Other than that, I don't know much about her."

Alden rubbed his chin. "He's changed his game if he has employed a witch. Is she here tonight?"

"I don't know." She looked around nervously. Thinking the witch might be nearby had Josephine's hands growing warm again. "Skulthorpe sent her to be rid of me a week ago."

"And you eluded her," he remarked. "You are dangerous yourself, little pirate."

Josephine's heart began to pound when he called her a pirate again. Did he know that she was an immortal pirate or was he only saying that because of her costume?

"I wasn't alone," she explained. "I wouldn't be here if it weren't for some very good friends."

Alden stepped forward and gently gripped her shoulder in a fatherly sort of way. "You misunderstand, my dear. *You* are dangerous to them. You are the threat. I believe that's why Skulthorpe collected you. As long you remain under his thumb, he will continue to use you and your powers for his schemes."

"What does that mean?" she asked. "How am I a threat to him?"

He gave her a perplexed look. "You are a *pirate.*"

"How do you know this?" Josephine gasped.

Alden looked away, as if he were recalling an old memory. "I saw you once when I was meeting your father. It was just four years ago. Joseph had smuggled in a shipment of molasses for us from Jamaica. It was just a glimpse, but I remember that you had the same brown eyes as him. And I suspect the same determined spirit. He was a good friend of mine for many years. His death was a great loss to us."

"Father was a Patriot?" Josephine muttered, mostly to herself. She'd always believed immortal pirates were independent souls, never committing to any country over another. Was that why he had stolen those prototypes from the British ships?

"Joseph was a lot like you. He knew that to stand against the Brotherhood was to stand with the colonies. The man was our eyes and ears on the seas."

Josephine's eyes widened. How did she not know this? "But why?"

"Joseph understood the need to be free. That's all the colonials want. And once you are no longer Skulthorpe's puppet to command, you will be free as well. The power you possess threatens everything he's built for himself."

Josephine wrapped her arms around her middle. "And just what is one lone pirate going to do for anyone?"

"To be a pirate is to be alone," Alden gently explained. "Stop being afraid of who you are. You could be the hope that your kind, that *all of us*, have been waiting for."

All of us? What did that mean? Was Alden talking about the Patriots? How did he know so much about immortal pirates? If there were other immortal pirates out there - if Josephine was not truly the last - where had they gone?

Swallowing those questions, instead, she asked, "What is Skulthorpe's endgame? What does he want? The death of all pirates and Patriots?"

"I think it's much more than that," Alden answered. "What does every powerful man want more of? Power? Money? Land? To say that he's won?" He shrugged. "The British do not want a war with the American colonies, and most of the Patriots do not want that either. Many have been working to resolve our differences with diplomacy, but there are still those who believe that war is the only way. There are also those who would benefit greatly from that war, depending on the outcome. How Skulthorpe might benefit ... that is a question you must find an answer to, Miss Teversin. What does he have to gain?"

Josephine cleared her throat nervously. This was not at all how she'd envisioned this conversation. "I will keep that in mind," she said, wringing her hands.

"Did I satisfy your curiosity?" he asked, folding his arms across his chest.

"Hardly."

His expression softened. "My dear, you have a good heart, like your father. I will pass the word that our meeting tonight should be postponed. In the meantime, if you have any plans to travel over the next few months, I would steer clear of Boston if I were you, or any major ports of entry." He gave her a wink.

What did that mean? Did it have something to do with the shipments of tea that Mattie and Margaret were talking about earlier?

"You should return to the ballroom before Mr. Runik finds us here." He gave her a little push between her shoulder blades to get her moving. "Good luck, Miss Teversin. I look forward to seeing you again."

Josephine headed back toward the doors that led to the ballroom from the veranda. So many new thoughts were whirling in her mind, she didn't know where to begin. She needed to speak to Oliver as soon as possible.

Although there were hundreds of guests mingling and people coming and going from the gardens, Josephine had the sense that she was being watched again. Stepping back into the ballroom once more, she glanced around. Nathaniel was not in the midst of the costumes, which was a relief. Hopefully, he was too busy with his own personal assignment to bother with her at the moment. Finally, Josephine spotted the one man for whom she had been looking. Oliver had found her and he was in his perfect disguise of Mister Lewis Brown.

THIRTY-FOUR

Nathaniel watched from a distance as Josephine reemerged from the gardens, Alden Howard not far behind. It was now perfectly clear that the woman was up to no good. And to think, he had actually been ready to trust the wench. His suspicions should have been raised as soon as he'd caught Beau at the masque and then seen him fleeing. Had Josephine planned that entire fiasco?

Following from a distance, Nathaniel continued to stalk Josephine as she made her way inside. Stopping only for a moment to search the room, Josephine meandered slowly through the crowd, clearly trying not to draw any unwanted attention. Careful to stay hidden, Nathaniel watched Josephine approach a gentleman near the entrance to the ballroom.

Why does that man look familiar? Nathaniel thought.

As he continued to watch the two speak to each other, a memory flashed through his mind of the same man asking Josephine to dance at the Harvest Festival soiree a few weeks ago.

What is his name? Nathaniel thought carefully for a moment, then it came to him. Brown. Lewis Brown.

Did Josephine know this Mr. Brown? At the soiree, she acted as if she'd never met the man. And she'd never spoken of any other friends or acquaintances in Charlestown, besides Oliver and Geneveive. Nathaniel snorted. *The girl has already lied to me this evening. Why wouldn't she lie about this too?*

Moving slowly in their direction, Nathaniel continued to watch them. When he was within a hundred feet of them, the onyx began to buzz against his chest. He'd nearly forgotten that he'd been wearing it. Nathaniel stopped to look around the room, but there was no way to know where the witch might be in the midst of so many strangers. Every single guest was wearing a costume: the perfect way to hide in plain sight.

Suddenly, Lewis Brown gripped Josephine's arm in a tight hold and began leading her out of the ballroom. Thoughts of meeting with Alden and Jasper Howard fled his mind as he followed the duo out into the east wing of the manor house. Josephine was not resisting, but something was making him uneasy. He checked for all his devices and for the two loaded pistols he'd smuggled in to be sure he was prepared for every possible scenario.

Even as the couple continued into a more secluded area, his onyx still hummed. And then he knew. Nathaniel cursed under his breath and drew his pistol.

JOSEPHINE WAS RELIEVED that phase four of her non-plan could be done away with. Alden Howard had assured her that he would cancel the secret gathering that would take place toward the latter part of the evening. Even if they decided to meet after all, sending Oliver disguised as Runik *or* sending the real Runik into a secret meeting with the Patriots was dangerous. The rumors of things being done to faithful Loyalists like Nathaniel Runik were unspeakable. She wanted neither of her men to be subject to such brutality.

Once she had reached Oliver-in-disguise by the entryway to the ballroom, she whispered, "You won't be needed tonight after all."

He surveyed the crowd. "Why is that?"

"Mr. Howard is postponing his secret meeting."

"You spoke to Mr. Howard?"

Josephine frowned. What a strange thing to ask. She'd told Oliver yesterday that she was planning to meet with the Patriot.

"Of course. I warned him about Skulthorpe, as I said I would do. Remember? Don't ask me how, but he already knows Runik is a hunter with the Brotherhood. And he knows I'm a pirate, too."

"How could he know about Runik?"

"Well, I imagine Mr. Howard heard it from Sophia and Beau." Josephine dropped her voice to a whisper. "Sophia is secretly working for the Patriots. I knew I could trust her."

"I see."

The muscle in Oliver's jaw clenched. Josephine didn't know what to make of that reaction to her news. He was probably just on edge from Josephine putting herself at risk speaking with a Patriot.

Josephine waved away her concern. "Regardless, if Nathaniel goes to that meeting, I'm not sure what they'll do to him. If you disguise yourself as Mr. Runik and take his place … we just can't take the chance. Mr. Howard wouldn't harm you, but who knows what the others will do."

Josephine stared up at Oliver, who at that moment looked entirely like Lewis Brown. He was still eyeing the crowd with a scowl on his face.

She added, "I also warned them that the witch might make an appearance tonight."

His green eyes flashed to hers. "You told Mr. Howard about a witch?"

Josephine scanned the crowd, searching for Nathaniel. He was probably looking for her. "I told you I was going to. Oliver, really. If you didn't want me to reveal it, you should have told me yesterday. But I think it was the right thing to do."

Oliver narrowed his eyes. "What else happened this evening? Did you uncover the Patriots' big plans?"

"Maybe, but that's not important. Nathaniel and I had a good talk before the ball. I believe he may be changing his mind about me." Josephine sighed. "After he finds out what I've done this evening, he's going to be vexed, but I didn't know any other way to convince him that Skulthorpe is his enemy and not the Patriots here in Charlestown."

"Runik is warming up to you?" Oliver's voice was sharper than usual.

Josephine's brows knitted together. "Warming up to me? I suppose … we might be friends. I don't know. There may be too much dirty water under the rudders for that. I don't think he'll be running charities for pirates after all this, but it was a start."

Oliver's eyes churned with anger as he stared down at her.

Josephine flinched at his fury. "Oliver, whatever is the matter?"

She gasped as Oliver suddenly wrapped his fingers around her arm in a bruising grip. He yanked her away from the ballroom, down a deserted corridor in the east wing of the mansion.

"Oliver, what has come over you?" she asked, surprised by his odd reaction. "Did you not hear me? You don't need to worry about the plan tonight."

Far from prying eyes and ears, she hoped that Oliver would finally explain his abrupt behavior. But before she could blink, he pushed her up against a wall and had his hand around her throat, choking her.

"I'm not Oliver," he snarled.

Josephine kicked and clawed at his arms, fighting for breath. Lewis Brown smiled down at her with cruel delight, his green eyes cold and hard. His fingers squeezed her neck, digging into her flesh. As she thrashed about, her hat tumbled to the floor and her hair came undone. This was clearly not her Oliver. Whoever it was, he was overpowering her easily and the loss of air was weakening her. Just as black spots began to fill her vision, her fingertips grew hotter. A burning flame in her gut coursed through her arms, blasting her assailant back. Gasping for breath, Josephine crumpled to the floor.

"Josephine!" Nathaniel shouted.

She looked up to find Nathaniel sprinting to her side, a pistol in his hand. When he reached her side, he pulled her to her feet. She had never been so glad to see him.

"Is he gone?" Josephine croaked.

Nathaniel glanced up and down the corridor. "For now."

"I thought it was Oliver in disguise."

"You don't say?" he drawled. Nathaniel took her by the hand and pulled her further down the abandoned hall, away from the masquerade. "It was the witch, and she disappeared when you blasted her. That was a timely bit of magic, I might add. I didn't realize you had such power."

Rubbing her tender neck, Josephine coughed and drew in another ragged breath. "It was not deliberate, I assure you. It just explodes out of me sometimes."

"It saved you from being strangled to death."

"Wait," she said, her voice still sounding strangled. "A witch? How did you know?"

"I'll explain later," he said. "We need to hurry before ..."

Rounding a corner into an adjacent hallway, Josephine and Nathaniel stopped dead in their tracks as the witch emerged from a cloud of black smoke.

"That is exactly what *I* would like to know as well," the witch sneered. She pulled back the hood of her cloak to reveal her identity.

Nathaniel uttered a foul curse while Josephine simply gaped at the woman. Standing before them was Eleanor - but not the kind and sweet lady Josephine had come to know. This Eleanor had a vicious gleam in her eyes and a scowl on her face. Her brown locks hung down past her shoulders, loose and wild. The cloak she wore covered a scarlett dress beneath.

"Eleanor? It *was* you?" Josephine accused.

"Do you know how long I have been waiting for this moment?" A cruel smile spread across Eleanor's face.

"B-but it can't be. Oliver said the witch's name was Tempest."

With a flick of her fingers, Eleanor transformed into another woman with bright red locks and a round face. Josephine gasped when a moment later, Eleanor's body swelled up into Garreck Skulthorpe's form. With another wave of her hand, she was back to being the wild, dark-haired witch.

"You see?" Eleanor sneered. "I can be anyone."

"You're the witch who works for Mr. Skulthorpe," Nathaniel muttered.

"Right you are," she said with a wicked smirk. "Garreck Skulthorpe has so enjoyed stringing you along in his plans. He has more patience than I do, however. All those weeks of being near you without being free to kill you was pure agony."

"How did you get inside this house?" Josephine asked. "Genny was supposed to -"

"This medallion, of course," she gloated. "Its magical charm protected me. Whatever protective barrier she placed around Willow Stone Place recognized the medallion and allowed me to pass."

"Oliver." Josephine's heart clenched. "You stole his glamour."

"Right again," she replied.

"But why? You had no quarrel with Oliver all these months, living below his flat as Tempest."

"I didn't have a quarrel with him ... until he brought you back to stay. I might have left him alone had he not recognized me in the alley. Something had to be done about him."

"What did you do to him?" Josephine said through gritted teeth.

"You have bigger problems than Oliver at the moment, Josephine," said Eleanor.

"Where is he?" she asked more forcefully, her hands warming with magic again.

For a second, Eleanor actually looked worried. The blast of power Josephine had unleashed on her a few minutes ago must have surprised her.

"I'm not going to ask again, Eleanor ... or Tempest ... or whoever you are."

Eleanor sniffed. "Fine. Mr. Skulthorpe has him. He wanted leverage just in case you manage to escape tonight. Though I really think he's over-estimated you." Eleanor's wicked laugh filled the empty hallway. "Did you honestly believe I would not notice Oliver all week posing as Mr. Runik, watching you while we danced and strolled about? He couldn't keep his eyes off you. Pathetic," she spat. "I knew that the *real* Nathaniel

Runik would never look at you with *love* in his eyes." Eleanor smirked, her eyes shifting between Josephine and Nathaniel. "How could Runik look at you with anything but contempt after what happened to his father?"

The blood drained from Josephine's face and her heart began to pound in her ears.

"Tell me, Josephine. Does Runik know the truth? Does he know the part that *you* played in his father's murder?"

Nathaniel dropped Josephine's hand and backed away as if she had the plague. She didn't know which feeling was worse: the fact that Oliver was in the hands of her worst enemy or that Nathaniel was about to find out her most terrible secret.

"Why are you doing this, Eleanor?" Josephine asked, her voice catching in her throat. "We were friends."

"Friends?" Eleanor scoffed. "It's called *acting*, Josephine, just as you have been doing this last month. Skulthorpe has been a useful ally."

"That man will never keep the promises he's made you," Josephine warned.

"You think he made promises, pirate? He's paying me, but I would have done all this for nothing. I had my own score to settle with the Pirate of Blacktail Cove. Imagine my disappointment when I found out he was dead." Eleanor narrowed her eyes. "But Skulthorpe gave me just the opportunity I needed to cause pain to his *precious* daughter ... Blacktail's most valuable treasure."

Josephine blinked in confusion. Revenge for what? How did Eleanor know her father?

"It was going to be so delightful, making you think that your dear Oliver had killed you. You ruined that plan, but no matter. The hunters are on their way. They're probably lying in wait for you right now." She turned her malicious gaze to Nathaniel. "Perhaps Runik should save them the trouble. Wouldn't that be best?" She quirked her eyebrow at him. "Garreck Skulthorpe would reward you beyond your wildest dreams if you rid the world of the Very. Last. Pirate."

Josephine's throat tightened as dread consumed her heart. Skulthorpe had no need for either of them anymore, it seemed. He was counting on Nathaniel's hatred of her and all immortal pirates to make his decision for him. Skulthorpe would single-handedly turn Nathaniel into a cold-blooded murderer and do away with Josephine in one blow. The hunters could be rid of Nathaniel afterward, whether he'd fulfilled the task or not.

The coldness in Nathaniel's stare had Josephine cringing. She had no way of knowing how he would respond to this brutal assignment, but listening to Eleanor's cruel laughter at their sad predicament made her blood boil and her fingers tingle. Josephine did not want her magic to hurt Nathaniel by mistake. Gritting her teeth, Josephine forced her power back.

Reaching beneath her coat, she drew her pistol. Nathaniel had been expecting it because he reached for his own. When they each raised their weapons, Nathaniel's was regrettably aimed for Josephine's heart. Josephine's was meant for Eleanor.

Taking a step back, Eleanor mocked her. "Do you really think you can kill me, Josephine? From what I have heard, you wouldn't have the stomach for it." She turned to Nathaniel. "Go on, Runik. Do what needs to be done."

Josephine peered up at Nathaniel and gulped. *Would he really do it?*

A glimmer of hope filled her when she saw his dark brows pinch together. His resolve was faltering.

Josephine pulled the hammer back on her pistol and fired. Eleanor disappeared in a flash, but Josephine hadn't fired directly at her. Josephine had aimed for the spot three feet to the right, where she'd predicted the witch would reappear. The musket ball must have hit its mark because a howl of pain filled the corridor. Dark smoke filled the corridor again and Eleanor vanished from their sight for good.

"Don't have the stomach, eh?" Josephine muttered to no one in particular. "Take that, you back-stabbing spit-weasel!"

The shot had not been a fatal one, but she hoped it was enough to leave Eleanor wounded.

Lowering her smoking pistol, Josephine turned to Nathaniel. "Well, if you're going to shoot me, you'd best get on with it."

Holding her breath, Josephine stared at the pistol aimed at her chest. Nathaniel's arm dropped but an inch and her eyes flew up to his. A storm of confusion and doubt was churning in his steel-gray eyes, his loyalty to the Brotherhood warring with his better judgement. For a dreadfully long minute, he stared at her with uncertainty.

Finally, Nathaniel blinked, as if he were coming out of a trance. His chin dropped to his chest and, with a deep sigh, he dropped his arm.

Josephine let out the breath she'd been holding and the knot in her chest loosened. "I'm going, then," she said softly, returning her pistol to its holster at her lower back. "I have to find Oliver."

Josephine picked up her skirts and jogged back toward the party. Perhaps she could blend in with the dancing enough to escape across the gardens. She must get back to Skulthorpe's estate to find out what had become of Beau and Sophia, to make sure they were safe. Afterward, she would head back to Captain Culligan's townhouse to figure out how to find Oliver.

As she reached the foyer, everything was just as it should be. Guests were still milling about, dancing and laughing boisterously, as if nothing out of the ordinary had happened. Josephine thought she might be able to leave without anyone noticing, until someone grabbed her from behind. Over her shoulder she recognized the black suit and white cravat.

The hunters had arrived.

THIRTY-FIVE

"Your time is up, Pirate," the hunter hissed in her ear, dragging her back, away from the bustling crowd.

Josephine resisted the urge to use her powers and jammed her elbow into his stomach instead. The man doubled over and groaned.

"Oliver's right. I *do* have bony elbows," she said. While the hunter was hunched over, gasping for breath, Josephine drew her pistol and clubbed him over the head.

She had only run ten feet when another man in a dark suit appeared out of the crowd. His hand reached out to grab her. Before she was forced to do something truly violent, like hit him with her magic, his body went limp. The hunter collapsed face-down to the floor for what seemed to be no reason at all.

She gaped down at the man, confused by his loss of consciousness.

"Josephine!" Beau exclaimed. He stood to her left about twenty feet away, grinning triumphantly. In his hand was one of Barnaby's napshots.

Josephine raced over to him and threw her arms around his neck. "Beau, I'm overjoyed to see you! But now, you must escape. Eleanor was here. She's -"

"A witch? Yes, Madame Sophia told me. Sophia has instructed me to see you safe. She's waiting for us at the Skulthorpe estate."

Josephine glanced around, hoping she didn't spot any black suits. "There will likely be more hunters waiting for me outside, but they aren't looking for you. Don't draw attention to yourself. Get back to the estate as fast as you can. You and Sophia pack as much as you can carry and I will meet you there. I'm going to need all the help I can get."

"You can count on me, my dear." He kissed her cheek. "Be careful."

"Stay safe, Beau," she pleaded, hugging him tightly.

"What about you?" he asked, giving her a once over. "Is your pistol still loaded?"

"Unfortunately no." Josephin tapped her sword belt. "Don't worry. I still have my cutlass and my hopelessly erratic pirate magic. I should be fine."

Beau's eyes went wide with awe. "Pirate magic? Really? That ought to be sufficient." He gave her a wink and then marched away.

After he had disappeared into the crowd, Josephine was, once again, grabbed from behind.

"Oh, you blasted hunters!" she cursed.

"It's just me, you foul-mouthed woman," Nathaniel scolded, dodging her elbow. He gripped her arm and began dragging her up the stairs to the second floor.

"Nathaniel!" she sighed with relief.

"Come along!" he commanded sharply.

Together, they ran up the stairs and away from the throng of guests below. "Are we climbing out a window?"

He gaped at her in astonishment. "Are you mad? There are no trees close to the house. We cannot just jump!"

"Then why are we going to the second floor? Besides, there's no need for jumping," she said, pulling out her trusty gloves. "I have these."

"Where did you get those?"

"What does it matter?" she snapped. "We can use them. Should we shimmy down from the front, side, or back of the house?"

"If I was doing the hunting, I would post men at every exit to catch you as you fled."

"Which exit will they least expect us to leave through?"

Nathaniel frowned. "Probably the front."

"Then out the front we go."

Nathaniel continued to drag Josephine behind him, muttering under his breath as they searched for an adequate escape. He entered a simple guest bedroom, strode to the window, and peeked out.

"It looks clear, but that does not mean hunters aren't waiting by the front door for this very reason," he pointed out. "See across the drive, that corn field there? That's where we should flee. We'll lose them in the field." Nathaniel opened the windows and peered down at the ground.

"And how are we going to get back to town?" she argued. "It was an hour by carriage."

"We'll have to wait until the hunters clear out before we can manage it."

"That's not fast enough," Josephine argued. "We should nick a couple of horses and run before the hunters realize we're gone."

"That's a terrible plan!"

Josephine lifted her chin. She had to find her Aunt Genny, collect Beau and Sophia, and then get back to the docks to rescue Oliver. "If you don't want to come along, then I shall go alone."

Josephine unraveled the spool of cord from her gloves and tied the end to a bedpost. Slipping her hands into the gloves, Josephine gripped the cord, climbed out the window, and lowered herself to the ground. Sophia and Beau had known what they were doing when they had created her costume. Josephine didn't have to worry with petticoats tangling around her ankles and tripping her up. The man's breeches and the dark frock she wore were perfect for making an escape from the hunters. Any watchful eyes would have trouble spotting her in the shadows.

She was about to make a run for the cornfield when she heard

Nathaniel signal with a soft whistle. Josephine looked up and smirked. Nathaniel was climbing out the window. Crouched down in the shrubs, watching for hunters, Josephine heard Nathaniel muttering curses as he climbed down the cord. He landed with a thud beside her.

"Decided to join me then?" she whispered.

Nathaniel glared at her. "I'm a dead man already, since I didn't kill you, remember? I can't stay here. And we are *not* stealing horses."

"Is a hunter against stealing now?"

"It's not the stealing that bothers me," he explained. "Horses are loud and leave tracks. The hunters will have us outnumbered and surrounded before we can make it a mile down the road. From the window, I saw the stables and carriages being watched, so that plan is out, regardless."

Josephine sighed, trying to think of another argument, but came up with nothing.

For good measure, Nathaniel added, "It is a distance to walk, but two hours will make little difference at this point. Oliver is already gone and could be well on his way to New York by now on Skulthorpe's ship."

"All right!" she hissed. "We'll do it your way."

He peered around at the front yard leading to the cornfield. "The way is mostly clear. Run straight across the lawn and into the field, but …"

"Aye," Josephine agreed. They would be exposed as they ran the distance. "What if we created a diversion of some kind? Those carriages are just sitting there. Could we not frighten the horses and send them running?"

"I don't think we could get them to move. The carriage wheels will be locked - but maybe a fire would do it."

"Good idea," she said, getting excited. "Oh, but don't hurt those innocent horses."

Nathaniel gave her an incredulous look. "Now is not the time for sentimentality, Josephine."

"What about the barn over there," she suggested. "Surely setting the barn ablaze would work."

"There are horses *in* the barn!"

"But they could be rescued," she pointed out.

Nathaniel held up a hand. "Stop talking. I'll be back in a moment. Do *not* move."

Rolling her eyes and nodding her agreement, Josephine watched Nathaniel disappear into the shadows. A few minutes later, fire was spreading through the brush and grass until the flames were climbing up the side of the barn. Stable hands and servants began running to try to stamp it out.

"Oh, my!" Josephine remarked. "How did he do that?"

"Quite simple, really," Nathaniel muttered.

Josephine gasped and nearly jumped out of her boots at his silent return. "Stop sneaking up on me!"

"Quit dawdling! It's now or never, Josephine."

Everyone's eyes were on the fire. This was their chance. He clasped her hand and led her toward the corn field. They were halfway across the lawn when a shot rang out from the trees just east of the house. Josephine yelped and instinctively ducked as a musket ball blasted a small hole in an empty carriage behind them. At least ten hunters poured out from the surrounding brush and trees, all armed with pistols and muskets.

"Run!" Nathaniel shouted as the hunters gave chase.

More shots fired behind them. These hunters were not inept. They would certainly wound one of them if they kept shooting.

While the hunters paused to reload their pistols, Josephine remembered the string of pearls around her neck. They needed one more diversion, something to slow the men down. Halting for a moment, she gave the necklace a quick yank.

"What are you doing, you foolish woman?" Nathaniel yelled.

"Don't wait for me! Go!"

All Josephine needed was a few seconds. The necklace finally in her hand, she turned and flung the beads directly into the path of the hunters giving chase. The moonlight sparkled off the pearls' smooth surfaces as they sailed through the air. Once they hit the ground, the beads scattered brilliantly in every direction. A few of the men skidded to a stop, turned, and fled from the dangerous pearls, warning the others of the imminent danger. Other hunters kept running, focused on their prey and unaware of the peril that awaited them. And just as Sophia had warned her, within five seconds, the beautiful spheres exploded beneath their feet.

Josephine didn't wait around to see how badly the men were injured. She raced after Nathaniel into the corn field to hide.

NEARLY TWO MILES from Willow Stone Place and the masked ball, Nathaniel stopped. Josephine was behind him, doubled over and gasping for breath. They were well-hidden within the rows of corn stalks and far from any spying eyes.

"Let's wait here," he suggested, sinking to the dirt. He removed the mask from his face and slung it to the ground in frustration. "I believe we've lost them for now. They'll most likely lie in wait for us back in town in places that we're most likely to go. At least, that's what I would do."

Sitting down just a few feet from him, Josephine took off her mask and rested her head on her knees. They waited together in mutual silence for at least fifteen minutes, listening to make certain they had shaken the hunters from their trail.

The quiet did nothing to soothe Nathaniel's ill humor over the evening's blunders. From the moment they'd arrived at the masquerade, Josephine had been deceiving him. Even the kind words she had spoken to him in the coach sounded like bitter poison. When the witch had spoken of his father, Josephine had gone deathly pale. The little pirate had always defended the Pirate of Blacktail Cove vehemently, so Nathaniel could only assume that she'd been lying to him after all.

He could no longer keep silent about it.

"You owe me an explanation," Nathaniel growled. "For everything."

Josephine raised her head, her dark hair loose around her face and shoulders. "I know," she whispered.

"I was beginning to trust you."

"I know. And you still can, Nathaniel."

"Can I?" he snarled. "I saw you speaking with Alden Howard. He is one of the most notorious Patriot rebels in the southern colonies."

She turned her guilt-ridden eyes away. "I was trying to help you. To help *us*."

"You gave *us* away to our enemies," he said through gritted teeth.

"Alden is not *my* enemy. I am neither a Patriot nor Loyalist." She pointed her finger at him. "And he has known about you for some time, Nathaniel, but has done nothing. He knew you were a hunter and Skulthorpe's spy."

He shook his head. "That's not possible."

"Madame Sophia has been working for the Patriots," she explained. "I suspected it today when she armed me more heavily with Barnaby's devices, but Alden confirmed it. *I* am not the reason your plans went awry."

"If they have known about me then why not expose me or capture me?"

"I don't know," said Josephine. "Alden knew I was going to steal his note a few weeks ago, which was just a decoy, by the way. And I have a feeling Sophia knew we might be ambushed tonight as well."

Nathaniel narrowed his eyes. "What about Beau? Is he a spy for the Patriots too or did you just use him to distract me?"

"He works for Sophia."

Nathaniel shoved himself onto his feet, muttering a curse under his breath.

"I'm sorry for deceiving you, but I knew you wouldn't approve of my actions," she admitted. "I was willing to risk myself to get some answers."

"It was foolish and dangerous."

Josephine sighed. "Perhaps it was foolish, but in my heart, I knew I could trust Alden Howard, and my instincts were right. Sophia had already smoothed things over with him. He knew all about me. He knew I was a pirate."

Nathaniel folded his arms over his chest and glowered down at the little pirate sitting in the dirt. "Just what did you think would be accomplished by speaking with Alden? Did you honestly believe he would tell you their plans?"

"Of course not," she said. "Don't be an idiot. I actually went to warn him about Garreck Skulthorpe's plans."

Nathaniel gritted his teeth and stalked away from Josephine. When he pivoted to face her again. Josephine was on her feet, braced for another quarrel.

"I don't understand why this surprises you, Nathaniel. Who was it that sent the hunters after *both* of us this evening? I have lived in fear of Skulthorpe since before you and I met. He has no honor in him. And regardless of what he's told you, he's not trying to prevent war with England here. He's *instigating* one. And he's killing innocents along the way." With a piercing glare, she added, "That includes *my* father … and *yours* as well."

Taking a challenging step forward, Nathaniel jabbed his accusing finger at her. "You leave my father out of this! It was *your* pirate father that -"

"*It wasn't my father who killed him! It was me!*" she shouted.

Josephine's hands were curled into fists by her side and her chest heaved, breathing hard from her fury. An icy chill crept up Nathaniel's spine, keeping him frozen in place. His mouth went dry as he stared at her.

She took a deep breath and lowered her eyes. "Father had nothing to do with it. I was the one who got your father killed."

Her confession hung in the air like an ax waiting to fall on them both and chop them to bits. He ignored the smell of the oncoming rain and the wind gently blowing the cornstalks back and forth. He refused to dwell on her trembling lip and how she couldn't look him in the eye. Without a word, he turned his back on her again. The pain of losing his father flared inside him, like a dagger piercing him deep in his gut all over again. The day he'd become a hunter, he'd packed all of his anguish away. He'd harnessed the anger and turned it into a desire for revenge.

As storm clouds swirled overhead, Josephine began confessing everything that had happened that terrible night; how Joseph had been away and wasn't there to receive the letter from James.

"I didn't know he was your father, Nathaniel. I didn't know why he was writing to mine."

"That's not possible," he said gruffly, peering back over his shoulder. "My father would never consort with pirates."

Ignoring his argument, she went on. "The letter explained that he was waiting for Father at the Bulls Head Tavern in New York. It wasn't that far from the docks." She faltered and shook her head, searching for the words to say. "I shouldn't have gone. If I had waited, Father would have known what to do ... but I went, and when I arrived ..." A sob hitched in her throat and raindrops began to sprinkle down around them.

Nathaniel scowled as she spun a story of how his father had been sent there as bait and how she'd been ambushed. "The Bulls Head Tavern is a popular place for hunters, but it's not the sort of place my father would go."

"I know that now, because as soon as I mentioned the name James, all hell broke loose. There were too many of them. James was there. He tried to fight them off when he saw me being taken, but one of the hunters shot him."

He shook his head. "You're lying."

"I saw it with my own eyes, Nathaniel."

Tears and rain streamed down Josephine's face. He did not want to believe this tale. It could not be true that one of the very men he'd worked with in the Brotherhood had killed his own father—and his employer had arranged it.

"I can see your uncertainty," she said. "It's easier for you to believe Skulthorpe. He's English and a Loyalist, just as you are. You've taken on his prejudices toward pirates. He's poured his hatred of them into you, but not all of it is warranted, Nathaniel. I make no excuses for other pirates that have gone down a bad path, but my father was not one of them. Skulthorpe lied to you about what really happened." Face contorted with grief, she said softly, "My father traded his life for mine. Did you know that?"

Nathaniel swallowed, refusing to answer. He hadn't known that piece of information.

"He turned to sand right in front of me. I had to watch them both die ... and Skulthorpe laughed, as if it was all a joke. Nathaniel, that man does not care about you or the other hunters. Skulthorpe only cares about himself. He only wants to cause other people pain."

Nathaniel was at a loss for words. He simply stood like a statue and stared at her through the cold rain that was soaking them both to the bone.

"When Oliver and I found out you were James' son, I was heart-broken all over again. Skulthorpe had James killed just to draw you into his Brotherhood. What better hunter could there be than one who wants revenge? He chose you specifically to be my warden, didn't he?"

Nathaniel's brow furrowed in thought. Skulthorpe knew that Nathaniel hadn't wanted to be her charge, but he'd insisted. He'd told Nathaniel that he had the perfect temperament for the job. And no one refused Garreck Skulthorpe's orders.

When Nathaniel finally met her eyes, she nodded, the look on his face confirming her suspicions.

"He knew the connection between us." Josephine snorted. "If I were a betting woman, I'd say that he set this whole evening up so that we would both be eliminated. He has no further use for either of us. We were just a means to an end in his game."

Josephine scooped up her mask and gazed up at him, grief churning in her warm brown eyes. "I don't expect you to ever forgive me for my foolishness, and I accept all the blame. Like I said in the carriage, I understand why you've hated me, even though it was for the wrong reason. Just know that you will *never* hate me more than I've hated myself over this."

Without another word, Josephine brushed by him, disappearing into the shadows. He stood frozen to the spot between the stalks of corn, the truth like heavy stones in his stomach.

THIRTY-SIX

J osephine ran through the brush, pushing branches out of her way, scraping her hands and arms on thistles and thorns. Her feet caught on roots jutting out of the ground that she couldn't see through the tears blurring her vision. She couldn't get away from Nathaniel fast enough.

The pirate magic in her soul was her compass, pointing her back toward the wharf and hopefully to Oliver. How was she to reunite with Aunt Genny? She had known that Genny was sneaking around on the outskirts of the manor, but Eleanor had still managed to evade her defensive charms. Unless ...

No, Josephine could not believe Aunt Genny had been captured or killed. It was already unbearable to even consider what was being done to Oliver in the hands of the hunters. Nathaniel had warned her that Oliver might be on a ship headed to New York with Skulthorpe.

Her knees buckled and hit the dirt, a sob catching in her throat. Reaching inside her heart, she felt the steady tethers of her soul; the ones that bound her to the sea and reached for Oliver. They were secure. Josephine took a deep breath, knowing without a doubt that those tethers would snap like an anchor line if Oliver was killed.

Don't even think it, she scolded herself.

Swallowing the lump in her throat, Josephine picked herself up and kept moving. Staying off the road was her main priority, but it was impossible to stay hidden throughout her journey back to Charlestown. She raced across a few open fields and through some wooded areas, avoiding the swamps.

As she entered the next clearing, a prickle of unease spread through her body and the hairs on the back of her neck stood on end. She was being followed. Could it be Eleanor, coming to finish the job? Or maybe a hunter picking up her trail? It was possible it was only Nathaniel. He was most likely making his way back to town as well, but hopefully he would call out to her before she could run him through with her blade.

Josephine pulled her cutlass free of its scabbard. The weight of the beautiful instrument in her hand was like being reacquainted with an old friend. It might have been easier to deal with an enemy if she had managed to reload her blasted pistol back at the manor. Regardless, she refused to go down without a fight. Josephine's magic was still unreliable, so she had to rely on her stealth and steel.

Ducking into some brush, Josephine waited for her stalker. When she began to hear the sounds of rustling grass, she flipped the night vision lenses down over her eyes and prepared to attack. She had no idea what to do if Eleanor appeared. With only a wound in her shoulder, the witch was certainly not dead. Was Eleanor powerful enough to heal her own injury so quickly?

The person pursuing her was approaching and being awfully noisy about it. Very unlike a hunter. Nathaniel was skilled enough to stay silent as a predator. This person was either exceedingly stupid or someone courageous with a lot of power.

"Josephine? Is that you?" a familiar French accent called out behind her.

Josephine spun to face her. "Blimey, Aunt Genny! Why are you sneaking up on me like that?"

"I did not think I was sneaking so much. I was making plenty of noise, *non*?"

"How did you find me?"

"I am not without some skill." She grinned and winked, not giving anything else away. "Where is Oliver?"

Josephine threw herself into Genevieve's arms. "The hunters have him. He never made it to the masquerade." Tears began to well up in her eyes again. "We must get back to the Skulthorpe estate. I don't know if he will even be there, but we cannot leave him in the hands of those hunters."

Genny stroked Josephine's hair as her father would have done to comfort her. Here in this moment, she missed him terribly. He would have known what to do.

"Do not cry, darling," Genny said. "We will get all wet again."

Sniffling and wiping her eyes, Josephine nodded her head against Genny's shoulder. While Josephine was ready to fall apart, Genny was as strong and confident as ever.

"And we will get him back, *oui*? We will find him." She held Josephine at arm's length and looked her in the eye. "But first, you know what you must do."

"I do?"

"*Oui*," she said, cupping Josephine's face with her hands. "It is time for you to become who you were born to be."

"So you must change me as you did Father?" she asked, completely puzzled.

"*Non*! All that your father was is inside you," she said, pointing to Josephine's heart. "You have been so frightened of it for three years. Trying to keep it locked up. Stifling the urge to go to the water. Terrified of the power you have inside you and afraid that Oliver would not come with you." Genny embraced her again. "Do not be afraid of these things. These powers of yours - you will learn to control them when you learn to accept them. And Oliver? He will be by your side as long as you want him there."

Josephine stepped out of her arms and shrugged. "I don't have a ship, Aunt Genny, or a crew. If Skulthorpe has Oliver, then Captain Culligan could have been killed as well. How will I find him? Skulthorpe could have taken Oliver anywhere."

Genny took hold of Josephine's hands. "When we reach the wharf, you will know what to do."

"Let's go, then," she said. "The Skulthorpe estate is not far from here, I believe."

"Bah! No need to walk," she said, gripping Josephine's fingers. Genny whisked them away into the night by magic, disappearing from the abandoned field and reappearing at the end of the drive to the estate.

"How did you do that, Aunt Genny?" gasped Josephine.

"All true witches can do this," she explained, shrugging her shoulders. "Just because you have never seen me do it, does not mean I cannot. It is wasteful magic, *non*? Why poof around when I can simply walk?"

"Eleanor … Tempest, or whoever she is, seems to do it quite frequently," Josephine pointed out.

"She is a stupid woman," said Genny, wagging her finger. "She poofs and poofs, and everyone knows she is a witch! No one knew I was a witch. Not even you."

"Can you poof us into Headquarters," Josephine asked, gesturing to the mansion in front of them.

Genny shook her head. "That is not a good idea. Someone could be waiting to do us harm. Best if we walk from here."

Hand in hand, they walked up the drive to Skulthorpe's Charlestown estate.

Genny studied the mansion. "It looks as if no one is home."

"Even so, hunters might be lurking."

It did seem that the estate had been abandoned. Not a candle was lit inside the mansion, and the front door was wide open.

"I told Beau to wait for me with Sophia," Josephine whispered. "I truly hope nothing has happened to them." But even as she said it, dread crept over her like deadly tentacles. When Josephine had thought she was speaking to Oliver, she'd inadvertently told the witch about Sophia and Beau's allegiance. She hoped the witch was far from here, recovering from her gunshot wound.

"There is nothing to do but go and see," said Genny.

They stepped lightly over the threshold of the dark foyer. Goosebumps rose on Josephine's arms at the eerie silence, leeching all warmth from her skin. Genny found a candlestick near the ballroom entrance and lit it with a flick of her magical fingers. The orange glow cast sinister shadows along the corridor as it illuminated their path.

"Maybe down in Headquarters?" Josephine suggested, speaking in the quietest whisper.

Her palms began to tingle with barely contained power as she led the way through the ballroom, through the solarium, and into the library. Genny was right on her heels. Tugging down on the little statue once more, Josephine pulled her cutlass free again, just in case hunters awaited them below. When they reached the bottom of the circular stairs, Josephine saw a still form sprawled on the floor of Headquarters.

Lifting a hand to cover her mouth, Josephine whispered, "No, Sophia!" The cutlass fell to the floor with a clatter as she rushed to the woman's side, carefully turning her over to check for a pulse.

Genny knelt down beside her. "Is she breathing?"

Josephine placed her ear to Sophia's chest but could hear nothing. A breath hitched in Josephine's throat at the loss. Sophia had not been the kindest person, but Josephine knew now that she'd been working against the man who had been manipulating them all.

"Eleanor killed her."

Gasping in fright, Josephine turned to find Beau sitting motionless on a chair near the dressing room, completely shrouded in darkness. Josephine padded across the floor and crouched in front of him.

He sniffed sorrowfully. "If I had been here -"

Clasping his hand in hers, Josephine interrupted, "I'm to blame for this. If I hadn't asked you to come with me tonight, she might still be alive."

"No," Beau argued, squeezing her hand. "Sophia urged me to go. You saved my life, my dear." His shoulders rose and fell in a deep, sorrowful sigh. "I would be lying there beside her if I had been here, so don't you apologize. I just wish she hadn't faced that witch alone."

"There weren't any hunters here when you returned?" Josephine inquired.

He shook his head. "The mansion is empty. They must have all gone to the ship after we left for the ball. The servants have all turned in for the night."

"What about Barnaby?"

"He's not here, either. In the days leading up to tonight, Sophia and I confiscated as many devices and weapons as we could without drawing attention to ourselves." He gestured to the bag resting by his feet.

Swallowing her own urge to sit and cry, Josephine wrapped her arms around her friend. "I am grateful to you both. Every weapon she gave me tonight saved my life."

"That would have made her happy," Beau said, smiling sadly. Sniffing and stiffening his spine, he said, "We should not linger." He slapped his hands against his knees and rose from his seat. "Madame would not want us to wallow in our grief. She would want us to stay the course and finish the job."

"She sounded very wise, *monsieur*," Genny told him, placing a comforting hand on his shoulder.

"What should we do with her body?" Josephine whispered to them. "We cannot leave her here."

"I would suggest burning the place down to spite Skulthorpe, but the servants would be harmed," Beau pointed out. "Better if we leave quietly."

"I will bury her," Genny replied. "Will that suit everyone?" Without waiting for an answer from either Josephine or Beau, Genny began to mutter an incantation. Sophia's lifeless body disappeared before their eyes. "There, now."

"Where did you send her?" Josephine asked, staring down at the floor where Sophia had been lying.

"She is buried in the garden outside," Genny answered. "I could not move her far, but she will be at peace, *oui*?"

Josephine nodded. "I suppose that's best."

Slinging his bag over his shoulder, Beau wiped his eyes with the backs of his hands. "I think Madame knew her time was up," he said, turning to Josephine. "Before I left for the ball, she gave me strict orders to look after you. I thought she meant for the evening, but now …" He sniffed and lifted his chin defiantly. "Wherever it is we must go, Josephine, I am coming along."

"Of course," Josephine said with a nod. "I couldn't do without you, Beau."

Together, they walked out of the mansion. Promising herself that she could mourn later, Josephine blinked back tears. There had been enough crying for one day.

Standing on the front porch, Genny frowned and placed a hand on Josephine's shoulder. "What do you feel, Josephine? Where is Oliver?"

"I don't know."

"Of course, you do," Genny insisted. "Look inside yourself. Let your magic guide you."

Josephine swallowed and closed her eyes. She sensed Oliver's trepidation on the end of the tether that joined their souls, but he was being taken further and further away. "He's not in Charlestown. Skulthorpe must have taken him as a hostage."

"They'll be using him to draw you into a trap," said Beau, rubbing his chin.

"I think they will find we are not so easily trapped," Aunt Genny said with calm resolve. "Come. It is time to go down to the docks."

THIRTY-SEVEN

N athaniel stood in the cornfield alone, staring into the shadows. He was a fugitive from the hunters and the Brotherhood with few options left. Free of his obligations to Mr. Skulthorpe, it would not be difficult to find passage back to England, but the thought of making the voyage through the winter months made Nathaniel cringe. A month or more on the Atlantic was not his cup of tea. What did he have waiting for him in England? A family he'd been estranged from because of his eagerness to join the hunters. No. There was no going back to his old life.

What about Mr. Skulthorpe? He was guilty of having Nathaniel's father murdered and had nearly convinced Nathaniel to murder Josephine.

Nathaniel wiped a hand down his face, wondering what he should do. He was honor-bound as an Englishman and soldier to bring Skulthorpe to justice, but how would he ever find the man? Skulthorpe had the resources to sail anywhere.

Josephine.

It was true, Nathaniel's trust in the girl was shaken, but she would do anything to save Oliver. To find the boy, she'd need to track down

Skulthorpe. That was all Nathaniel wanted from her. To catch up to the blackguard, he needed a fast ship.

He needed a pirate.

As soon as Genny had transported them back to the remains of the Kraken's Lookout, Josephine put on her masquerade mask and kept the night vision lenses down. It was well past midnight and the docks seemed to be abandoned. Anyone on board their ships was likely asleep, and everyone else was in a tavern, drinking rum. They crept silently to the wharf, passing by the ships that were docked. Josephine was wound tighter than an anchor line. Water splashed against the pier and the swaying ships creaked against their docking lines. Josephine flinched at every sound.

"Calm down, Josephine," Genny whispered. "You are skittish as a bird."

"Rightfully so," Josephine replied. "What if they've done something to Oliver?"

"The magic in your blood would alert you if he were harmed, darling."

"You sense things with your blood?" Beau asked, eyes wide in astonishment.

"Only certain things," Josephine corrected.

Beau shook his head. "Still, that's incredible, Josephine. Did Sophia know?"

"I never told anyone about my magic. Not even Nathaniel. I didn't want Skulthorpe to find out." Josephine sighed. "He'll find out soon. Eleanor will tell him."

"Don't think about that now," said Genny, squeezing Josephine's hand. "We must deal with the challenge in front of us first."

Josephine gulped and gripped her cutlass tighter. "Father might say this is foolish. Two women and Beau walking right into a trap that we know is waiting for us."

"But we are not ordinary women, *oui*?" she smirked.

Josephine rolled her eyes. "Yes, I'm sure my magic will blow the entire pier to dust if I'm attacked."

Beau chuckled. "We have faith in you, my dear."

"*Oui*," Genny agreed. "We must get you out to the pier - to the water. That is where you are strongest."

Elbows linked, they continued on despite Josephine's growing fear. The three of them made it to the outset of the pier that she had always enjoyed visiting, under normal circumstances at least. As they started down the long wooden dock that jutted out into the harbor by a good hundred meters, Josephine had the strongest sense of déjà vu. The storage warehouse on the pier was the perfect place for hunters to hide in wait, just as Nathaniel had done that fateful night he'd abducted her.

A cloud of heavy fog hung over the harbor from Josephine's earlier bout of tears. The ominous silence surrounding them filled her with a chill of dread. Clutching her sword, Josephine searched her surroundings as they crept toward the bay.

"This is not good," Josephine whispered. "We'll be surrounded if we walk out onto the pier. There's no escape except to jump in the river and swim."

"Don't you worry," Beau said, encouraging her. "We've come this far."

Josephine gave him a skeptical look. "Beau, just what are *you* going to do if we get attacked? How am I supposed to protect you?"

"Protect me?" Beau drew a pistol from his belt and winked. "I was a crack shot in a duel. No one wanted to challenge me back in England."

"Oh!" Josephine replied, gaping at him. "Well, that's something, isn't it?"

Genny turned and cupped Josephine's cheeks. "No matter what happens to us, you must get to the water. Do you understand, Josephine?"

Josephine nodded but an unease settled like heavy lead in her stomach. How could she leave her friends behind to face an unknown danger alone?

Tightening her grip on her sword, Josephine kept walking, searching the fog for threats. They had just reached the warehouse when a pistol fired. Josephine screamed and bright-white light promptly exploded from the palms of her hands, creating a temporary shield against the musket ball. The first two hunters emerging from the warehouse were lifted off their feet and thrown back, crashing through the wall of the building.

"Kill the pirate and the witch!" another male voice bellowed, drawing Josephine's attention.

Hunters in their black suits swarmed the pier. Five of them raced down from the bayside road, blocking their escape. At least ten others had been hiding inside the warehouse. The hunters sprinted toward them, pistols and swords drawn. Aunt Genny whipped her hand around, flinging a spell in their direction. The pistols backfired on them as they pulled their triggers.

Josephine felt her fingertips warm again as the hunters closed in.

"*Go*, Josephine!" Genny shouted.

"But, Aunt Genny -"

"You *must* get to the water! *Go!*"

Genny's forceful commands sent Josephine sprinting down the pier, boots pounding on the wooden slats. She was so close, she could feel the spray of water on her face. Just when she'd nearly reached the end of the dock, a dark figure emerged through the fog. Josephine slowed to a stop immediately. Could it be?

"Nathaniel?" she called.

A mixture of relief and dread ran through her. Surely if it was Nathaniel, he wouldn't kill her. He could have pulled the trigger when Eleanor had commanded him to at the masque. Was he ready to prove his loyalty to Skulthorpe and the pirate hunters after all?

"No, I'm afraid not," the hunter replied, stepping out of the mist to reveal himself.

Though it greatly resembled him, it most definitely was not Nathaniel. Before she could challenge him, another Hunter stepped up behind her, leaving her alone, two against one. Skulthorpe and his hunters had lured her to the dock, which had been the plan all along.

With her back to the water, Josephine slid the dagger from her boot. Though she'd practiced fencing against two opponents in the past, she was uncertain how her skills would hold up against two highly trained hunters. Josephine would have to be quick. Dagger in one hand and cutlass in the other, she awaited their attack.

THIRTY-EIGHT

Nathaniel rode the ten miles back to the White Pearl Wharf at a gallop. He'd stolen a horse from the Howard estate, ignoring the fact that it had been Josephine's idea to do so. She'd been headed back to the docks, but Nathaniel knew her efforts would be short-lived if the hunters had beaten her there. Those men knew she would return to the White Pearl Wharf because he had told them she would back when he was loyal to them. It was the first place she would go to commandeer a ship.

She'll be destroyed, he thought. Nathaniel's stomach clenched with fear for the girl that he hadn't known he possessed.

It took him nearly half an hour to reach the quay, and by then, the fight had already begun. The witch, Genevieve, was taking on a bulk of the hunters with her powerful magic and was overwhelming them easily, like a cat playing with mice. Beau, surprisingly, was hunkered down behind some crates, shooting and reloading his pistol in record time, killing hunters one by one as Genny kept them busy.

Nathaniel kicked his horse into a gallop once more when he did not spot Josephine in the melee. The ringing of steel on steel coming from the pier caught his attention. Nathaniel pulled on the reins, steering his mount toward the dock.

Once he had reached the pier, Nathaniel dismounted and ran past the warehouse into the fight. Through the fog, he could see Josephine holding off not one, but two very skilled Hunters with her sword and dagger. He recognized the men. Ashford and Phelps had both been with the Brotherhood for several years before Runik had joined them.

The gold trim on Josephine's crimson coat glimmered in the moonlight as she crossed blades with the men. She ducked as Ashford swiped his sword over her head. She twirled away toward Phelps and smashed the hilt of her cutlass into his face. Phelps stumbled backward, a bit stunned, blood trickling from his nostrils. Josephine blocked Ashford's blade with her own and then kicked him between the legs. Ashford doubled over and nearly fell to his knees. Josephine was using every dirty trick in the book.

Phelps recovered and jumped back into the fray. His sword rang out as it struck Josephine's. She stumbled back a few steps, but managed to hold onto her cutlass. Another swing of his sword and Phelps had knocked Josephine's dagger out of her hands. The small blade clattered to the wooden slats of the dock. Ashford, finally able to stand upright again, moved in to corner Josephine on the edge of the dock. There was nowhere for her to go.

"You've lost, Pirate," Phelps snarled. "Drop your sword."

Josephine never wavered. She swiped her cutlass back and forth to keep them back and lifted her stubborn chin. "You'll kill me whether I have a sword in my hand or not. I'd rather go down fighting."

Nathaniel strode toward them. Pirate or not, he would not allow Josephine to die tonight. He drew his sword, prepared to engage in a temporary alliance with the little half-pirate. Hearing Nathaniel's approach, Ashford whirled to face him. Phelps kept Josephine at sword-point but was watching Nathaniel and Ashford closely.

Ashford's lip curled. "Runik. The hunters will never trust you again."

Nathaniel clenched his jaw at the man's words.

"You're a dead man," Ashford confirmed.

Josephine took full advantage of Nathaniel's timely distraction and leapt at Phelps with renewed vigor. Jolted out of his stupor, Phelps only just blocked the swing of her sword. She spun and sliced his shoulder with the curved blade of her cutlass. Phelps growled and retreated to regain his balance.

Ashford advanced toward Nathaniel, a deadly gleam in his eyes. Their blades crossed again and again. Nathaniel was confident and parried Ashford's thrusts without difficulty. They circled each other a few steps and Nathaniel lunged once more, attempting to put Ashford on his heels. His opponent anticipated the move. Ashford's blade sliced across Nathaniel's chest. His frock and waistcoat took most of the damage, but his flesh burned from the surface wound. Done with polite swordplay, Ashford pulled a pistol from his belt.

"You shouldn't have interfered, Runik." Ashford took aim at Nathaniel's heart.

Josephine heard the click of the hammer and screamed Nathaniel's name. She left Phelps behind and raced toward Ashford. Sensing her approach, Ashford turned and fired his pistol at Josephine instead. Nathaniel cried out in horror as Josephine jerked back from the impact. Her body hit the pier with a thud.

Rage surged through Nathaniel. He gained his footing and lunged toward Ashford, finishing the Hunter in two strokes. Phelps charged, but Nathaniel disarmed him easily and thrust his sword through Phelps' torso, just under his rib cage.

Racing toward Josephine, Nathaniel dropped to his knees beside her. Leaning over her still form, he wiped her tousled brown hair from her face.

"Josephine!" With trembling hands, he began removing her coat and outer garments to find the wound. *There's no blood. Why is there no blood?* Nathaniel thought. She had been shot at such a short range. Perhaps he'd been mistaken. Had it only been a flesh wound? Nathaniel swallowed back the dread he felt. He knew that Ashford had been aiming for her chest.

"*Monsieur?*" a voice called out to him.

Nathaniel peered over his shoulder to see Genevieve and Beau sprinting toward them.

"What happened?" she asked.

Beau and Genny knelt down beside Josephine and stared at her lifeless body. Nathaniel continued unbuttoning her waistcoat and, as if she knew he was stripping her bare, Josephine groaned and opened her eyes.

Giving Nathaniel a perplexed stare, she asked him, "Did we win?"

———

JOSEPHINE FELT like she'd been kicked in the chest by a horse. Not that she'd ever felt the like before, but she was sure this pain would be close enough. Nathaniel, Aunt Genny, and Beau all stared down at her with anxious expressions on their faces.

"What … happened?" she coughed.

Nathaniel heaved a sigh of relief. "I thought you were … you are a reckless woman! He *shot* you! How are you not dead?" He nearly yelled the last.

"Aye, he did shoot me, but I don't think I'm wounded. You hunters all have twitchy fingers." Josephine tried to laugh but it came out as choked coughing instead.

With Beau and Genny's help, Josephine sat up. She undid the laces of her shirt and showed them the protective corset she'd worn underneath her costume. The musket ball was there just below her chest, squashed flat into the durable weave.

"It felt like I was shot, but I'm all right," she reassured him, holding her middle. "It just knocked the wind from my sails." Josephine stilled and eyed Nathaniel. "Why are you here?"

His arrogant air was back in full force. "You will need my help if you are planning a rescue attempt. I have decided that I will be your ally in that mission."

"My ally?" Josephine said, quirking her eyebrow.

"Well, I have no one else on this bloody continent that I can trust." His jaw ticked at the confession. "In return for my services, you will help me seek justice for my father."

Josephine thought about this for a minute. It would be dangerous to get involved any further with the Brotherhood, but they were already in up to their necks. Even she had to admit that having another skilled spy would be extremely helpful in her plan to retrieve Oliver from the monster's grasp. With a nod, Josephine accepted his proposal.

"I don't mean to throw cold water on this reunion," Beau said. "But we might want to get on with things. The hunters that escaped could come back with reinforcements."

"All right, then," Josephine murmured. "If you'd be so kind as to help a girl up?"

Nathaniel clasped her hand and hauled her to her feet. She doubled over, still in an extraordinary amount of pain. Pressing her hand to her chest seemed to help, but she would be bruised for days.

"Let's go," she groaned, straightening up again. She gathered up her sword and dagger from the ground and strode toward the water. When she reached the edge of the pier, she looked back at Genny, who gave her an encouraging smile. Her eyes shifted to Nathaniel. She saw his jaw tighten, but there was no going back for Josephine. She could not avoid her destiny.

Turning to face the wide expanse of the harbor, Josephine was unsure of her next step. When a man decided to become an immortal pirate, a witch would do most of the work, but Aunt Genny had told her that she would know what to do.

All that your father was is inside you, Genny had told her.

Then it came to her. Sheathing her cutlass, she took hold of her dagger. Josephine had her father's blood and it tied her to the sea.

"What are you doing?" Nathaniel asked, staring at her blade with wide eyes.

"Don't worry, I'm not going to stab you," Josephine said with a grin.

Without hesitating, she dragged the dagger down the palm of her hand, covering the blade with her blood, and then chucked the dagger out into the bay as far as she could throw it.

"Bloody hell, woman," Nathaniel muttered.

Josephine didn't respond. She stared out at the water and waited.

After a moment, Josephine turned to Genny. "Did it work?"

Nathaniel folded his arms across his chest. "Yes, after purposefully slicing your hand open, that was somewhat disappointing. I assumed there would be some sort of sign in the sky or flames coming up out of the water."

Josephine rolled her eyes at him.

"That is ridiculous, *monsieur*," Genny replied, waving his sarcasm away. "The power is inside you. Call them."

"Call them?" Josephine asked, frowning.

Aunt Genny nodded. "*Oui*, your ship, your crew. They are waiting."

Josephine peered out toward the glimmering water again and reached inside for her tethers. The ones that reached for Oliver were stretched taut, aware that he was being taken further and further away. The others - there was something different about them. Closing her eyes, Josephine mentally grasped hold of them and began pulling steadily on those anxious cords.

Nathaniel muttered a curse beside her, but she ignored him. A moment later, the anticipation was gone. Only the tethers themselves remained, strong as rigging on a ship.

When Josephine opened her eyes, she gazed in pure wonder. Out in front of her and swiftly approaching the wharf was her father's ship.

"The *Nepheria*," she whispered, marveling at the sight. The ship was a wonder; a large, beautiful brigantine with two square-rigged masts. The white sails sparkled in the moonlight, as though the ship had not been hiding under the Atlantic for three long years. "I thought it had been forfeited to the British Crown all this time. My father's magic kept it safe?"

"*Oui*," Genny grinned. "It has been waiting for you for a long time, darling. Oh, and here they come." She pointed back toward the warehouse.

Out of the fog behind them emerged a group of men, all walking purposefully with bags over their shoulders. Nathaniel reached for his sword, but she quickly stayed his hand.

"It's Father's crew." Josephine swallowed the lump in her throat and corrected herself. "*My* crew."

Sure enough, Captain Culligan and Jett led the way, with the rest following behind; all the men who had pledged blood oaths to her father. The only person missing was Oliver.

"Miss," Jett greeted her.

"It's Captain now, you dung beetle," Culligan scolded, smacking him on the back of the head.

"Aye," he said, standing a bit taller. "*Captain* Teversin."

Josephine's eyes pricked with emotion. "He made you wait for me."

"Aye," Cully replied. "He knew that one day you'd be needin' a crew."

She eyed the men, remembering them all fondly. She couldn't help but notice that some of them were giving her wary looks. It had been three years since she'd sailed, and she was just a young girl. Josephine would be foolish to think they would follow her blindly.

"I can see the doubt in your eyes," she said, studying each face. "Anyone wanting to be released from the oath can go without condemnation or punishment. That was always Father's way. But if you stay …" She lifted her chin and gave them each a stern look. "… we're on a mission to rescue Oliver. That means chasing down Father's killer. This is our chance to bring him to justice. It will be dangerous, so any man not willing, leave now."

The uncertain few glanced at each other.

"I'm with you, Captain," Jett said. "I ain't leaving Oliver to them hunters." He turned and glared at the other men. "And anyone who don't come with us … I say you're a coward."

Josephine bit back a smile, her heart nearly bursting with overwhelming joy at his loyalty to her. The men who had been wavering reluctantly nodded, grumbling their assent.

"But what about this dog?" Jett pointed at Nathaniel, fingering his pistol.

Josephine glanced at Nathaniel, whose jaw was clenching again. "He's with us. No harm is to come to him," she said, her words sharp, brooking no argument.

"But ain't he a hunter, miss? … uh … Captain?" another one of the crew hissed. "A bleedin' redcoat?"

"He's a rogue agent."

Behind them, the *Nepheria* docked at the pier perfectly. Josephine admired her lovely brig for a moment and the magic that bound them together.

Cully took a step toward her. "What are your orders, Captain?"

Josephine narrowed her eyes and shouted, "On deck, men, and make ready to set sail!" The crew took off at a run with their meager possessions in tow, scrambling to prepare the ship.

"Aunt Genny, are you coming with us?" Josephine asked, turning to her guardian.

"Without the tavern, I have nothing waiting for me here," she said. "Besides, I am always ready for an adventure." She smirked at Josephine and then strode toward the brig. Cully was waiting to help her up onto deck.

Beau stepped up beside them. "Mr. Runik," he said by way of formal greeting.

"Mr. Hopwood," Nathaniel replied. "Are you thinking of joining us? What is in your bag?"

"Barnaby's devices," Josephine informed him.

"You stole our devices?" Nathaniel huffed.

"We're on the same side now, you idiot," Josephine scolded.

"Oh. Right." He cleared his throat and nodded at Beau. "Well done, then."

"My lovely, that was really something!" Beau said, some excitement back in his voice. "But I am simply famished. Did we think to pack any food?"

"Oh." She actually hadn't thought of food in a while. "We'll see to it at once."

"Aye, aye, Captain Teversin! Oh, this is going to be exciting!" Beau marched down the pier and hopped aboard the ship, still muttering about food.

"Captain Teversin," Nathaniel murmured, stepping forward to face her. "Not the Pirate of Blacktail Cove then?"

"That was my father's title," she said sadly.

"Perhaps, then," he said thoughtfully and with a grin, "the *Petticoat Pirate?*"

Josephine giggled. "Pirates do not wear petticoats, Mr. Runik."

Nathaniel raised an eyebrow, his steel-gray eyes flashing in amusement.

"All right, perhaps this one does. And what about you? A rogue redcoat?"

He snorted. "The Petticoat Pirate and the Rogue Redcoat. Who would have thought?"

Josephine's smile disappeared. "What do you think Skulthorpe will do to Oliver?"

Nathaniel cast his gaze out to the horizon. "He'll do whatever he must to punish you," he murmured, unable to meet her eyes.

Josephine gulped. "Then we must make haste."

After giving her one last piercing look, he walked away and boarded the *Nepheria,* Josephine following close behind him.

Once the *Nepheria* had set sail, Josephine took her place at the wheel. Her dark hair and burgundy coat billowed out behind her with the wind.

"Do we have a destination, Captain Teversin?" Cully asked, sidling up next to her at the helm.

Josephine bit her lip, thinking of the many places Skulthorpe might lead her. Nathaniel had mentioned something about New York, but Skulthorpe might have been lying to throw them off course. Josephine recalled her meeting with Alden Howard at the masque. He'd hinted that something significant might be happening soon at one of the major ports; an event that Skulthorpe might be meddling with.

Josephine turned the wheel, adjusting their course. "Boston."

To be continued...

If You Enjoyed This Book, Please Leave A Review Here

ACKNOWLEDGMENTS

Huge thanks to Maddy Glenn, who never fails to help me polish my work until it shines. Christian Bentulan, once again, your cover art blows my mind. You make people want to pick up my book in the first place. Miranda and Sophie, thank you for reading through my work and giving me such amazing advice and critiques. I couldn't have done it without you. Bobby, Caleigh, Mom, Dad, Tina, Melvin, and the rest of my amazing family...you never stop believing in me! To Corbyn, who was the first teen to read this work from its roughest draft. You gave me hope that this book would be something amazing. There are too many incredible people from my writing community on Twitter to ever name them all, but thank you for your unfailing support and encouragement.

ABOUT THE AUTHOR

C.R. Pugh is a young adult writer who lives just outside Dallas, Texas. She's a sucker for science fiction, fantasy, and happy endings after a long drawn out adventure with several gut-wrenching cliffhangers. In her spare time, she watches home improvement shows and endless Disney movies.

https://authorcrpugh.wixsite.com/home

Made in the USA
Columbia, SC
23 August 2022